MW01277975

A DEATH IN FRENCHTOWN

George B. Gelman

VANTAGE PRESS
New York

FIRST EDITION

Copyright © 1998 by George B. Gelman

Published by Vantage Press, Inc.
516 West 34th Street, New York, New York 10001

Manufactured in the United States of America
ISBN: 0-533-12536-7

Library of Congress Catalog Card No.: 97-91039

0 9 8 7 6 5 4 3 2 1

For Janet, Lois, Andrew, and Judy.

Prologue

It was a cool, clear evening in early June at a lakeshore and in a modest cottage a young girl lay sleeping. Her bedroom window was slightly open and had she been awake, she would have heard the incessant screeching of the cicadas. The rays of an early rising moon lit up her face whose features were those of a young child, and her slender body, boyish in form, lay clad in a worn nightgown. She did not awaken when the bedroom door opened and she did not see the short, thin man slip into her room.

He approached her bed and stared down at her sleeping form and, placing his hand on her stomach, he leaned over and whispered to her: "Wake up, honey, it's your daddy." Her eyes opened as he sat down on her bed, his hand still resting on her stomach. She could smell the strong beery odor on his breath and she started to open her mouth as if to scream.

"It's all right, honey, your mommy wants me to talk to you about becoming a woman." His hand slid up her body and touched the buds of her slight breasts and he lay down beside her. She started to whimper and he leaned over and placed his lips on her mouth, stifling any sound. His hand moved down her body to her hairless mons and pulled up her nightgown until her body was completely uncovered. He lifted his lips from her mouth but no sound came out.

"Now, honey, just lie there and be quiet and I'll show you how a man can make a woman happy." His lips touched her neck and slid down her body to her breasts as his fingers began to separate the lips of her vagina. He gently probed the opening with his fingers. She gasped and then started to cry. "Did I hurt you, honey? I didn't mean to do that. I'll be more careful and you'll see how good it's going to feel."

His lips passed from her breasts to her stomach and then to the opening of her vagina. Slowly he began to insert his tongue into the opening. The young girl became dimly aware of a tingling sensation spreading upward inside her body. As the probing and licking continued, her mind became numb.

1

Finally, he lifted his head up. "Did you like that, honey? Daddy will do that for you anytime you want. Now what will you do for your daddy?"

"I don't know, Daddy, I'm scared. Can't I go to sleep?"

"No, honey, it's all right, you'll see. It's just you and me and we're going to have a lot of fun together." He opened his pants and took her hand and placed it on his penis which was fully erect. "Do you know what that is, honey?"

She was cringing now but she said: "It's your thing, isn't it? I saw it once when you were coming out of the toilet, but it's so hard. What do you want me to do, Daddy?"

"Just you lay there, honey, and Daddy will take care of everything. All you do is lay back and spread your legs a little bit more."

Leaning on his elbows he stretched himself out over her now trembling body. His fingers separated the lips of her vagina and slowly he placed his penis into the opening and began to ease himself into her. There was no one to hear her screams as her hymen shredded, and thrust by thrust he penetrated deeper and deeper. The screams ebbed into sobs and then she lost consciousness as he continued thrusting. When he came he lifted the slender body off the bed and, his passion spent, he collapsed on top of her.

ONE

The river flows through the Valley of the Delaware and along its banks are towns and villages where once ferries, and now bridges, transported traffic across the river. Frenchtown is a sleepy Delaware River town nestled in the middle-reaches of the Delaware Valley. It has but modest pretensions; while once it had flourished on trade with the surrounding farmers, that had disappeared by the turn of the century and now, some ninety years later, the sleepy village had become quaintly charming. Its main street, Bridge Street, sported antique shops, art galleries and framing studios, artsy gift stores and restaurants catering to the tourist trade, a pizzeria, and a motley collection of stores catering to the locals, including a unisex barber shop, the great majority of whose customers and employees were grossly over-weight. The local population numbered some fifteen hundred re-siding in an area of a square mile of mostly late Victorian homes largely converted into two and three-family dwellings. Within the past decade there had been a minor influx of artists, musi-cians, and a few writers. Otherwise, the population was blue col-lar, hard-working and drinking, and honest. On the weekends and holidays when the weather was pleasant tourists paraded along the two short blocks of Bridge Street gazing in the win-dows of the shops which catered to them, and bikers congregat-ed around the Bridge Cafe on the left bank of the river.

Local crime consisted mostly of speeding, driving under the influence, spousal and girl friend abuse, barroom brawls occa-sionally ending in a knifing, soft drugs, vandalism, a weekly break and entry, and as winter neared, the theft of snow plow blades. The Frenchtown police had almost enough expertise to deal with that level of criminal behavior. The department con-sisted of a chief whose principal activity was to drive a patrol car and scowl at the tourists and locals alike; a sergeant and a pa-trolman, both fifty pounds overweight, who spent most of what passed for their duty time parked inside a cemetery gate or on side streets and parking lots waiting to pounce on speeders and passing out tickets, the revenues from which went a long way to support the Frenchtown budget.

And then there was Gus Bass. The town fathers had placed Gus in charge of criminal investigations and supplied him with an imposing array of the latest technological equipment consisting of a telephone, a manual typewriter, and a hand-held tape recorder with four cassettes. Since he didn't wear a uniform they didn't have to give him a uniform allowance and instead gave him his own office, if a cell measuring six by eight feet could be called an office. Gus had worked as a cop in the Trenton Police Department for ten years and had been a detective there for almost two years and two months when he was shot in the foot and was given a small disability pension and asked to find other employment.

Gus made few demands on his present employer. Officially, he was a part-time employee, received no health insurance or other fringe benefits, and was paid eleven dollars an hour plus overtime for anything over forty hours a week. And that is how Gus knew the chief could read, because the chief could spot any overtime on Gus's timesheets and put a string of x's together. The "x" was the only word Gus had ever seen the chief write in the two years he had known the man.

Gus never complained about the timesheets or not getting the overtime which got the chief's x's. He was not a whiner; having passed the age of forty, he had accepted what he was and where he was and that was twenty pounds or so overweight and an over-the-hill part-time cop in a hick town. He had once been an athlete with a good body, which had now gone to pot. He often remembered his high school coach telling him that he slouched too much when he was sitting down and that he would have all kinds of back problems by the time he was middle-aged. The coach had been right on the money; while he didn't think of himself as middle-aged, his back was almost literally a real pain in the ass. The only thing Gus had going for him was that he had never married and so he had no ex-wife looking for alimony and no one was after Gus for child support. There had been a few close calls but they had never been able to get a DNA match.

The first call came in at 3:30 P.M. on a Friday, June 3, which also happened to be Gus's forty-second birthday, a non-event he

4

had decided to ignore completely. At the time, he was sitting at his desk typing a criminal referral form for the Hunterdon County Prosecutor's Office for one George Walters who had managed to leave his driver's license next to a broken rear window of an unoccupied dwelling. George, upon noticing his loss the next day, had walked into Gus's office that morning to report the loss. By a strange coincidence, George had a rap sheet with four prior B&E arrests and two convictions, for which he had served a total of ninety days in the county lockup over in Flemington.

It took Gus about ten minutes of quiet conversation with George to extract an inculpatory statement. It seemed that George was lost just about a block from his mother's house and was trying to get information as to his whereabouts. He rang the doorbell of this house but got no answer. So he decided to go around to the rear to gain entry only to use the telephone to call his mother. The back door was locked but there was a window near it and he decided to use a small screwdriver he happened to have with him to pry open the window but the window broke and his screwdriver happened to fall inside. George realized that it might look suspicious if his screwdriver were to be found inside a house with a broken window and besides, it probably had his fingerprints on it. George had been watching too much TV; he didn't know the Frenchtown PD had no equipment to lift fingerprints and Gus figured that maybe it was just as well George didn't know that.

So George put his hand inside the window to retrieve his screwdriver. Just as he recovered it he heard several dogs barking loudly and quite close by. George figured that he best find out where he was some other way. But as God was his witness he had never entered the house and had not taken a thing. And for the life of him he just couldn't figure out how he dropped his driver's license next to the window.

"Are you sure you didn't lose it, George, when you climbed through the window?"

"Mr. Bass, I swear I never went into that house except to get my screwdriver."

"Well, let's see what we got here George. You broke a window, right?"

"But, Mr. Bass, that was an accident."

"And then you reached in through the window to get your screwdriver, isn't that right, George?"

"But that's all I wanted to get. I didn't want anything from that house. And besides, there wasn't anything in it worth anything, anyway."

Gus decided to ignore that statement. George couldn't help it; George was the end product of too much in-breeding which was not exactly uncommon among the local population.

"Okay, George, let's see what we got here. You broke the window, that's a break. And then you reached in through the window to recover your screwdriver. George, that's a break and entry if I ever heard one."

George seemed to nod as if in agreement, and Gus, suppressing a smile, said: "George, I'm not going to place you under arrest, although I probably should. I'm going to report this to the county and let them decide what they want to do. Just make sure you stay around Frenchtown, or for sure we'll have to get out an arrest warrant for you. Do you understand what I'm telling you, George?"

"I sure do Mr. Bass, and I want to thank you. You're a decent guy. I'm always telling everybody you are."

"Well, thanks, George. I appreciate that and I'll call you when I hear from the county."

TWO

So Gus was in his office when the call came in at 3:30 P.M. A Mrs. Gladys Hartwick, 222 Ridge Road. Her son Bobby, aged six, had not returned from school at three o'clock. She had gone down Ridge to the path through Veterans Park near the foot of Ridge Road which she did every day to meet him and walk him home or downtown to shop with her. But today Bobby wasn't there. She had seen two of his friends, the Aaron boys, coming up the path and Bobby usually was with them, but he wasn't there and they hadn't seen him. She had run through the park and across Creek Road to the school but couldn't find anybody who had seen Bobby. She ran back home and called his friend Jimmy's house, but he wasn't there and Jimmy's mom said that Jimmy hadn't seen him either. By the end of the narrative she was hysterical and screamed out: "Where is Bobby, you've got to find him."

"Look, Mrs. Hartwick, just calm down. Call your husband and I'll be there in less than five minutes." He hung up and immediately dialed the Frenchtown Elementary School. He knew Margaret Shipley would not have left and she answered the phone on the second ring. Gus recognized Margaret's voice; they had first met when Gus had talked to the kids at the school about the signs which read "Drug Free School Zone" and how to deal with strangers who approached them and to write down license plate numbers.

Peg was the assistant principal at the Frenchtown school and had introduced Gus to the kids at the assembly program. After that Gus and Peg had been seeing each other off and on for about six months, frequently eating and occasionally sleeping together, more for company than love.

Before Peg could finish saying Frenchtown Elementary School, Gus broke in: "Peg, this is Gus. I'm down at the station and I just had a call from a Mrs. Hartwick who says her son Bobby didn't come home from school this afternoon and none of the kids in the neighborhood have seen him. She's upset and I'm going over to her place to get more information."

"That's strange. Bobby Hartwick didn't return after lunch recess and I was just about to call Mrs. Hartwick to find out if Bobby was sick. She really should have called us."

Gus grimaced. "All right, Peg. I'm leaving now for the Hartwicks. Check with the kid's teacher and find out if she knows anything about what might have happened to the kid. Call me at the Hartwick's as soon as you find out anything. By the way, do you know if Bobby has any brothers or sisters?"

"There's a younger brother, about three, I think. Mrs. Hartwick was here a few weeks ago asking about a pre-school program."

"Okay, call me as soon as you can. Maybe I'll stop in tonight. How about seven?"

"Fine, Gus. I'll see you then and I'll call you at the Hartwick's after I speak to his teacher."

Gus's transport was not only an unmarked car, it was also his own car, for which Frenchtown reimbursed Gus at the rate of twenty-five cents per mile, even though the IRS allowed thirty cents a mile. So Gus had to keep exact records of mileage traveled on Frenchtown business. They had to be exact because the chief spent at least an hour each week checking Gus's mileage against town and county maps computing the exact mileage against Gus's trip sheet, and if Gus's mileage was over, it got the "x" treatment. But Gus didn't complain about that either.

The ride to 222 Ridge Road was 0.8 miles, down Creek Road past Veterans Park to King Street and then up King and a left on Ridge. The street was lined on both sides with two story frame houses dating from the late 1920s when it became fashionable to seek elevation rather than proximity to the river. The houses were built on 75-foot lots which at the time were considered to be "estates." Over the years the "estates" had been converted to two-family dwellings and No. 222 was the tenth house on the left, gray clapboard with yellow shutters and freshly painted. There was a large front porch separated down the middle by a railing to serve two families. The number "222" was next to the door on the left side of the porch, and as Gus went up the steps he noticed a small bike with training wheels leaning against the porch railing. When he reached the top step, he could see Mrs. Hartwick standing just inside the glass-fronted door which she

8

opened as he walked across the porch. Gus could see she was a thin, flat-chested woman, probably in her late twenties, about five-two with straight, ash blond hair which hung down to her shoulders, and a thin sharp featured face dominated by piercing blue eyes. Her complexion was blotchy and her eyes were swollen. She was wearing what his mother would have called a house dress, no jewelry, and well-scuffed loafers.

Gus put on one of his better smiles. "Mrs. Hartwick, I'm Gus Bass. Have you had any word about Bobby?"

Her thin voice came in sobs. "No, none at all. I've been calling everyone I can think of and no one has seen Bobby. I've tried to reach my husband but he's on a job somewhere and his boss has sent someone over to tell him to come home."

"Mrs. Hartwick, when did you last see Bobby?"

She turned and started walking into the front hall. After a brief pause she stopped and, turning to face Gus, said, "Right after he ate lunch. He was a little late and Ricky, that's my three year old, has a cold and was fussing a lot, so I didn't walk Bobby down Ridge. I stayed on the porch until Bobby got to the path through the park. I saw him start down the path and waved to him and he waved back and went down the path. That was the last I saw him."

Following her into the narrow hall, Gus said: "Do you usually let him go back to school alone?"

Her voice seemed calmer now. "Usually he goes back and forth to school with the Aaron boys but sometimes, like today, if he misses them, then I just watch him from the porch until he heads down the path."

"Did you see anyone else on Ridge when Bobby was walking back to school?"

She shook her head. "No, there wasn't anyone else around. Bobby's friends, the two Aaron boys, had already left."

"Where is Ricky now?"

Pointing toward the staircase at the end of the hall, Gladys said, "He's upstairs playing in his room. He's already asked me where Bobby is and I told him he was at a friend's house."

Gus glanced toward the stairs and then back at Gladys: "Can you think of anyone Bobby might have gone home with?"

Without hesitating but in a sharper voice Gladys replied:

"No, I've called everyone I could think of but Bobby isn't with any of them."

"Mrs. Hartwick, are you sure Bobby went back to school after lunch? You see, I've already checked at the school and they said Bobby didn't come back after lunch."

Gladys gasped and seemed to shrivel, leaning against the wall for support. The sobbing started again and she covered her face with her hands. "Oh, no, no, no. Why didn't someone tell me?"

Gus put his hand on her shoulder trying to comfort her and said: "They thought he might have gotten sick and they were waiting to hear from you. As a matter of fact, when I called the school they were about to call you to find out what had happened to him."

At that moment the telephone rang. Gus said: "That may be for me. I've asked Mrs. Shipley to call me here if she found anything out. Where's the phone? I'll get it."

Gladys pointed toward the back of the front hall and Gus walked down the hall and picked up the phone.

"Gus Bass here. Who is this?"

"Gus, it's Peggy. Look, I've spoken to Bobby's teacher and she says Bobby definitely didn't come back to school after lunch and she reported it to the office. She says that Bobby didn't seem to be sick during the morning and he was certainly all right when he left. As a matter of fact, she noticed him walking with the younger Aaron boy towards the park on their way home for lunch. That's all I can tell you. What's going on?"

Gus paused before he replied: "Look, I'm not sure now, but I'll call you as soon as I have anything."

"I'll make some more calls and see if I can find out anything. Where will you be?"

"Try me at the station. If I'm not there just go home and wait for me to call, okay?"

"Sure, Gus. Please be sure to call, I'm worried."

"So am I. Speak to you later." Gus hung up and went back to the front of the hall. Mrs. Hartwick wasn't there. He turned to his right and walked into a small parlor room almost barren of furniture except for an oversize television, a lazy-boy chair mounted on a swivel base, and a small table in the corner. There

10

were blinds on the two small windows but no curtains, no pictures on the walls, and no adornment of any kind. Mrs. Hartwick was sitting in the lazy-boy, her head bowed. Gus walked over to her and knelt down and spoke calmly. "Look, Mrs. Hartwick, I'm sure there's nothing wrong. We'll find Bobby but you've got to pull yourself together and help me."

Without looking up, Gladys said almost matter-of-factly: "I'm never going to see him again. I know something's happened and you won't tell me. Where is he?"

"Look, Gladys. It's maybe twenty minutes since you first called me. I don't know where Bobby is, but we're going to find him for sure and he's going to be all right. But you have to help. Look, I don't know what Bobby looks like. Can you describe him for me?"

Gladys Hartwick now straightened up in the chair, and she seemed to be staring straight ahead, looking right through Gus. When she finally responded her voice was mechanical, like the voice that gives you the number when you call information. "Bobby is forty-six inches tall, weighs about forty-eight pounds. He has brown eyes and brownish-blond hair. I don't know what else to tell you. He's just an average little boy."

"What was he wearing when he went back to school?"

The response was in the same mechanical voice: "A yellow long sleeve polo shirt and jeans. It's warm out. And his blue sneakers, but no socks. He hates to wear socks."

Gus stood up and stared down at Gladys. She must have been aware of Gus's movement for she looked up but continued to look straight through him. He thought to himself she must be in shock and he had no idea what he should do next. Finally, he said: "Look, Gladys, maybe it would help if I had a picture of Bobby. Tell me where to look and I'll get it."

With that Gladys rose from the lazy-boy and went over to the small table in the corner. She opened up a folder and turned to Gus with a picture in her outstretched hand. "Here's Bobby. That's all I have."

Gus walked over to her and took the picture from her hand. The picture was reasonably clear and Gus could see a small face, smiling and very animated, with dark blond, shaggy hair. The boy was cradling a large plastic water pistol in his arms and Gus could see that he had a slightly chubby body.

"Gladys, when was this picture taken?"

Again the robotic response: "About three weeks ago. We were having a party for Ricky. It was his third birthday."

"I would like to take it with me. We'll need it to show to people."

"It's all I have left. Will you bring it back?"

"Of course, I'll have copies made." The phone rang again and Gus went down the hall to answer. "Hello, Gus Bass here. Who's calling?"

"This is Bob Hartwick. Where's my wife? What's going on there?"

"Mr. Hartwick, this is Gus Bass. I'm with the Frenchtown Police Department. Everything is all right but I would like to see you as soon as you can get here. Your son Bobby is missing and we're about to start a search for him."

"Where's Gladys? Let me speak to her."

"Just a moment, let me get her. . . . Gladys, it's your husband. He wants to speak to you."

Gladys came out of the parlor and walked down the hall to Gus who held out the phone to her. She didn't reach for the phone but put the back of her hand to her mouth and started to fall. Gus reached out with his free hand and caught her. "Look, Mr. Hartwick, I think it would be a good idea for you to come home right now. Your wife is upset and I've got to get things going. How soon can you get here?"

"It'll take me ten minutes at least. Is Ricky there?"

"I haven't seen him but your wife says he's upstairs playing in his room. I really think everything is going to work out okay, but your wife needs someone to look after her. Is there anyone I can call before you get here?"

"I don't know. You might call Becky Aaron, she's just a few doors down. She knows Glad and maybe she can help. I'll leave now. Where will you be?"

"I'll be within yelling distance. My car is in front of your house and just give a call. I'll go down to see if I can get Mrs. Aaron up here."

Gus hung up the phone and half-walked and half-carried Mrs. Hartwick back to the parlor and sat her down in the lazy-boy. Her hands covered her face as she slumped down in the chair. After a long minute her eyes opened but she didn't see Gus, who knelt down and spoke gently to her: "Gladys, please stay here a few minutes. I'm going to get Mrs. Aaron and I'll be right back. Is that all right?"

Gladys seemed to nod and Gus immediately left. As he went down the steps he realized he wasn't sure exactly which was the Aaron's house. He started to go back and as he did he saw a small boy running down the steps of a house three doors down the street. He turned and yelled out to the boy: "Hey, is your name Aaron?"

The boy turned quickly and seemed to be sizing Gus up. Gus realized the boy must be thinking about the talk Gus had given about being approached by strangers. "Hey, Aaron, this is Gus Bass. Remember me, the cop who spoke to you at school? I want you to go back in and ask your mother to come out. I need to speak to her. Would you please do that for me?"

Gus wasn't sure whether the kid recognized him or if he was just scared, but the boy quickly turned and ran up the steps and disappeared through the door. He heard a yell, "Mommy, there's a man out there."

Within seconds a tall heavy-set, frowning woman walked cautiously through the door and onto the porch, clad in a halter top and slacks. Her brunette hair was drawn back in a bun. Gus strode toward her and she opened her mouth, prepared to scream. Gus beat her to it. "Mrs. Aaron? I'm Gus Bass from the Frenchtown PD. Could you please come over to the Hartwick's? I need someone to stay with Mrs. Hartwick for a few minutes."

Becky Aaron stared at Gus, uncertain what to do next, and then she started down the steps and walked towards Gus, who now attempted to smile. "Look, Mrs. Aaron, Bobby Hartwick is missing and Mrs. Hartwick is very upset. Her husband will be home in a few minutes and I need someone to stay with her while I can get something organized. Can you do that?"

Becky Aaron's hand shot up to her mouth as she gasped: "Of course, let me tell my husband and I'll be right there."

She disappeared into her house and was back on the porch and running down the steps towards Gus in less than thirty seconds. "What happened? I knew something must be wrong. The boys told me that Gladys couldn't find Bobby and had gone running down the path to the school."

Gus tried to continue his reassuring smile. "I'm not sure anything has happened. Apparently Bobby didn't make it back to school after lunch and Mrs. Hartwick hasn't any idea where he is. Please go in and stay with her at least until her husband gets home, he's on his way now. I've to go make some calls."

"Of course. Is she all right?" Gus's words then registered on her and her jaw sagged. "You mean Bobby's been gone since lunchtime? How can that be? Didn't anybody tell that poor woman?"

"I don't know yet how it can be. All I know is that the school says he didn't come back after lunch and Gladys says she saw him going down the path through the park after she gave him lunch. Look, I think Gladys may be in shock, just look after her and check on Ricky. I think he's upstairs in his room."

Becky Aaron ran up the steps into the Hartwick house and Gus heard her call out for Gladys. He turned and went to his car, reached in, and grabbed his cellular phone, paid for by Gus and not the Frenchtown PD, which had only recently installed radios in its two patrol cars. Gus dialed headquarters and was about to hang up after several rings when he heard Sgt. Ralph Krantz's unmistakable voice: "Hello?"

"Krantz, how many times have you been told to answer 'Frenchtown Police Department?' Jesus, get off your ass and get me the chief quick."

"Is this Bass? Don't you yell at me, who the hell do you think you are.

"I know who I am, you dumb bastard. Get me the chief."

"He's not here, but when I see him you can be sure I'm going to tell him what you called me."

"I don't give a shit what you tell him. Where is he?"

"I'll tell him that too, and I don't know where he is and if I did know I sure as hell wouldn't tell you."

"Look, asshole, we've got a six-year-old kid who's missing and if you can't get the chief to call me back on my car phone, I'm going to call in the Prosecutor's Office, the State Police and maybe the FBI. Do you understand what I'm telling you?"

14

"Look, Bass, I don't give a fuck who you call. I've had it up to here with you."

Gus, whose voice had been rising in volume throughout the encounter, now smiled as he lowered his voice: "That's fine with me, Krantz. Just remember this call is being taped and you can explain it to the chief." With that, Gus hit the end button and dialed Chuck Fahy's direct number at the Hunterdon Country Prosecutor's Office.

THREE

Gus had worked with Fahy several times over the past two years and respected Fahy as a competent and dedicated cop. Fahy was the chief of detectives of the County Prosecutor's Office and had spent his entire career as a prosecutor's detective conducting field investigations, preparing cases for the grand jury, and assisting lawyers in the prosecutor's office at trials. Fahy had a Marlboro-man type craggy face atop a six-foot-four body. His physical size and booming voice could be intimidating and he had learned law enforcement the hard way, on the job. He was looked upon by his staff and lawyers in the county as being honest and fair. He had only one quirk known to Gus. He refused to carry a gun or any other weapon except for an old-fashioned six-cell flashlight. Gus had heard that Fahy had used the flashlight only once, to knock a gun out of the hand of a hold-up suspect who didn't want to be apprehended.

Standing orders of the prosecutor required local PD's to notify the prosecutor's office immediately of any felony or violent crime. But Gus's chief's orders were that Gus had to call the chief first to get permission to call Flemington. Gus knew he would catch hell for jumping the gun, but let the chief explain where he was and why he hadn't left word at HQ where he could be reached.

Gus recognized Chuck Fahy's voice as soon as he answered. And Gus could tell he wasn't anxious to take a call at four on a Friday afternoon.

"Chuck, this is Gus Bass over in Frenchtown."

"Well, Gus, I haven't heard from you for awhile. How's everything going over there? What can I do for you?"

Gus glanced up and down the street and almost in a whisper said: "I think we've got a problem. About three-thirty this afternoon I got a call from a Mrs. Hartwick that her six-year-old son hadn't come home after school and she couldn't locate him. I checked with the school and they said he never returned to school after the lunch break. I'm up at the kid's house now, and the mother says she saw the kid go off to school at about twelve-forty-five, and that's the last time anyone seems to have seen the kid. I've called my chief and he's not around. The only one I can locate is that idiot Krantz and I need help quick to start canvassing the neighborhood and searching the area. It doesn't smell right."

There was no response for a few seconds and then Fahy said: "I don't like the smell of it either. Look, Gus, I don't know how many of my guys I can get over there right now. It's Friday and some have left early, but I'll do what I can and head over to you in a few minutes. Where will you be?"

"I'll be around the Hartwicks' house at least until the husband gets home from work. That's 222 Ridge Road. I'll start checking with the neighbors, but I don't think too many are home from work yet."

"You do that Gus and I'll see you in twenty minutes."

Gus put the phone back in his car and decided to try the house at 218 first. There were no cars parked in front or in the driveway and Gus got no response when he knocked at either of the two front doors. He glanced down at the next house, 214, but it also seemed to be deserted, so he walked back to the Hartwick house and into the rear yard which was neatly mowed, the grass lush and well-kept flower beds bordering the rear of the house. Gus continued walking to the back of the yard which was bounded by a tall, dense hedgerow of hemlock and forsythia whose bloom had long since faded. As he made his way through the meshed-together branches he found himself at the edge of an embankment, about thirty feet or more above the northerly end of Veterans Park. Gus was amazed by the density of the trees which rose above him and the undergrowth below. In the two years or so that he had lived in Frenchtown, he had never been beyond the playground at the park's southerly end. He remembered something about a nature trail up at this end, and now he understood why. Despite his vantage point, he couldn't see any of the ground below.

As he turned and walked back to the front of the house, a pickup truck turned into the driveway. A short, slender man wearing jeans and a jean shirt with the embroidered name "Bob" over the left front pocket quickly dismounted and started toward the house.

Gus called out: "Mr. Hartwick?"

The man stopped and turned to face Gus. "Yes, are you Mr. Bass?"

Gus tried but couldn't quite make the same smile he had given Becky Aaron. "That's right. Could I have a few words with you before you go in?"

"I want to see my wife. Can't it wait?"

Gus tenderly put his hand on Hartwick's shoulder and said: "Mrs. Aaron is in there with her now and I just need a few minutes." Gus related the story Gladys had told him and added: "Your wife is really shook up so you just go in and stay with her and as soon as I find out anything I'll call you. The prosecutor's office will have some men over here soon to start a search. We're going to get Bobby back."

Bob Hartwick ran up the steps and Gus walked back to his car, picked up the phone, and called headquarters. After five rings he recognized the chief's nasal whine: "Frenchtown Police Headquarters, Chief of Police Robert Winters speaking."

"Chief, this is Gus. I'm . . ."

The chief's voice reflected his anger. "Bass, where the hell are you and what's all this bullshit about a missing kid? And I want you to stop riding Sergeant Krantz all the time. You get your tail back here right now or else."

Gus tried to remain calm: "Chief, I think you had better hear me out. I'm over at the Hartwicks' house, up on Ridge. And it's not bullshit, their kid is missing since lunch time." Gus sketched out what he knew and then added: "When I couldn't get you I called Fahy over in Flemington and he's on his way here now with some of his people to start a search for the kid."

Gus could picture in his mind the chief's face as he barked into the phone: "Who said you could call Fahy? You know you have to clear that with me first. I'm calling him right now and he had better keep his ass out of my town unless I call him and as for you, I have had it with you. You're out and I mean finished."

"Chief, it's a little late to call off Fahy. He just pulled up. I

18

think you had better come over here so you can tell him to get back to Flemington yourself, in person."

Gus hung up and walked over to Fahy's car as it pulled up to the curb. Just behind Fahy another county car rolled up and Gus recognized Bert Williams, the only black investigator in the Prosecutor's Office, and Sam Carter, Fahy's number one detective.

Before Fahy could get his door open Gus was alongside the car: "Chuck, I'm sure glad to see you, but I've got to tell you the chief is probably on his way over and he's madder than hell I called you in without clearing it with him. As a matter of fact he told me I'm through."

As he opened the door and got out Fahy was grinning and he said: "Don't worry about that, Gus. I'll deal with him and if he really means it, you got a job with me. You better give me a rundown on what you have so far."

As Gus opened his mouth, the chief's car sped up the street and screeched to a halt alongside Gus's car. The door swung open hard, banging into the side of Gus's car and bouncing back catching the chief square in the nose as he emerged. The blow was hard enough to knock the chief back into his seat. Gus and Fahy looked at each other and doubled over. Williams and Carter who were walking toward them stared at the chief holding his nose and started laughing. For sure, the chief was a favorite over in Flemington.

More slowly this time the chief reemerged from his car, stood up, squared his hat, and strode over to Fahy and Gus, mustering what he considered his foremost scowl. "Fahy, you may be boss over in Flemington, but this is my town and you don't come in here unless I call you first. Now I want you and your people gone, now."

Fahy was about six inches taller than the chief and his voice about six octaves lower. Like all big men who knew their business, he rarely raised his voice except to make a point that had to be made. He looked down at the chief and said very quietly: "Chief, I'm taking over this investigation. And Bass here is going to be working directly for me and reporting to me. I want you to get back in your vehicle, turn it around and get back to your headquarters or wherever else you hide out and stop interfering

19

with me and my men. If you don't so help me I'll have you called before a grand jury for obstructing an investigation. Do I make myself understood?"

The chief's lower jaw was now moving from side to side and Gus could hear the teeth grinding while the chief struggled to control himself. His eyes were bulging, but no sound came from his mouth. Fahy's voice dropped another octave. "I want you to leave now! And I want you to call Krantz and that other asshole you've got working for you and tell them to get over here immediately and report to me. If you're not gone in five seconds I'll have Williams take you over to see the prosecutor and you can explain to her what's going on here."

With that, Fahy turned his back on the chief and taking Gus by the arm started walking toward the Hartwicks' front steps. Gus glanced over his shoulder at the chief, whose body was now rigid with his hands clenched into fists. Williams took two steps toward the chief who turned to face Williams and snarled: "Stay away from me, you black bastard, or I'll . . ."

Fahy turned abruptly and in two strides had the chief by the front of his jacket. His voice now rose in volume: "You know, I can't spare Williams, come to think of it. So I want you to get into that car and drive yourself straight to Flemington and report to Prosecutor Stevens. I'm calling her with a report. If I don't hear from the prosecutor in thirty minutes, I'm calling the state police to have you picked up."

The chief's jaw dropped. He tried to speak but no words came out. Finally, he turned and strode back to his car. As he opened the door to get in, his head twisted back toward Fahy: "Fuck you, Fahy and that dike prosecutor you got over there." He slid behind the wheel and backed down Ridge, leaving rubber on the street.

Gus gulped and said: "Chuck, do you think he's really going over to the prosecutor?"

Fahy's grin spread nearly from ear to ear: "I hope so, because she's not there. She left early to go to the shore for the weekend. Now let's get down to business. What have you got so far?"

"Not a hell of a lot. The mother is in shock and a neighbor is in with her. The father just got home. There's no one home at the two houses south of here and I checked the rear yards as far

20

as I could see and there's nothing there. I think we should check out the park pretty quick. It's a long shot but he might have decided to play hooky and gone up into the woods and got lost."

Fahy's frown signaled he didn't think much of the idea. He said: "If I remember the layout of the Park, Creek Road runs along the westerly side, doesn't it?"

Gus nodded. "That's right. The kid would follow the path through the playground area and then have to cross Creek Road and walk up Creek Road to get to the school." Gus paused: "Yeah, I get it, anyone with a car on Creek Road could have picked the kid up, and if that's what happened we ain't' going to find him unless we get a break. I've got a picture of the kid taken about three weeks ago and a physical description and the clothes he was wearing. I think we should get it out on the teletype."

"Yes, I think we should do that. Give the picture to Williams and the description and tell him to get over to the office and get it out to the state police. I'm going in to the house and introduce myself to the parents. Come in as soon as you're finished."Gus walked over to Williams and Carter, pulled out his notebook and Bobby's photograph. He handed the photo to Williams and said: "Bert, this was taken three weeks ago, and I promised I would get it back to the kid's mother. Can you have copies made and bring it back?" He gave Bert the kid's description and asked: "Is there anything else you think you need?"

"That should be it, Gus. I'll get it on the wire and I'll be back here in a half-hour at the most. I'll catch up with you guys later. And Gus, how the hell do you put up with that motherfucker?"

"That's easy, Bert. I don't need the money."

"Lucky you, man. That foot shot down in Trenton was your big break. I'll be right back and I'll see if I can get some more guys over here." With that, Bert got in his car, U-turned on Ridge, and was gone.

Gus and Carter turned and started toward the steps. Carter was the first to speak: "You know, Gus, some day I'm going to run into your chief at the right time and place and that prick will be pissing up his asshole for a good long time."

"Let me know, Sam, I want to be there."

They entered the house together and found Fahy in the little parlor with the Hartwicks and Becky Aaron, who stood up when she saw Gus. "Mr. Bass, is it all right if I go home now? I've got to get supper for my family."

Gus looked at Fahy and it was Fahy who answered: "That will be all right, Mrs. Aaron. You run along home and feed your family. If we need you later one of us will come down and fetch you."

"No need to do that, just give me a call." She turned to Gladys, knelt down, and took her hand, squeezed it and was out the door.

Gladys Hartwick was still sitting in the lazy-boy, her husband on one knee beside her. Fahy was the first to speak: "Mrs. Hartwick, have you told us everything you know?"

The Hartwicks looked up quickly. Mrs. Hartwick's face was contorted but it was her husband who spoke: "What else can she tell you, she's told you what happened. When are you going to start looking for Bobby?"

Fahy put his hand on Hartwick's shoulder. "We'll have a search under way very soon, but I have to tell you that it's more than four hours since anyone last saw him and there's a real possibility that somebody could have taken him a long way from here in that amount of time. Mrs. Hartwick, when you were watching Bobby go down the street did you happen to see anyone walking on the street or maybe a car passing by?"

Gladys's face tensed and the words were almost spit out: "I told Mr. Bass I didn't see anybody on the street, walking or in a car. The street was empty except for Bobby and me."

"I know you told Gus that, but it's very important and I want you to keep thinking about it to see if you can't recall seeing anyone or anything unusual. Will you do that?"

Fahy then turned to Bob Hartwick: "Is it all right if I call you Bob?" Hartwick nodded and Fahy continued: "Bob, I know you have a young boy in the house. Is there anyone you can call to come over and help you out for awhile?"

"I can call my mother. She lives on the other side of the river in Lumberville and I'm sure she can get over here pretty quick."

"Fine, you do that and we'll get back to you as soon as we have any information."

FOUR

Gus, Chuck, and Carter walked down the front steps and as they reached the cars Fahy paused and said: "I see what you mean Gus. That woman gives me the creeps too, but for now we'd better get going on what we have." Fahy turned to Carter and said: "Sam, I want you to go over to Creek Road and start house-to-house above the park. See who was home between noon and 2:00 P.M. and if they saw any cars or people on Creek Road, especially headed north from the park. And ask them if they happened to be in Veterans Park or passing by around twelve-thirty or thereabout. Do you have a description of the kid?"

"Yah, Chuck, I made some notes when Gus gave the kid's description to Bert. Where will I catch up with you?"

"That's a good question." Turning to Gus, he said: "Gus, I think most of the work is going to be done over here for now and we should get some place big enough to set up as a situation room. We'll need some telephones and a desk or two. I don't suppose you got that kind of space at your headquarters?"

"You must be kidding, Chuck. Besides, I don't think we'd be welcome there. I think we could set up shop in the council chamber in the municipal building. It's right next door to headquarters and it's certainly big enough for what we'll need, all we'd have to do is get some phones in there. I'll give Mary Trantino a call, she's the borough clerk, and I'm sure she'll cooperate. She's been around this town forever and she's the one who gets things done around here."

"That'll be just fine, Gus. You get that going and I'll call the prosecutor and give her a rundown. She should have reached the shore by now and she'd want to know about this."

Fahy walked to his car, picked up his cellular and dialed. "Ms. Stevens, glad I got you. This is Chuck Fahy. How's your weather there?...Glad to hear it. The weather here was fine, too, until I got a call awhile ago from Gus Bass over in Frenchtown. You know him?...Well, I think he's a smart cop and certainly the only cop they've got over here...I think we've got a child abduction. . . . No, not a kidnapping. The family certainly isn't wealthy and there is nothing to indicate someone might have picked him up for ransom or anything like that. It doesn't look good, the kid has been missing since lunchtime. I'm trying to get the boys from the office over here to start a search and do a house to house job. It's going to mean overtime, is that all right with you? . . . Fine, and I think it would be a good idea to have an assistant prosecutor available. Anyone you want me to call? . . . Thanks, you can tell him to try me for now on my cellular and I'll check in with him later. . . . You do, too, and I'll call you in the morning. What would be a good time? . . . Oh, and by the way, I almost forgot. I had a little run-in with the chief over here. It seems he doesn't want our office on his turf, if you know what I mean. It's the same old story with that jackass and I told him to go over to your office and wait to see you. I doubt if he did, but at least he's out of our hair for now. . . . Okay. If I see him I'll be sure to do exactly that. Have a good weekend, I hope I'm not spoiling it."

As Chuck ended his call, Gus was standing alongside of him. "Ms. Stevens has given us full authority to get all the manpower we need and she's assigned Ben Harris to us if we need any legal input. He's a bright guy and I'm glad we have him. How did you make out with the clerk?"

Gus grinned. "She's getting it set up. She'll have the council chamber ready for us and a couple of phones and typewriters set up in there for us to use. I asked her if she knew anyone who uses the playground during the day, and she is going to check that out. What's next?"

Fahy nodded and said: "I think it's time to head for the park and start looking there. We'll leave the cars here and walk down and follow the path the kid took. Let's time it to the path and then through the playground. It'll give us an idea how much time the kid could have been seen by the neighbors or anyone who happened to be around at the time."

They heard the squeal of tires and a county car screeched to a stop alongside them. Fahy said: "Well, Bert's back. He sure made good time. I'm just glad I wasn't in that car with him."

As Williams got out, Fahy walked over and said: "Look, Gus and I are going to head down to the park and start looking be-

24

fore it gets too dark. Sam is working Creek Road house to house and I want you to stay here on Ridge and do the same. Find out if anyone saw the kid leave the house after lunch or if they happened to see any cars on Ridge around that time. When the guys from the office get here have one of them help you here, and send the others over to Creek Road to help Sam. Okay, Gus, let's get going."

Gus looked at his watch: "Right, it's five-fifty-eight and thirty seconds." The two of them started down the street walking at what they thought a kid's speed might be who was late for school. It took them just a minute to reach the path which led down a low embankment and into the playground area. Twenty seconds later and they were into the park and in another twenty seconds had reached Creek Road. "Okay, Chuck, that's a little under two minutes to reach Creek Road from his house, if he got this far."

Looking into the expanse of woods beyond the playground Fahy said: "You know, Gus, this park is a lot bigger than I remember it. For now it's just you and me and we've got less than two hours of decent light left so we had better get started into those woods up there. Let's start about ten yards in from Creek Road and walk north. Try to stay about five yards from me and we'll go up to the creek and then move over and head back. Okay?"

Gus nodded and the two walked off almost in step and reached the woods in half a minute or so. The first five or ten yards were easy going, but as they went further, the trees, the vines and the undergrowth got thicker and their pace slowed down. It took them almost thirty minutes to reach the course of the creek closest to the road for which it was named. They stopped at the bank of the creek and looked at each other. Their shirts were torn and their hands full of nicks and scratches from the briars and vines. Gus asked: "Should we try crossing the creek?"

Fahy shook his head. "I don't think so, Gus. At this rate we won't even cover the lower end before it gets dark. So let's just move up this side and head back toward the playground."

They walked a few yards up the course of the creek and then reversed direction. The trip back to the playground clearing took even longer and produced nothing. The two men looked at each other, shrugged, and moved over and started back into the woods.

The trees and the undergrowth became even more dense and with the light fast fading, they realized it was hopeless to continue. They could barely see each other and could easily have missed anything more than a few yards to either side. About half way back to the creek Chuck yelled over to Gus: "I'm putting a penknife in this tree to mark how far we got. Let's head back and check out with the others."

As they emerged from the woods, Fahy said: "Damn it, Gus, that's about the thickest woods I've seen around here. How far does it go like that on the other side of the creek?"

Gus shrugged his shoulders. "I'm not really sure, but I would guess at least another half mile and from what I could see over there, it's even worse on the other side."

Fahy shook his head and said, "If we're going to do this right, we should have at least ten guys working this area and I don't have that many people. We'll have to call in the state guys or get some volunteers here in the morning."

They stepped up their pace back to Ridge Road and spotted Bert Williams at the door of a house almost directly opposite. Fahy yelled across: "Anything yet, Bert?"

"Not a thing, boss. There aren't that many people home. It's Friday night and they're probably hitting the bars early. I've only spoken to three people so far, and not a one of them was home between twelve o'clock and one o'clock. Cal Amster is working the upper part of Ridge and I sent Billy Howland over to help Sam."

"Good. When you finish up this end, go and help Cal up above. When you're done, come over to the municipal building next to their headquarters, and if you happen to run into the chief, I don't want you to say a word to him. Got that?"

Fahy turned to Gus and said: "You go over to the municipal building and I'll be right there. I want to tell the Hartwicks where we'll be and then I'll take a run up Creek Road and see if those guys have come up with anything."

Gus nodded and the two of them got into their cars and headed down Ridge.

FIVE

Gus pulled into his regular spot at headquarters. He could see the chief's car wasn't there, but Krantz' patrol car was in its assigned parking space. He figured he would stick his head in and find out where the chief was. As he opened the door, Krantz stood up, his jowls, which dominated his face, shaking. "Bass, I didn't think you would show your face around here for awhile. The chief said you were finished, kaput, and he doesn't want you in headquarters. You fucked up good this time."

"Actually, Krantz, I'm not staying. We're running this investigation out of the council chamber next door. I just stopped in to find out where you and your fat buddy, Schumacher, have been. Fahy told the chief to tell you to get your asses up to the Hartwicks' and he wanted me to find out what the hell happened to you."

Still yelling, although he was no more than a foot in front of Gus, Krantz screamed: "Is that so. Well, the chief says we have more important things to do than screwing around chasing after some lost kid or taking any shit from Fahy. He says that we take our orders from him and we do what he tells us to do. As a matter of fact, I'm going out on patrol right now, what do you think of that?"

"You mean you're going to sit on that fat ass of yours down in the cemetery. Well, if I were you I would check in with Fahy first and tell him what you told me. He'll be next door in a minute and I'm sure he would like to hear what you and the chief have to say."

Krantz quickly lowered his voice. "That suits me fine. I don't kiss anyone's ass like you, you prick."

"See you around, Krantz." Gus quietly closed the door and started laughing as he headed next door to the municipal building and walked into the council chamber. Mary Trantino was there talking on the telephone as he entered. She waved a hand at him and Gus could see other telephones spread out on the

27

councilmen's desks and two typewriters. Mary turned to Gus as she hung up.

"Gus, guess who that was! Hazel Stevens, the prosecutor. She wants to get in touch with the mayor. She left a number for the mayor to call and she told me, off the record, that the chief has been superseded or something like that and to make sure to tell the mayor that he keeps the chief away from your investigation. Gus, what's going on with the chief?"

Gus smiled. "That's a kind of long story, but let's just say that Fahy and the chief had some words about my calling the prosecutor's office in on this, and Fahy wants the chief out of his hair for now. Have you seen the chief?"

"No, I haven't laid eyes on him. I've been busy getting these phones and stuff set up for you and clearing things with the mayor so you guys could use this place. And I've been making some calls around to women I know who have little kids who might have been in the playground this afternoon. What's this all about anyway?"

"All I can tell you now, Mary, is that the Hartwick's older boy has disappeared. He's been gone since about one this afternoon. We've searched through the park, but we came up with nothing. Some of Fahy's guys are going door to door, and they should be checking in here soon. Tell me, Mary, did you come up with anything from any of the calls you made?"

Visibly upset at the news, Mary said: "Oh my, how awful." After a pause she continued: "Well, I've got two possibles. There's Jane Darrow who lives down on Harrison Street. She's got two small kids and she takes them to the playground often on nice days. She was there today, but she's not sure of the time, it could have been well after lunch. And there's a Sally Westerbrook over on Thompson Street, just off Creek Road. She was out shopping but her husband thinks she might have had her kid over at the park today. They all want to know what's going on, you know what a small town this is. There will be a lot of rumors going around just from the calls I made."

"I wouldn't worry about that. There will be a lot of talk going around soon enough. Look, if anyone asks you, just tell them you don't know anything and you're just doing what you have been told. Okay?"

Just then Fahy walked into the council chamber. Gus called out: "Chuck, come on over and let me introduce you to Mary Trantino. Mary, this is Chuck Fahy, I'm sure you have heard of him."

Fahy extended his hand—about twice the size of hers—and said: "How do you do, Mrs. Trantino. You certainly have been a big help and I want to thank you for what you have done."

"Believe me, Mr. Fahy, it's nothing at all. Just give me a ring if there's anything else you need, and I'll be right over. Gus has my number. If you don't mind, I had better get home now and see to my family."

"Well of course, and I don't think we'll have to disturb you. Enjoy your evening."

Mary walked out of the chamber and Gus could see by her stride that she was quite pleased with herself and probably smitten by Fahy, who turned to Gus: "We may have a lead. A woman up Creek Road about a quarter of a mile from the north end of the woods was out in her front yard pruning some shrubs and she says she saw a pickup truck she didn't recognize a little after one this afternoon traveling slowly up Creek Road from the park. She's sure of the time and she gave us a pretty good description of the truck, a dark blue Ford pickup, F-150. She didn't get a license number, but it definitely had the new issue Jersey plates. She couldn't give us a good description of the driver, just that he was a white male, with dark, longish hair. But she says he was driving with one hand and seemed to be pushing something down on the front seat with his other hand. It might have been a dog, but it could also have been our kid. You know, I think we can forget about the park for now. Someone picked up that kid, most likely offered him a ride to school, and the kid went with him because he was late. I'm going to call the state police and see what they can do with that truck."

Gus frowned. "You know, Chuck, half the vehicles in this county are pickups and probably half of them are Fords and half of them are some color of blue. It's worth a shot, but we'll have to get awfully lucky to get anything useful out of that."

"I hear you but that's all we have to go on for now. Are these phones working?"

"Mary was using one as I came in, so I guess they are. By

29

the way, Chuck, Mary told me that she got a call from the prosecutor before I got here and your boss is reaching out for the mayor. But she told Mary, off the record, that the chief is to stay away from us. I think Mary was pleased as all hell."

Fahy smiled: "That Hazel Stevens is a good woman. She's got bigger balls than any prosecutor I ever worked for."

Just then, Fahy's guys walked in. Sam Carter was almost bursting. "Hey, boss, we got another sighting of that blue pickup about six houses up from the first one. Same description of the vehicle but not much on the driver. New Jersey plates and he seemed to be picking up speed. This woman was taking out her garbage and she says she's sure the truck is an '88 or '89, because her son has the same truck. She says it's not from the neighborhood and the time matches with the first lady's."

Cal Amster couldn't resist: "Geez, Sam, you mean Hillary Clinton's in on this, too?"

With but a slight grin, Fahy snapped: "All right, Cal, cut the crap." Turning to Sam he said: "That's good work. Now we know at least we're not dealing with a mirage." Fahy sat down at the mayor's desk and dialed the state police barracks over in Flemington. Aside from the prosecutor's office and a few local PD's, the state police provided law enforcement presence for the rest of the county which covered almost 450 square miles with a population of over a hundred thousand. There were a total of one hundred ten cops in the local PD's and sixteen detectives and investigators in the prosecutor's office. That's the way the local politicians wanted it, and if it weren't for the state police, a lot of the county would have no cop presence. All of the major crime investigations were run by the prosecutor's staff which was also responsible for photo id-ing and fingerprinting arrestees, as well as interrogations, crime scene photography, witness statements, and everything else required to run a criminal investigation.

"Hello, this is Chief Fahy from the prosecutor's office. Is Captain Sloss still there? . . . Good, put me through would you. . . . Hi, Bob, this is Fahy. You're certainly working late tonight. How come?"

"Well for an old guy like me, it's kind of hard to see the clock, so I just hang around until someone kicks me out. What the hell are you doing, you're no spring chicken either."

"I won't argue with that. Look, I'm over in Frenchtown and we've got a situation here. A kid has been missing since about noontime, and we think he was snatched by some creep. The only lead we have right now is a dark blue Ford pickup with the new cream-colored Jersey plates which was spotted by two people leaving the area where the kid disappeared. From the description we got it was a Ford F-150, 1988 or 1989. The driver was a white male with long, dark hair. It's only a hunch but we think the guy is probably from nearby, though probably not from Frenchtown. I know it's a long shot, but could you get to one of your buddies at Motor Vehicles and get us a list of pickups in the county matching that?"

"That will take a lot of old buddying, but I'll see what we can do. They got a lot of computers down there and if I can find the right people we might get it by tomorrow but don't count on it. By the way, I saw the type from your office this afternoon, is this on that case?"

"Yeah, Bob, it is and it doesn't look too good right now. Listen, while you're at it, can you have one of your guys check with SCI and get a rundown for us on known child molesters in the area? Maybe, if we're lucky, we might get a match with the pickup."

"You got it friend. I can guess you're short-handed over there. Can I get you any warm bodies to give you a hand?"

"That's good of you, Bob. There's not much we can do tonight, but I could use some of your guys tomorrow morning first thing. Three or four would be a big help."

"You got it, pal. Where do you want them and when?"

"We're operating out of the municipal building in Frenchtown. If they could be here at eight tomorrow morning that would be a big help. Oh, and by the way, the chief here is out of the loop for now, so tell your guys to report directly to me."

"Is that jerk giving you any trouble? It would be like him."

"I think we've got that under control for now. If you get anything, you can reach me at this number, nine-nine-eight two-six-two-two. There will be somebody here through the night, so give us a call."

"You got it buddy, it's been good talking to you."

Fahy hung up the phone and said to Sam: "Call Noreen

31

Walsh and ask her to get at least one court stenographer over here as soon as possible and to have two here by nine tomorrow morning. Then call those ladies from up on Creek Road and ask them if they could get down here in about an hour or so to give us statements. I want to nail down their description of that vehicle while it's still fresh in their minds. Oh, and call the Sheriff's Office and tell them I want their K-9 unit here not later than seven-thirty tomorrow morning."

Gus said: "Chuck, Mary Trantino came up with two women with small kids who use the playground during the day. Is it all right if I go and check them out?"

"Fine, Gus, take Cal with you and if they have anything, bring them back and we'll take a statement here."

"I just have to make one phone call. I promised Peg—that's Mrs. Shipley, you know the principal at the school—I would let her know what's going on." Gus picked up one of the phones and dialed Peg's number at home. "Hello, Mrs. Shipley? This is Gus Bass. . . . Yeah, I know. . . . Look, we're working out of the municipal building and we'll be here for some time. . . . I don't know when, but you can reach me here at nine-nine- eight two-six-two-two in about an hour. I'll call you later, if you don't mind, and see if you have heard anything. Will that be all right. . . . Fine."

As they started to leave, the door to the council chamber opened and a broad-shouldered man wearing a white apron walked in carrying a load of pizza boxes. They stared at him and he grinned. "Hey, I'm from Napoli's pizza. Mrs. Trantino called and said there were some guys over here who need something to eat and she asked me to bring these over. I didn't know what you wanted, so I got one pepperoni, one with sausage and mushroom, and one with broccoli and clams. It's on the house."

The six of them looked at each other and at the pizza boxes. Gus was the first to speak: "Guys, this is Frankie, and he makes the best pizza this side of Trenton. Frankie, just set them down and we'll take care of them."

With a great flair, Frankie put the pizza boxes down on the mayor's desk and started to leave. He turned at the door, and looking at Gus, said: "I don't know what's going on, but if you guys need any food any time, just give a ring. It'll be on the house."

When the door closed, it was Fahy who spoke. "Look guys, the pizzas will keep. Let's get going. On your way back, maybe you could pick up a few beers to go with the pizza."

As they started toward the door again, it opened and in walked a short, round-faced elderly man with a monk-like fringe of white hair around the crown of his head. He was carrying a cooler and walked over to Gus.

"Hello, Mr. Bass? Mary Trantino called and said you fellows could use some beer. I've got three six packs here, on the house. Anything else you need just let me know." He put down the cooler next to the mayor's desk and strode out the door.

The prosecutor's men turned and looked at Gus. Sam Carter laughed: "Gus, it's some town you run here."

"It ain't me, guys, that's Mary Trantino. The people around here will do anything for her."

They finally got out the door.

SIX

Within the next two hours the Creek Road ladies had been in and were gone, having given their statements to Noreen Walsh. The playground mothers had been interviewed and they had drawn a blank with them. Neither one had been at or around the playground between twelve and one and they had no leads on anyone else who might have been. Noreen had insisted upon taking the reports of each of the detectives with the promise that they would have typed copies of everything by ten the next morning. The pizza and half of the beer had been consumed and the men were just sitting and stuporishly staring at one another.

Finally, Fahy stood up and said: "We might as well wrap it up for now, there's nothing more we're going to get done tonight. I want someone to volunteer to stay here on the phones and let's all be back here by seven o'clock in the morning. How about you, Billy, can you stay?"

"No problem, boss. If anything comes in I'll call you first thing."

As they were going out the door Fahy nudged Gus and said: "I'm going to stop off and see the Hartwicks and tell them where we're at. You get home and get some rest. Tomorrow is going to be a long day."

SEVEN

As soon as Gus was in his car, he called Peg. She answered sleepily. "Peg, it's Gus. Sorry, I guess I woke you up, but we just broke for the night. . . . No, nothing's turned up, just one lead on a truck that was in the area, that's all we got. Is it too late for me to come over? . . . Be there in five minutes."

Peg lived in a white, shingled ranch house, a few miles out of Frenchtown on the Pittstown Road. The house, complete with mortgage, was Peg's share of the equitable distribution that ended her marriage to a real loser. As she told Gus early on in their relationship, the distribution was the first and only thing equitable about her marriage. She had been divorced for over ten years, and at thirty-eight and a vivacious, amply endowed, hazel-eyed brunette, she was still getting offers but was determined never to make the same mistake again. That didn't make Gus unhappy; he had no interest in making the mistake for the first time.

Peg was at the door when Gus pulled up. As he walked in, she put her arms around him then stepped back and looked into his eyes. "Gus Bass, you look all in. Is it that bad? Get off your feet and I'll get you a drink." Gus plopped onto the couch and, resting his head on the back cushion, closed his eyes. Peg was back within a minute with a Stoly on the rocks and put it into his hands. Gus looked up and murmured: "Thanks."

Peg sat down next to him and started stroking his hair. "Gus, it's going to be all right, you'll see. Even if some jerk took him, I'm sure he won't hurt him. He'll most likely just keep him overnight and let him go in the morning." Gus sipped his drink slowly, still leaning his head back, his eyes closed. "Gus, isn't there anything I can do?"

Gus's eyes opened but were unfocused. "You don't understand, Peg. This is my worst fucking nightmare come true all over again."

"What do you mean, Gus? I don't understand, what kind of nightmare? Has anything like this happened before?"

35

Gus sighed: "I really don't want to talk about it, Peg."

Peg cupped her hand around Gus' chin and turned his head toward her: "Gus, if there's something eating at you, you've got to talk about it. Is it some case you had before?"

"Not really. It goes back way before Trenton, it started in 'Nam."

"You were in Vietnam? You know, you never told me that. What happened to you there, can't you tell me?"

Gus turned away and, shaking his head, said: "Peg, you really don't want to know. It was horrible, and it's been in my dreams ever since. There are nights I just don't want to go to sleep 'cause I know that dream will be there. It's like it is part of me and it won't let me go."

"Is it something you did, Gus?"

"Oh no, not me, for Christ's sake. It was something I saw and couldn't do a goddamned thing about. It was all over when I got there."

Peg put her arms around Gus' shoulders and turned him to face her. "Then you've got to talk about it. It's the only way it will ever let go of you, Gus, tell me what it is."

Suddenly Gus started to sob. At first he spoke haltingly but the pace picked up quickly and the words came out as if he were in a trance. "You know, Peg, My Lai wasn't the only massacre in 'Nam. That's the one that got all the headlines because they shot up so many. But there were a lot of other little My Lais all over the place. When I went over there at the end of sixty-nine, they were still doing these search and clear operations. They called it the Phoenix Program or some goddamned thing. They were going to pacify the countryside and make it safe for the farmers. What bullshit. I was in an MP platoon that was attached to an infantry regiment working with a South Vietnamese division in Quang Tri. We were supposed to follow along after recon patrols and look for stragglers and goof-offs and try to round up the gooks who decided they wanted to go home, not that I blamed them."

Gus paused and took a long sip of his drink. "One day we set out about an hour or so after the patrols had left. We were gone maybe two hours when we heard what sounded like a gun fight going on up ahead of us. This chicken shit looie who had just hit

'Nam and took over our platoon ordered us to stop and take cover. We laid around for a good half hour after the firing stopped and then he tells us it's safe to move. So we move out. We went about a mile, maybe less, and we come up to a little hamlet, just maybe a dozen or so shacks in a clearing alongside a rice paddy. We couldn't see a thing moving as we got nearer. And then I saw the first one, a kid no more than five or six. He was lying face up on the ground in front of this hut. The back of his head had been blown off and he must have had six holes in his body from being hit by gunfire. I turned away, I couldn't look at him. And then I saw what must have been his mother lying just inside the hut with a baby in her arms. The baby's skull was blown open and the mother's guts were hanging out. I puked right there. This prick comes up behind me and says, 'Must be VC. Move out.' The whole place was the same way. I counted at least a dozen kids and babies, every one of them shot from the front. The mothers were all dead, too, shot from the front. Not a man in the entire village. These bastards had just walked in and killed women and little kids for no reason at all.

"I lost it. I ran over to that bastard and I screamed at him, 'These aren't VC, this is murder and you know it. If you don't report it, I'm going to, so help me.' He just looks at me and says they're VC and he's reporting it that way. Then he yells over to the sergeant, 'Get me the body count.' I started screaming and went after him. A buddy of mine grabbed me, and the prick says you're under arrest and ordered two of the guys to take me back to base."

By now tears were trickling down Peg's face but Gus had stopped sobbing.

"When we got back, they put me in this holding area for a couple of hours and then this captain who was supposed to be from divisional intelligence comes along and has me taken over to their headquarters. He sits me down and tells me that he heard what had happened out there and had gotten reports in from the field. He said that one of the recon patrols had taken fire from somewhere near those shacks and one of the guys from the patrol had been hit so they had no choice but to return fire and clean out the place. I told him that was a crock of shit, that there wasn't a VC or even a man in the place and every one of those kids and the women had been shot close up and from the front, that it was nothing but outright murder. So then he goes into this bullshit about how things happen in a war that maybe shouldn't happen, but there isn't a damn thing anybody can do about it. These people just happened to be in the wrong place at the wrong time and our guys were scared and one of them had gotten hit, and you can't expect them to simply walk away from it. I told him I wanted to file a report on what I saw. He says you better not do that, it'll go real bad for me and that I would be kept over there for a long time after my tour was up, and I'd probably spend time for assaulting an officer and maybe a lot of other charges. If I behaved myself, he would personally see to it that no charges would be brought and he would arrange for a transfer out of my outfit to an MP battalion near Saigon and I wouldn't have to see what goes on in any field operations."

Gus started sobbing again. Peg put her arms around his neck and pulled his head on to her shoulder.

"Gus, honey, that was bad, I know, but you had nothing to do with it. You can't blame yourself for what they did."

Gus pulled away from her and sat upright. "Peg, you don't understand. I took the easy way out. I never reported it. And so I ended up in Saigon rounding up drunks and potheads until they shipped me home. But you know you hear things, and one of the things I heard was this same fucking recon team pulled the same fucking thing two, maybe three weeks later and murdered another ten kids. So maybe the first ones weren't my fault, but the next bunch sure as hell were because I didn't report the first one to save my own ass. And I've been living with that for the last twenty years. I see those little bodies lying all around and I dream about them and they're not dead and they're screaming at me to help them and I didn't."

Gus put his head down between his knees and Peg wrapped her arms around his limp body and cried with him.

"Gus, Gus, it wasn't you who killed those kids and you can't go on punishing yourself for what someone else did, don't you see that?"

He sat upright and he stared straight ahead.

"There's more to it, Peg. Down in Trenton, before I made detective, I had a situation on a domestic violence call. I went to

38

this apartment and there was this guy and a woman, they weren't married, I don't think, and they were both drunk or high and they were beating each other up pretty good. While I was in the place, I heard some crying from another room. So I went in and there were two kids maybe two or three years old lying on a bed in filth. When I walked over to them I could see bruises all over their bodies and I knew they had been beaten. I confronted that guy and the woman about the kids and they said the kids had gotten banged up falling down the stairs. I knew that was bullshit so I put them both under arrest and called headquarters for some backup. The desk sergeant who took the call said I was out of my mind, that it was for family services to deal with and just file a report on it and let the two of them go. I told him to come over and look at the kids himself if he didn't believe me, and he said it was an order and I should get the hell out of there. So I did and I called those assholes over at family services and reported it. Two days later, that guy killed the younger of the kids. So now tell me that wasn't my fault either."

"Gus, I can't tell you anything. You have to convince yourself." She took his face in her hands. "You are a good human being, Gus Bass, and stop blaming yourself for something you didn't do. Please, honey, do it for me. I love you, Gus." She stopped as Gus looked up. "There I said it and that's the first time I've said those words to anyone for almost twenty years. Gus, you're really a good person and that's part of why I love you, I think."

Still crying, Gus's face broke out in a grin. "Peg, you don't have to tell me you love me. I'll get over it some way, don't worry. But now that you mentioned it, the fact is I have been in love with you, at least I think so anyway, for the past six months. I just didn't think you ever wanted to hear it."

"Gus, you may be a good person, but you are awfully dumb about some things." She leaned over and kissed him softly on the lips.

EIGHT

The phone next to Peg's bed rang at exactly 6:08 A.M. Peg pushed herself up and stared at it for a moment, then reached over Gus and picked it up.

"Hello."

"Peg, this is Mary Trantino. It's important, is Gus there?"

"Well, yes he is. He just stopped by on his way into town. Just a minute, I'll get him." Cupping her hand over the phone, she poked Gus hard on his shoulder. "Gus, it's Mary Trantino for you, she says it's important."

Gus shot upright and grabbed the phone. "Mary, what's up?"

Gus could hear the anxiety in her voice as she said: "Gus, you'd better get down here right away. They found the body of a boy over in the woods above the park, and the chief and Krantz are over there along with a lot of people from town."

Gus groaned: "I'm on my way, Mary. Do me a favor and call seven-eight-one seven-oh-eight-oh, that's Fahy's home number and tell him what you told me." Gus slammed the phone down and quickly rolled off the bed. Putting on his shirt he said: "Shit, those idiots are going to fuck up the works. They found the kid's body over in the park and it sounds like there's a circus over there. Sorry, Peg. I'm out of here. Call you later." Gus jumped into his pants and shoes—he had never taken off his socks—and ran out the door.

On the way, Gus called the council chamber. Billy Howland answered and Gus yelled: "Billy, you'd better get over to the park right away. The chief and Krantz are there with a bunch of civilians and they'll make a mess of the crime scene. Didn't they check in with you?"

"No, they didn't. I heard it five minutes ago from Mrs. Trantino. I've called the boss, and he's on his way. I got a call into the medical examiner and he should be here soon. I woke up Carter and he's on his way, too. I tried to reach you, but Trantino said she would get you. Where are you?"

"I'm on the way. I'll meet you there in two minutes."

40

As Gus pulled up alongside the park, Howland was running up from the municipal building and together they ran into the woods that abutted the embankment which rose up to Ridge Road. They followed a trail and after a few hundred yards or so saw several civilians milling about in the woods. A few yards farther on they saw the chief bending over the body of a small boy lying face up on the ground next to a large spruce tree. The body was naked and, even from that distance, Gus recognized Bobby Hartwick's face.

The chief was touching the body and talking to Krantz who had his notebook out and was scribbling in it. As Gus approached, the chief looked up at him and grinned. "Well, mister hot shot detective, it took you long enough to get here. You and that bunch from Flemington must have been out having a good time last night. We found your body for you."

Gus screamed: "Chief, get away from that body or you'll screw up the crime scene, don't you realize what you're doing?" Turning to Krantz, Gus started to push him towards the civilians: "Get these people out of here. What's the matter with you?"

Krantz, still on his haunches, stared at him and seemed paralyzed, with his notebook in hand and pencil poised in a writing position.

Gus took two steps toward the closest civilians and shouted: "All right, I want everyone to turn around and get out of here. Don't touch anything, just leave quick."

The crowd started backing up. At first there was some muttering, but they seemed to realize Gus was right and they shouldn't be there. They quietly left, headed back in the direction of the playground. Gus turned back to face the chief, who was now standing erect above the boy's body. His face was contorted and he yelled: "Bass, I want you out of here, right now. Krantz and I found this body and I'm in charge of this investigation. Get your ass out of here."

As Gus began to speak, he could hear the sounds of people charging through the woods in back of him. He turned and saw Fahy and Sam Carter running toward them. Gus breathed a sigh of relief.

Fahy in his deepest voice said: "Gus, what's going on here? What were all those people doing we just passed?"

41

Gus shook his head: "I don't know, Chuck. You'd better ask the chief."

Fahy strode up to the chief and reached out and grabbed him by the tie. "Winters, what's going on? When was this boy found and by whom?"

"I don't know that it's any of your business, but if you want to know, Krantz got a call about thirty minutes ago. Isn't that right, sergeant? A young lady from the other side of Creek Road was walking her dog along the trail over there when the dog must have picked up the scent. She followed the dog over here and saw the body under this tree here and she ran home and her mother called headquarters. Krantz got the call and we came over to check it out."

By now Fahy's complexion had turned beet red. "What do you mean, under the tree? How did the body get out here?"

"Well, naturally, Krantz and I pulled the kid out to see who it was and to make sure the kid was dead."

Barely able to control himself, Fahy's voice seemed almost like a physical force. "Oh shit, you mean you actually moved the body? Don't you know you can't move a body before the medical examiner says so? Don't you realize what you've done? You were told yesterday to stay away from this investigation."

The chief's face paled and Gus could tell by the sudden change in the chief's expression that he knew he could be in trouble.

Fahy turned to Carter. "Sam, I'm arresting this man for obstructing a criminal investigation. Take him over to the municipal building and get a statement from him. I want to know exactly what he and Krantz saw when they got here and exactly what they did to the body before we arrived. Read him his rights first."

Fahy now faced the chief: "Winters, I don't want any more trouble from you. Just go quietly along with Carter and do as he tells you. If you expect any consideration from me, you'd better give Carter a full statement and don't ask for a lawyer first."

Turning to Krantz and in a quieter voice, Fahy said: "Sergeant, I'm not arresting you just now. I want you to get down to that playground area and you have one job: keep all civilians out of the park and the playground. As soon as my men get here, have one of them take over for you and pass the rest of them through. Then I want you to go over and tell Carter exactly what happened here this morning. Do you understand that?"

Krantz nodded as if in a trance and took off faster than Gus had ever seen him move before. He passed Carter and the chief before they had gone ten yards.

Fahy and Gus knelt down and started to examine the body of the little boy. Fahy said: "There's no question, that's the Hartwick kid. You agree, Gus?"

"Well, I never saw the kid alive, but that's the boy in the picture we got from the mother. Oh shit! Chuck, look, his penis has been cut off."

Fahy, who had been examining the upper part of the torso, glanced down at the boy's hips and saw the stump of what had been a penis. Immediately above the stump he saw three round puncture wounds in the boy's abdomen in the shape of a triangle, with the apex at the top just below the navel. There was very little blood on the body that Fahy could see. He looked over at Gus, who was rocking back and forth on his heels, his eyes closed, obviously in pain.

Fahy tried to comfort him: "Gus, I know what you're feeling, but it's not your fault. This kid was most likely dead before you ever got the call from his mother. Pull yourself together, we're going to get this bastard and when we do he's not going to any diagnostic center."

Gus opened his eyes. "I know you're right, Chuck, I'm thinking if I only got the call earlier, or maybe if I had gone down into the park right away. I know there always are ifs and maybes, but for Christ's sake, a little kid like this, it really blows my mind." He paused and then said: "I suppose I had better go and break it to the parents. They probably have heard something already and they'll be going crazy."

Pulling Gus to his feet Fahy said: "Gus, I can hear some of the guys coming now. Just wait till they get here so we can get this place secured and I'll come with you."

Within seconds Captain Sloss appeared leading several troopers and more men from Fahy's office. "We heard on the way in, Chuck. How bad is it?"

As he stepped away from the body, Fahy said: "Take a look

for yourself. He was mutilated, but I think it was done after he was killed. There are bruise marks on the throat so he may have been strangled first. Can you guys get some tape to mark off this area? The body was moved already so we had better mark off a pretty large area."

Sloss looked bewildered: "What do you mean the body was moved? Who the hell did that?"

Fahy shook his head and said: "Winters and Krantz got here first. When Gus and Billy arrived there were already a bunch of civilians around and Winters said they had found the body under this spruce and pulled it out. We don't have any details yet, but I sent Carter back to take a statement from Winters. Bob, you could do me a big favor if you went down and helped Carter with that asshole. I put him under arrest for obstructing this investigation and he'll probably give Sam a hard time, but if you're there he'll know we mean business."

Sloss nodded. "Good for you. It's about time somebody gave it to that jackass." Turning to his men, Sloss said: "Chief Fahy is in charge here and take your orders from him. Get some tape and secure a circle about twenty yards or so around the body and keep your eyes open." Looking back at Fahy, he said: "I'm going to call in for some more help, is that all right with you?"

"Thanks, Bob, we can use all the help we can get. We're got a lot of ground to cover here and I want an asshole and elbows job on all of this ground. I'll catch up with you later. Gus and I are going to go up to see the parents now." Fahy gestured to Bert Williams and Cal Amster, both of whom had their camera bags with them. "Okay, get started with the pictures. Cover an area at least twenty yards around this tree and I want every inch under that tree. And while you're under the tree, keep an eye out for any signs of blood. When you're finished report back to me at the municipal building. The rest of you work with the troopers. Have you got evidence bags with you?" They nodded, and Fahy said: "Let's get it over with, Gus."

NINE

Gus and Fahy worked their way back to the playground. There was now a crowd of civilians milling around on Creek Road, and Krantz and two more troopers were hard at work keeping them out of the playground. A short dark-haired woman, whom Gus recognized as a reporter for the *Del Val News*, moved past one of the troopers and headed for Gus: "Hey, Bass, give us the story. Is it the Hartwick kid up there?"

Gus looked at Fahy, who walked over to the woman and said: "Ma'am, we can not give you any information at this time. I'm calling the prosecutor and I'm sure that she will have a statement to make in a few hours at most and we will contact you as soon as she is ready. Is that all right?"

Looking up at him the reporter asked: "Aren't you Chief Fahy from the prosecutor's office? Can you tell me who is in charge of this investigation and what's going on with Chief Winters?"

"The prosecutor's office is in charge of every major crime investigation. That's SOP. I'm afraid I can't tell you anything further, you'll have to wait until the prosecutor gets here. I'm sorry but we have to go now."

Fahy called one of the troopers over. "Officer, I want you to get barricades set up at this end of Creek Road and up to the next cross road above here. I don't want any traffic coming through here and keep all the civilians off the roadway."

Gus and Fahy left together in Fahy's car and drove to the Hartwicks' house. In the car Fahy dialed Hazel Stevens's number at the shore. "Ms. Stevens? . . . Sorry to bother you so early but we found the body of the Hartwick boy this morning. . . . Yes it's a homicide and we're getting questions from the press. I promised that you would make a statement this morning. When do you think you could get here? . . . . Good. I'll meet you at the Frenchtown municipal building at eleven and fill you in on what we have so far. . . . Yes, the Medical Examiner should be here any minute and we'll have the body moved as soon as he finishes at the scene . . . Fine, I'll see you soon."

As they pulled up in front of the Hartwicks' there was a small knot of people standing in the road talking in hushed tones. The two men ignored them and mounted the steps. Becky Aaron was standing at the door and stepped out on the porch. She was red-eyed and tears streamed down her cheeks. "Mr. Bass, is it Bobby?"

Gus nodded: "I'm afraid so, Mrs. Aaron. How are the Hartwicks?"

Becky sighed: "Those poor people, I don't think they slept at all last night. Bob's mother is here, but she's not much help. And I've got little Ricky down at my house playing with my boys. I'll stay here with Bob and Gladys as long as I can."

Gus patted her on the shoulder. "That's good of you, Becky. We'd better be going in."

Gus and Fahy found the Hartwicks in the kitchen at the rear of the house. A matronly, heavy-set bleached blonde woman was sitting at the table with them drinking coffee. Bob Hartwick stood up as they entered, his face was ashen and his eyes were half closed. "This is my mother, Alice Degroat. Mom, this is Mr. Bass and Mr. Fahy." He paused, trying to find the words to ask the question he was afraid to ask. "Is it . . . I mean we heard something was going on down in the park. Is it . . ." and he stopped.

Fahy said: "Yes, Mr. Hartwick, I'm afraid it is."

Hartwick slumped down into his chair and put his hands over his face, his body heaving with sobs. Gladys Hartwick sat up straighter in her chair, staring blankly ahead. Gus looked at the grandmother who was sitting with her shoulders thrown back. She glared at Gladys and screamed: "I told you and told you to watch your kids. What else do you have to do? Now look what's happened. What kind of mother are you?"

Bob Hartwick half stood up and yelled: "Shut up, Mom, don't you ever say anything like that again, or so help me I'll shut your mouth for good." Turning to Fahy, his voice breaking, he asked: "Can you tell us how it happened?"

"We don't know yet. The medical examiner should be here any minute, and then we'll have to take him over to the medical center. We'll know more then. I hate to ask you to do this, Mr.

Hartwick, but we'll need you to come over later to make a positive identification. I'll have one of my men pick you up as soon as we are ready. Will that be all right?"

Hartwick slumped down in his chair. "I guess so. Do I really have to, aren't you sure it's Bobby?"

"Yes, we're sure, but the medical examiner will require an identification from the next of kin. Look, Mr. Hartwick, why don't you take your wife upstairs and make her lie down. I think it would be a good idea to have your doctor come over and give her a sedative. If you want, we'll make the call for you."

Hartwick shook his head. "No, that's okay. I'll call him."

Becky Aaron came into the kitchen and lifted Gladys from her chair, put her arms around her, and walked her out into the hallway and up the stairs. Bob Hartwick followed them. Gus and Fahy looked over at Mrs. Degroat. She was just sitting in her chair dry-eyed and looking bewildered. Gus looked at Fahy and shrugged and they left her there.

TEN

When they walked into the council chamber Carter had just finished the chief's statement which Noreen Walsh had taken down. Krantz was sitting across the room waiting his turn. He was obviously crestfallen and uncertain what would happen next. Fahy walked over to him and put his hand on Krantz's shoulder: "Look, sergeant, just relax and give Carter your statement. We need to know as much as you can remember about the murder scene. Do you have the name of the girl who called in the report?"

"Sure, Mr. Fahy." He pulled out his notebook and read: "Janice Miller, two-ten Third Street. She called it in at quarter of six."

Turning to Gus, Fahy said: "Gus, get up to the Millers' house and see if the girl will come down here and give us a statement." Gus left and Fahy walked over to where Sloss was sitting.

His head shaking, Sloss said: "Chuck, it's unbelievable. The kid was lying under the tree face down with his side up against the trunk. You know it had rained pretty good last night and the chief didn't want to get his clothes dirty crawling under the tree, so he told Krantz to reach in and pull him out into the open. When Krantz got him out, the chief rolled the kid over on his back."

Fahy shook his head in disgust. "Did they see any marks on the back before they rolled him over?"

"Carter asked him that and from what I could make out they did see a lot of scratches and scrapes and there was dirt in them, but that's about it. He's not too observant, for Christ's sake, he didn't even know the kid's penis was missing. Oh, and one of my boys called in from the scene. The medical examiner got there ten minutes ago and he's finishing up now. They've called the ambulance corps to move the kid's body over to the medical center for an autopsy, if that's all right with you." Fahy nodded. Sloss went on: "Chuck, I've notified all troopers patrolling in the county to stop all trucks matching that description you gave me yesterday. They're going to check licenses and registrations, home

48

addresses and try to find out what the drivers were doing yesterday. They've been told not to jump the gun or pull anybody in, just radio the information in to the barracks and we'll sort through it. Delaney from my crimes unit is going to put it all together for you."

At that moment, an elderly, white haired gentleman entered the chamber and walked quickly over to where the chief was sitting. After a few words with the chief, he strode over to Fahy. "I am Mayor John Hartmann. Are you Fahy and is it true that you have arrested Chief Winters? On what charge, if I may ask?"

Fahy smiled and said: "Yes, I'm Fahy and this is Captain Robert Sloss, who is in charge of the state police barracks in Flemington. Mayor, I know you are concerned about your chief, but we are investigating the murder of a six year old boy who lived in your town and we've got our hands full just now. I'd appreciate it if you could wait for the prosecutor to get here, she's on her way over. By the way, I certainly want to thank you for letting us use your council chamber. It has really been a big help to us."

A slight grin came over the mayor's face. "I've heard about you, Fahy, and they're right, you are a good politician. In the meantime though, what do we do for a police force over here? I see you've got Krantz here, too. Is he under arrest? For God's sake, that leaves us only with Schumacher, and he's still wet behind the ears."

"No, Mayor, he's not been arrested, we just need to take a statement from him and as soon as he's finished, you can have him back."

Sloss then spoke: "Mayor, I know you're shorthanded. I'm going to call the barracks and have them send over two more patrol cars to help out. You know there will probably be a lot of people heading this way, reporters and thrill seekers and whatever. If you need any more help just contact me or call the barracks and ask for Lieutenant Delaney."

The mayor's smile got broader. "I can see you and Fahy make a good pair, Captain. The two of you should run for office. I'll get out of your hair now." He shook hands with them and left without so much as a glance back at the chief.

They could hear an ambulance siren a short distance away. Fahy went over to the window. "They're on their way over to

Flemington now. I imagine the guys from the scene will be checking in here pretty soon, but I don't think they'll have too much for us." Fahy walked over to the chief: "Winters, you are through here for now. I want you to go next door and sit in your office. When the prosecutor gets here, I'll send for you."

The chief stood up and said, almost apologetically: "Look, Fahy, I'm not going to ask you for any favors. I may have screwed up over there, but before this is over, you're going to need me to help. I've been around this town a long time, and I know the people better than anyone else."

"Chief, if I think you can be of any help, you can be sure I'll ask you. In the meantime, I think it would be better if you went over to your office." The chief looked over at Sloss and started to say something. He must have thought better of it, because his mouth snapped shut and he walked stiffly from the room.

The door had barely closed when it swung open again and Mary Trantino walked in bearing two large cartons. She was followed by another woman and a man, each of whom was carrying two large thermoses. Mary smiled at Fahy: "Mr. Fahy, I know you and your men haven't had any breakfast so I've rounded up some coffee and danish from the deli over on Race Street. If it's all right with you, we'll be back later with a fresh supply."

Fahy smiled and said: "Mrs. Trantino, I spent two years in the army and I've got to tell you, you're the best mess sergeant I've ever seen." Mary beamed as she looked up at Fahy, who was at least a foot taller than she. "By the way, I'd like you to meet Captain Sloss, he's in charge of the state police over in Flemington. Captain, this is Mary Trantino, the borough clerk here in Frenchtown, and don't get any ideas. I found her first." Mary's face turned beet red as she offered her hand to Sloss.

"Mrs. Trantino, it's a pleasure to meet you. We're really very grateful to you, and if this big Irishman here steps over the line, you just let me know and I'll take care of him."

Still beaming Mary said: "Captain, I think I can handle him. I'm half Irish myself and I know his type. By the way, the two of you really did a job on the mayor. I ran into him a few minutes ago, and he's now a big fan of yours." Turning to leave she said: "Remember to let me know if you need anything."

Fahy walked over to where Carter was sitting with Krantz

and Noreen. "Boss, we've finished up here and Krantz' story is the same as Winters's. He said he didn't see any blood or anything else under the tree when he crawled in to pull out the kid. He looked for footprints, too, but there was nothing he could see. The rain last night was pretty heavy and if there was anything there, it would have been washed out. Is there anything else you can tell the chief, Krantz?"

Krantz shook his head. "I don't think so. I've told you everything I can remember. Look, Mr. Fahy, the chief didn't mean any harm. We were both excited about finding the kid, and I guess we just weren't thinking about anything else except whether he was alive. I'm real sorry if we screwed up anything."

"I'm sure you are, Krantz, and I don't think it was your fault. But I've got to tell you, cops are supposed to think. That's part of the job, too. I want you to run along now. The guys out there can use some help keeping things in line. There's only one other thing. Gus Bass isn't the enemy here, and I think maybe you owe him an apology. Anyway, I want you guys to get along and start working together. You know he's a really good cop and we have to stick together."

Krantz smiled and said: "I'll try, Mr. Fahy, but it won't be easy, I can tell you that."

As Krantz left, Fahy's men and the troopers began filtering in. By the expressions on their faces, Fahy could tell that they hadn't come up with anything. It was Amster who spoke for them: "Boss, we went over every inch of that ground for more than twenty yards around that tree and on down the trail back to the playground. There wasn't a damn thing. A lot of footprints because the ground was soft from last night's rain. We found cigarette butts, but they must have been dropped there this morning by the civilians who were up there. We crawled under that damn spruce tree with the laser gun, and we didn't turn up a thing. Zero. A complete blank. No blood, no fibers of any kind, just leaves and spruce needles. Sorry."

"That's okay, Cal, not your fault. We have to go with what we're dealt. Look, help yourselves to the coffee and danish and get off your feet for a while. I expect Ms. Stevens here soon and I want to get ourselves organized before she gets here."

Sloss was hanging up the phone as Fahy walked over to him.

51

Sloss's face had now broken out in a broad grin: "Chuck, we may have something. SCI has come up with two men in the area who have records for child molesting. One of them lives right here in Frenchtown and the other over in Locktown in Kingwood. The Frenchtown guy is named Henry Baumgart and the last address they have for him is Twelfth Street. Did four years for sexual assault on three boys. He was released five years ago. The other guy is Ralph Frohmeyer. Convicted in nineteen eighty-nine for abduction and sexual assault of an eight-year-old boy. Released from that fucking diagnostic center five weeks ago. We've got an address in Locktown. I'm sending a patrol car over there to keep an eye on his house. Do you want him picked up?"

"Not just yet, let's get the chief in here first and see what he knows about this local guy. Funny, I don't remember either of those cases. Maybe they weren't in the county. Eat up quick guys, as soon as the prosecutor gets here I think we'll move this operation over to Flemington. This place is too public."

Just then, Gus came in alone and walked over to Fahy and Sloss. "Chuck, I met with the girl, Janice Miller. She is only fourteen and she is really shook up. The kid was still crying when I got there and the mother wouldn't have any part of letting her come down to give us a statement. I figured we didn't want any more hassles here so I interviewed her there." Gus pulled out his notebook and started reading: "Miss Janice Miller, aged fourteen, two-ten Third Street. She lives there with her mother and grandmother, father is deceased. At about five-thirty this morning her dog, a Jack Russell named Bert who sleeps on her bed, woke her up to be let out. She saw it was a pretty morning and so she thought she would take Bert for a walk. She walked along the edge of the playground and followed the nature trail up on the easterly side of the wood. After she had walked a short way up the trail, she is not sure how far, the dog ran off into the woods and started barking like crazy. She tried to get him to come back to her but he wouldn't so she worked her way through the woods to where she could see the dog. He was under a large spruce tree and still barking. She separated some of the low branches trying to see what the dog was barking at and she saw the back of a small, naked child. She couldn't tell whether it was a boy or girl, she could only see its back which was all scratched up and dirty. She said she knew the child must be dead, so she reached down and picked up the dog—he's only a little guy—and she ran home and woke up her mother. The mother says she called headquarters at about five-forty-five or so and spoke to Krantz. That's all she knew and the mother insists we not bother her anymore."

Fahy nodded: "Well, that checks out with the story we got from Krantz and the chief. I don't see any reason to bother her anymore today, but when things calm down a bit, we'll have to bring the girl over to Flemington to give us a formal statement. Grab yourself something to eat while you can. We've got a full day ahead of us."

The phone rang and Sloss picked it up. He spoke for a few minutes and turned to Fahy with a big grin: "Chuck, everything is set up at this guy Frohmeyer's house. We've got an unmarked car about a hundred yards down the road and another one about two hundred yards down on the other side. But get this: the first guy there cruised by the house and he spotted a blue Ford pickup sitting in the driveway around the back of the house. He isn't sure of the year or the model, he didn't want to take a chance of being seen. I've asked Delaney to get everything they have on this guy down in Trenton faxed up to us and we should have a complete file over in Flemington within an hour."

Fahy broke out in a broad grin. "Sloss, you old bastard, if you weren't so ugly I would kiss you. This guy is almost too good to be true. Let's bring him in right now. Carter can go over to meet your guys and have him brought over to Flemington. And we've got to check out that truck. He's had a chance to clean it up already, but maybe not."

Fahy paused for a moment and turned to Walters: "Walters, I want you to get hold of Ben Harris and tell him we need a search warrant for the truck. Meet him over at the office. Carter will be there by the time Harris is ready and he can give you the information Harris will need for the warrant."

Turning to Howland Fahy said: "Billy, would you go next door and ask Chief Winters to step over here? Now, Gus, what do you know about a creep named Henry Baumgart, lives here in Frenchtown on Twelfth Street. Convicted for sexual assault on three boys. Served four years and was released five years ago."

Gus shrugged his shoulders: "That's before my time, Chuck.

Never heard of the guy since I been here. Did you get that from SCI?"

Fahy nodded: "Yep, him and a guy named Frohmeyer who lives over in Locktown. That one was released just five weeks ago. Did almost five years for abducting and sexually assaulting an eight-year-old boy. We're having him picked up and I think we should round up this Baumgart."

Billy Howland came walking in with Chief Winters in tow.

The chief was smiling as he said: "Did you want to speak to me, Fahy?"

"Yes I do, Chief. I'l like you to help us out if you can. What do you know about Henry Baumgart? I'm told his last known address is on Twelfth Street here in Frenchtown."

The chief's face registered bewilderment. After a slight pause he said: "Yes, I do know the guy. I check up on him every so often since they let him out. That must be a good four, maybe five years ago. What do you want to know?"

"Anything you can tell us, Chief, starting with the case and what he's been doing since he got out."

"As I remember it, we got a call from someone in the prosecutor's office up in Warren. They wanted Baumgart picked up and held for questioning, so I think it was Krantz who brought him in. When he got here I recognized the face as someone from around town, but so far as we knew he'd been clean here. Not even a speeding ticket. I'd say he's about fifty years old now, a small guy, sort of heavy, and mostly bald. When the Warren guys got down here that time, they quesitoned him here. His car had been identified by the license plates and they had him for picking up kids, three young boys it was, I think, and getting the kids to give him a blow job. Just picked the kids at random and would get them into the car to show him the way to some place or other. Then he would give them candy and money and he would dump them off."

"Did he physically assault any of them, any kind of violence?"

Shaking his head, the chief said: "Not that I heard of. I sat in when they questioned him and nothing like that came up, but you'd have to speak to them up in Warren about that. As soon as they started questioning him, he caved in and admitted everything."

54

"Would you happen to remember the names of the guys who came down from Warren?"

"Not offhand. I might have them in the files, but I doubt it."

"What's he been doing since he got out?"

"The first few years he was working over in the ceramics factory, but that closed down quite a while ago and I think he's working as a car salesman over in Flemington, but I'm not sure which dealer. He lives alone and so far as I know he doesn't seem to have any close friends. He keeps pretty much to himself and as I say, we haven't had any complaints about him."

"Thanks a lot, Chief, you've been very helpful and if you could find the names of those Warren guys, I'd appreciate it. By the way, does he own any kind of truck?"

"Not that I know of. I've only seen him driving a car with dealer's plates on it." With that the chief left and headed back to his office.

After his departure, Fahy walked over to Gus. "Did you hear that? What do you think?"

Gus shrugged. "The MO doesn't fit, but then who knows. If he got desperate enough to pick up a kid in his own town, he'd have to know there would be a good chance of the kid's identifying him and he'd have to get rid of the kid."

Fahy was rubbing his brow. "Right. Suppose you and one of Sloss's guys go and pick him up. Tell him you'd like to ask him a few questions and take him over to the barracks in Flemington. I'll have Sloss get one of his people from the crimes unit to work with you. Carter and the rest of them will have their hands full with Frohmeyer. Keep in touch. I'll be back at my office in less than an hour. Oh, here's Ms. Stevens now. Come on over and meet her and we'll brief her so she can make a statement and get rid of the press people."

Hazel Stevens was a tall, slim and handsome woman who obviously was no stranger to aerobics. Always well groomed, today she was wearing an olive green silk pants suit with a white silk blouse and gray pearls with matching earrings. Even though it was only early June, she already had the beginnings of a Jersey shore tan. Out of law school and a judicial clerkship, she had spent two years in the AG's office in the criminal justice section. From there she had opened up her own office in Clinton and done

55

well right from the start. She ended up representing a couple of towns and planning boards and was second in line to become the first woman president of the county bar association when she got the prosecutor's appointment three years ago. Now with a woman governor in office, the word was out that she would get the next judgeship in the county. Some of the bar leaders were grumbling about that. If she got the job, that would mean two of the three judges in the county would be women and the old guard were having enough problems adjusting to the idea of having one woman judge to patronize. As Gus walked over to meet her he was impressed. She didn't look like any prosecutor he had ever seen.

Ms. Stevens walked directly up to Fahy and was frowning as she said: "Chuck, you look all in. I called the office on the way in. I guess this is as bad as it gets. I can't conceive of anyone doing that to a little child. How are the parents?"

"It's good to see you, Ms. Stevens. I'm really glad you're here. The father will be okay, I think, but I don't know about the mother, she doesn't seem to react at all. What can you expect? We didn't tell them the whole story about the boy. They've had enough of a shock already."

"Oh, I see you have Captain Sloss with you. I noticed several troopers outside. I'm sure you can use help on this one and if there is anything you need from the state just let me know. I still have some friends there."

Fahy grinned: "Sloss has really been pitching in and he's got the people down in Trenton lined up at their computers. We've been getting some real help there. Look, I think it's about time for us to move this operation over to Flemington. This place is too public. I thought if you could give the press a statement, that will hold them for a while so we can get out of here and get some work done. If it's okay with you, we can go into one of the offices here and fill you in on where we are. By the way, this is Gus Bass. He's with the Frenchtown PD and he got the first call on this and he and I have been working together ever since. If it's all right with you, I'd like to have Gus and Bob Sloss sit in with us."

"Of course, you're the boss on this, Chuck. I'm just here to help out."

Fahy called Sloss over and the four of them went into Mary Trantino's office. They emerged after twenty minutes and Stevens said: "Let's get the press in here and I'll give it to them." Sloss said: "I'll get them in, Chuck," and with that he was out the door. In less than two minutes, he came back into the chamber trailing in his wake seven or eight noisy people who started yelling even before they were in the door. Gus recognized the brunette and a young man from the *Del Val News*. Hazel Stevens seemed to know the rest because she greeted them by name. She squared her shoulders and then began: "If you'll just hold it for a minute, I have a statement to make. I'd ask that you hold any questions until I have finished. Is that all right?" They quieted down quite abruptly, surprising Gus.

"At three-thirty on Friday, June 3, Detective Bass of the Frenchtown Police Department received a telephone call from Mrs. Gladys Hartwick who lives at two-twenty-two Ridge Road in Frenchtown. Mrs. Hartwick reported that her six-year-old son, Robert Hartwick, Jr., had not returned home from school that afternoon. Detective Bass upon further investigation learned that the boy had not returned to school after the lunch recess. The boy's mother reported that he had left home after lunch at about twelve-forty-five and she last saw him going down the path from Ridge Road leading through Veterans Park. Detective Bass immediately notified my office and detectives Charles Fahy and other officers from my office together with Detective Bass commenced a search of the neighborhood. Several persons were interviewed without results. The search was discontinued last night at about eight-thirty P.M."

"This morning at about five-forty-five A.M. Sergeant Krantz of the Frenchtown Police Department received a call from a Mrs. Miller that her daughter had been walking her dog in the woods above the playground and had found the body of a small boy. Chief Winters and Sergeant Krantz responded and confirmed the discovery of the body. Chief Fahy and Captain Sloss of the state police were contacted and arrived at the scene by six-fifteen A.M. The body has been tentatively identified as that of Robert Hartwick, Junior. The medical examiner has removed the body to the Hunterdon Medical Center but we have had no report as yet as to the cause of death."

"The staff of my office together with Captain Sloss and the major crimes unit of the State Police are developing leads but there are no suspects and no one is in custody at this time."

"We will have no further statement to make until after we have heard from the medical examiner. Are there any questions?"

The woman from the *Del Val News* was the first with her hand up. "Ms. Stevens. We have heard a rumor that Chief Winters was arrested early this morning by you. Can you tell us what that's all about?"

"I'm sorry, I have no comment to make at this time. I can tell you, however, that Chief Winters is now cooperating fully with my office in this investigation."

The next hand up was that of Frankel from the *New York Times* Trenton bureau. "Madam Prosecutor, there are reports that the boy was mutilated, can you confirm that?"

"No, I cannot. We have had no report from the medical examiner as to the cause of death or the condition of the body and I think it would be a grave mistake for anyone to speculate about that at this time."

"Ms. Stevens, I'm Roger Perkins from the *Star-Ledger.* Can you tell us why the boy's mother waited until three-thirty to call if the kid was missing since almost one o'clock?"

"Mr. Perkins, as I said before, Mrs. Hartwick saw her son off to school after he had lunch. She was not aware that he wasn't in school until he didn't return after school was out."

"If the boy didn't return after lunch, why didn't someone at the school call his mother to find out why he wasn't back?"

"I'm not sure I can answer that question. Mr. Bass, can you help out?"

Gus gulped. He had never spoken at a press conference before and he looked at Fahy, who just shrugged. Gus cleared his throat and said: "We checked with the school and they were just about to call Mrs. Hartwick when I called. That's all we know at the present time." Gus looked at Fahy who nodded his approval.

Hazel Stevens took charge again. "I think we have given you all the information we have at this time. We would appreciate your cooperation in one matter, however, but I'll take no further questions. An F-150 blue Ford pickup, nineteen eighty-eight or eighty-nine model year, bearing New Jersey license plates, was seen in the vicinity of Veterans Park yesterday. We would appreciate your asking your readers to call our office, seven-eight-one four-three-four-three with any information if they saw such a vehicle in the vicinity of Frenchtown yesterday between noon and two P.M. Thank you very much and we will contact you as soon as we have anything further to report."

As Hazel Stevens started to leave the reporters tried to close in on her. Fahy and Sloss kept them at bay while she got out the door. The *Del Val News* reporter cornered Gus as he tried to follow the prosecutor. "Gus, what is this about the pickup truck? Where exactly was it seen and who saw it?"

"It's Grace, isn't it?" She nodded and Gus went on: "I'm afraid I don't know the answers to your questions. You'll have to speak to the prosecutor or Chief Fahy. I'm sorry, but I have to go now." He half ran out the door and caught up with Fahy and Sloss.

"Captain, which of your men can go with me to pick up Baumgart?"

Pointing in the direction of Krantz Sloss said: "Take Frank Cuccio, he's the guy standing over there with Krantz. And you better take both cars and head toward Flemington. Meet him up at the Corner Store, leave your car there and the two of you double back and pick up Baumgart. Otherwise, one of these reporters might get it in his head to follow you if you head straight up to Twelfth Street from here."

Gus nodded: "Got it, Captain."

"One more thing, Gus. Cut the captain bullshit. It's Bob to you."

Gus grinned at him and went to pick up Cuccio. The two of them left and Fahy, Sloss and the rest of the prosecutor's people followed right behind. Before leaving, Sloss sent one of his troopers to stay up at the Hartwick house and watch over them. Four troopers remained downtown to help out with the crowd of people who were already showing up to get in on the act and maybe, if they were lucky, get interviewed for one of the local TV newscasts.

ELEVEN

The Corner Store was a local institution. Located two miles up the hill from Frenchtown on the road to Flemington, it was the meeting place and hangout for the blue collar crowd in that part of the county as well as the place where everyone, blue collar, white collar, professionals and corporate executives got their papers, cigarettes, milk, eggs, bread, morning pastries, fried egg sandwiches, and coffee. Open from 6:00 A.M. to midnight, the Corner Store was stocked with a little of anything and everything anyone might run out of, from motor oil and shotgun shells to soda, ice, potatoes, onions, tomatoes, macaroni, frozen hot dogs, and hamburgers. It also doubled as a fast food restaurant at lunch time, featuring the Corner Store's answer to Big Macs: hamburger patties slowly simmered for hours on end in a large pot of home made onion soup.

Gus dropped his car off at the far end of the Corner Store's parking lot next to the sign which read: "Parking $5 per hour, $70 per day." After going in and telling Big Sam that he had to leave his car there on police business, he left with Cuccio in the trooper's patrol car. They headed out 519 and then back into Frenchtown from the north to Twelfth Street. No one was following them as they pulled up in front of Baumgart's house, a small, two-story frame structure. Gus got out, walked up the porch steps and rang the bell. After the second ring, he could see a man's face peering out at him from an adjoining window. A thin, high-pitched voice called out: "Who is it?"

"Are you Henry Baumgart? If you are, I'd like to speak to you for a few minutes."

"Who are you?"

Gus could see enough of the man's face to see that he matched the description the chief had given. "Mr. Baumgart, my name is Gus Bass and I'm from the Frenchtown Police Department. I need to speak to you for a few minutes. Will you please open the door?"

The face disappeared from the window and the door opened.

When Baumgart appeared, Gus thought to himself: for once the chief got it right, Henry Baumgart was indeed a short, stout, balding man. And he was every bit of fifty. Gus could see that the man was terrified and his hands were trembling.

Baumgart blurted out: "If it's about that boy, I didn't have anything to do with it."

Gus was taken by surprise and after a slight pause he said: "What boy would that be, Mr. Baumgart?"

"I don't know what boy. Someone called me a little while ago and said that some boy had been found murdered. That's all I know, I swear."

"Well, Mr. Baumgart, I'm sure you had nothing to do with it. You know it's a little awkward for me to be standing out here talking like this. It'd be a whole lot better if you'd just come along with me and answer a few questions for us. It wouldn't take long and we'll have you back here in no time. How about it?"

Baumgart's face seemed to shrivel. "Why do I have to do that? Just ask Chief Winters, he'll tell you I had nothing to do with it."

Gus nodded: "Well, actually, Mr. Baumgart, it was the chief who sent me up here to ask you to come over and speak to us."

"He did? Well, I don't know. I have to go to work soon. You know, Saturday is our busy day and I work on commissions so I really can't stay very long."

"Where do you work, Mr. Baumgart?"

"Over in Flemington. I'm a used car salesman for one of the big dealers over there."

"Well, I think it will work out just fine. As a matter of fact, we have to go to Flemington because the chief will be over there. We'll drive you over and when we're finished we'll just drive you to your job. If you need a ride back, we'll have a car pick you up."

Baumgart wrung his hands and after a long pause he finally responded: "I guess that will be all right. Just let me go in and finish dressing and I'll be right out."

"That will be just fine, Mr. Baumgart, I'll be out at the car."

Henry Baumgart noticed the car parked in front of his house. "Isn't that a state police car? Are you the state police?"

"Oh, that. No, I'm Frenchtown PD. You see my car is laid up, and I had to ask this state cop for a ride over here. You know, he's just my chauffeur, that's all."

Baumgart's whole body was trembling now as he walked stiff-legged back into the house. Gus thought something had shaken this guy up pretty good and he was afraid Henry might try to bolt out the back door, so he decided to walk around the back of the house. But in a few minutes he heard Cuccio calling him and when he returned to the front of the house, Baumgart was standing alongside the patrol car.

As they neared the Corner Store on their way to Flemington, Gus asked Sal to stop off at his car so he could make a phone call. He dialed the Prosecutor's Office and was put through to Fahy immediately. "Chuck, this is Gus. We've got Baumgart, but I have to tell you he is pissing in his pants. I told him that Winters was waiting for him over in Flemington. That's the only way I could get him to come quietly. So, could you have someone call Winters and ask him to go over to the barracks?"

"I'm glad you called, Gus. We've had a change of plans and I think you should bring him over to my office instead of the barracks. I'll have someone call Winters and get him to come over. When you get here, park Baumgart with Cuccio and come to see me."

"Will do. We should be there in ten minutes. This guy Cuccio drives like Bert Williams."

TWELVE

Gus had underestimated Cuccio; it was exactly seven minutes later that Cuccio pulled the patrol car into the lot at the rear of the prosecutor's office across the street from the Hunterdon County Courthouse, a handsome 19th century plantation style building, with a white-columned portico. The courthouse was famous as the site of the Hauptmann trial in the 1930s for the kidnapping and murder of the Lindbergh baby and in its first floor lobby there was a large showcase containing souvenirs and photographs of that epic event which had made Flemington the focal point of world news for several weeks.

The prosecutor's office was located to the rear and across the street from the courthouse, in a two-story red brick building which had been the county jail when it was built in the 19th century. Today it was a rabbit warren of tiny offices and awkward narrow corridors. Gus figured that the offices had probably been converted from the original jail cells. At the rear of the building a one-story annex had been added which served as the grand jury room.

Gus found an empty office for Baumgart and Cuccio and went in search of Fahy. He found him in the grand jury room along with seven or eight of the guys from Fahy's office as well as Sloss and Lt. Delaney. Fahy was hanging up the phone as Gus walked in. "That was the medical examiner. Dr. Sanchez gave me some preliminary findings. He hasn't started the autopsy yet. He says that when he started his examination at the scene there was full rigor mortis present and based on the rectal temperature reading he got he says the time of death was between noon yesterday and six P.M. last night. He'll know better after he has examined the contents of the stomach and gets accurate information on the temperatures last night. He said there are bruises on the kid's neck that were made before he was killed, but he doesn't think the kid was strangled or choked to death. His hunch is that the kid was asphyxiated with a plastic bag and the bruises were made by someone holding the bottom of the bag around his neck. There are numerous scrapes and cuts to the body, but these were inflicted post-mortem. He thinks the body was most likely dragged through the woods or over rough ground. The penis was definitely cut off after death, and the same for the puncture wounds to the belly. That's about all he can give us now and he'll call in as soon as he has anything more that might help. Oh, and one more thing, he said the boy was definitely not killed where we found him. He was dumped there some time later."

Fahy paused and then went on. "Before we start questioning these creeps, I think we ought to start a preliminary time line and try to brainstorm a scenario that fits what Sanchez has given us. Howie, suppose you be the secretary and put up the time line on that chart over there. Okay, we know the kid was in school in the morning. Gus what time do they recess for lunch over there?"

"I checked that out. The kids leave at exactly twelve."

"Okay, that's where we start, Howie. Twelve o'clock P.M., June 3, kid leaves school for lunch. Now we timed how long it would take him to walk from his home down to Creek Road, and that was just over two minutes. I would guess it's about another three or four minutes from the road to the school, that about right, Gus?"

Gus nodded: "Sounds right, but I'll check it out first thing tomorrow."

"Do that. Howie, put down twelve-o-five P.M., kid arrives home. Now the mother says he had lunch and was late leaving to go back to school and had missed the Aaron kids. She believes he left at about twelve-forty-five or thereabouts. Gus, what time are the kids due back after lunch?"

"At twelve-fifty."

"Well, if he was late and it only takes six or seven minutes to get back to school, then he probably left home at twelve-forty-five or maybe even a few minutes later. Okay, Howie, put down twelve-forty-five, kid leaves home for school. And we know it takes two minutes to reach Creek Road, so put down twelve-forty-seven, kid arrives at Creek Road."

Sloss spoke next: "But Chuck, we don't have a sighting for that time. The last time the kid was seen was when his mother saw him head down through the park. We don't know that he ever reached Creek Road."

Fahy frowned. "True enough, Bob, but for now we have to use these times to be able to question anyone and check out any alibis. So we have to assume that the kid reached Creek Road, 'cause that's the most likely spot for some one to grab him. You agree?"

Sloss was shaking his head and nodding at the same time. Finally, he said: "I'll buy that for now, but it seems weird that no one saw anything. After all, this is broad daylight and during the lunch hour and there should have been people around somewhere."

Fahy nodded. "That's something we have to work on. I want to get four guys over to Frenchtown this afternoon to cover the entire area around Creek Road, the playground and the stores there to see if anyone was around who might have seen something. Sam, would you get a detail out to cover that?"

Sam shrugged and said: "Boss, this is the weekend and there are going to be a lot of tourists over there and outsiders who wouldn't have been there on a week day. Maybe we ought to wait until Monday to check that out."

"Well, we can at least go door-to-door today and tomorrow. You're more likely to catch people home. We'll save the stores and the downtown area until Monday."

"So where are we? We've got the kid at Creek Road at twelve-forty-seven. No one sees him. Let's assume for the moment that he's grabbed there. We got a sighting of the pickup truck at about one o'clock on Creek Road about a half mile from the playground. That fits roughly with the scenario so far, although it wouldn't take that long to get to the Fenster house where she saw the pickup. If it's Frohmeyer, he lives in Locktown. It would take him maybe fifteen minutes, probably less to get from his house to Frenchtown. If he picked up the kid, he could have been back home by one-fifteen or one-twenty. What happened to this kid, it wasn't done in the open; for sure, it was done inside a house or somewhere no one could see them. If it's Frohmeyer, he probably would take the kid back to his house, and kill the kid there. I can't see him wandering around with the kid in his truck. So, when we question Frohmeyer, we've got to find out where he was from noontime yesterday on until six, which is the latest the kid was killed. Everyone agree?"

Gus looked up and said: "That's okay for the grab and killing him, but how does he get the body back, and why the hell would he take the risk of driving the kid back to Frenchtown and dumping the body way up in the woods there? He'd have to be a looney to take a chance like that. He'd have to park the truck or whatever he was driving and then hike through the woods with the body and dump it where we found it. Geez, Chuck, you know what those woods are like, it would take him a good half hour to get from Creek Road to where we found the body and then back to his truck. That doesn't make sense. He could have dumped the body anywhere without taking that kind of risk."

Fahy shrugged. "I can't quarrel with that, Gus. But the key word is 'looney.' Who knows how a guy like this thinks. What it means is we got to find out what he was doing and where he was from noontime yesterday right on until daylight this morning. If he's the guy, he would have brought the body back when it was dark. Anybody who did it had to dispose of the body sometime last night. One more thing: whoever did it, he had to park somewhere while he dumped the body. He sure as hell wasn't going to carry a body out in the open. Gus, if he came back last night, is there anyplace next to the woods where he could pull off Creek Road and be out of sight?"

Gus's eyes squinted as he was trying to recollect the course of Creek Road: "There may be one or two places along the road where you could pull off, and if you drove in a bit, at night it would be pretty hard to spot a vehicle from the road."

"That's another assignment and we'd better check it out right away. It rained like hell last night and there could be tire tracks left in those spots. Bob, I'm running out of men. Do you have any spares to send over and check those areas out for us?"

It was Delaney who answered. "We sure do. I'll put a call into Kevin Givnin right now. He's the best at finding any kind of tracks or ground impressions and he's got all the equipment to make casts of anything he finds."

"Thanks, Al. If he has any trouble finding those spots Gus is talking about, tell him to get hold of Krantz. He'll certainly know any good snooze spots along that road."

Fahy's face now lit up: "That brings us to Baumgart. We've got to question him for the same time frame, except that he lives right there in Frenchtown and he wouldn't need as much time to get to his house or back to the woods. When you think about it, the woods right there in Frenchtown would be a more logical spot for him to dump a body than Frohmeyer. It would be a lot closer to his house and he would probably know the area better."

Gus spoke up: "But why would he bother to drive all the way over there? If he killed the kid, he would have done it at his house, and that's close by the river. Wouldn't he just wait until night and carry the body down to the river and dump it there?"

Fahy shook his head. "There you go again, Gus. Who says the guy has to do the most sensible thing? You've got to remember that you're dealing with a nut to begin with so you have to assume he might do anything. But you got a point. If it was Baumgart, he would have taken the kid to his house. So there is another assignment: we've got to check with his neighbors and find out who was home yesterday and if anyone saw him around. I'll get Smitty to take that on as soon as we break up here. Any other suggestions?"

Again it was Gus who spoke: "How about a search warrant for Baumgart's house and his car?"

Fahy turned to Sam Carter: "How about it, Sam, think we have a shot at that?"

Sam shook his head: "I doubt it, boss. Harris is giving us a bad time with the Frohmeyer search warrant. Says he doesn't think the guy's record and a sighting of a similar type of truck in the area is enough probable cause. He wants us to work on the guy first to see if we can't get his consent. With Baumgart, we wouldn't have a chance at all. Does anyone know what kind of car he drives?"

Gus said: "We haven't questioned him at all yet, but when I picked him up I saw an Olds Omega parked in the driveway with dealer plates and I would think it was his 'cause he works over here as a used car salesman."

"Then you work on him, Gus, and see if you can't get him to go along with a consent search." Fahy turned to Howie: "All right, put down at the bottom of that time line five-forty-five A.M., June fourth, body found in woods above Veterans Park. Now we've got to fill in the blank between then and twelve-forty-five P.M., June third. That's a lot of time to cover so let's start questioning these guys. If it's okay with you, Bob, I thought Delaney and I would take the first shift with Frohmeyer and you and Sam take the second crack at him. Gus, how about you and Howie taking the first dibs with Baumgart, and Sam and I will be the second team with him. Does everybody have copies of that picture we got from the mother? Good, let's go."

THIRTEEN

Gus led Howie back to the room where he had parked Baumgart. As they got there, Chief Winters was just about to enter the room.

Gus approached the chief and said: "Chief, Fahy asked you to come over to talk to Baumgart before we start the questioning. He's really jumpy, and I told him that you would be here. Maybe you could just talk to him and take the edge off a bit. Fahy wants to see if the guy will consent to a search of his car and house. Maybe you could help us out there. The guy mentioned your name a couple of times when I picked him up and I think he might listen to you."

The chief smirked. "I told that guy he was going to need me before this was through. Isn't he man enough to come and ask me himself to help out?"

"I'm sure he would have, Chief, but he and Delaney have already started questioning another suspect and he can't break away yet."

Sloss was close enough to overhear the exchange and walked over to the chief. His scowl more than matched anything the chief had ever been able to manage. "Now I want you to listen to this 'cause I'm only going to say it once and for the last time. This isn't some kind of ego game we're playing here, and I don't give a damn about who's king of the hill. We're trying to investigate a murder. You know you've got the reputation of being the biggest pain in the ass we've got in the county, and if you want to stay in deep shit, just keep it up. They're trying to find the guy who killed a kid in your own town, and you're just blowing smoke up everyone's ass. If you don't start behaving yourself it won't be just Fahy who's after you, it will be me. And believe me, you don't want me all over you. From now on, you do what you're told and if you don't, it won't be just the prosecutor of this county who's on your case, it will be me and the AG's office. Do you understand?"

The chief's adam's apple rose and fell twice. His face grew

pale and, to Gus's surprise, he looked up at Sloss and said: "I'm sorry, you're right. I guess I have been acting like an asshole." He turned and opened the door and went into the office.

Sloss grinned at Gus. "Maybe he's gotten the message, but don't hold your breath." He turned and walked on down the corridor.

When Gus and Howie walked into the room, Cuccio got up and left; there wasn't room enough for all of them. Winters was already sitting in a chair opposite Baumgart and Gus heard him say: "Henry, these men would like you to answer some questions about where you were yesterday, and they would like you to let them go and search your house and your car. Would you let them do that?"

Baumgart's eyes were cast down as he said: "Why do they want to do that, Mr. Winters, you know I didn't have anything to do with what happened to that little boy. Why are they after me?"

"They're not after you Henry. They're just doing their job. Look, I know you have nothing to hide, but you have to convince them, too. All they want to do is to make sure you are not involved and the best way to convince them is to let them check out your house and your car. They're not going to find anything, I know that, and when they don't, they'll let you alone. That's pretty reasonable, isn't it?"

Baumgart's brow knitted and his head sank down. Without looking at the chief he said: "I don't know, Mr. Winters. You know, when I did that time for that other thing, the guys in there told me I was a fool for telling anybody anything. So now I'm not sure what I should do. Maybe I should speak to a lawyer."

The Chief started to stand up. "Well, if that's what you want, Henry, I'm sure that's okay with them. Of course, it's going to take some time to get a lawyer over here; you know it's a Saturday afternoon and those guys are out playing golf or something. So if you want to hang around here, I'm sure they will just wait. Won't you, guys?"

Gus nodded his assent and Winters continued: "How about it, Henry, do you want to speak to a lawyer?"

"Mr. Winters, can I speak to you alone?"

The chief looked over at Gus and then Henry. He said: "I'm

70

sure that would be okay if that's what you want." Gus and Howie stood up and walked out. A few minutes later the chief came out and said: "He's got a problem. He says he's got a lot of child porn in his house and maybe some in his car, too, he's not sure. He says he uses the stuff to jack off with so he doesn't go after kids anymore. He's afraid you'll get him for having that stuff. He swears he never made any of it, he just buys it through the mail. If you'll agree not to charge him for having it, he says he'll consent. What should I tell him?"

Gus responded: "I don't have authority to tell him that, we'd better check it out with Fahy. Give me a few minutes and I'll get back to you." With that Gus went off down the hall. He was back in five minutes and told Winters Fahy had given his okay, no charges would be filed for possession of pornographic materials. The chief went back in and stuck his head out a few seconds later and told them to come in.

It was the Chief who spoke. "Henry, I want you to tell these men what you just told me, okay?"

Looking Gus in the eyes he said: "That's right, Mr. Bass, I agree you can search my house and my car and anything else you want. But if you find any pictures of boys and stuff like that, you're not going to charge me with having it, is that right?"

Gus nodded his head: "That's right, Henry. So long as you understand if we find anything else connected with this case, we can use it as evidence. Do you understand that?"

Now Henry was nodding: "Yes, I do, but you're not going to find anything, I swear it."

"That's good, Henry, we'd just like you to sign a little statement Mr. Walters will write out that you agree to let us make the search. Is that all right with you?"

Howie went out and returned shortly with a printed form and gave it to Baumgart. After what seemed a half hour but was only a few minutes, Baumgart took the pen and signed the form. The chief said: "Henry, you've done the right thing, and I want to tell you, you won't regret it. Now I've got to go, and I want you to cooperate with Mr. Bass and this gentleman and answer their questions."

Baumgart's face paled as he said: "Mr. Winters, aren't you going to stay with me?"

The chief reached out and put his hand on Baumgart's shoulder: "No, Henry, I've got to get back to Frenchtown now, but don't you worry about anything. Just answer their questions and everything will be all right."

Howie handed the signed form to the chief and asked him to give it to Sam Carter. As the chief walked out, Henry began to visibly shake. Gus said: "Henry, would you like a drink of water or maybe a soda or a cup of coffee?"

Henry shook his head which he was now holding between his hands. Gus said: "Look, Henry, I'm not going to read you your rights or anything like that because you're not under arrest or even a suspect. We just want you to answer some questions and then you can go about your business. This interview will be tape-recorded so that we'll have a record of everything we say here. Okay?"

Henry nodded and as he looked up his face brightened a bit. "What do you want to know?"

"Well, for openers, how long have you been living in Frenchtown?"

"Except for the time I did on that other thing, I've lived there all my life. As a matter of fact, I was born in that house where you were this morning. That's the only place I've ever lived."

"Henry, have you ever been married?"

Baumgart's face reddened. "No, I never got married. I lived with my mother and grandmother and my aunt Mary. It was my grandmother's house, you know, and when she died, my mother owned the house and I lived there with her and my aunt. Aunt Mary died and then, when my mother died, she left the house to me and I've been living there alone ever since."

"What about your father, Henry, where is he?"

Baumgart frowned. "I don't remember my father. I really don't know what happened to him. They told me he had died, been killed in the war, but you know I never did believe that. Maybe he just took off or something before I was born."

"You never saw your father?"

"Well, if I did, I don't remember him. It was always just my mother and my grandmother and my aunt."

"How far did you get in school, Henry? By the way, you don't mind my calling you Henry, do you?"

A slight smile appeared on Baumgart's face for the first time as he said: "No, I like that. Can I call you Gus?"

"Absolutely. And Mr. Walters here is 'Howie,' okay?"

Baumgart's eyes seemed to brighten. "I'm pleased to meet you, Howie. Now what did you want to know? Oh yes, school. Well I went to school in Frenchtown. In those days, the high school was right there in Flemington, they didn't have the regional school, you know, and I graduated there. You know, I was second in my class and the principal wanted me to go on to college, but my mother said she couldn't afford it even if I got a scholarship. You know, I should have gone to college, but I didn't."

"So what did you do after you finished high school?"

"I got a job up at the paper mill in Milford. I worked in the shipping department but I really didn't like it very much. After a while, I got a job in the office there checking the shipping memos against the invoices. Then I was a billing clerk and over the years I was in charge of billing. And I was making good money. Then mom died. That was ten years ago. Then I got into that trouble up in Warren. That was eighty-five and I got out in eighty-nine. That's the whole story of my life. It isn't very much is it?"

"What have you been doing since you got out, Henry?"

"For the first six months or so, just some odd jobs here and there and then I got a job at the ceramics plant in Frenchtown. Just like before, I started out in shipping and then I was a billing clerk in the office. I thought that would be it for the rest of my life, but then some English outfit bought the company and they shut down the place. It's still sitting there, they haven't sold it or anything. Just sits there empty. Why did they buy the place if they're just going to close it? It doesn't make any sense."

Gus nodded: "I agree, Henry, but I sure don't know what goes on with those guys. So what did you do then?"

"Well, for a while, not very much of anything. Then I got a job selling used cars over here in Flemington. To tell the truth, I don't like it very much, I don't have the stomach for it. You got to tell a lot of little white lies about the cars, and the buyers are telling you all kinds of lies about what they want and what they can afford. You know, you con them and they con you and that

73

kind of thing. I've become pretty good at it, though, and I've been making good money. So I can't complain. Plus, I get a free car to drive."

"Is that the Olds I saw in your driveway?"

"That's it for this week, anyway. I usually get a different car every week or two."

"Well, Henry, that kind of brings us up to yesterday. Did you work yesterday?"

At first, Henry didn't answer. There was a long pause and he started looking around the room, but there wasn't too much room to look at. Finally, he said: "No, I was off yesterday. I'm working today and tomorrow. You see if you work Saturday and Sunday, you get Friday off. You only work two out of every three weekend days; they count Fridays as weekend days, because a lot of people go hunting for cars on Friday afternoon and evenings."

"That's interesting Henry. I never knew that. So what did you do yesterday?"

Henry shrugged his shoulders: "Mostly, I just hung around the house, did some laundry, went to the cleaners, and bought some food up at the A&P. You know that place robs you blind. You can go over to the Acme here in Flemington, and the prices are twenty or thirty percent less. That A&P really has a racket going."

Gus nodded. "Yeah, I've heard that, too. But Henry, what I need from you now is like a kind of diary. What time did you get up, what time you left the house and that kind of thing. Isn't that right Howie?"

Howie closed in: "Look, Baumgart let's cut the crap. We ain't interested in all this bullshit about the A&P or where you went to school or whether you fucked your mother. Where were you yesterday starting with when you got up in the morning and every fucking minute after that, you hear me?"

Gus stood up and glared at Walters: "Howie, what's the matter with you? Henry wants to tell us everything, isn't that right, Henry?" The trembling started with Baumgart's hands and soon his whole body was shaking. "Damn it, Howie, now look what you done. Why don't you just get out of here and leave me and

74

Henry alone for a bit so we can have a nice quiet talk. Go get me a coffee or something. Would you like anything, Henry?" Henry's head was now on the table, and Gus winked at Howie, who stormed out of the office and slammed the door.

It took Henry a good two or three minutes after the door slammed to lift his head up and there were tears in the corners of his eyes. "Why does he have to say things like that, Mr. Bass, about my mother. He's really not a nice person, you know."

"As a matter of fact, Henry, he's not a bad guy. He's just upset about what happened to that little boy. You know whoever killed him must have hurt him pretty badly. It wasn't easy to look at the body and Howie really wants to get the guy who did it. We all do, but Howie has taken it very hard. You see he has a little boy just about the same age as the Hartwick boy. So you can see why he is upset, can't you?"

Baumgart was sitting upright again. "Yeah, I suppose so but why does he say things like that about my mother and me?"

"He really didn't mean it Henry and when he comes back I'll make him apologize, you wait and see. But now Henry, how about telling me when you got up yesterday, okay?"

"I'm not sure, Gus. You sure you don't mind me calling you Gus?"

"Of course not, Henry, everybody calls me Gus."

"What's your real name, Gustave?" Henry winked at Gus.

"If you really want to know, it's Augustus."

Henry laughed. "I can see why you want to be called Gus. Were you named after somebody important?"

"As a matter of fact, I was named for Caesar Augustus, you know, the Roman emperor. My father had read a book about him just before I was born and I guess he wanted me to become an emperor or something. He was a bit weird, my old man was. How about you, Henry, who were you named for?"

Baumgart shook his head. "Gee, I don't know that I was named after anybody. Maybe my father, but they never told me his name so I'm not sure. I always hated the name Henry, I always wanted to be called Hank but somehow nobody ever did."

"Well, from here on it's Hank with me, okay?" Gus paused and then continued: "Now Hank, we've got to talk some business here, 'cause I want you to get over to your job and make some money today. How about it, Hank, when did you get up yesterday?"

"I think it was about eight or around there, 'cause I was watching television until quite late the night before, you know the Letterman show. He does some clever things on that show."

"Yeah, I've watched a few times myself. So what did you do when you got up?"

"Well, I woke up at about eight and I stayed in bed for awhile just thinking about what I was going to do to pass the time for the day."

"So what did you think about, Hank?"

"Not very much, there's not much I do anyway, even on my days off."

"So how long did you stay in bed, Hank?"

"Maybe an hour or so, I'm not sure."

Gus frowned: "An hour? Gees, Hank, that's a long time just to stay in bed thinking."

Henry's face reddened again and his head lowered. "Do I really have to tell you, Gus?"

"Gee, I wish you would, Hank. I need to know what you were doing all day long. The head guy over here calls it a time line or something like that. He makes these big charts and he expects us to fill them in for everybody we question."

"I never heard that before. A time line? That's interesting. You know I think I would have liked being a detective, it must keep you thinking all the time."

"Not all the time, Hank, but most of the time. So what were you thinking about in bed yesterday, Hank?"

Henry looked away from Gus. Finally he said: "Please don't tell anybody else, Gus. You promise?"

"It all depends, Hank. If it doesn't have anything to do with the case, mum's the word."

"Well, I was masturbating myself."

"Gee whiz, Hank, there's nothing wrong with that, a lot of guys do it. I bet you woke up with a hard on and figured you might as well not waste it. Does that happen often, Hank?"

"To tell the truth, yes it does, almost every morning."

"Is that what you use those pictures for you were telling Chief Winters about?"

Henry's face became pale. "Did Mr. Winters tell you that?"

"Well, he had to, Hank. I had to tell the head guy here about that stuff so he wouldn't charge you with anything for having it around. Okay, so you were in bed for about an hour— and I don't think I have to tell anybody what you were doing— which means you got out of bed about nine. What did you do then?"

"Well, I took a shower and then I made myself some breakfast."

"So how long did all that take?"

"Oh, I guess I finished breakfast about ten or so, and then I went for a walk along the river. You know the river is pretty high after all the rain we've had, and I like to watch the birds down there."

"Well, when did you get back from your walk?"

"I guess that would be about maybe eleven or a little later. Then I hung around the house watching TV for a while until I went out shopping."

"And what time would that be Hank?"

"Probably about twelve-thirty or maybe a little later, I'm not sure."

"Well do you remember what you were watching on television just before you left?"

"I think it was the news from Philadelphia, Channel ten, the station that has the computer weather map, you know the one I mean?"

Gus nodded. "Yeah, I've seen that, it's pretty good. If I remember right, Hank, that news comes on at twelve and goes off at twelve-thirty. Did you watch the whole half-hour?"

"Well, I remember watching that weather part, and I don't know if I watched the end of the news. Why is that so important?"

"It's just that damned time line I have to fill out, Hank. So did you leave right after the weather?"

"Yes, I'm pretty sure, and then I went uptown to the cleaners to pick up some shirts I had there."

"I guess you went right up Harrison to get there, isn't that right?"

"Oh, yes, I went straight there. So then I went to the A&P to pick up some stuff for lunch."

"How did you get to the A&P from the cleaners, Hank, did you go over Race Street and then a ways along Creek Road, you know past the playground?"

"I'm not exactly sure, but I might have gone that way. Anyway, I went to the A&P and I was there maybe ten or fifteen minutes. I didn't get too much there. And then I went home and made myself some lunch."

"Okay, Hank, let's see where we are now. You left the house probably a little before or after twelve-thirty and you went to the cleaners. Say five minutes to get there and five minutes to get your shirts and get back in the car and head to the A&P. So let's say you were headed toward the A&P about twelve-forty and you might have been driving past the playground about twelve-forty-five give or take a few minutes. How does that sound?"

"I guess that's about right, Gus. You really think about these things, don't you? I never would have been able to figure that out by myself. Did you have to go to school to be a detective?"

"No, as a matter of fact, it isn't something you can be taught, you just pick it up with the job. Tell me, Hank, did you see anybody as you were driving over to the A&P, anybody you knew, maybe?"

"Gee, I don't think so. I don't really know many people."

"Did you ever see the Hartwick boy before?"

Henry's face seemed to shrivel up and he bit on his lower lip. "Mr. Bass, I thought you were my friend. I didn't know that boy and I didn't have anything to do with that."

"Hank, I didn't say you did, did I? I'm just trying to find out if you saw anybody when you were driving over to the A&P, that's all. You see we know the Hartwick boy was there at about the time you were driving by and I thought he might be someone you knew whom you might have seen, that's all. Are you sure you didn't see anybody as you drove over to the A&P, a small boy perhaps?"

"I told you, Gus, I don't know many people and I don't recall seeing anybody."

78

"Okay, Hank, so you got to the A&P about twelve-fifty, let's say, and you stayed there maybe ten or fifteen minutes. So you left there a little after one. Where did you go then?" Gus paused and then said. "By the way, did you happen to see anyone you knew while you were in the A&P?"

"No, I didn't see anybody I knew. I was only in there a few minutes and then I went straight home and I made myself some lunch. I suppose you want to know what I had for lunch?"

"Not really, Hank. I just want to know how long you stayed in the house that afternoon, that's all. By the way, did you happen to see any of your neighbors when you got home from the A&P? You know, anybody you might have said hello to or anything like that?"

Baumgart shook his head: "I don't recall seeing anybody. You know I live at the end of the street next to the river, and the neighbor next door works all day, so he wouldn't have been home."

"Does he live there alone?"

"No, he's married, but his wife works too, so she wouldn't have been home. And I certainly wouldn't have said hello to her anyway. We haven't spoken a word to each other since that trouble I got into. She's a real bitch. As a matter of fact we never did get along even before that. She's got a cat and it's always hanging out around my house and digging up my plants and stuff and she won't do a thing about it. I used to complain, but I don't bother anymore."

"I don't like cats either, Hank, they're a pain in the ass. Not like a dog. You have any pets, Hank?"

"Just some goldfish. I got them when I got out. I like to watch them swimming around, and they're easy to take care of, just give them a little food a couple of times a day."

"So, Hank, what did you do all afternoon, just stay in the house and watch the goldfish? Didn't you go out at all?"

"Maybe for a little while. I know I watched TV, one of those programs on twelve about dolphins and how smart they are. I love to watch them jumping out of the water and doing all those tricks they do. And then I read a little and I took a nap. I slept almost 'til dinnertime."

"What time did you get up from your nap, Hank?"

"I guess about five or something like that."

"What did you do then, did you leave the house?"

After a long pause, Baumgart looked around the room, and then at Gus. "You got to promise you won't tell, Gus. I masturbated myself again."

"For Christ's sake, Hank, twice in one day? What happened, did you wake up with a hard on again?"

"Yeah, that's right, I always wake up with an erection."

"Always? That's amazing, Hank. How come?"

Baumgart's face was now flushed. "It's something, isn't it? I told the doctor down in Avenel, so I guess it's all right if I tell you. It's because of my Aunt Mary. She would take care of me while my mother and my grandmother were working. They left the house early and my aunt would wake me up in the morning and get in bed and play with me. You know she would rub me down there and tell me how she would make it get bigger. And she used to suck it, too, sometimes, but not all the time. And when I got older, she used to masturbate me a lot. Like when I came home from school for lunch, she used to do it. And if I was sick and stayed home from school, she used to stay in bed and play with me all day."

Gus's jaw dropped. "Holy shit, Hank. What did your mother say about all this?"

"She never knew anything about it. My aunt told me it was something special that aunts did for little boys, but it was a secret thing and I couldn't tell anyone about it, not even my mother, so I never told her."

"And your mother never knew anything? How old were you when all this started, Hank?"

"As early as I can remember. I know it was before I started school. I don't think my mother ever knew anything about it."

"What about your grandmother? Didn't you tell her?"

"No, Aunt Mary said I couldn't tell anyone, so I didn't."

"How long did this go on, Hank? How old were you when it stopped?"

"Well, it never stopped . . . until she got sick and died."

"How old were you when she died?"

"I was in high school. I guess I was about fifteen or so."

"And your aunt masturbated you all that time?"

"Well, not for the whole time. You see, when I got bigger and started to grow hair down there, she said it was time for me to learn how to be a man and she made me get on top of her and she would put me inside her and make me come that way. Sometimes she would tell my mother I was sick and I had to stay home from school and then she would get into bed with me and make me do it with her sometimes four or five times a day. And you know I really hated it. She smelled bad, you know, and she used to make me do all kinds of things to her I didn't want to do. To tell the truth, I was really glad when she died. And you know when I told that doctor over in Avenel about it, he told me that's why I probably like boys, because of all the things my aunt did to me and made me do to her."

"That's quite a story, Hank, and I'm glad you told me. But we'd better get back to that time line now. So what time did you leave the house after all that?"

"Well, I made myself some dinner and I left at about eight or so to go up to the video store to rent a movie I wanted to see. I came straight back home and I watched the movie, and then I watched some television and went right to bed."

"What time would that be, Hank?"

"Oh, I went to bed kind of early because I had to go to work today. I would guess about eleven or before."

"And you never left the house after you got back from the video store, is that right?"

"Absolutely, I was in the whole night and I didn't leave the house until you came and got me this morning."

"By the way, Hank, who was it who called you about us finding the boy?"

"Do you really have to know?"

"I'm afraid so, Hank. Is that a problem for you?"

"I guess not. It was Chief Winters and he told me some people would probably be coming over to ask me questions because of that trouble I was in before. He told me not to tell anybody who called me about it, but I guess it's all right 'cause you guys work together, don't you?"

Gus nodded his head vigorously: "Oh, we sure do."

Just then the door opened and Howie came in with coffee for Gus and a soda for Henry. "Look, Baumgart, they didn't have any diet soda, so I got you regular coke. And here's a straw. How's he doing, Gus?"

"Just like I told you, Howie. Hank has been very cooperative and we filled in his whole time line for yesterday right up until this morning, isn't that right, Hank?"

Henry took a small sip of his soda. "I'm kind of tired from all of this talking, Gus. Can we stop for a while?"

"Sure thing, Hank, that's a good idea. Why don't you just stay here with Howie while I go and speak to the head guy. Is that all right?" Henry nodded and Gus left.

FOURTEEN

Gus went down the hall in search of Fahy and found him in his office with Delaney drinking coffee. Their faces were drawn and they looked haggard. Neither one even looked up when Gus walked in. Gus looked at them, shook his head, and said: "So how did you make out with Frohmeyer?"

Fahy's face was sagging as he said: "Not very well, to tell the truth. That one is a tough nut, although I think he's scared shitless, but he doesn't give you anything at all. How did you make out with Baumgart?"

"You know Chuck, like my old man used to say, the more I see of other people the better I like myself. This guy is a nutcase if I ever saw one. Howie and I did a Mutt and Jeff on him, and when I threw Howie out, he opened up. He says he is clean on this and I think I believe him. But here's the thing, he was uptown during the noon hour and he admits he was driving by the playground at about twelve-forty-five on his way to the A&P. He says he didn't see anybody and no one saw him. He picked up some stuff at the A&P and then went home, made himself lunch, watched TV, took a nap, had dinner, and then went out to pick up a video about eight last night. Stayed home all night and didn't leave the house until we picked him up this morning. No one saw him when he got back to the house from the A&P and no one saw him at the A&P unless someone at the checkout can place him there. You put it all together, and he doesn't have any alibi at all so we can't eliminate him. He was near the park when the kid disappeared and he went out again last night and he could have disposed of the body then. I just don't think he did it, that's all. The poor bastard is all screwed up. Says the shrinks over in Avenel told him he liked boys because his aunt used to jerk him off when he was a little kid and then she made him fuck her when he got older and he hated it. And you know what? When you hear him tell it you kind of believe him."

Fahy's face sagged even further and then he said softly: "Well we've got someone checking with the neighbors and let's get somebody over to the A&P and check with the cashiers there to see if they spotted him. What time would that be, Gus?"

"He says about one and no later than quarter after one. I'll see if I can get a picture of him and show it to the cashiers who were working yesterday."

"I want you to stay with him, Gus. I'll get Cal to take a Polaroid and have him get over to Frenchtown with it and check that out. I'd say if they can identify him and place him there around one, he's got an alibi. What do you think Al?"

Al nodded: "I agree. If he had picked up the kid at the playground he sure as hell wouldn't have gone to the A&P with him. But it all depends on when he was there. He could have taken the kid home, killed him and then gone to the A&P after that. Gus, when you go back, ask him if he saved his cash register tape. If he has it, it will show the time they checked him out."

"Will do. Either of you want to sit with this guy and see what he's like?"

Fahy said: "Yeah, I think I would like to take a crack at him. Just let me get Cal in there first and get his picture."

"I've got to take a leak anyway. I'll be back in a minute."

As Gus started out, Sloss and Sam Carter walked in, shaking their heads. It was Sloss who said: "Son-of-a-bitch, I wish it were the old days, I'd get that bastard to open up. He's just blowing smoke up our ass. All he'll say is that he was drunk all day and doesn't remember a thing. And now he wants a lawyer."

Fahy said: "You didn't do any worse than we did, Bob. We got the same shit, too. And he won't consent to any search of anything. But you know his mother owns the house and the truck is registered in her name. Sam, why can't we get her consent if she owns them? Won't that stand up?"

"It might. Let me check it out with Harris." Sam got up and went out looking for Harris. Gus left with him, looking for the men's room.

As he was about to go back to Baumgart, Gus met up with Fahy. "Gus, you'd better come back to my office. Dr. Sanchez is on the phone and he's got the first autopsy report. We better hear what he has to say before we go back to your boy." Gus followed Fahy back to his office.

Sloss had the phone in his hand and said: "Doctor Sanchez,

here's Fahy now, I'm going to put you on the speaker phone if you don't mind."

The disemboweled voice they all heard said: "Chief, how are you? Your men just left and they've got the autopsy photos. The father was in and he made a positive ID before I started the autopsy, so you've got the right kid. What a mess."

Fahy: "Good to hear from you, Doc, what do you have for us? Anything more on the time of death?"

"Yes, I can do better on that. Death occurred between noon yesterday and two o'clock at the latest based on the body temperature readings I've taken and the extent of rigor mortis in the body. The boy ate a meal before he died, not very much, I think a peanut butter and jelly sandwich and some milk. From the stomach contents, I'd say he died probably within thirty minutes or so of the time of that meal. Does that tie in with what you have?"

"It sure does, Doc. So what you're telling us is that if he ate at twelve-thirty, he was dead by one o'clock."

"That's about right, give or take fifteen minutes. The cause of death was definitely asphyxiation. I found what we call petechia, or small hemorrhages, in the conjunctivae and the eyelids, plus congestion in the liver and the lungs. That's definitely asphyxiation, no doubt about it."

"Could he have been strangled, do you think?"

"Definitely not. Those bruises on his neck you saw were made before death, but he wasn't strangled. There is no injury to the larynx, no fingernail marks on the neck and not enough damage to the throat and the musculature to be a strangulation. There was no fluid in the lungs, so he wasn't immersed in water. I'm convinced the boy was suffocated and most likely with a plastic bag. As I told you before, I think the bag was placed over his head and the neck bruises you saw resulted from someone holding the bag around his neck to make sure he suffocated. Any problem with that?"

"Not at all, Doc, what else is there?"

"The body was placed or dragged into the woods after death. How long after I can't say yet. I found evidence of pseudoabrasions caused by ant bites, and blowfly eggs in the eyes and nose. The eggs hadn't hatched yet but I have collected specimens and

I will have an entomologist study them and he can give us a better fix on the time factor. There are literally hundreds of scratches and skin abrasions all over the body, but they were inflicted after death, some from the ants and the rest probably by his being dragged through the woods and underbrush to where the body was found. So far as the autopsy is concerned, I made the standard Y incision and I've got specimens of the organs and blood for analysis, but we won't have the results back for a few days. I can tell you that there was no evidence of any semen in the mouth or anus, so there wasn't any sexual assault committed either before or after death, at least there is no evidence of any. There was definitely no penetration of the anus at any time."

"How do you account for that, Doc?"

They could hear Sanchez laughing: "Chief, that's your job. I can only tell you what I found."

"Sorry, Doc, I should know better. It's just that I'm puzzled. We're questioning two guys who have a possible connection with this, and both of them have records for molesting small boys and from what you say, they don't seem to fit if you know what I mean."

"I don't know what to tell you, Chief. It's possible of course that someone took the boy intending to assault him sexually and killed him accidentally before he did whatever he intended to do. I can't help you out there. Good luck, Chief, you've got a tough one on your hands. As soon as we get the lab results back on the specimens I'll give you a call. In the meantime, I'll get my written report over to you by late tonight or first thing in the morning. Is there anything else I can help you with?"

"I guess not, Doc. If I think of anything I'll give you a call."

There was silence in the room after Fahy hung up. No one said anything, they just stared at each other. Finally, it was Fahy who spoke: "Well at least we've got some idea about the time of death, and so far as I'm concerned, these two birds are likely candidates for it. I say we keep going with what we have and try to get Frohmeyer's house and truck searched and check out Baumgart's alibi. Anybody got any other ideas?"

No one spoke and finally Fahy said: "Sam, stick with Harris and see if we can't get a search going on Frohmeyer. I'm going to see Baumgart."

FIFTEEN

Gus followed Fahy down the hall to Baumgart's room. When they entered they found Baumgart slumped over the desk. Howie was standing over him, his face beet-red. Gus spoke first: "Howie, what's going on here, is Hank all right?"

Howie winked at Gus and didn't reply. Gus said: "No, I mean it, Howie, what happened to him?"

"Nothing very much. He doesn't like it when I insult his mother. This guy is a real piece of shit, and if I have anything to do with it, he's going to get flushed down the toilet."

Now it was Fahy's turn. "Howie, I think you had better get out of here now. I want to speak to Mr. Baumgart without you." As Howie opened the door, Smitty was standing there.

"Mr. Fahy, could I have a minute with you?"

Fahy walked out and closed the door behind him. "What's up, Smitty?"

"We just got back from Frenchtown. Billy and I searched his house and his car and you won't believe what we found. This is the biggest collection of child porn I've ever seen or even heard of. There must be a hundred or more notebooks crammed full of pictures of kids. And you know what? He's got them sorted out by pose, by age, by what's going on, you name it. Christ, it's gruesome. Where the hell does he get this kind of stuff? It's all boys, not one girl in any of them. And the boys are like from maybe four or five on up to maybe ten years old. You know he's even got them sorted out by hair color, can you imagine anything like that? He's some sick son-of-a-bitch, I tell you."

"Where have you got the stuff?"

"We put it into cartons and they're bringing them in now. I brought along a sample for you." Smitty handed Fahy a three-ring black, loose-leaf notebook.

"All right, Smitty, make sure everything gets inventoried. Did you find anything else, any kid's clothes, anything to link the Hartwick kid being in the house or car?"

"Not a thing, Chief. We went over both the car and the house carefully. Billy had the laser and we checked for hair, fibers, and prints. We lifted prints from all over the house and the car, but there's nothing that would be a kid's print in the lot. Most of the prints look like the same person and they're most likely Baumgart's. A few partials here and there which I'll have checked out with Gary. Is he around?"

"He's somewhere in the building. Thanks, Smitty. Tell the guys we'll assemble in the grand jury room about six, would you?"

Fahy turned and went back into Baumgart's room carrying the notebook. Henry was sitting up and his face was flushed. When he saw the notebook in Fahy's hand he stood up and yelled at Gus: "You promised me, Gus, they wouldn't touch my collection. You lied to me. You're just as bad as that other guy." Henry slumped down in his chair and put his head between his hands and began to sob. Fahy gestured to Gus and Gus walked around the desk and put his hands on Baumgart's shoulders.

"Hank, I didn't lie to you. This is Chief Fahy and he'll tell you in person, face to face, that he's not going to charge you with possession of this stuff, isn't that right, Chief?"

"Absolutely, Hank. Gus didn't lie to you and neither will I. We're not going to say a word to anybody about the porn we found and there will be no charges filed against you for possession. You've got my word on that. If you want, I'll bring the prosecutor in here and she will confirm that."

Henry looked up quickly. "You mean the prosecutor is a woman? You're not going to show my collection to her, are you?"

"Not if you say no, Hank. We're just going to put the stuff away, and after a while we'll burn it and that'll be the end of it."

Henry's face paled. "You mean you took my whole collection and you're going to keep it? Gus, you never told me they would take it away from me. Why do they have to do that?"

Fahy answered, "It's very simple, Hank. We can't let you keep that kind of stuff. It's contraband and we have to confiscate it even if we don't charge you with having it. And what if somebody else came along and saw the stuff? You know, like Chief Winters or some other cop. They could arrest you on the spot and there's nothing we could do about it. Believe me, you're much better off this way."

"But Chief Winters knows I've got a collection. I told him about it."

Fahy's face straightened up: "When did you tell Winters that? Did he ever see your collection?"

"Oh, I told him a couple of years ago. He used to come around my house and check up on me, and I told him that I was staying away from boys and everybody else because I had this collection and I didn't need to get messed up anymore. I didn't show it to him. He just said it was okay, and I shouldn't show it to anyone. I don't understand, if Chief Winters said it was all right for me to have it, why can't I keep it?"

Gus looked at Fahy and shrugged. Fahy said: "Look, Hank, I've told you. It's against the law to have that kind of stuff in your possession no matter what Winters says, and we can't let you keep it. That's the end of that. I'm sorry, but that's the way it is. Now, Hank, Gus here has been telling me about your activities yesterday and I just want to go over a few details with you, do you mind?"

Henry didn't look up, he just nodded.

"Now we've got to know exactly what time you left your house to go uptown yesterday and everything you did until you got home again."

"But I already went over that with Gus. He's got it all down, haven't you, Gus?"

"Yes I do, Hank, and Fahy won't be long with you. He just wants to tie things down precisely so we can get you out of here, that's all. Am I right, Chuck?"

"Absolutely. Now you left the house a little before twelve-thirty and you went up to the cleaners, right?" Henry nodded. "And you picked up some shirts at the cleaners, and then you drove over to the A&P and bought a few things. By the way, did you happen to save your receipt from the check out?"

"I usually do."

"Do you know where it would be?"

"It should be in the kitchen somewhere. I don't think I threw it out."

"Good. Now how long did it take to pick up those shirts, and what route did you take to the A&P?"

Henry paused briefly and his voice was almost a whimper:

"Like I told Gus, no more than five minutes to get up to the cleaners and park. Another five minutes to pick up the shirts and then I drove up Bridge Street, over Race to Creek Road, and then up Creek Road to the A&P on Sixth Street. That's all I can remember. You know I wasn't looking at my watch or timing myself."

"And if you went over Creek Road, you certainly had to drive right by the park there, isn't that right?"

"Sure I did, but why is that so important? Gus kept saying the same thing. What's supposed to have happened at the park yesterday, anyway?"

"Well, I'm going to level with you, Hank. You see we have good information that at just about the time you were passing by the park yesterday, Bobby Hartwick disappeared from that same park just as he was about to cross Creek Road on his way back to school. Now so far, you're the only person we know who was passing the park at just that time, and you certainly had the opportunity to pick up that boy, didn't you?"

Henry put his hands over his face and started to sob. The words that came out of his mouth were barely intelligible. All Gus could make out was "No, no, no..."

Gus broke in at once. "Hank, believe me Hank, no one says you did anything like that. If we thought that, we'd have to read you your rights and get you a lawyer and all that crap. I told you that when we started. The chief here isn't accusing you of anything. He's just trying to find out if you might have seen the boy, that's all. Isn't that right, Chuck?"

"Oh, absolutely. You heard me, Gus, did I say he picked the boy up?"

"No, you didn't, Chuck. I just want Hank here to understand that. You do, don't you, Hank?"

Still holding his hands over his face, but in a more controlled voice, Henry said: "But that's what you're thinking, that I picked up that kid and killed him. I swear to you, I never saw that kid and I wouldn't do anything like that. Don't you understand, I love little boys. I would never hurt them."

Before he could stop himself, Fahy blurted out: "Yeah, Baumgart, we know how much you love little boys. What about those kids up in Warren County, did you love them, too?"

Henry violently threw his whole upper body down on the

90

desk and was now sobbing uncontrollably. Gus looked over at Fahy who stood up and said: "You can have him, Gus. He's a creep and I don't want anything more to do with him. Sooner or later we'll get the goods on him, and when we do, he's going to get the needle and I'm going to be there and watch it." Fahy went out, slamming the door.

A good five minutes passed in silence except for the sobs and the moans coming from Henry. As he began to grow quiet, Gus reached across the desk and put his hand on his head. "Look, Hank, crying isn't going to help. If you did it, then as your friend, I have to tell you it would be better if you got it off your chest and told us now. Maybe it's not too late to do something for you. You're sick, I'm sure of that, and we can get you some help."

Henry's moaning stopped. "Gus, I thought you believed me. I didn't do it. It's too late to help me anyway. That's what the doctors up in Avenel told me. I'm too old to change, that's why they said I should just masturbate whenever I got the urge, and so help me, that's all I've ever done. I haven't been near a boy since I got out. Someone's got to believe me."

"I'd like to believe you, Hank, it's just that it's too much of a coincidence that you happened to be passing the park just when that kid disappeared, you know what I mean?"

Henry's face paled and he straightened up in his chair. "Mr. Bass, I want to go home now. I'm not under arrest, am I? If I'm not, I want to go home."

"Well, Hank, let me check on that with the boss. If he says it's okay, I'll have someone drive you over to Frenchtown, is that all right?" Henry nodded and Gus left the room in search of Fahy.

He caught up with Fahy as he was about to go into the grand jury room and he said: "Chuck, I'm worried about this guy. He's really shook up and now he says he wants to go home if he's not under arrest. What should I tell him?"

Fahy shrugged his shoulders and, casting a sidewise glance at Gus, said: "Well we certainly don't have enough to arrest him on anything other than the porn. I could get the prosecutor to nix the deal I made with him and hold him on that charge. What do you think?"

Gus frowned: "To tell the truth, Chuck, I don't like it. I just don't think he had anything to do with that kid, and if he's not crazy already, arresting him now will put him over the edge for sure and he'll end up in the looney bin and we'll never get at him again."

Fahy nodded: "You're probably right, Gus. Get someone to take him home and then come on into the grand jury room. We're going to have a meeting to see where we are and make assignments for tomorrow."

SIXTEEN

By 6:15 the entire staff, except for Sam Carter, was assembled in the grand jury room, together with Sloss and Delaney and a few troopers and Ben Harris. Fahy spoke first: "All right, here's where we're at. Baumgart is definitely a possible. He admits riding by the park at just about the time the kid disappeared. His only possible alibi is when he went to the A&P and that's being checked out. If he's lying about that, he's got to be our number one candidate. Smitty and Billy did the search on his house and car and came up with nothing. He collects kiddy porn—he's got a ton of the stuff—but so far that's the only thing we've come up with by way of physical evidence. We shook him up good, but I've let him go home. Let him stew about it over night and we'll bring him back first thing tomorrow morning. Gus, I want you to pick him up and bring him back here. What do you think, Ben, can we bring him back in?"

"How long did you have him today?"

"Altogether, maybe six hours, but the questioning wasn't continuous. We gave him breaks and fed him soda. He wouldn't eat anything, isn't that right Gus?" Gus nodded. "And as soon as he wanted to quit, we let him go."

Harris shook his head: "You have no physical evidence, and I would say if he doesn't come in voluntarily, you're dead in the water. You never mirandized him, did you?"

Gus spoke up. "No, I told him he wasn't a suspect or under arrest and I didn't have to read him his rights."

"Well, you're cutting it pretty fine. If you bring him back, you better mirandize him."

Fahy continued: "That brings us to Mr. Frohmeyer. Have you gotten anything from him, Bob?"

Fahy shook his head violently. "The same bullshit. He started drinking in the morning just after his mother left and he was drunk all day and doesn't remember a thing. Says that's all he has been doing since he got out, staying as drunk as he can get. Chuck, have you heard from Sam about a search?"

93

"Not yet, he's still over there. He should be calling in any minute now. How about it, Ben, can we get by with her consent?"

Harris grinned and said: "Sometimes you guys amaze me, Chuck. You come up with questions that belong on a law school exam. I'll skip the lecture, but with some exceptions, if you get the property owner's consent to the search, it will stand up. It all depends on whether the suspect has a legitimate expectation of privacy as to what you're searching. Like his room and anything which is personal to him in the house. So far as the truck is concerned, if the mother owns it and she drives it, too, I think her consent will stand up. But remember it has to be informed consent and in this case I think she better be told that you are looking for evidence of her son's possible involvement in a crime. Does Sam know that?"

Now Fahy grinned: "When he calls in, I'll make sure to tell him. Come to think of it, you'd better tell him yourself and explain the drill to him. What about questioning him, how long can we keep him tonight and can we bring him back tomorrow?"

"I don't suppose you mirandized him, either, did you?"

"I didn't, how about you, Bob?"

"Hell no. I'd like to finalize the creep."

They all laughed and Ben said: "I didn't hear that, Captain, and I don't think anyone else did either."

Sloss's face hardened: "Well, that's good, 'cause if you find that turd squashed in the road, just remember I didn't have anything to do with it."

"I'll plea bargain with you on that one, Bob."

The phone rang and Fahy picked it up. "Good work, Sam. I'm going to put you on the speaker. Ben Harris is here and you tell him."

"Hello, Ben?"

"I hear you Sam, what did she say."

Sam was excited as he said: "She may be his mother, but there ain't no mother love there. She says we can search all we want and she hopes we find something so she can get rid of him again. Says the best thing that ever happened to her was his being put away, but it wasn't long enough. How about it, Ben, can we search?"

"Sam, you had better get it in writing and spell out that we are searching for her son's possible involvement in the commission of a crime. Find out if she drives that truck at all and if she does, include the truck and the registration number of the truck as well as the address of the house and everything else you need to identify what you're going to search. Is there a garage there?"

"Not a garage but they've got a kind of small barn out back. It's a big piece of property, about seven or eight acres, I'd guess."

"Okay, make sure you describe the barn and include all the grounds in the description. For the time being, though, don't search his room or if he has a desk or something like that in the house, stay away from that. Got that?"

"Right. Anything else we got to be careful about?"

"That's about it. Happy hunting and here's Chuck."

"All right, Sam, I'm sending Williams and Walters over there to help you out. Bert will have his camera with him so get pictures of anything you find before you remove it. They'll have the laser, too, so give it a real going over. If you need any more guys, just give a call. We'll keep the creep here for at least another three hours so he'll be out of your way. If we have to let him go, I'll call you before we do."

Fahy hung up and said: "All right, Williams and Walters get over there. We'll wait up for you, so get back here as soon as you're finished." Fahy then turned to Harris: "How about it, Ben, can we keep him for another three hours or so?"

"If you can get him to stay voluntarily, there's nothing wrong with that. Get him some dinner or something. Come to think of it, you could have a couple of guys take him over to the National for dinner, and that will sound a lot better. It'll show he was treated well and not being kept in custody."

"Whatever you say, Ben, but I hate to buy that creep a meal on the county. How about it, Bob, want to take your friend to dinner?"

"Don't even joke about it, Chuck. I think I'd probably slip some poison in his food if I got the chance. Send some of your guys, they can use a free meal on what you pay them."

"You're getting too predictable in your old age, Bob. I knew you were going to say that. Just remember I gave you your opportunity and you refused. That's about it guys. Why don't the rest of us break and get some food ourselves and get back here by about eight."

Gus caught up with Fahy as he was going out the door. "Chuck, do you think you need me anymore tonight? I'm kind of all in and if there's nothing more you want me to do tonight, I'd just as soon go home and pack it in."

Fahy put his arm around Gus's shoulder: "Sure, Gus, you've had a long day. I don't think there's anything more you can do around here tonight, so you go on along. Just leave a number where we can reach you if anything comes up. If not, I'll see you back here tomorrow with your friend, Hank."

"Chuck, he's no friend. I just kind of feel sorry for the guy."

"I know that, Gus. Maybe I feel the same way myself."

SEVENTEEN

Gus got a ride over to the Corner Store and picked up his car. But he didn't go straight home. He detoured over to Pittstown Road and stopped at Peg's. The front light was on as he pulled up into the driveway and by the time he got out, Peg was at the front door holding it open for him.

Peg wrapped her arms around him as she said: "Gus, what happened? You look like someone's been hitting on you all day."

"That's just about right, Peg. I guess you know we found Bobby Hartwick this morning after I left here."

"Yes, I spoke to Mary. She told me all about it. It was pretty bad. Do you know how it happened?"

"All we know is someone smothered the kid in a plastic bag. Then they cut off his penis and punctured his belly and dumped him in the woods where we found him."

Peg gasped: "Oh, God. He was such a pretty little boy. Who could do anything like that?"

"I don't know, Peg. We picked up a couple of perverts and we've been questioning them all day. One of them lives in Frenchtown, a guy by the name of Baumgart. A mousy, little man with a record of molesting young boys. He's a sorry specimen of a human being. He was all screwed up by his family and I could almost feel sorry for the bastard, he's so pathetic. We really put him through the wringer but I don't think he did it."

By now they were in the house and Gus was sitting on the sofa. Peg asked: "Gus, have you had anything to eat? Let me make you something. How about a drink?"

"I could use a drink for sure. I don't think I could eat anything, but thanks, just a drink will do."

Peg was back in a minute and handed Gus his Stoly. "You said there were a couple of people you were questioning. Who were the others?"

"Just one other, a guy from Locktown by the name of Frohmeyer. He's got a record, too, and he got out only a month ago for abusing a young boy. But I didn't spend any time with him. I was with Baumgart the whole day. They didn't get anything out of Frohmeyer, claims he was drunk the whole day and doesn't remember what he did. When I left, they were doing a search of his house and his truck. It turns out he has a pickup that matches the description of the truck they saw going up Creek Road from the park after the kid was taken. I didn't wait around for them to get back."

"What did you do with these guys, are you holding them?"

Gus almost sneered as he said: "We had to let Baumgart go. We had nothing to hold him on, but I'm going to pick him up first thing tomorrow and take him back and question him some more. But he's a dead end, I'm sure of that. They've still got Frohmeyer over there waiting for the guys to get back from the search. They're wining and dining him, but from what I hear, they won't get anything from him. Funny thing, they got his mother to agree to the search 'cause she owns the house and the truck. When they asked her permission, she didn't just go along with it; she said she hoped that would find something so they could put him away. How's that for a loving mother?"

"Speaking of mothers, how are the Hartwicks taking it?"

"I don't know. I haven't seen them since early this morning when Fahy and I went up and told them their son was dead. Christ, that was a scene. Nobody should have to do that. It's inhuman. We had to go in cold turkey and tell them. They had heard that a kid had been found in the park and we had to tell them it was their kid. How's that for a job?"

"Gus, I don't know how you can do it. I don't know how anybody can do it, for that matter. I know I couldn't. The worst I ever have to deal with is telling parents their kid isn't going to pass his grade, and then I feel like shit. I can't imagine how you can tell parents their kid has been murdered."

Gus took a long swallow of his Stoly. "Well they already had to know it because of what they had heard. All we did was to confirm it. And you know the grandmother was there, the husband's mother, and when we told them, she started screaming at Mrs. Hartwick, that it was her fault, she didn't watch her kids. I could have killed that woman. Can you imagine saying something like that to a mother who's just been told that her son was murdered?"

"Gus, my poor Gus, you've really been through it, haven't you?"

"You know, Peg, another day like this and I'm finished. They can take this job and shove it. And then, after that scene with the parents and the grandmother, I had to spend the rest of the day with this Baumgart and break him to get his story. For a time I thought he was the one, but he isn't and all I did was to get the poor bastard really screwed up. He was a basket case by the time he left the office."

"How about Fahy, what does he think?"

"I think he agrees with me that Baumgart's clear, but he has some doubts. He wants to check out his alibi. I tell you, Peg, I think we're chasing our tails. The autopsy report came in and the kid wasn't sexually molested at all and the only leads we have are a couple of queers. It just doesn't smell right to me. Fahy seems to be convinced that the kid was snatched by a queer, but it doesn't add up. Why would a guy take the kid in broad daylight and kill him and then bring him back and dump him in the park? It just doesn't make any sense to me."

"Gus, you're just getting yourself all worked up. I don't care what you say, I'm making you something to eat. You just finish your drink, I'll be right back."

It was not more than ten minutes when Peg returned to the living room. She found Gus stretched out on the couch fast asleep. She went to the bedroom and got a light quilt and covered him up, kissed him gently, and turned out the lights.

EIGHTEEN

Gus woke up slowly, uncertain where he was. The first light of dawn was barely illuminating the room and by the time his eyes were fully open, he recognized Peg's living room and he could make out the silhouettes of the trees outside the front window. Then he remembered talking to Peg, but for the moment nothing else. With a rush, the events of yesterday came back to him and he moaned softly. Sleep was over so he sat up slowly on the sofa and stretched and immediately felt a sharp pain in his back. He stood up and wobbled slightly. He thought to himself he was too old to be sleeping on sofas, even Peg's sofa. He went to the kitchen, opened the fridge, and got out the coffee can, thinking that Peg was the only person he ever knew who kept the coffee can in the fridge. He wondered if that really made any sense, he could never tell the difference between her coffee and any other. By now he could see the fast-rising dawn from the kitchen window and the sky was already a brilliant reddish gold and the clouds were clearly visible and beginning to turn bluish-gray against the lightening sky. It was going to be a hot day, and as he loaded the coffee pot he wanted the day to be over and to go back to sleep. But he knew that wasn't going to happen. He poured two glasses of juice and went into Peg's room. She was already stirring as he sat down on the side of the bed and leaned over and kissed her cheek: "It's juice time, honey, and the coffee's on."

Peg rolled over and opened one eye and then the other. She murmured: "What time is it?"

"In the army, it's bugle time. In Frenchtown, it's almost six o'clock. You want to go back to sleep?"

She murmured: "I don't think so. Just let me lie here a bit and I'll get up."

"Sure, honey. I'll put the juice right here and the coffee will be ready when you are." He kissed her shoulder and went back to the kitchen and poured himself his first cup of coffee. After a few minutes, Peg walked sleepily into the kitchen. "I'll take that

100

coffee now. You know, you keep weird hours. I don't know how you do it."

"It used to be okay, but I'm getting too old for it now. Especially having to sleep on sofas."

"I'm sorry, Gus, but you really passed out and I thought it would be better just to leave you there. Did you sleep all right?"

"I must have. I woke up not knowing where I was. Peg, I'd better be going. I got to get home and change and go pick up Baumgart and take him over to Fahy's office. Look, I'll call you first chance I get. What'll you be doing today?"

Peg shrugged. "I've got no plans. I might go shopping over in the mall and things like that, but nothing special. If I'm not here just leave a number for me on the machine." She walked over and put her arms around him and said: "Gus, I really do love you. Please, for my sake, don't let this get to you any more than it has, okay? Keep your distance from those people."

"I wish I could. It's not easy, but I'll try, honestly, Peg. And tonight I'm taking you out to dinner. How about that Chinese restaurant down in Lambertville?"

"Sounds good to me. Call me and let me know when you're coming."

NINETEEN

Gus's apartment was in a small townhouse project—the only one in Frenchtown—just off Trenton Avenue. When Gus walked into his apartment he realized he hadn't been there for more than two days and the apartment already smelled musty. He never had been much of a housekeeper and as he entered the tiny kitchen he realized from the strong odor that he had not taken the garbage out when he last left the place. He reached under the sink for the deodorizer can, sprayed it around a bit, and took the garbage out after he sprayed that, too. As he threw the garbage bag into the dumpster, he saw his next door neighbor, an elderly widow, whom Gus knew only as Mrs. Radcar, staring at him from her kitchen window. The window was open and Gus said: "Good morning, Mrs. Radcar. Aren't you up early?"

"At my age, Mr. Gus, it doesn't make any difference when you get up. Sleeping and being up are pretty much the same. But I'm sorry to see you having to take out your garbage. A nice man like you should get a wife and let her take out the garbage."

"Mrs. Radcar, if I got married then I'd just be taking out the garbage for two instead of one."

Mrs. Radcar shook her head. "Nonsense, I never let my Phil take out the garbage, not even once in almost fifty years. You know, Mr. Gus, if you just took off twenty pounds or so you would be the best looking man around and you'd have to fight off the girls who'd be after you. Why even now, that school teacher lady I've seen you with is really after you. Why don't you marry her? She's not a young chicken but she's certainly a good looking woman."

"I'm sure she would thank you for that Mrs. Radcar, but I don't think she's interested in getting married."

"Well, why don't you just ask her and find out. I bet you never did, did you?"

"No, but I'm going to think about it, I promise you. Say, Mrs. Radcar, while we're talking, did you ever know a family by the name of Baumgart? I understand they lived in Frenchtown for

102

a long time and I thought you might know them. There's a guy named Henry Baumgart. You know him?"

"Let me think, 'Baumgart.' Didn't they live up on Twelfth Street?"

"That's right. Henry still lives there, as a matter of fact."

Mrs. Radcar nodded: "I knew the old woman, I guess that would be the grandmother. She's been dead a long time now. And I knew his mother at least to say hello to. They kept pretty much to themselves but they were hard working people. I don't think the mother ever married. You know in those days, that was a scandal, to have a child and not be married. I remember there was a lot of talk about who the father was, but I don't think anyone really knew, except her I guess. It happened during the war, and there were a lot of soldiers around picking up young girls in those days, so who knows. Why do you want to know about the Baumgarts, if you don't mind my asking?"

"Oh, I don't mind your asking. I happened to run into Henry yesterday and I was wondering if you might know him. That's all."

"Well, him I really don't know at all, so I can't help you there. Are you working on that poor boy's murder, is that how you met him?"

"Well sort of. Look, I have to run now. They'll be expecting me over in Flemington and I still have to shower. Thanks, Mrs. Radcar, you've been very helpful."

"You go along, Mr. Gus, and don't forget what I said about the garbage."

After Gus had showered and changed, it was almost eight and he decided it wasn't too early to pick up Baumgart. The drive to 12th Street took but a few minutes and as Gus pulled up in front of the house, he was relieved to see Baumgart's car parked in the driveway. He knocked several times on the front door and got no answer, so he decided to walk around to the rear of the house. The rear door which led into the kitchen was partly open and Gus walked in and called "Hank" in a loud voice but there was no response. As he proceeded down the darkened hall he walked into the feet of a body suspended above him. Gus screamed, at first from fright and then despair. There was Baumgart hanging by what looked like heavy braided sash cords from a second floor beam, his body suspended over the staircase bannister. Gus dashed up the steps and grabbed him to relieve the pressure of the noose. As he did so, one look at Henry's face told him he was dead and had been for some time. Rigor had already set in and the face was a grotesque mask. Still, he leaned his head against Henry's chest listening for a heart beat. There wasn't any and no carotid pulse. Gus released his hold on the body. An overwhelming sense of guilt emptied Gus of any other feeling and he sat down on the stairs. His thoughts became ugly and distorted. Later, he wasn't sure how long he had just sat there on the steps, but with the passage of time, he realized he had to call Fahy and let him know. He walked down the stairs, found a telephone in the kitchen and dialed Fahy's office. He was put through immediately.

"Chuck, it's Gus. I came over to pick up Baumgart, and he's dead. He hung himself sometime last night. You better get over here quick and get the medical examiner."

"Gus, take it easy. I don't want you to do a thing in there. Go outside and sit in your car and just watch the house and we'll be there in fifteen minutes. Are you all right?"

"I'll be okay. Just get here."

Gus hung up the phone and went out the kitchen door. It was already a warm, sunny day and he walked in the direction of the river. As he reached the river bank, he saw a pair of ducks with their brood entering the water and the sounds of birds were everywhere. He thought to himself: This is what Henry liked to do, but he isn't going to do it anymore. That poor, miserable little bastard never had a life. And then Gus thought, *Who am I to say he never had a life? What kind of life have I ever had? Everything's passed me by, too, I'm just as hopeless as he was. What have I ever done to make a life for myself or anyone else?* And then, for the first time in as long as he could remember he thought about a God who might be judging him and his life. His last confession had been before he left for 'Nam, But even then he had known it was hopeless for him to believe in any kind of God as a protector or healer. God couldn't exist or he would never have let happen what he had seen happen. And what about his own little brother, where had God been? He had really wanted God to be there then, but He wasn't and Gus had given up on

Him. From the time of his brother's death, faith had left him to deal with his guilt alone.

He walked back to Baumgart's house only a minute or two before Fahy and his gang arrived. Fahy was first out and ran up to Gus and grabbed his arm. "You okay, Gus? You look like shit. Where is he?"

Gus nodded in the direction of the house. "The front door's locked but the back door is open and he's in the hallway hanging from a beam. He's been dead for at least several hours, there's a lot of rigor in the body."

"Was there any note?"

"I didn't see any, but I didn't look around. I just called you and then I got out of there. So now what do we do, Chuck?"

"Just keep going, that's all we can do. You have any ideas?"

"No, I'm out of ideas. Oh, shit, this is all we need now. Here comes the chief."

The chief's well-ornamented official car stopped within a few feet of where they were standing and the chief got out. Gus noticed that the chief was careful about swinging his door open. As the chief strode up to them, he barked out: "What the hell are you guys doing here now, find another body or something?"

Fahy answered. "Well, Chief, I'm afraid we have. Looks like Baumgart killed himself. My people are in there now checking it out and we'll have the medical examiner here in a few minutes."

"Why the hell did he do that? Did he kill the kid?"

This time it was Gus who answered. "I don't think so, Chief. I didn't see any note or anything like that when I was in there, and he sure as hell didn't confess when we questioned him yesterday."

"Then why the hell would he kill himself? Did you guys do something to him?"

There was a long pause before Fahy answered. "Don't be a jerk, Winters. Of course we didn't do anything to him. As soon as he said he wanted to leave, he left. As a matter of fact, we even drove him home."

"Listen, Fahy, you asked me to help you set this guy up for you. Now he's killed himself. I want to know what the hell's going on. I've had enough of you throwing your weight around and I'm entitled to some answers."

"Well, we don't have answers for you. I don't want another hassle with you, Winters. Just leave us alone, you've already caused us enough problems, remember?"

"All right, if that's the way you want it. But I'm telling you I'm going to call in the attorney general's office on this and I'm going to get some answers before this is finished."

"You do that. In the meantime, just get the hell out of here."

"One more thing, Fahy. Who the hell is this asshole Bass working for? He's not on my payroll anymore, so he better not be giving me any more of his fucking time sheets. Is that clear?"

"Is that right? Good, he's working for me. There's one more thing, Winters. We took a statement from Baumgart yesterday after we picked up his collection of porn. He told us you knew all about it and told him it was all right with you. He also told us you called him yesterday morning to warn him we were going to pick him up. Is that true?"

The chief stepped back from Fahy. He paused and then he grinned openly: "How you going to prove that one, Fahy? That little prick is dead. If that's what you think you got on me, you know how far you'll get with it." The chief turned his back on them and left.

Fahy looked at Gus. "How the hell did that piece of shit ever get to be a cop? If it's the last thing I ever do I'm going to have his ass, I swear it. Come on, Gus, we had better go in and see what they've found."

Gus followed Fahy up the steps and into the house. Bert Williams and Amster were taking pictures of the scene. Carter was walking down the stairs and when he saw Fahy he said: "Boss, we found a note. It was on a table in the hall upstairs. I didn't touch it, it was lying open on the table. Just one sheet of paper. You had better take a look."

Fahy followed Carter up the stairs with Gus trailing behind them. Straight ahead of them was the table with a single sheet of lined notebook paper resting on it. Carter stepped aside and now Gus could with difficulty read Baumgart's words:

Dear Aunt Mary,
They think I killed that boy but I didn't and they won't believe

me. They took everything away from me. I'm sorry. I'll see you soon.

Henry

Gus turned and walked down the stairs and out the front door. After a few minutes Fahy came and joined him. "Gus, he was over the edge for a long time. This was going to happen sooner or later. It was just a matter of time, so don't go blaming yourself. You played it by the book and so did I."

"If that's supposed to make me feel better, Chuck, forget it because it doesn't. I knew the guy was sick, and I didn't let it stop me for a second. And you know what? If I had to do it all over again, I'd probably do the same fucking thing. That's what bothers me. It's the job and I just want out."

"I know, Gus. I've felt the same way I don't know how many times. But somebody has to do it, and sometimes people get hurt."

"That may be so, but I don't want to do the hurting, that's all. Look, I'm responsible for what happened to that poor bastard, and you know it."

Fahy grabbed Gus's shoulders. "I don't buy that Gus, but it's what you believe that counts. If you really think about it, I'm the one who called the shots, not you, and I can live with it. Now that's the last word I'm going to say on this. We've got a lot of work ahead of us and I want you with me. We're having a meeting over in the office at noon and I expect you to be there. That's an order. Oh, here comes Sanchez, so snap out of it."

The medical examiner's car stopped in front of the house and Dr. Sanchez emerged with a broad grin on his face. "Well, Chief, what have you got for me now? At the rate you're going, I would be better off working on piece rates than a salary."

"Well, Doc, at least it's not a kid this time and I don't think you'll have any problem with the cause of death. It's a guy named Henry Baumgart and we were questioning him yesterday on the Hartwick case. We sent him home last night, and when Gus Bass here came over this morning to pick him up, he found him strung up. He left a note and it certainly looks like a suicide."

"You guys are certainly playing rough these days, aren't you? Well, let's go in and take a look."

Fahy grimaced. "Doc, your sense of humor stinks sometimes, and this is one of them."

The medical examiner put his arm around Fahy's shoulders and the two of them turned and walked into the house leaving Gus standing in the road.

TWENTY

Gus got into his car and started driving just to get away and without any destination. He drove through Milford and headed up the road along the river, a narrow, one lane road that twisted and turned along the river's course. He pulled into a layby and got out and walked over to the sloping bank of the river and sat down. All around him life imposed itself upon his senses. A doe and two fawns were grazing on the lush grasses only a few yards from where he sat, ducks and geese were swimming with their young, squirrels were scurrying about or raised up on their haunches nibbling and staring at him, birds were calling for their mates, the wild dogwoods were almost flaunting their beauty at him. He stared at the water rippling in the slanting rays of the morning sun and bowed his head and wept. He lost all track of time as he stared at the water flowing past.

He heard the sound of a car on the road just above him. The car stopped and a young man leaned out the window: "Are you all right, mister? Do you need any help?"

Gus stood up and turned to face the voice. "I'm all right, but thanks for asking anyway. That was nice of you."

"That's okay. Is there anything I can do?"

"No, I was just resting a bit, but thanks anyway. Listen, you have a nice day."

The car drove off and Gus walked slowly back to his car feeling better than he had since he had gotten that damned call. He picked up the phone and dialed Peg's number. She answered on the first ring. "Peg, it's Gus, can I stop over for a few minutes?"

"Sure, Gus, I didn't expect you to call. Has anything happened?"

"I'll tell you when I see you. I'll be there in a few minutes."

Gus glanced at his watch as he pulled into Peg's driveway. It was already eleven. Peg's door was open and he walked in and called out: "Peg?"

"Be right there, Gus. Just putting the last load in the washer." Gus went into the kitchen and sat down. When Peg turned around, she said: "I thought you were going to pick up that guy and take him over to Flemington. How come you're back so early?"

"Baumgart killed himself sometime last night. When I got there I found him strung up from a beam on the second floor. He left a note for his Aunt Mary. Christ, she's been dead a long time ago. He says in the note that he didn't kill the kid but we don't believe him. How's that for a mess. And if that isn't enough, the goddamned chief shows up and starts accusing Fahy and me of hounding the guy to death. What a way to start a day."

"Gus, you've got to give up this job. You're not cut out for it." Putting her arms around him and hugging him tightly, she said: "Did you eat anything since you left here? Let me fix you something."

"No, there isn't time. I've got to be over in Flemington by noon. Fahy is having another skull session to see where we go from here. You know, Peg, when this one's over, I think I am going to quit. But God knows when it will be over. I think we're just chasing our tails around. If the kid wasn't molested there's got to be another angle to this case, but I'm damned if I know what it is."

"Gus, when this is over I think you ought to dig ditches or something."

"I don't think so. I'd end up finding buried bodies and I'd be right back where I am now. Look, I'd better be going. Remember, we've got a date for dinner. I'll call you before I leave Flemington."

"Fine, honey, I'll be back here by four if you need me for anything."

TWENTY-ONE

Gus walked into the grand jury room just before noon. Fahy's staff was already there, most of them looking like zombies. Gus said: "You look like you guys had a late night. What went down with Frohmeyer?"

It was Sam Carter who answered. "We had a merry old time at his place. Didn't get finished until after midnight, but we came up with something. He had at least two pounds of high grade marihuana stashed in the barn out back. And we found forty pieces of crack in a bag under the seat in the truck. And the truck has one of those big tool boxes mounted on the flatbed behind the cab. We found yellow fibers in that box which might match up with the kid's shirt. Fahy's got samples on their way down to the FBI lab for analysis. The only problem is that we don't have anything to match them up with unless we can find the shirt the kid was wearing."

"How about prints, anything there?"

"Nope, not a thing. All we found was the fibers. We're going to have to go back and speak to Mrs. Hartwick and find out where she bought that shirt and the brand. That will help them at the lab and maybe they can come up with a match that way."

Fahy walked in with Sloss and Delaney. Sloss walked over to Gus: "I hear you had a bad time this morning. You okay?"

Gus nodded. "I think so, so long as we don't find any more bodies lying around today. How late were you here last night?"

"I called it quits about two or so. I can't take these late nights any more at my age. Geez, my old lady was all over me this morning about it. Said she's going to have me on a curfew if I don't behave. You ever been married, Gus?"

"No, I still take out my own garbage." Sloss grinned and Gus told him about his talk with Mrs. Radcar.

"You're right about the garbage. I've been married more than thirty years and I still take out the garbage."

Fahy stood in front of the grand jury foreman's desk and started off: "I want everyone up to date. You all know about

Baumgart. Dr. Sanchez says it was definitely suicide. He hung himself at about midnight last night. We checked the note for prints, and the only ones on there were Baumgarts. And the handwriting on the note seems to match up with samples of his we found in the house. Sanchez is listing it as a suicide on the death certificate, so that's it so far as Baumgart is concerned. We've got his whole interrogation on tape and I'm preparing a report on what happened for the prosecutor. Anybody have anything to add?"

Bert Williams spoke up. "Boss, do you think he could have killed the kid? You know that note reads like he was a psycho."

"I don't think he was our guy. He was looney-tunes all right, but I'm convinced he didn't kill the kid. Gus is too, and he spent the most time with him, isn't that right, Gus?"

"Yeah, there's no question in my mind. He wasn't anywhere near that kid."

Fahy continued: "For those of you who missed the fun and games last night, we've got Frohmeyer under arrest on drug charges, possession with intent to distribute. I suspect that he was going to use the drugs to lure kids. It sure didn't take him long to start up again. That kind of tells you how much good they do over at Avenel. Those treatment programs are all just bullshit to satisfy the bleeding hearts. But we did find yellow fibers in his tool box which might be from the kid's shirt. We'll get a report from the FBI lab in a few days. We've confiscated the truck because of the drugs we found in it and Gary and Smitty are taking it apart piece by piece. We measured the tool box and he could have hidden the boy's body in there and that might account for the fibers we found. Let's hope so. It's about all we got going for us on him for now."

Gus asked: "What about tire marks? Did they find anything useful over along Creek Road?"

"They found a few treads in one of those spots you mentioned and got some casts, but nothing matches up with Frohmeyer's truck. There wasn't anything useful in the other areas, at least nothing you could use to identify the tread."

"Has anyone questioned Frohmeyer this morning?"

"No, we had to mirandize him when we arrested him for the drugs and he said he's not talking anymore without a lawyer. We

112

called the public defender's office and they're sending someone over to hold his hand. We're going to arraign him this afternoon on the drug charges and Harris is going to ask for two hundred fifty thousand dollars bail but he doubts whether the judge will go for that much. Harris thinks fifty thousand dollars is all we'll get on a drug charge. Sam spoke to his mother this morning and she wants him kept in so he probably isn't going to make bail anyway. So there's not much more we can do with Frohmeyer for now. Sam, how about you and Gus going over to Frenchtown and speaking to the parents. See if you can find out about the shirt the kid was wearing. Maybe she has another one like it she might have bought for the boy when she got him the yellow shirt."

Fahy continued: "So far as the time line is concerned, we've narrowed that down to an hour and fifteen minutes between twelve forty-five Friday and two o'clock. Bob says we should be getting a list of blue pickups registered in the area from motor vehicle by late this afternoon or first thing tomorrow and then we'll start checking those out. Al, do you have anything on the stops your guys made on the trucks on Friday?"

"Yeah, it was faxed over here this morning. They stopped about thirty blue Ford pickups within a ten mile radius of Frenchtown and got the drivers' names and addresses. Some poor bastards got stopped twice, and one guy was stopped three times. He must have been wondering what the hell was happening to him."

"Well, that will give us something to do this afternoon. Let's get a detail organized and start interviewing them. Al, you got any guys who can give us a hand?"

"Oh, I can get you at least five or six guys, no problem. When I left the barracks this morning, the boys were volunteering to do anything we needed on this one. They're hot to trot. I'll make a call over there now and get them started on the first fifteen on the list, and your guys can handle the rest, if that's okay."

"Can't ask for anything more than that, Al. We owe you on this. I've got to hang around here for a while. The prosecutor's called a press conference at two o'clock and she wants me here for it, but I'll get our guys going on our end of the list right now. Anybody got any other ideas?"

It was Gus again. "You know, Chuck, I've still got a problem with the kid being dumped back up in those woods. For sure, the kid wasn't dragged up there from the playground in broad daylight. If the kid was just picked up there at the playground why bring the body back to Frenchtown? I know I said it before, but it just doesn't figure."

"I hear you, Gus, but that's where we found the body and if the killer didn't bring him back, how did he get there?"

Gus frowned. "You got me there, Chuck, but I'm going to work on that angle if it's all right with you. After we see the parents, I want to stay in Frenchtown and go through those woods again and see if I can work something out."

"Be my guest, Gus, and if you figure anything out, let me know. I guess we had better get going now."

Gus followed Sam Carter over to Frenchtown to the Hartwick house. There were several cars parked near the house, mostly with Pennsylvania plates. They walked up onto the porch and could see that there were several people inside the house.

Gus looked at Carter and said: "Maybe this isn't such a good time, what do you think? Just then, Bob Hartwick spotted them and walked out onto the porch.

"Hello, Mr. Bass. Would you like to come in? We've got a lot of family here, but I'm sure we can make room for you."

"Mr. Hartwick, this is Sam Carter from the prosecutor's office. He was here the other day, but you might not remember him. Actually, we need to speak to your wife and get some information from her if we can. How is she holding up?"

Hartwick shook his head. "Not too good. She's upstairs in bed. The doctor's given her sedatives and she just sleeps a lot."

"That's probably the best thing for her for now. We hate to bother you, but maybe you could help us out. It's about the shirt Bobby was wearing when he disappeared. Your wife told me it was a yellow, long sleeve shirt. Do you know the one she meant?"

"I think so. We were both together when we bought it over in Flemington in the mall, at the kid's store there, but I forget the name of the store."

"Would you happen to remember the brand of shirt it was?"

"No, I never look at those things, my wife just picks them out. Why, is it important?"

"Well, it may be. You see, we found some yellow fibers in a

truck and we want to see if we could match them up with the shirt Bobby was wearing."

"You mean you've got the guy who did it?"

"No, Mr. Hartwick, I can't say we do. To be honest with you, we have questioned someone, but we don't have any evidence yet. That's what we're working on. Do you remember if your wife bought another shirt like the yellow one at the same time?"

"Yeah, I think she bought a blue shirt that time. I'm pretty sure of it. A yellow and a blue shirt, I think they were both the same except for the color."

"Do you think you could get us the blue shirt so we can check the brand?"

"Sure. You want to come in?"

Gus looked at Carter and then at Hartwick. "No, Mr. Hartwick, I think it would be better if we waited out here."

"Okay, I won't be long." Hartwick turned and went back into the house and Sam and Gus went to the side of the porch while they waited for him to return. He was gone about five minutes and came back out with a blue shirt in his hand. He was crying as he handed it to Gus. "This is the blue shirt. I'm sure it's the same make as the yellow one. It looks it, anyway."

"We're sorry to put you through this, Mr. Hartwick, but it is important to our investigation. Would you mind if we took it with us?"

"You might as well. We don't need it any more, do we?" He turned and went back into the house. Through the door, Gus could see him walking slowly up the stairs and he and Carter went back to their cars.

Gus handed the shirt to Sam and said: "Sam, would you take it back to Fahy? I want to hang around here for awhile."

"Sure, Gus. You going down into the park?"

"I think so. I just want to take a look around. Tell Chuck I'll be in touch." Sam got into his car and left. Gus drove down to the municipal building and parked there rather than the police station. He walked over to the playground and then into the woods near the embankment and soon found the nature trail. He followed the trail until he saw the big spruce tree off on his right. He looked past the spruce and could just make out the embankment about ten yards or so beyond it. He made his way through the vines and undergrowth, ducking under the low lying branches until he reached the foot of the embankment. He looked up but couldn't make out very much because the trees climbed right up the embankment to within a few feet of the top. Not sure of why or what he was looking for, he started climbing the embankment, clutching tree limbs and trunks to pull himself up. It was tough going and his hands were chewed up by the time he reached near the top. He looked up and stopped and gaped at what he saw. It was the bottom of a hedge row of hemlock and forsythia. He stopped and said to himself "It can't be," but he knew it was the hedges at the Hartwicks' backyard. He reached up, clawing the ground until he got to the top, and pulled himself over. He stood up and pushed his way through the hedge row and found himself standing in the Hartwicks' backyard. "Shit, this can't be. The kid was dumped right at the foot of their backyard. This is crazy, it's unbelievable. Why didn't we make this connection before?"

Gus didn't want to go near the Hartwicks' house and he walked down several backyards until he reached what he thought was the Aarons' house. He walked through the yard to the front of the house and went up and knocked on the front door. The younger Aaron boy came to the door and stared at him. "Hi, Aaron, remember me, Gus Bass? I was here the other day. Is your mother home?"

The boy didn't say anything, he just turned and went down the hall. Gus heard him say: "That man is here again. He wants to see Mom."

A man came walking down the hall to the door and said: "Did you want to see my wife?"

"Yes, Mr. Aaron. My name is Gus Bass and I'm with the Frenchtown PD. Could I have a word with Mrs. Aaron?"

"Well, she's not home now. She's up at the Hartwicks' looking after Mrs. Hartwick. Can I help you?"

"Maybe you can. Look, I know the Hartwicks moved here about a year or so ago. Do you have any idea where they moved from?"

"I know they're from the other side of the river, somewhere over in Upper Bucks, but I'm not sure of the name of the town. Maybe Durham or Springtown, somewhere up there I think.

Why do you want to know? If it's important, I'll go over and get Becky, she'll know."

"That's all right, Mr. Aaron. I just need the information as part of the background for our investigation. It's not that important. Tell Mrs. Aaron I may call her later to get the name of the town. Sorry to have bothered you, you've been very helpful."

"Any time, Mr. Bass, and I'll tell Becky to expect a call from you."

Gus walked down Ridge and cut through to the playground and across Creek Road to his car. He got in and just sat there thinking, trying to figure out for himself what it all meant. He sensed the location of the boy's body had a lot to do with his death and how he had died and he was more certain than ever that no one who had abducted that boy would have placed the body there by accident. It had to mean something, but he couldn't see what. After what seemed like an hour but was only fifteen minutes he decided to call Fahy and tell him he had an angle. When he got through to the prosecutor's office, it was Howland who answered. Fahy was still tied up with the press conference and so he left word for Fahy to call him back in the car. He drove over to Peg's house, but she wasn't back from the mall, so he just sat in the car in her driveway.

He had been there for a good half-hour before his car phone rang and it was Fahy. "How you doing, Gus. Come up with anything?"

"I think so, Chuck, but I'm not sure what it is or what it means. I went back up into the woods to that spruce tree and I climbed up that embankment which is about ten yards from the bottom of that tree."

"How the hell did you manage to get up that damned hill? I didn't know you were a billy goat."

"Believe me, it wasn't easy. But when I got to the top, you know where I was?"

"Still in Frenchtown, I'd guess."

"Yeah, but in the Hartwicks' backyard. That boy was dumped right at the bottom of their own yard. How do you figure that?"

There was a long pause before Fahy answered. "I don't know, Gus. What're you driving at?"

117

"Damned if I know, but I can't believe it's just a coincidence we find the body so close to their house. Somebody put it there for a reason. It's got to be somebody who knew them and has some grudge against them we don't know anything about. And if he knew the family, maybe that's why the kid went off with him without any fuss. What do you think?"

"I don't know, Gus, it sounds pretty far-fetched to me. Why would anybody kill a kid just because he has a grudge against the family? It doesn't make any sense."

"Well, how do you explain the location of the body? It can't be just a coincidence. Somebody had to have some kind of reason to take that kind of risk to bring the body back there. Look, if it's all right with you, Chuck, I'd like to follow up on this."

"How you going to do that?"

"Well, I know they moved to Frenchtown about a year ago. I found out they used to live in Upper Bucks and I'd like to go over there and start checking up on their background, you know, see if they had any enemies or anything."

"It's all right with me. We're not getting anywhere over here on this end anyway, so go to it. Just keep in touch and let me know how you're making out. See you, fella."

TWENTY-TWO

After he hung up on Fahy, Gus waited in his car for almost another half hour before Peg returned home. As he sat, he berated himself for not having taken a key when Peg had offered it to him. He remembered he had refused at the time because he thought it would create a kind of permanent relationship which he wanted to avoid. He thought to himself that was pretty stupid. If he had a key, he could be inside right now watching the Phillies' game and they were playing Atlanta. His car radio was on the blink so he couldn't even get the score. The longer he sat the more he kicked himself and he decided that when Peg showed up he was going to ask her for a key, just in case of emergencies like this.

Peg's car pulled into the driveway abreast of Gus. Gus's first thought was, *Geez, she's a pretty woman and I'm an idiot.* He got out as she was opening her door and walked up to her, put his arms around her and gave her a big hug then kissed her on the mouth. Peg pushed him away. "What's that for?"

"Oh, nothing, I was just glad to see you, that's all. Where you been?"

"I told you I was going shopping this afternoon. The mall was really crowded, you'd think people had nothing to do but go out shopping. You been waiting long?'

"Almost an hour, but now that I see you it was worth it."

"Maybe I ought to keep you waiting all the time."

"As a matter of fact, now that you mention it, maybe I ought to have a key to your place so I won't have to wait around for you all the time."

"Wait for me? Since when have you ever had to hang around waiting for me? And I wanted you to take a key, but you wouldn't take it, remember?"

"Yeah, but you didn't force me to take it, so I didn't."

"Why should I have to force you to do anything? If you wanted a key, you should have taken it."

"Yeah, I guess you're right. Do you still want to give me a key?"

Peg laughed and kissed his cheek. "You really are a little boy sometimes. Of course I want you to have a key. Come on, help me in with the packages and let's have a drink. Remember you promised to take me out to dinner tonight."

As they went in to the house Gus noticed that Peg didn't stop to unlock the door as they went in. "You mean to tell me you went out and left the door unlocked? You mean the door was open all this time?"

"You never tried the door? You're some detective, you are. I never lock the door if I go out during the daytime. Only at night, when I go to bed."

Gus took the packages into the kitchen and ran over to the television set. As the sound came on he heard the announcer say: "That's all from the Vet, be sure to tune us in on Monday night when the Phillies will host the New York Mets. Game time seven thirty-five. So long for now."

Gus shouted: "What the hell was the score, you jerk? Who won?" After a brief pause, the first of four consecutive commercials came on. Gus banged the power button in disgust and walked back into the kitchen.

"Peg, if it's all right with you, I'll take that key now."

"Sure, Gus, there are two or three spares in the junk drawer. Help yourself."

Gus opened the drawer and saw at least fifty keys in a tangled mass. "Peg, how the hell do you know which are the house keys?"

"Just grab a handful and try them out. The ones that fit the front door are the house keys."

Ten minutes later Gus came back with a big smile on his face. "I found one. But what are all the other ones for?"

"To tell the truth, I don't have the slightest idea. I just save all the keys I've ever had. You never know when you might need one."

Gus groaned and shook his head. "Honey, I'm hungry. How about eating early?"

"Come to think of it, I haven't eaten since this morning. Just let me fix my face and I'm ready."

On the drive down to Lambertville Peg asked Gus how the day had gone. He told her about the visit to the Hartwicks and getting a matching shirt. Then he said: "You know, Peg, I think I may have come up with a new angle. After we got the shirt I went up into the woods to the tree where we found the boy. I walked straight over from the tree to the embankment and climbed up it, and damned if I wasn't in the Hartwicks' backyard. What do you think of that?"

"That's interesting, Gus, but I haven't the slightest idea what it could mean, do you?'

"I'm not sure, but I just don't think it could be a coincidence that the boy's body was dumped right at the foot of their backyard. We know he wasn't killed there, so why bring the body back to that spot? Whoever did it would have known the kid would have been reported missing and there would be people out searching for him. Christ, Fahy and I were up in those woods looking for the kid until it got dark. So I figure whoever did it had to have some strong motive to take the risk of being seen by someone. I've been thinking that it could be someone who had some grudge against the Hartwicks and killed their kid for revenge and this was his way of letting them know it."

"Gus, that sounds way out, even for you to come up with. And how do you know it was a he, why couldn't the whoever be a she?"

"No way. What woman would do that to a kid? I can't buy that."

"But if you're looking for someone with a strong motive, why couldn't it be a woman who had the grudge. You know maybe it was some girl that the father jilted or something like that. Or she could have something against Mrs. Hartwick. You know women can be just as violent as men, especially when it comes to dealing with kids. You ought to read some of the studies that have been done on that, it would amaze you."

"All right, I'll check up on the women as well, but I just don't see it. Fahy thinks I'm going nowhere with it anyway so I might just as well go the whole nine yards. I'm going to start on the background of the family first thing tomorrow. Did you know that they moved over here from someplace in Upper Bucks only about a year ago?"

121

"Yes, I knew that. They lived over in Durham. When they enrolled Bobby in class here, his mother naturally told us where they had lived and where he had gone to pre-school so we could get his records."

"Well, how about that? I should have known to ask you. What else would be in your records?

"Not a whole lot you'd be interested in. Just medical history, vaccinations, any behavior problems we would want to know about, that kind of thing."

"Would you know how long they had lived in Durham or where they lived before that?"

"Offhand, I wouldn't remember, Gus, but I can check the records tomorrow and let you know."

"That would be great, honey. If I knew who I was working for I'd hire you as my assistant. How about it?"

"Work for you? Not on your life after what I've seen this job does to you. And what do you mean you don't know whom you are working for, what happened to Frenchtown?"

"Well, this morning, after we found Baumgart, we had a run in with the chief. He told Fahy he didn't want to see anymore of my fucking timesheets, and that's a quote."

"Can he do that, Gus?"

"I don't know, but to tell you the truth I don't give a damn. I never want to see that bastard again, anyway."

"Does Mary Trantino know about this? I'm going to call her when we get back and tell her. You know she likes you and she can talk to the mayor and I'll bet he will take care of the chief."

"You can call her, but tell her not to do anything just yet, I want to think things over. Besides, Fahy says I've got a job with him anytime I want. I just don't know whether I want to do what I've been doing."

"Gus, that's the smartest thing you've said in a long time."

Gus reached over and put his hand on Peg's thigh and gave a squeeze. Peg leaned over and kissed him on the cheek and Gus's hand slipped up her thigh and he squeezed a little harder. "Watch it, fella, or we ain't ever going to get to that restaurant."

"That might not be a bad idea at all."

"I'll tell you what, Gus, let's head back and pick up a pizza and go home. I lost my appetite for Chinese food anyway. How about it?"

Gus glanced in the rear view mirror, make a U-turn in the middle of Route 29 and in five minutes they were back in Frenchtown.

TWENTY-THREE

Peg's alarm went off at 6:30 Monday morning. Gus never heard it and didn't stir. When Peg stood up, she looked down at Gus and said to herself: "Do I really want this guy in my life?" Then she thought about last night and smiled. It might not be such a bad idea at that. She bent down and kissed him lightly and then went to put on the coffee.

By the time Peg got out of the shower Gus was sitting in the kitchen, coffee cup in hand. "Honey, what do you do with your garbage?"

"What the hell are you talking about, Gus? What difference does it make what I do with my garbage? You know you're a looney."

"It was just something my neighbor, Mrs. Radcar, was talking about yesterday. She said I ought to get married so I wouldn't have to take out my garbage."

"Are you telling me that's a reason to get married?"

"Well, that's what she said. She said she was married for fifty years and she never once let her husband take out the garbage. It kind of made sense."

"Gus, maybe you ought to marry Mrs. Radcar. What else did she say?"

"You sure you want me to tell you?"

"Why not?"

"You asked for it. She said you were really after me and you were pretty good-looking even if you're not a young chicken and I should marry you." Gus started laughing.

"What's so funny? So what if I'm not a young chicken? I can still make you crow, you old rooster. You were sure crowing a lot last night." She paused for a moment and started laughing uncontrollably until there were tears streaming down her face. "Gus, I want to meet your Mrs. Radcar and give her a kiss. Did she really say I was pretty?"

"That's right, and I believe her." He reached over and started to pull her bathrobe open.

"Don't start in with me, Gus, we don't have time. I've got to get over to school and you've got to get going on that crazy idea of yours."

"I wasn't starting anything, honestly. I was just telling it like it is that's all. To tell the truth, I'm all crowed out anyway. I'm getting dressed and I'm out of here. I'll call you later and find out what you got in the records on the Hartwicks. Is that okay?"

"I guess I'm on Fahy's payroll now, too, so give me a call. When will you be getting back tonight?"

"Depends on how far I get, but I'll call you by five or so."

TWENTY-FOUR

Gus figured he might as well start at the top and so he headed across the river and up over the hills, picking up 611 into Doylestown, the Bucks County seat. He found his way to the district attorney's office and introduced himself to the receptionist, asking to see the chief of detectives. In a few moments a middle-aged woman came out and asked him what his business was and then she disappeared. She came back shortly and said: "Right this way, if you please, Chief Spahr will see you." He was ushered into an office at least three times the size of Fahy's office and Gus noticed there was carpeting on the floor. He thought to himself, These guys certainly know how to live.

A tall, gangly man stood up from behind the desk. He had reddish-blond, thinning hair and the map of Ireland on his face. "What can I do for you, Mr. Bass? Won't you be seated." That was not a question but an order, and Gus decided he better sit.

"Chief, I don't think we have met before. I work out of the Frenchtown PD, but right now I'm working with Chuck Fahy over in the Hunterdon prosecutor's office. You know him?"

"I most certainly do. I haven't seen him in quite a while, to be sure. Are you by any chance working on that murder you had in Frenchtown last week? That was a nasty business. I heard the little boy was mutilated, is that true?"

"Well, he was asphyxiated first, and he was mutilated after he was dead."

"Have you arrested anyone yet?"

"We picked up two guys who had a record of child molesting, but so far we've drawn a blank, and that's why I'm here. We're trying to trace the background of the parents, it might possibly have some connection with the case."

"If there's anything we can assist you with, just say the word and we'll do it, of course."

Gus thought to himself, This guy doesn't talk like a cop, he sounds like an English teacher or something. Gus figured he had better elevate his grammar and his vocabulary. "That's certainly good of you, Chief Spahr. We need all the help we can get on this nasty business. Could you tell me if you have any record in your office of the boy's family. The name is Robert Hartwick, Sr. And the wife's name is Gladys. I have it from a reliable source that they moved from Durham to Frenchtown about a year ago."

"Give me a moment and we will check on that for you." He dialed an extension and asked for a search to be made under the names of Robert Hartwick and Gladys Hartwick. He looked up at Gus and asked: "Would you care for a cup of coffee while we are waiting?" Gus nodded and Spahr continued: "Cream and sugar?"

"Straight black, if you would," Gus said with a polite smile.

After the order had been given to "Gertrude," Spahr said: "How is old Fahy doing, isn't he ready to retire? He's getting on in years, I should think."

"To tell the truth, Chief Spahr, I think we'll all be ready to retire after this case is finished."

"As bad as that, is it? Well, as my old coach used to say, don't let it get your dauber down." A faint smile appeared of Spahr's face and Gus said to himself, *What the hell is a dauber? I never heard of that one before. Maybe it was his tiddlywinks coach or something. Geez, I'm in a different world here.* He decided to return the smile, not knowing what to say about his dauber.

Gertrude arrived with the coffee and before Gus had half-finished his cup, Spahr's phone rang. Spahr nodded his head a few times and hung up. "I am afraid, Mr. Bass, we have nothing for you on either one of the Hartwicks. Indeed, we don't have any record of any Hartwick anywhere in our files. I'm truly sorry."

The disappointment was obvious on Gus's face. "Well, it was a long shot anyway, just thought I would give it a try. Do they have a police department up in Durham? Maybe I could try there."

"No, I am afraid Durham doesn't have a police department. The state police provide coverage there. If you wish, I could call Lieutenant Schoop at the Dublin Barracks. He's in charge of their crimes unit and he might be able to assist you."

"Well, Chief Spahr, I've imposed on you enough. I'll just work my way up there and speak to some people along the way, if that's all right with you."

"Of course, Mr. Bass." Spahr paused and continued: "And when you see that old fart Fahy, tell him Andy Spahr said he's still the dumbest Irishman he's ever seen." Spahr grinned and Gus stared at him. Spahr went on: "Fahy called and said I should expect you to come over. He said you were a diamond in the shit and I should put on the dog for you. You know, I think you fell for it."

Gus's jaw dropped and then he started to laugh. "I should have known from that goddamned Irish face that you were full of shit. I've got to admit, you sure had me fooled. I owe Fahy one." Gus put out his hand and Spahr grabbed his arm.

"Fahy's right, you are a diamond in the shit. Look, before you go chasing your tail around Upper Bucks, stop in and see a woman by the name of Shirley Mason. She's the clerk up in Durham and she can probably give you what you're looking for. In the meantime I'll call Schoop and see if he has anything. If he does, I'll get in touch. Where can I get you."

"Thanks, Andy. I'll be in the car most of the day so try me on the car phone. The number's nine-three-o one-o-two-six. That's a nine-o-eight number. Good meeting you."

"Same here, Gus. I'll be in touch one way or the other."

TWENTY-FIVE

Gus headed out on 611 to Durham. A few miles out of Doylestown, the landscape began to change to large manorial estates with elegant stone houses, some of ancient vintage and some recent expressions of money chasing a heritage. Then he was into real farm country of more modest dwellings and imposing barns and silos. Here and there cattle grazed serenely in lush pastures and fields of corn stalks were sprouting up. Mares were out to pasture with their foals, and sheep with their lambs beside them. Having been born and raised in Trenton, Gus had come to think of Hunterdon as some kind of paradise, but this was something else again. Then he thought, Here I am trying to find the snake in all this grass. Why am I doing it? Christ, I ought to be a farmer. That must be the life. And then he thought of last winter and what it must have been like to be up here on a farm taking care of all those animals in that snow and crap. Farming might have some downside too, even if it didn't have Chief Winters.

Eventually Gus found the old Durham Road and came to the Durham town hall, an ancient stone mill which now served as the post office and the seat of local government. The place seemed to be deserted when he pulled in but he tried the front door and to his surprise it was open. He walked down a narrow hall and called out: "Anybody home?"

"Hello, I'm in here. Who is it?"

Gus had to duck his head as he walked through a doorway into a low-ceilinged room. Behind the desk with a neat little sign that read: "Shirley Mason, Town Clerk," was an elderly woman with snow white hair and bright, twinkling blue eyes.

"Are you Mrs. Mason?"

"That's what the sign says, but it's Miss Mason."

Gus held out his hand. "Pleased to meet you. My name is Gus Bass and I'm from over in Frenchtown. I'm with the Frenchtown Police Department and Chief Andrew Spahr down in Doylestown said you might be able to help me. I'm trying to check up on a family who used to live here and now lives in French-town."

Miss Mason gave Gus a pleasant smile as she said: "I'd be happy to tell you anything I can. What is the name of the family and what did you want to know?"

"It's Robert and Gladys Hartwick. I've been told they moved from here about a year ago. I'm just trying to get some background on the family."

"Oh, those poor people. I read about what happened to their son. What a tragedy that must be for them, to lose two children like that. I don't know how they can live through it."

His jaw dropping, Gus said, "Do you mind if I sit down? Did you say two children? No, it was just Bobby who was killed. Their other son, Ricky, is fine so far as I know. Did something happen to him since I left this morning?"

"I didn't mean Ricky, he's such a sweet little baby. So was little Bobby. No, I meant their first son, Jimmy. He died so tragically, it must be seven or eight years ago, right here in Durham."

Gus shook his head. "You mean they had another son who was murdered?"

"Oh, no, he wasn't murdered or anything like that. I don't know all the details, but his mother found him dead right in the house. He had suffocated himself. And he was only a year and a half old. It was so tragic. We all wept for them, they were such good people and to have something like that happen. And now this. It's just horrible."

Gus sat there stunned not knowing what to say. Finally, he said, "Miss Mason, where were they living when their first son died?"

"Oh, they were living in a house they rented just off Easton Road. That's just east of here. Why, is that important?"

"I don't really know. Probably not. You wouldn't happen to know how the boy came to suffocate himself, would you?"

"Well, I didn't get any of the details, you know. I only heard that he smothered himself while he was playing with a plastic bag or something like that." She paused and then said: "Oh yes, now I remember. It was a bag from a record album."

"Didn't anybody investigate what happened?"

"Why yes, of course they did. It was someone from the state

police barracks up in Dublin. We don't have any police department here, you know. There wouldn't be anything for them to do if we did, thank God for that."

"Can you tell me anything about Gladys Hartwick?" Was she always from around here?"

Miss Mason paused, looked up at the ceiling, and then at Gus. "I think her family was from around Lake Nockamixon. Her mother moved here with Gladys, it must be fifteen years ago at least. I think her parents had divorced or separated before they moved here. Anyway, I never recall seeing Gladys's father."

"How about Bob Hartwick, was he from around here, too?"

Miss Mason shook her head. "No, his family lived down in Lumberville. I happen to know that because Bob and Gladys were married right here in town hall and the mayor did the wedding, so I had to do the paperwork, you know fill out the marriage certificate and all that. They were awfully young and they were really in love with each other. I don't think Bob's family was too happy about the wedding, especially the mother. But you can't please everybody."

"What did Bob Hartwick do for a living then?"

Miss Mason paused before responding: "As I remember, he worked as an electrician for his father. Then, right after little Jimmy died, Bob's father died and Bob was working as an electrician for other people in the business."

"This is a kind of tough question, but I have to ask it. Did either of them have any enemies, or any kind of problems with neighbors or anyone else you can think of?"

"I'm not sure what you're driving at, Mr. Bass. So far as I know, they were just a quiet, young couple and they kept pretty much to themselves."

"No problems of any kind then?"

Miss Mason again paused. "Look, Mr. Bass, I don't like to gossip. Can I kind of talk off the record?"

"Absolutely. I'm not taking any of this down. I'm just trying to get some background, that's all. Nothing you tell me goes any further, you've got my word on that."

"Well, there was some talk for awhile that Bob Hartwick was chasing after women. I don't think it was anything serious, just going around flirting and things like that. But then, not long before they moved, there was a story going around that he was seeing a girl who lived over in Springtown and that was causing some problems at home between them. That's what I heard, anyway. It could just be a lot of silly gossip, you know how things can be in a small town like this. People talk about anything just to have something to say because otherwise they wouldn't have anything to talk about."

"I know what you mean. It's the same way over in Frenchtown. Look, I won't bother you anymore. You have been very helpful and I really want to thank you. If something else should come up, would you mind if I call you?"

"Of course not, Mr. Bass. You can always reach me. If I'm not here you can get my number from the book. And I must say, if we ever have a police department here in Durham, I hope we get someone as nice as you to run it."

"Why, thank you, Miss Mason. That's very nice of you to say that. Just let me know if you ever want to hire a cop, I'll make myself available."

By the time Gus got out of the old mill, it was already midafternoon and he realized he hadn't eaten anything all day, just the two cups of coffee. He looked at the pleasant landscape around him and wondered to himself how so much shit could go on in a place as beautiful as this. It just goes to show, it ain't where you are but who you are that counts the most. He got into his car and almost immediately the phone rang. It was Spahr.

"Glad I caught you, Gus. Schoop is not in his office, he's testifying before a grand jury up in Newton on some case that ended up over on your side of the river. I spoke to his number one guy and he says there was some kind of case involving a family named Hartwick a long time ago, but he couldn't find the file. There's no use of your going up there until tomorrow. Schoop will be back then and you should give him a call before you go up. How did you make out with Mason?"

"I think I found out more than I want to know and I'm not sure I know what to do with it. The Hartwicks lived here all right, and they had a kid who smothered himself in a plastic bag when he was only a year and a half old. I don't know if I told you this, but the medical examiner thinks that Bobby Hartwick was smothered with a plastic bag, too. How does that grab you?"

"I know what you're thinking, Gus, but it could just be a co-incidence or maybe just bad luck."

"To tell the truth, Andy, I'm not thinking anything. I'm kind of numb and I'm hungry as hell. I haven't had anything to eat yet today and it's beginning to get me. My mind doesn't work too well on an empty stomach. Is there any place to eat around here?'

"If you're still up in Durham, I know a place just down the hill in Riegelsville. It doesn't look like much, but the food's good. A gal by the name of Sally runs it and just tell her I sent you and she'll take care of you. What do you figure on doing when your mind starts working again?"

"Geez, I don't really know. I've got to find out more about that other kid and start digging deeper into the family. You know your Miss Mason told me that the Hartwicks were having some problems when they left here. Seems like he was chasing some girls and may have settled on one in particular. The word is that the wife made him move the family over to Frenchtown to break it up. I want to check into that some more. It's always possible that the girlfriend had it in for the wife and went after the kid for some kind of revenge. Who knows, maybe she saw it on some fucking TV program. It's a crazy, fucked-up world we live in, so anything is possible."

"Listen, Gus, you'd better go and get yourself something to eat before you get committed to a nut house. I'm going to call and leave word with Schoop's office to expect you first thing tomorrow morning. You want me to meet you up there?"

"That's up to you, Andy. It might help. You know the guy and I don't. If I can talk Fahy into it, I'll bring him along and you two can have a reunion."

"You're on. Tell Fahy I want to see that dumb Irish kisser of his. Maybe I'll see you tomorrow."

Gus tried to follow Spahr's directions and ended up getting lost. Eventually he found his way down to a road along the river and found Riegelsville and Sally's place. Spahr was right, it didn't look like much and besides, it was closed. He started to get back in his car when the door opened and a buxom middle-aged woman stuck her head out the door and said they closed for lunch at two. Gus said he was sorry to bother her, but Andy Spahr had told him this was the best place to eat in Bucks County and he just thought he would give it a try.

Sally's face lit up. "Andy Spahr sent you? Why didn't you say so in the first place? You come on in and you'll find out he was right about my food."

Gus had no second thoughts about that invitation and he followed her in and sat down at the lunch counter. "My name is Gus Bass, and you must be Sally."

"That's right, I'm Sally and if you know Andy, you must be some kind of detective, too, I guess. It so happens I had Spahr's favorite on the menu today, split pea soup with chunks of ham. There's still some left, how about starting with that?"

"I don't care if it's his favorite or not, it happens to be mine, and can you make it a bowl?"

"Sure, there's enough left. And then you're going to try my lamb stew, how's that?"

"Sally, you've got a way with words." Sally disappeared into the kitchen and returned in a few minutes with the soup.

"By the time you finish that, the stew will be heated up for you. You know stew is always better when it's heated up again. What brings you up to these parts, if I may ask?"

Gus looked up from his soup. "Well, I'm from over in French-town and I've been checking into some people over here for a case I'm working on." Gus returned to his soup.

"And who might you be checking up on, maybe I know them?"

"It's a family by the name of Hartwick. They used to live up in Durham before they moved to Frenchtown. You know them by any chance?" Gus started breaking up crackers into his soup.

"If you want more crackers, I've got plenty of them. Yeah, I know the Hartwicks. That was their son who was killed the other day, wasn't it? Young Gladys, as a matter of fact, she asked me for a job waitressing when she got out of high school, but I didn't have any need at the time and she got a job down in Upper Black Eddy, I think. If you want to know the truth, I wouldn't have given her a job even if I needed someone. I never liked her looks. She was an odd one, if you ask me. But I must say, I really feel sorry for the girl, that's two children now she's lost. I can't imagine anything worse happening to a mother."

"Sally, would you happen to know anything about Gladys's

mother? Is she still alive?"

"You mean Henrietta Wilkins? She's been dead at least five years. That woman ate herself into her grave. She just kept getting heavier and heavier and one day she just upped and died. That woman spent too much time in her kitchen, if you ask me."

"What about Mr. Wilkins? Is he still around?"

"So far as I know, he was never around. When Henrietta and Gladys moved to Durham he wasn't with them. Least I never saw him. I heard Henrietta got a divorce from him after they moved here."

"How old was Gladys then?"

"I'd say she was around fifteen or so."

"Would you happen to know where they came from before they moved to Durham?"

"I heard Gladys say once that she grew up around Lake Nockamixon. That's about all I know."

Gus pushed the empty soup bowl away from him and it was immediately collected by Sally. She came back carrying the largest bowl of stew Gus had ever seen. "Gee, Sally, I don't know if I can eat all that much."

"Well you just start and we'll see what happens."

Gus started and had downed half of the bowl before he paused for a rest. "Sally, that's the best stew I've ever eaten. What's your secret?"

"That I ain't telling. If you want my stew, then you have to come here to eat it."

"That's good enough for me. Tell me, are you open for dinner too?"

"Just Fridays and Saturdays, and we stop serving at eight. You can bring your own bottle if you want something to drink. But not at lunchtimes. I don't believe in drinking before dinner."

Gus returned to the stew and ended up finishing the bowl. "Sally, that was just great. I really appreciate your taking the trouble, but if you want to know, I don't feel guilty about it. It was too good."

Sally smiled. "How about a cup of coffee and a piece of banana cream pie, that's one of my specialties you know. Did Spahr tell you about it?"

"Sally, I'm a sucker for banana cream pie, but forget the coffee. I've had my quota for today."

The bowl disappeared and Sally returned with what had to be a double slice of pie, about five inches high and six inches wide. Gus's eyes bulged. After a half dozen forkfuls he had barely made a dent and he stopped for breath. "Geez, that's good pie, Sally. I might even finish it after I rest for a minute. Say, did you happen to know Gladys's husband, Bob?"

"Oh, yes, I know that one. He used to work for his father until the father died. That was just after they lost the first child, little Jimmy. He was named after Bob's father, you know. Anything special you wanted to know?"

"Well, I heard that Bob was chasing after girls and maybe one in particular."

Sally nodded. "You know, when I first met that boy he used to come in with his father for lunch when they were working up around here. He was such a little fella, shy as could be. Then the next thing I knew, he had married Gladys and they used to stop in here together once in a while, and they seemed to get on well. He began to open up a bit, you know what I mean? He would talk to you and make jokes and that kind of thing. After Jimmy was born, I began to hear things about his running around a bit but no one in particular. Then a few years ago, he started up with a young girl who lived over in Springtown and Gladys found out and they were having lots of problems. The next thing I knew, they had moved over to Frenchtown?"

"What happened to the girl in Springtown? Did he drop her?"

"I don't really know. I kind of lost track of them after they moved. At least I didn't hear anything more."

"Sally, would you happen to know the name of the girl in Springtown?"

"Why do you have to know that?"

Gus tried to be nonchalant as he said: "It might be useful, you never know. Look, she won't ever know who told me, you have my word on that."

"So long as you give me your word, all right. It's Jean Albertson."

"Would you happen to have an address for her?"

"Now, look here, Mr. Bass, did you come in here to eat or to question me?"

136

Gus grinned. "Maybe both, but mostly to eat."

"Well, to answer your question, I don't have an address, but if you go up that way and ask, you'll find her. Now if you're finished with that pie, I had better clean up and get out of here. I expect my grandson over for dinner, and he's got an appetite like yours so I had better get home and start some cooking."

"You mean to tell me Sally, you leave here and go home and cook?"

"Of course. What do you think I do? Besides, this is business, when I cook at home, it's for family."

"Well, I just hope they eat as well as I have. Thanks, Sally, it really has been a treat for me and I'm coming back this Saturday with a bottle of champagne and we'll have a drink together."

"You get out of here, Gus Bass. You're worse than that Spahr ever was."

TWENTY-SIX

Back in his car, Gus glanced at his watch and saw that it was almost 3:30. There was enough time left to try to track down Jean Albertson and even if he didn't get to see her, he could find out where she lived. He got out a map and saw he was only about five miles or so from Springtown, so he headed out Durham Road going west. As he got to the intersection of Route 412, he found a gas station of sorts and pulled in. An elderly man with a full beard came out of the garage wiping his hands on an oily rag. "What can I do for you, Mister?"

"Fill her up with regular, and could you check the oil."

"I always do. That's part of my job."

"Where I come from, they never do, not even if you ask."

"You must be from the city. Out here we take care of our customers."

"That's good to know, but as a matter of fact, I'm not from the city. I only live across the river in Frenchtown."

"Well they should know better then. Where you headed for, if you don't mind my asking?"

"Now that you ask, I'm not sure. I'm trying to locate a woman by the name of Jean Albertson. Do you know her?"

"Let's say I know the family."

"Do you happen to know where Jean might be living now?"

The old man paused and slowly looked Gus up and down. Finally, he said: "Why do you want to know?"

"Well, I'm trying to get in touch for a friend of mine. He asked me to look her up and say hello, but he didn't give me the address. Just said she lived in Springtown. So here I am."

"Your friend ain't too bright, is he? Around here we don't have any address, just a box number."

"Yeah, I guess that's so. You wouldn't happen to know her box number, would you?"

Again there was a pause. "Are you a bill collector or something?"

"Hell no. I'd as soon collect garbage or go back into the army before I'd do that kind of work. No, I'm just supposed to deliver a message for a friend who knew I was coming over this way, that's all."

"Well, you've got kind of an honest face, so I guess it's all right for me to tell you. She lives in a trailer up on Snake Hill Road. You just go left out of here and you find Snake Hill on your right about a mile or so down. Hang a right and go about another mile or so and you'll see a blue trailer on the left. That's where she lives."

"That sounds easy enough. A left, a right, and she's on the left. I think I got it and many thanks to you. I hope I run into you again some time soon."

"That will be ten-fifty for the gas, and your oil's okay."

Gus paid up and a few minutes later found himself on an isolated dirt road opposite a blue trailer set deep into the woods. There was a postal box on the side of the road without a name, just the number 454. He didn't see a car around and there was no sign anyone was home, but having come this far he figured he might just as well give it a try and went up to the door and knocked. There was no answer and he went to have a look around the place. There wasn't a whole lot to see, no flowers, no shrubbery of any kind, just weeds all over and an empty garbage pail out back. But there were a lot of birds flitting about in the trees and through the woods he saw a doe with her fawns kind of staring at him. He yelled at them: "Take it easy, I'm just looking around," but they didn't respond, just kept staring. He walked back around the front of the trailer and got into his car. As he was about to turn the key, a blue Ford pickup pulled up and drove into the gravel area in front of the trailer. A tall, young, attractive woman with a sizeable bosom got out and looked over at him. Not bad, he said to himself, I guess Bobby likes them big all over.

The woman called out: "You looking for someone? What are you doing up here?"

"Are you Jean Albertson?"

"Who wants to know?"

"Fair enough. I'm Gus Bass. I'm with the Frenchtown Police Department and if you're Jean Albertson, I'd like to have a word with you."

"What for?"

"Can we go inside and talk? It won't take long."

"No, we can talk out here. How do I know who you are?"

"Here's my badge." He pulled out a beat-up black leather pouch, opened it, and showed her his badge. "Okay?"

"I still want to know why you want to talk to me. I haven't done nothing so why are you bothering me?"

"I'll be right up front with you, okay? You know a guy named Bob Hartwick?"

"What if I do? What's that got to do with anything?"

"Did you know his son Bobby was murdered Friday over in Frenchtown? Look, wouldn't it be better if we went inside and talked? I could use a drink of water if you don't mind. It's taken me a while to find you and I've been driving around most of the day. How about it?"

"I guess it will be all right. But don't try pulling anything on me. Cop or no cop, I can take care of myself."

Inside the trailer, Gus could see it wasn't any palace. There were piles of dishes in what passed for a sink and bags of garbage on the floor next to it. The place stank of garbage and cigarette smoke. Gus asked: "Do you mind if I sit?"

Jean scowled and said: "Sit anywhere you want, it's all right with me. Just say what you have to say and get out of here."

"Believe me, I don't intend to stay any longer than I have to." Gus found an empty chair in the tiny kitchen and sat down.

"You really want that water, or were you just trying to get yourself in here?"

"Yeah, I really want a drink, I'm thirsty as hell."

"The glasses are in the cabinet over there. Help yourself."

Gus got a glass and reached around the dishes in the sink to get to the water tap. He sat down again. "Do you mind if I call you Jean?"

"That's my name, why should I mind? Look, ask me what the hell you want to ask and get out of here. I've got better things to do than talking to you."

"I'm sure you do, Jean, and I'll get out of your hair as soon as I can. First off, I hear from several people you and Bob Hartwick had a thing going between you. Is that true?"

Jean's eyes narrowed to tiny slits and she glared at Gus with contempt. "Who's been feeding you that bullshit? I know the guy and that's it."

"From what I hear, you know him pretty good. That's no crime you know, at least not anymore it isn't." Gus stared hard at her, fixing on her eyes. "I heard that Bob's wife found out and was raising all kinds of hell. As a matter of fact, she made your boyfriend move out of Durham over to Frenchtown. Any truth to that?"

Jean hissed her response. "You know what, ass or Bass or whatever your name is? I don't like your questions and you can just get the hell out of here."

"Look, Jean, I don't want to hassle you. I just need answers to some questions. If you're going to play hardball, it's all right with me. I'll just go out in my car and call my friend Andy Spahr down in the DA's office and he'll be up here quicker than you can clean your dishes and then you'll be down in Doylestown answering his questions. You want to play it that way, just say the word and I'll be glad to leave. This place stinks anyway. So what's it going to be?"

Jean sat down in the only other chair in the kitchen and took out a cigarette. She lit it and blew the smoke in Gus's direction. Finally she answered. "I always heard that you cops were pricks. I can believe it. So what if Bobby and I were friends, what's that got to do with anything? Yeah, that bitch found out and she really hassled him, tried to get him away from me. But he came back anyway. So what? She couldn't give him what he wanted and I could. I'm sorry the kid is dead, not for her, but for him. He really liked that kid. Maybe now he'll wake up and clear out. She's no good for him."

Gus knew he had gotten a straight answer and he wasn't sure he liked it. He stared for a moment at her before he spoke again. "When did you two get together again after they moved over to Frenchtown?"

"It wasn't that long. He was back here last fall and we just picked up where we left off like nothing had happened."

"Did his wife know about it?"

"Oh yeah, she knew. Bobby told me they were having awful fights. She said she was going to leave him and he could have his kids and see how long I would last taking care of him and his kids. I'm telling you she was a real bitch. She didn't give a shit for him or the kids. She just wanted to have a nice house and have everybody think she was a lady."

"Jean, I don't want you to take this the wrong way, but I have to ask. Where were you last Friday, from about noon on?"

"What the hell are you getting at?"

"I'll tell you straight out. The kid was snatched by somebody between noon and one o'clock on Friday and then he was murdered. A blue Ford pickup, just like the one you have, was seen leaving the area where the kid was last seen. There it is. I got to know where you were on Friday around noon-time."

"You lousy bastard. You think I had anything to do with what happened to little Bobby? You got to be out of your mind."

"Somebody killed that kid, and if it's the last thing I ever do, I'm going to find out who did it. Now you'd better tell me where you were on Friday and cut out all the crap."

"I ain't telling you nothing. Get the hell out of my house. And you can go and call your friend Spahr for all I care. I got nothing to tell you. Get out of here."

Gus stood up. "All right, Jean, if that's what you want, you got it. I'll be out in my car and I'm going to wait five minutes and then I'm calling Spahr and I'm going to get your boyfriend Bobby over to Doylestown and we'll get some answers, that I guaran-fuckin-tee you." Gus walked out of the trailer and got in his car.

He smiled when he saw the trailer door open. He looked at his watch and his timing was pretty good, only three minutes. Jean came over and he rolled down the window. "It's your turn, Jean. How we going to play it?"

She glared at Gus. "All right. Just leave Bobby alone, he's got enough to deal with. Look, I'll tell you where I was but you can't tell Bobby. Do we have a deal?"

"I don't give a shit what you were doing so long as it doesn't have anything to do with that kid. You understand where I'm coming from?"

"Okay. I was with another guy Friday. He's an old friend of mine from up in Easton. We spent the afternoon together right here in this trailer. I wasn't anywhere near Frenchtown. I was right here in this trailer, you got the picture?"

"Yeah, I got the picture. Now I want a name to go with that

picture or else the picture ain't worth shit. You got the picture?"

"Look, he's married to a friend of mine. What are you going to do if I tell you his name?"

"I don't give a shit who you're screwing, Jean. So far as I'm concerned, you can fuck the whole of Bucks County and you can take on the Jersey side of the river, too. I won't bullshit you. I'm going to check with him and find out if you were here, and if that's the case, that's it for me."

"Boy, I hate you pricks. His name is Jerry Haas."

"And where can I find this Jerry Haas?"

"He lives in Easton. He's in the phone book."

"All right, you stay right where you are. I'm going to call him right away. You got a number for him?" Jean gave him the number and Gus dialed. "Hi. Is Jerry home? . . . Fine, could I speak to him? . . . Tell him it's a friend of a good friend of his. . . . Sure I'll hang on. . . . Jerry Haas, my name is Gus Bass and I've got a friend of yours with me. . . . Who? Why, her name is Jean Albertson." Gus turned to Jean, "Jerry says hi." Jean grimaced. "Jerry, Jean says hi, too. . . . Now that you two have said hi, were you with Jean up in her trailer this past Friday afternoon from about noon on? . . . No, Jerry, this isn't a game show, I want a straight answer, and either it's yes or no, which is it? . . . Fine, Jerry, now tell me when you left the trailer. . . . About five or so? . . . Well, Jerry, you gave the right answer to the question and that makes you eligible for the asshole of the year prize. Been nice talking to you Jerry. Have a nice day." Gus disconnected and looked up at Jean and said: "See how easy that was? Now you can go in and wash your dishes and take your fucking garbage out. So long, Jean, it's been nice meeting you. Have a nice day."

TWENTY-SEVEN

It was now after five and as soon as he left the trailer, Gus called Peg and told her he was on his way to his place to change and would be over to see her at about seven. Peg was anxious to know how he made out, but he put her off. "It's been a long day and I've got a lot to tell you. I can't give you the whole story over the phone and there's no point in starting unless I tell you the whole works. Want to go out to dinner?"

"No, I picked up some things at the Acme and I'm making you dinner here. You could pick up a bottle of wine on your way over. Make it red. I can't stand that white stuff. It tastes like vinegar."

"You got it, honey, but the guys who make the white stuff would be pretty pissed off if they heard you say that. You have any Stoly left?"

"I'm sure there's at least half a bottle, that should hold even you. Anything else you wanted, maybe me for instance?"

"It's crow time, baby. Get ready and, hey, have a nice day."

"Gus, you're nuts, but I guess you know that."

Driving back, Gus put in a call to Fahy, but he was out. Carter said Fahy was over at the medical examiner's office and wouldn't be back for at least an hour. Gus asked: "You guys get anywhere with Frohmeyer?"

"His lawyer won't let us get within a hundred feet of the bastard. Sometimes I think the whole system is crazy. For Christ's sake, here we are paying for these asshole public defenders and what the hell do they do? Stop us from doing what we should be doing, and this prick Frohmeyer just sits there and laughs at us."

"Anything back from the FBI yet?"

"Nope, not a thing. The word is not before Tuesday afternoon at the earliest. How did you make out today over in Bucks? I heard Fahy set you up with Spahr."

"Yeah, they got me all right. That Spahr is a hell of an actor, I could have sworn he was some kind of queer. But he's a real good guy and he got me going in the right direction and maybe we're on to something. Tell Fahy to call me at nine-nine-two three-one-seven-o when he gets back and I'll give him a run-down."

"When will we see you?"

"Probably first thing tomorrow morning. I'll see what Fahy says. See you, Sam."

Gus got into and out of his apartment, having showered and dressed, without running into Mrs. Radcar. He was at Peg's by seven and when he walked in he could smell onions and garlic cooking. He knew he was in for another good meal, if he had the room for it. He decided he better not tell Peg about his lunch.

"That you, Gus? I'm in the kitchen. Come on in and help me with the stirring."

"You didn't have to tell me where you were, I could smell you from the car." Peg was standing at her range top with a wooden spatula in her hand. He walked over and gave her a hug. "What you cooking?"

"It's a recipe I made up for a pasta sauce. No meat, just two kinds of mushrooms—real fancy mushrooms, shitake and oyster mushrooms I got over in the Acme. I bet you never had them before. I've got a few secret ingredients in it. But best of all, it has very few calories and practically no fat. You know, Gus, I think it's about time you went on a diet. You're beginning to get a gut on you."

Gus took in a deep breath, contracting his stomach. "I don't know what you're talking about. I haven't had a thing to eat since I left here this morning, just a cup of coffee."

"Well if you ask me, you must be drinking some real fattening coffee. I could swear your gut is a lot bigger than it was when you left here this morning. Here take this spatula and stir this while I put up the pasta."

Gus looked at the instrument she had put in his hand. "Why do they call it a spatula? It's just a piece of wood with some slits in it. Why such a fancy name?"

"Gus, what difference does it make what they call it? Just stir the sauce before it starts sticking." Gus starting stirring with one hand, a Stoly in the other.

Twenty minutes later, Gus had opened and poured the wine

and they sat down to eat. Peg gave Gus a bowl filled to over-flowing. "Here, my poor starving boy, *mangia*."

"Gee, I thought you were putting me on a diet. What's with this *mangia*? Is that what this is called?"

"Gus, *mangia* means eat in Italian? Didn't you know that?"

"I may have heard it once or twice, but I never knew what it meant. To tell the truth, I thought it was some kind of curse word." Gus bowed his head low over the bowl and started eating. "Peg, this is real good. Are you sure it's not fattening?"

"No, Gus, it's not fattening. You can eat all you want. Now tell me what you found out over in Bucks today."

Gus gave her a blow-by-blow account of the day's interviews, leaving out only a plate-by-plate account of his lunch at Sally's. When he finished he looked over at Peg and said: "So what do you think of that? They had another kid who was suffocated a year or so before Bobby was born. And they never mentioned a thing about it to us. It kind of makes you wonder, doesn't it?"

"Why should they mention it? From what you found out, it couldn't have had anything to do with what happened to Bobby. What are you getting at?"

"I don't know for sure what I'm getting at. But to have two kids in one family who die by being suffocated in plastic bags is too much of a coincidence. And I don't believe in coincidences anyway. You know, when I went over there this morning, I thought whoever killed Bobby could have had a grudge against the Hartwicks. And then when I found out about the girlfriend, I thought maybe she had a motive for revenge or something. She sure as hell doesn't like Gladys, but Bob Hartwick was still seeing her so where's the motive for her? Anyway, she's got an alibi for the time the murder had to have been committed, so that lets her out. I kind of struck out on that one, but I've got to find out more about what happened to the first kid."

"Gus, I think I see where you're going with this. It's almost too horrible to even think about, but I know parents do kill their kids. I've read some study that was done about it. It made me sick to my stomach at the time. Maybe I could get it for you if you think it might help."

"Would you, Peg? I'd like to see it. Christ, I know all about parents beating up their kids and abusing them and that kind

146

of crap, but this is different than anything I've ever known of. I'm not saying that one or the other of them killed Bobby, but it's something that's got to be checked out and I guess I'll have to do it. Fahy's absolutely convinced that it's got to be a child molester and he thinks it's a good bet it's Frohmeyer. All those guys over there in Flemington do, too. They'd like to get their hands on him, and I don't blame them for that, but he's got a public defender and they can't even ask the guy for the time of day. And they've been interviewing every poor bastard in the county who has a blue Ford pickup. That'll keep them going for a month at least."

"Have you told Fahy what you found out today?"

"No, he wasn't in when I called over there. As a matter of fact, I'm waiting for him to call me here. I left your number, I hope you don't mind." The words were no sooner said, than the telephone rang. Peg answered and handed the phone to Gus.

"Here, it's for you. It's Fahy."

Gus took the phone and in response to Fahy's first question proceeded to give him the same account of his day he had given Peg, again leaving out the details of his lunch. When he was finished, Fahy said: "Nice going, Gus, but didn't you shoot yourself in the foot? Oops, sorry about that, I forgot."

"Forget it. Although the way you set me up with your buddy Spahr, for that I owe you. Anyway, I haven't come up with anyone with a revenge motive, but it strikes me that something is wrong with the Hartwick family and the husband ain't the shy, retiring type I had him pegged for, you know what I mean?"

"So what angle you figure on working now?'

"I'm running out of angles. Right now I just want to find out all I can about the death of that first kid of theirs. I'm going back tomorrow and look up this guy Schoop at the Dublin Barracks. You wouldn't by any chance know him, would you?"

"I've run into him a few times. He's a good guy and he'll help you out if he can."

"Do me a favor and don't call him like you did Spahr."

Fahy laughed. "Gus, we just thought we'd have some fun, see if you'd catch on. Relax. Listen, I've got something for you. I just came back from Sanchez' office. They finished the first of the tests on the kid's stomach contents and guess what they found?

147

Barbiturates. He's trying to pin it down to a specific drug but somebody definitely gave the kid a barbiturate. That could connect up with Frohmeyer. He could have given the kid a dose to knock him out to keep him quiet while he got him out of Frenchtown. This guy is big on drugs, we know that, so it could tie in with him."

Gus grimaced. "Yeah, it sounds promising. Did they find any barbiturates when they searched his house?"

"No, but they weren't looking for it either. It could have been a prescription drug or something like that and they wouldn't have picked it up. I've got Carter on his way over there now to speak to his mother and do another search for any barbiturates. That's about it at this end. You want anyone to help you out tomorrow over in Bucks?"

"Gee, I don't think so. The most important thing is to see Schoop and I can handle that on my own. Besides, you're going to need all your guys checking out the pickups. How's that going?"

"Slow as hell, and we're not getting much out of it to tell the truth. When will I hear from you?"

"Will you be in the office all day tomorrow?"

"I expect so. If I'm not, someone will know where to reach me. Give me a call when you can."

"Will do." Gus hung up and looked at Peg. "Guess what, they found somebody had given the kid a barbiturate before he was killed. How does that grab you?"

"Who would do that and why would they?"

Gus shrugged his shoulders. "Fahy's got a theory that he was fed a barbiturate to keep him quiet when the guy snatched him. It doesn't make much sense to me. What does he do, say, 'Here kid, swallow this, it's good for you?' But Fahy thinks because the kid was given a drug that ties it into Frohmeyer because they found a load of drugs when they searched his place. Maybe, but it just doesn't make sense to me, not that anything about this case makes any sense."

"Gus, how about going to bed early tonight? We can just leave the dishes for the morning."

"Geez, Peg, I wanted to stay up to watch 'NYPD Blue.' That's a great program."

"For God's sake, Gus, don't you get enough of that? You have to watch other cops, too? Besides, that's on Tuesday nights. This is Monday, remember?"

"You're right, I thought it was Tuesday. I guess I ate too much."

"Gus, who are you kidding? You hardly ate anything. You didn't even finish the one bowl. What's the matter, didn't you like it?"

"Honest, Peg, it was great. I'm just trying to cut back on how much I eat. You're the one who said I had to go on a diet, you know."

"Gus, don't bullshit me. What did you eat for lunch?"

"Well, I did have a piece of pie and some coffee. But it was very late in the afternoon."

"What kind of pie?"

"Geez, I forget, maybe apple or something like that."

"How many pieces of this apple-or-something-like-that pie?"

"Just one piece, honestly."

"Gus, when you say 'honestly,' then I know you're bullshitting me. Come on, let's go to bed."

TWENTY-EIGHT

Gus woke up at 1:30 with a chest pain. It hurt like hell and he sat up in bed. The pain lessened a bit and he thought maybe it's not a heart attack. He belched and felt a little better so he got up and went into the bathroom. He found a package of alka-seltzer in the medicine cabinet and downed the concoction in two gulps. He stood at the sink for a few minutes and then it worked. Two good belches and the pain was practically gone. It had to be that banana cream pie, never again. Peg's right, I'm going on a diet starting tomorrow. The pain was all gone now, so he crawled back into bed and within seconds was asleep.

When he woke up the next morning, Peg was already gone. He found a note next to the coffee pot saying she had to leave early, but to call her during the day. He missed her already. He said to himself, This is getting serious, if I don't watch my step, I'm a dead duck. Well, maybe that's not so bad. Who knows?

By 10 o'clock he had found the Dublin barracks up in the wilds of Bucks County. He told the sergeant at the desk he was looking for a Lieutenant Schoop and that Andy Spahr had arranged for him to see the lieutenant. Two minutes later a short guy with a military bearing came walking out to the desk and introduced himself as Lieutenant Edward Schoop of the Pennsylvania State Police. Gus said to himself, oh shit, don't tell me I got another Chief Winters to deal with.

Gus said: "Lieutenant Schoop, I'm Gus Bass. I'm with the Frenchtown PD and I'm working on this murder we had over there last Friday. Andy Spahr told me you might be able to help us out on some background information about the Hartwick family and the death of their son back some years ago."

"Well, Bass—or should I call you Gus—you've come to the right place and the right guy. I happen to know all about that case. I was a sergeant then and just assigned to the barracks here when it happened. I conducted the investigation. Let's go into my office and I'll give you what I have on it. Andy called me last night and said you'd be up here today, so I got the file out for you. He said to tell you he couldn't make it up here this morning. How about a cup of coffee?"

"I'd like that very much, thanks. Just black. I told Chuck Fahy I was coming to see you today, and he says he's run into you a few times. Said to say hello for him."

"Yeah, we had a couple of matters we cooperated on some time back. Good man. You work with him before?"

"Nothing as big as this, just local stuff, but we got our hands full on this one."

By now they were seated in Schoop's office. It reminded Gus a bit of CO's offices he had seen in the army. An American flag in one corner, and instead of a regimental flag, a Pennsylvania state flag in the other. A metal desk with a linoleum top, an "in" basket and "out" basket and just one file on the desk. A picture of the Commander of the Pennsylvania State Police on one wall and of the governor on the opposite wall. And an asphalt tile floor. Yep, this was the army, all right.

After the coffee came, Schoop handed him the file that had been sitting on his desk.

"Here, take a look at it, there's not much in it. Read it, then I'll try to answer your questions if I can."

Gus opened the file and saw that it consisted of two sheets of paper and a death certificate. He read the certificate first: "James Hartwick, II, name, born May 18, 1985. Date of death, November 16, 1986. Place of death, Durham, Pennsylvania. Cause of death, asphyxiation by plastic bag, accidental." The certificate was signed by Alexander M. Wilson, MD.

Gus turned to the report and noted that it was signed by Sergeant Edward Schoop. He looked up at Schoop for a moment and then continued to read. Schoop had been summoned to the Hartwick house by a call from the coroner's office that a child had been accidentally smothered in a plastic bag at that location. Upon arrival he learned that the child's body had been removed by a local mortician at the direction of the attending physician, Dr. Wilson. Dr. Wilson had left and Schoop spoke to him by phone at the doctor's office after he interviewed the mother, Gladys Hartwick. The mother told him she had been in the kitchen cooking and her son, Jimmy, had been playing with his toys in the living room. She had checked up on him about fifte

151

minutes before and had continued her cooking. She realized that she hadn't heard any of his usual noises coming from the living room, so she went in to check up on him again. She found him on the floor unconscious among his toys. There was a plastic bag over his head. She pulled it off and his face was blue and he wasn't breathing. She tried giving him mouth-to-mouth but he didn't respond. She called the ambulance squad and then her family doctor.

The ambulance squad came and they tried to revive Jimmy but couldn't. Dr. Wilson arrived and he told her Jimmy was dead and there was nothing further that could be done. Dr. Wilson called the coroner's office and reported the death and told the coroner it was an accidental asphyxiation and that he would sign the death certificate that way. The coroner agreed, and his office called Schoop. In the absence of a body, Schoop asked Mrs. Hartwick to describe exactly where she had found her son. She pointed to an area next to a bookcase where there were a number of record albums with plastic covers.

The child's toys were scattered all over this area and Schoop found a plastic record album cover on the floor on top of some of the toys. Mr. Hartwick arrived after he had interviewed Mrs. Hartwick and he collapsed when he was told that his son was dead. The boy's grandmother arrived shortly after and upon learning what had happened became hysterical and was screaming that it was the mother's fault. Schoop called Dr. Wilson to return to the house to look after the father and the grandmother.

Gus looked up when he had finished reading. "You say in here that the father collapsed and the grandmother was hysterical. What about the mother, what was she doing?"

"That was the damnedest thing about it. She was like an automaton. Almost no reaction or emotion at all. She didn't scream or yell or do anything, just sat there and answered my questions. And when her husband came home, she didn't say a word to him, didn't try to help when he collapsed or anything. She just sat there. Then the grandmother comes in. And she's screaming at her, and she still just sat there. I figured she was in a state of shock and couldn't react to anything. That was some scene, I'm telling you."

"Did you ever get to see the kid's body to check out her story?"

"As a matter of fact, I tried to do just that. I went over to the mortician's place, but by the time I got there they had already started to embalm the kid, which I thought was pretty unusual to do it so quick, you know. But they told me they had to with a little kid like that because otherwise the body deteriorated very fast. So there wasn't anything I could see. I spoke to the doctor the next day and asked him if he had observed any marks on the kid's body but he said he hadn't. The ambulance squad had been working on the kid and it would have been useless to try to look for any marks because you wouldn't be able to tell when they were made."

Schoop scratched his head and then continued: "Gus, I'm going to level with you. I didn't like the whole set-up with that case. There was no crime scene, no body to look at, all you had was just people's words and that's no way to conduct an investigation of a death. If you want to know, I spoke to my boss after I filed my report and told him to speak to the coroner's office and tell them they shouldn't be signing off so quickly on a case just because a local doctor says a death is accidental. I wouldn't be telling you all this, but Spahr says you're an okay guy and I should tell you everything I know. And what I know is I never liked the bottom line on that one. As a matter of fact, you know I even took that plastic bag with me when I left the house, and I think I still have it in the evidence vault. Want to take a look?"

Gus's eyes lit up: "Holy shit, you still have it? Yeah, I'd like to take a look at it."

"Just sit tight for a few minutes and I'll go take a look. I'm probably the only one who could find it anyway. Help yourself to another cup of coffee, it's just down the hall next to the men's room. You know that's something new. We didn't used to have a men's room and a ladies' room in the barracks, but now that we have all these women troopers, we had to put in a ladies' room. Some of the old timers, if they saw that, they would piss in their pants."

"Now that you mention it, Ed, I think I'd better take a leak while I'm getting that coffee."

153

By the time Gus was half way finished with his coffee, Schoop was back carrying a redwell. He laid it on his desk and untied the string binding. He opened and removed a plastic bag and handed it to Gus. Gus took it and his eyes widened in disbelief. He looked at Schoop. "Ed, this is the bag?"

Schoop nodded. "That's the bag, all right. It's got my initials on it up in this corner."

"But this isn't one of those they use now on album covers, you know those, what do you call them, polystyrene. This is one of those old types, this plastic is stiff as hell. Is this the way it was when you found it?"

"So far as I remember it, yes, that's exactly the way it was, maybe except for the color. It's yellowed a bit."

"But this plastic is stiff. How the hell could a kid smother himself in this? I thought you were talking about the kind of stuff they use now, you know, like on the bags you get from the cleaners."

Schoop nodded: "Now you see what I mean that I didn't like this from the get-go. I thought so, too, at the time. How could it have happened? But I had nothing to go on, just fucking words. That's why I saved the bag, I think. Maybe some day somebody might want to look at it, and I'll be damned if you didn't finally get here."

Gus opened up the bag and turned it around in his hand. Suddenly, he saw it: Three small puncture marks in the shape of a triangle. He couldn't believe his eyes. His jaw dropped open, but he couldn't speak.

"What's the matter, Gus, you see something?"

Gus still couldn't utter words, he just stared at the triangle of holes in the plastic.

"What is it, Gus? You look like you seen a ghost. What are you looking at?"

"Do you see what I see, Ed? Were these holes there in the plastic when you picked it up?"

Schoop took the bag from Gus's hands and held it up to the light. "I see what you mean, Gus. Those holes had to have been there. I never noticed them, but what you're looking at now is just the way I found it. The only thing I did was to put my initials up here in the corner, that's all. What's so important about these holes?"

"It's like Yogi said: 'It's deja vu all over again.' Guess where there are three holes arranged just like these three? In little Bobby Hartwick's belly, that's where. I've got to call Fahy before we waste any more time chasing our tails around. He's got to see this or he wont' believe it. Ed, there won't be any problem with the chain of custody on this bag, will there?"

"I can't see how. I logged it into the evidence vault myself and no one has touched it since then, that I'm sure of. You're the first person who's seen it since I put it there."

"Good. Before you put it back, can you get someone to take a picture for me that will show up these holes in the bag?"

"That should be no problem, Gus, I've got a good crime scene guy right here and I'm sure he can do it."

"I'd appreciate that. And look, there's no possibility there was somebody else in that house the day the kid died, is there?"

"No way, it's in the statement you read. The mother was the only one in the house that morning. I asked her that specifically and that's what she said. Let me take this bag down to the photo lab and get that picture made up for you."

"Is it all right to use your phone, Ed?"

"Sure, that's what it's there for. I'll be back in about ten minutes."

Gus reached across the desk and picked up the phone and dialed Fahy's direct number. After three or four rings, it was one of the secretaries who answered and Gus asked for Fahy. "I'm sorry. Mr. Fahy is in conference with the prosecutor. Can I give him a message?"

"Please. Tell him it's Gus Bass and I have to speak to him. It's urgent. Have him call me back at this number, two-one-five nine-eight-two nine-nine-one-one and ask for Lieutenant Schoop. If I'm not here, tell him he can get me on my car phone. He knows the number."

Gus hung up and waited for Schoop to return. As he sat there he tried to review the facts he knew of Bobby's death in some kind of logical order to present to Fahy when he spoke to him. First, the boy left school at noon on Friday, June 3. He was alive

155

when he left the Aaron's younger boy and went home to eat his lunch. Gus realized that he had never questioned the Aaron boy to confirm that and made a note to himself to speak to the boy when he got back to Frenchtown. Gladys Hartwick admits the boy came home for lunch and he ate lunch. Dr. Sanchez says he ate a peanut butter and jelly sandwich and had a glass of milk no more than thirty minutes before he died. Someone also slipped him a barbiturate, most likely with his lunch. Gus made a second note to himself to check with Sanchez and see if it was possible to tell if the barbiturate was given to him in the food he had for lunch. Who was the last person known to see the boy alive? His mother. She says she saw him go down the path through the park at 12:45. But so far no one had been found who saw the kid leave the house, saw him on Ridge, or in the playground, on Creek Road or near the school. All this movement during the noon hour on a bright, clear sunny day, and no one sees the kid where he would have had to have been if he left the house and went back to school like she says. So she's still the last person who claims to have seen the kid alive, and we can't find anybody else who did. We've got nothing but her word to go on that he ever left that house.

Gus had gotten that far by the time Schoop returned with the bag. "He's developing the pictures right now and he'll have them for you in about twenty minutes. Not like the old days when we'd have to send stuff out to a lab and wait a day for pictures to come back. He says the holes will show up good in the shots he took. In the meantime, I'm putting the bag back in the evidence vault. Okay with you?"

"You bet, Ed. Look, while we're waiting maybe you could help me out on some background on Mrs. Hartwick. I've been told her maiden name was Wilkins and she's originally from around Lake Nockamixon. I think her mother's name was Henrietta, but I don't know her father's name. Her parents were separated or divorced by the time she and her mother moved down to Durham. Is there any way you could check to see if you have something on the family?"

"Well, I could run the name through the computer and see what comes up. You're lucky, we just finished up about six months ago putting all the old files into the computer and we're right up to date." Schoop picked up the phone and dialed. "Sally, I want you to check a name out for me: 'Wilkins.' From up around Lake Nockamixon. Mother's name was Henrietta, daughter's name is Gladys. We don't have any name for the father. Give me a call back as soon as you can." He hung up and said to Gus: "Now we'll see if those computers are as good as they say they are."

"Christ, Ed, I am really scared of those things. I tried to use one once when we first got them down in Trenton and the goddamned thing froze up on me. They had to call some guy in to undo whatever I did to it. I thought I was just following the manual they gave me for it, but the guy said the manual wasn't written for idiots and I should stay away from the thing. Since then, I've never touched one of those machines. Maybe some day I'll take a course or something and find out how they work. They are sure useful for some things. You know Captain Sloss from over in the Flemington Barracks?"

"I sure do. We put in a lot of time together and he's one hell of a guy to have around. Christ, he knows everybody there is to know."

"Yeah, like Fahy wanted to get the records on all the perverts in our area when we started this case and a list of all blue Ford pickups registered in the county. So he asks Sloss to get some buddies of his down in SCI and in motor vehicles on it. Sloss knows the guys who run the computers down there and damned if we didn't get everything back within hours. Before they had computers something like that would have taken a week if it ever got done at all."

The phone rang and it was Sally. Schoop hung up and said: "She's bringing over a file which she thinks has some stuff on the family you're looking for."

The door opened but it was Schoop's lab man with the pictures of the bag. He handed Schoop a dozen glossy eight-by-tens and said: "These ought to do it. I told you those holes would show up good. You can almost put your finger through them, they look so real. I've made two sets, one for each of you."

"They're perfect, Tom. That should do it." Schoop handed one set to Gus and said: "Tom, I want you to meet Gus Bass from over in Frenchtown."

157

"Nice to meet you, Gus. I hope these are okay. If you need any more, just let me know. I've got to get back to the lab and clean up now."

"Thanks a lot, Tom. I'll call you if we do. Nice meeting you."

As Tom started to leave a woman trooper walked in carrying a fairly thick file. "Here, Lieutenant, I think this is what you may be looking for. The name's Wilkins and there's a Henrietta and a Gladys Wilkins in it."

"Thanks, Sally. Say hello to Gus Bass from Frenchtown. Gus, this is my computer genius, Sally Tuttle. If you took a leak in your backyard ten years ago and it got reported, she'll have you in her computer. You have to be careful around her, Gus."

Gus laughed. "Sally, some day I'm going to come up here and have you show me how these machines of yours work. I was just telling your boss here the last and the only time I ever touched one, the damn thing blew up on me."

"Any time, Mr. Bass, just give me a call and I'll have you working a computer in no time. What you should do is go out and buy yourself a cheap one and try fooling around with it at home. And you can get yourself a one-two-three manual that's real easy to follow. They call it 'DOS for Idiots' and you can learn a lot all by yourself"

Gus and Schoop laughed and Sally looked at them quizzically. "Did I say something wrong?"

Schoop said: "No, Sally. Gus was just telling me before you came in that when he blew up the computer down in Trenton, the guy who came to fix it told him that computers weren't for idiots. It looks like maybe they are now."

Sally laughed and said: "It's nice to have met you, Mr. Bass."

"Let's go sit over at the table, Gus, and we'll look at this thing together."

The first entry in the file was a report signed by Sergeant Joseph McElroy, dated June 3, 1978. McElroy was called to the home of Mr. and Mrs. Roger Wilkins, Sr., Lake Nockamixon, on June 3, 1978. Mrs. Henrietta Wilkins had returned home from a visit to a friend's house at about 4:00 P.M. and found that her four year old son, Roger, Jr., was missing. Mrs. Wilkins had left the house at 2:00 P.M. Her husband, Roger, Sr. was at home along with her daughter Gladys Wilkins, aged fifteen. Mr. Wilkins had left at about 2:30 to visit some friends and Gladys was left to look after the boy. According to Gladys, the boy was playing in the yard with a small baseball bat and a ball. Gladys was in the den watching television. She says she checked up on the boy every so often, but couldn't say when she had last seen him before her mother got home. When Mrs. Wilkins returned she couldn't find her son and she and Gladys looked in the woods behind the house and checked along the lake shore. They then called the Dublin Barracks and McElroy arrived at their home at 5:05 P.M. Upon learning the above information, McElroy called for assistance to organize a search party. Additional officers were on the scene by 6:00 P.M. and commenced a search of the area around the easterly and southerly end of the lake. A pair of children's shoes and socks were found in a wooded area near the shore line about fifty yards from the Wilkins property. A scuba team from the Easton Barracks was summoned and they commenced a search at 6:55 P.M. At 7:15 the boy's body was recovered in approximately five feet of water about twenty yards from the shore where the shoes were found.

The body was brought ashore and resuscitation efforts were commenced but were unsuccessful. Dr. James Oldmayer arrived shortly after the body was recovered and pronounced the boy dead. Resuscitation efforts were discontinued and the body was transported to the coroner's office by local volunteer ambulance. Mr. Wilkins returned home after the body was removed and appeared to be in a highly intoxicated condition. It was not possible to take a statement from him at that time.

The following day Sergeant McElroy returned to the Wilkins' home and interviewed the father. He stated that he had left home at about 2:30 to visit his brother Hiram who lives near Pleasant Valley. He stayed at Hiram's house for about two hours and then he and Hiram went to a bar in Easton and had a few drinks. They didn't leave the bar until about seven and then he drove Hiram to his house and returned home. He stated that when he had left home that afternoon, his son was in the yard playing with a baseball bat and a ball he had given him for his birthday, and Gladys was in the den watching television. He told Gladys he was leaving and she said she would watch after Roger, Jr. According to Mr. Wilkins, the boy could not swim and never went into the water unless accompanied by an adult.

Gladys Wilkins was re-interviewed and she confirmed the time her father had left. She denied saying to him that she would watch the boy, but she was aware that her father had gone out. She didn't know where he was going or how long he would be gone. She assumed he was going to see his brother Hiram because he frequently went there. She also confirmed the time Mrs. Wilkins left and she knew she was going to visit a friend because her mother had told her so when she left. Gladys couldn't remember what programs she was watching that afternoon as she was doing homework and wasn't paying much attention to the television. She states that she definitely saw the boy playing in the yard not more than fifteen or twenty minutes before her mother came home and asked for him.

It was not possible to re-interview Mrs. Wilkins as she was heavily sedated. From other sources, McElroy confirmed that Mrs. Wilkins had visited a Mrs. Hester Johnson who lives near Harrow and had arrived there at about 2:15 or 2:20 P.M. She left Mrs. Johnson's house at about 3:30.

All neighbors within a mile of the Wilkins' residence were interviewed. No one reported any strangers in the area the day of the boy's disappearance nor did any one see the boy. No one was reported to have been fishing on the lake in the vicinity of where the boy's body was recovered, nor were there any boats seen in that area.

Examination of the boy's shoes and socks disclosed no evidence that he had them on when he entered the water. McElroy's opinion was that the ball the boy had been playing with had rolled into the lake and the boy had gone after it but took off his shoes and socks before he entered the water to retrieve the ball. No ball was found either in the water or on the shore.

McElroy concluded his report by stating his opinion that the death was an accidental drowning pending receipt of the autopsy report.

The file contained several additional reports of officers who had been at the scene as well as the scuba team members describing the exact location in which the body had been found.

The final documents in the file were the death certificate,

which stated that the death was caused by accidental drowning, and the autopsy report, which stated that the autopsy was conducted at the coroner's office starting at 9:30 P.M. on June 3, 1978. All anatomical findings as well as the condition of the lungs, which were distended with the presence of fresh water and torn alveolar walls, were consistent with death by drowning. The presence of foam in the airway established beyond doubt that the victim was alive at the time he entered the water. There were no marks or bruises on the body inconsistent with the marks which would have been caused during the effort to resuscitate the boy after he was recovered from the water. The report concluded that "This four-year-old white male died of submersion in fresh water and the death is considered to be accidental."

Gus looked up at Schoop and closed the file. "That's three she killed. She's a fucking serial killer. She should have been put away a long time ago. She got away with the first one, then the second, but she ain't going to get away with the third, goddamn it."

"Gus, how can you say she killed her brother? This one was an accident. You got nothing to go on for this."

"Accident my ass. Look at the date, June third. That's the same date she killed Bobby, for Christ's sake, that's no accident. And look how the brother died. Drowning. That's the same thing as smothering, only she threw the kid in the water instead of using a plastic bag. Three poor, defenseless kids, she killed them all. And that's all she's ever going to kill. You can bet on it. I'm going to nail her ass even if it's only for little Bobby. You should have seen him lying there. She wasn't satisfied to kill him, she had to cut his little prick off."

Schoop reached over and put his hand on Gus's shoulder. "Gus, take it easy. I'm not saying I don't agree with you, but calm down. It's a case, that's all. Look, you've done a great job on it, but don't go crazy. There's still a lot of work to be done before it gets wrapped up and you've got to be a professional and not go off half-cocked or people won't listen to you."

Gus sat and said nothing for quite a while. Finally, he looked up at Schoop and said: "Thanks, Ed. You're right, I am getting too mixed up with this. It always happens when the victim is a

161

kid, but this time I'm going to play it cool. Can I get a copy of this file? And your file on Jimmy Hartwick to take with me, do you think?"

"That's better. Of course you can. I'll have them run off for you right now. When do you figure on leaving?"

"I was just waiting for Fahy to call back. As soon as I get the copies I'm going to head back to Flemington and I'll lay it out for him over there with the pictures and all. God, what a fucking case this is. Who would have believed it?"

"It ain't over yet, Gus. There'll be a lot of people who still aren't going to buy it, accusing a mother of killing her own kids. You wait and see, if you don't get a confession out of her, you'll have a tough time getting her for anything. It's a tough sell. I'll get these copies run off for you, it will just take a minute."

Schoop returned shortly with an envelope containing copies of the two files and handed them to Gus. "Good luck. You're going to need it and if there's anything I can do just call. I'd like to nail her myself for Jimmy Hartwick. Maybe if I could have back then, she never would have had a shot at the last one."

"Ed, I don't have to tell you how much help you've been. I think you know it. The only good thing about this case is that I've had a chance to meet guys like you and Spahr. And if we can break this bitch, I want you to come over and get the statement from her on your case. We owe you that much and a lot more. I'll give you a call right after I've seen Fahy."

"Gus, you're one hell of a cop, you know that? I wish I had you over here with us. Take it easy, pal and remember what I said."

They shook hands and Gus left. Fahy still hadn't called back.

TWENTY-NINE

Gus wanted to get out of Bucks County as quickly as he could, so he headed to Upper Black Eddy and crossed the river into Milford. On the way he called Peg at her school but she was having a conference with some parents and couldn't be disturbed, so he went straight on to Flemington. When he reached the prosecutor's office, Fahy was still in conference with Ms. Stevens and he waited in Fahy's office.

At last Fahy came in and he looked depressed. "What's wrong, Chuck? You don't look so hot."

"The boss lady ain't too happy, either. We searched the Frohmeyer place and we couldn't find any form of barbiturate anywhere. And his public defender has gone to the prosecutor and is making all kinds of noise that we're harassing his client. Now she says maybe we're pushing Frohmeyer too hard and we'd better back off. If that's not enough, we got a call from the FBI lab and they say the fibers we got from the truck don't match up with that shirt we got from Mrs. Hartwick. That shirt was cotton and the stuff from the truck was some kind of blend of cotton and a synthetic. So we got nothing to go with, except I'm sure that bastard did it."

"You'd better sit down, Chuck. Frohmeyer didn't do it. He didn't have anything to do with killing that boy."

Fahy's eyes narrowed to thin slits. "What are you talking about, Gus? What makes you so sure?"

"Because the mother did it, that's why."

Fahy threw up his hands. "Gus, you're out of your mind. What the hell are you talking about? No mother kills her own kid, for Christ's sake. It just doesn't happen. You know, I kind of suspected that was going to be your angle going over there to Bucks, but you're chasing your tail as much as we are with Frohmeyer."

"That's not why I went over there, and you know it. I wasn't looking to nail her, I thought it just might be somebody who knew them and was trying to get even with them for something. This

163

just fell into my lap and believe me, I wasn't happy with it either, but you got to see what I got here." Gus opened the files and spread them out on Fahy's desk along with the pictures. "Number one, here's Schoop's report on the investigation he did of the death of Jimmy Hartwick, aged eighteen months. This goes back to November 1986. It wasn't any investigation at all. There was no body when he got there, the local doc and the coroner let the body be moved to the funeral home. There was no autopsy, there was nothing. All he had was Gladys's story that the kid was playing in the living room and stuck his head in a plastic bag and suffocated himself. She was supposed to be in the kitchen when this happened."

Fahy gulped. "A plastic bag? Are you kidding me?"

"I ain't kidding you, Chuck. A fuckin' plastic bag. And you got to see that bag. It's the old kind of plastic they used for record albums. You know that stiff kind of plastic, not the clingy kind they use today. And Schoop says he couldn't figure it out at the time, how the kid could have suffocated himself in a bag like that. But he had nothing to go on except, like he says, just words, and he couldn't really conduct an investigation. The local doc said it was an accident and the coroner went along with it and that was the end of it. Except for one thing. He picked up the bag and stuck it in the evidence vault and it's been there for almost eight years, just sitting there. And you know what he told me? He says he's been waiting all these years for someone to come along and want to see that bag. And here's the pictures of that bag his guy took this morning."

Fahy picked up the first of the pictures and dropped it on his desk. "Gus, is this for real? Are these three holes in the bag?"

"That's why I had the pictures taken. As soon as I saw those fucking holes, I knew she had to be the one. They're the same holes she put into Bobby's belly. You see that, don't you?"

Fahy didn't respond, he just sat and stared at the picture and then he picked up the next picture Gus had brought back and the one after that and the last one. "Gus, I never would have believed it. I'm not sure I believe it even now. What the fuck does it mean, those three holes? Let's get the autopsy pictures in here and see if it's the same."

"Go ahead, if you want. They're the same goddamned holes

we saw on the kid's belly, remember?"

Fahy nodded: "You're right, but we'd better show these to Sanchez and see what he says."

"There's more, Chuck. Schoop says when he took a statement from Gladys, she acted like an automaton, she showed no emotion at all. Does that ring a bell? He thought she was in shock, just like I did. And while he was there, Bob Hartwick got home and he collapsed. Then the grandmother, Mrs. Degroat, only she was still Mrs. Hartwick then, she showed up and the first thing she did was to blame Gladys. Does that ring a bell?"

Fahy didn't say a word, just sat there staring at the pictures and so Gus went on. "There's more, Chuck. Schoop dug up an old file on Gladys's family. Her maiden name was Wilkins, and they lived up on Lake Nockamixon. You know that area? Well on June third, nineteen seventy-eight, Gladys was home alone with her four-year-old brother, named Roger Wilkins, Junior. Her mother and father were out and she was supposed to be watching the boy. She was fifteen then. The boy drowned in the lake and according to the report Gladys was in the house watching television and never noticed the kid wasn't around. When her mother got home she tried to find the boy but he was missing. They found his shoes and socks down by the lake and then a scuba team found his body about twenty yards offshore. He was dead, all right. And the father said the kid didn't swim and never went into the water alone before. The guy who investigated figured the kid was playing with a ball and it went into the water and then he went after it and drowned himself. For Christ's sake, what four-year-old kid is going to stop and take off his shoes and socks when he's chasing a ball that went into the water? They did an autopsy but it didn't show up anything except the kid drowned and so they called it accidental. As sure as shit comes out your ass, she killed that kid, too."

"Gus, you're going off the deep end now. How could anybody prove that? And why the hell would she want to kill her own brother?"

"Who the hell knows why? I don't give a damn about why. She did it. And we don't have to prove it. All we have to do is get her for little Bobby. And I think we can get her for that with what we have right here. Did you notice the date her brother died?

June third, does that ring a bell?"

"What the hell does June third have to do with it? Oh, shit, I see. The same date Bobby died." Fahy paused and looked at the pictures again. Finally he said: "I'm not saying you're wrong on any of this, Gus. I think we'd better go in and see Ms. Stevens and lay it out for her and see what she says. Jesus Christ, Gus, when you come up with an angle, it's a lulu. I got to hand it to you, it's some piece of work you've done, but if you're right we still got a long way to go before we nail her. Believe me, Gus, this is going to be tough."

Gus gathered up the Bucks County files and the pictures and followed Fahy downstairs to Ms. Stevens's office. Along the way, they stopped off in the record room and Fahy picked up Bobby Hartwick's autopsy file. The prosecutor's door was open and they just walked in. Gus was glad to see her office was larger than Fahy's and she had a wooden desk, but no carpet on the floor. He thought to himself, *They live a lot better over in Bucks.*

Hazel Stevens looked up and could see by the expressions on their faces that something was afoot she didn't know about and she invited them to sit at the small conference table near the window. She started by saying: "Gus, I haven't seen you around the past few days, what have you been up to?"

It was Fahy who spoke first: "He's been over in Bucks checking out the Hartwicks and he's come up with a lot of material. I think he has identified the killer of Bobby Hartwick and it may be a shock to you. But I'm going to let him tell you what he has dug up. Go ahead, Gus, lay it out."

"Well, if that's the case, before you get started, I would like to get Ben Harris in here so he can hear it, too. We can use his input." Ms. Stevens went to the door which was still open and yelled for Harris to come into her office. He walked in and saw Fahy and Gus sitting at the conference table. He closed the door.

"Let me guess. You guys have come up with another body. Who's it this time?"

It was Fahy who answered. "As a matter of fact, Ben, Gus has come up with two more bodies, and they're long dead and buried. And they weren't killed here so we don't have to worry about making those cases. Gus will give you the picture. Okay, Gus, you've got the floor."

166

"I want you to know first I wasn't looking for any of this and I never figured who the killer was until I sat down with some people over in Bucks and talked with them and then I got the files on two old cases and some pictures from the state cops over in Pennsylvania at the Dublin Barracks." Gus then took them through the scenario he had put together in Schoop's office. He continued his narrative: "So, according to Gladys, she fed him lunch. The medical examiner says he ate a peanut butter and jelly sandwich and a glass of milk. But he also was given something else by somebody, a barbiturate. I asked myself, who could have given the kid a barbiturate and when? According to Sanchez, the kid was killed within thirty minutes of the time he ate lunch. And he had to be given the barbiturate before he died or else it would never show up in his blood."

Ben Harris interjected: "That barbiturate has been bothering me, too. I assumed it had to be given to him with something he ate or drank and all Sanchez found in his stomach were the sandwich and the milk."

Gus went on: "Now the mother says Bobby left the house to go back to school at twelve forty-five and the Aaron boys had already left so she sent him back alone. It's the noon hour on a bright, clear, sunny day. The kid walks down Ridge to the park, cuts through the playground to Creek Road, crosses the road and then walks up to the school grounds. But the guys have checked the neighborhood and everybody in the vicinity of where the kid had to have been if he did go back to school like his mother says. So far not a single person sighted that kid going back to school on Friday."

Gus paused: "So how do we know he went back to school like she says? We only have her word for it, and so far as I'm concerned that ain't good enough. If Sanchez is right about when the kid ate before he died, that kid could never have left his house alive. He was killed right there and there were only two other people in the house, his mother and his three-year-old brother."

"And how was he killed? Sanchez says he was suffocated, probably with a plastic bag. He wasn't strangled. It so happens that Bobby wasn't the first Hartwick kid who died suddenly."

Hazel Stevens's eyes widened. "Gus, are you saying they had another child who died before and they never said a word about that to anyone? Why didn't we find out about this before now?"

Gus's voice was getting hoarse. "To answer that question, the first kid died when they were living over in Durham so no one here knew anything about it. They just moved to Frenchtown about a year ago, and I guess they never told anyone. They didn't have too many friends here anyway. But what's important is the way the kid died. This was almost eight years ago and the kid's name was Jimmy Hartwick. He was eighteen months old and the mother claimed he stuck his head in a plastic bag when he was playing in the living room and she was in the kitchen cooking. Like I told Chuck, the guy who investigated that death, Lieutenant Schoop, he's with the Pennsylvania state cops, couldn't figure out how the kid could have killed himself the way she said it happened. So he picked up the bag and he kept it in the evidence vault over there all this time. A local doctor had been there before Schoop got to the house and the doctor called it an accidental death and the coroner went along with it. That was that, no autopsy, no nothing. Schoop didn't like it but there was nothing he could do about it."

Gus opened the envelope and put Schoop's report on Jimmy's death in front of the prosecutor. "These are pictures we took this morning of the plastic bag just as he found it eight years ago. See those three holes in the shape of a triangle? Now Chuck, show them the autopsy photos."

Fahy opened up the file and took out a large color photo of Bobby Hartwick lying face up on the autopsy table. Hazel Stevens turned pale. Gus continued his monologue. "There, see those three holes in Bobby's belly? I don't know what they mean, but whoever put those holes in that bag over in Durham, put the holes in Bobby. And there's only one person who was there both times who could have done it and that was the mother. And when you think about what Sanchez found, no one else could have killed Bobby except her, even if she didn't kill the first kid."

The prosecutor and Harris picked up the pictures and started reading Schoop's report. After minutes had passed, Ms. Stevens looked up at Gus and said: "Fahy said you found two more bodies. Who's the other one and when did that happen?"

"It happened on June third, nineteen seventy-eight. Gladys was fifteen and she lived over at Lake Nockamixon with her parents and a four-year-old brother, her name was Wilkins then." Gus then took them through the drowning. "And like the others, she was the only one who was there and just like with her first kid, she claimed she didn't see anything. That makes three small boys, all dead and she's the only one there all three times. I've got a copy of the whole file on her brother here and you can read it for yourselves."

Gus stood up and stretched. "Look, I'm kind of beat. I've been doing too much talking all day and I haven't had anything to eat. If it's all right with you, I'm going to go across the street and get a bite while you go through all of this stuff."

Hazel said: "Sure, Gus. Why don't you come back in about an hour and we'll talk some more." Gus left and went over to the National. He started with a Stoly on the rocks, no twist.

THIRTY

As he paid the check, Gus looked at his watch and saw that it was 4:30. He decided to call Peg before he went back to the prosecutor's office. He figured she would be at home by then and she was.

"Hi, hon, it's me. Look, I'm over in Flemington and I'm going over to another meeting with the prosecutor and it may be a late night. So don't wait up for me. As a matter of fact, I'll probably go over to my place and sack out. I need a change of clothes, anyway. What I've got on is beginning to smell a bit. . . . Well, I'm glad you'll miss me, 'cause I miss you already and it's still light out. . . . Hon, maybe it would be a good idea if I brought a change of clothes over to your place and kept them there for emergencies and things like that. Would you mind? . . . Okay, tomorrow night, but I'll call you during the day. Hey, by the way, do you know when the funeral is for Bobby? . . . Tomorrow? What time? . . . Will you be there? . . . Okay, I may see you there. If not I'll call. There's a lot going on with the case but I don't think I can tell you just yet. Maybe tomorrow. I love you, hon. . . . That's good. So long."

Gus headed back to the office and when he went in the receptionist told him to go into the grand jury room, everybody on the case was meeting there. Gus walked to the back of the building and when he entered the room, he saw most of the guys already there and Ms. Stevens was sitting in the foreman's chair and Fahy was standing in the front of the desk. Fahy was just finishing up when he saw Gus walk in and said: "Gus, I've laid it out for the guys, just like you gave it to us, and I think everybody buys it. Is that right?" Everybody seemed to agree, at least no one said he didn't.

Fahy went on: "So now the question is how and where do we go from here? You got any ideas, Gus?"

"We got to clean up the interviews with the neighbors and make sure no one saw the kid leave the house that day. Then we got to get the Hartwicks in and interview them and get statements. I just found out the funeral is tomorrow at eleven o'clock so we can't get them in until Thursday at the earliest, I would guess. What do you think, Ms. Stevens?"

"I don't know, Gus. Obviously, we can't bring them in until after the funeral and even Thursday may be a little too soon. Anyway I think we should start with the father first and work on him before we bring her over. And I would like to get a search warrant for the house to look for barbiturates and the boy's clothes she says he was wearing that day. They may still be in the house, at least it's a possibility. What do you think, Ben? Have we got enough to get a search warrant?"

"This may come as a surprise to a lot of you, but so far as I'm concerned we got more than enough to get a search warrant, even if the late Justice Brennan were the judge."

Ms. Stevens and Susan were the only ones who laughed, the rest of them just looked blank. Ms. Stevens continued: "All right, Ben and Sam can put together the affidavit for the search warrant. I think Gus had better sign it, since he got the files from Pennsylvania and interviewed the people there. I think we'll need one from Sanchez on the autopsy findings as well, don't you Ben?" Ben nodded in agreement.

"Chuck, I think you should get a team over to Ridge Road tomorrow morning first thing and get statements from all the neighbors who might have been home last Friday. A lot of them may be staying home tomorrow to go to the funeral, so it may be the best time to get them. We'll figure on bringing the father over here first thing Thursday morning and start questioning him. Gus, do you think you can set that up?"

"I think so. I thought I might go to the funeral and I could speak to him right after."

"Is there anything else we can get under way tomorrow?"

It was Gus who spoke up. "I've got to tell you, the only thing that's been troubling me is how she got the boy's body down to where we found it. She didn't have a car, so how did she get the body there? She couldn't go walking down the street with the body, for Christ's sake." Gus paused and said: "I'm sorry, Ms. Stevens, I didn't mean that. Well, anyway she couldn't do that.

171

So how did she get the body there? There's only two possibilities I can see. One, she just carried the boy out to the hedges in the backyard and dumped him over the embankment and he ended up where we found him, or two, she carried him down the embankment and placed him there. We've got to check that out. Go over that ground between the hedges and the tree and see if there's anything there which would show how she did it. It's my hunch she just dumped him and the body rolled down under the spruce tree. That's how all those scratches on the body might have gotten there. Either that or she just dragged the body on the ground when she went down the embankment."

Sam Carter interrupted: "But Gus, wouldn't she take a chance of being seen one way or the other taking the kid out the backyard? One of the neighbors could have seen her."

"Sure they could. But this was premeditated. She fed the kid barbiturate to knock him out so she could kill him. When I was there that Friday afternoon, I checked the two houses down the street from the Hartwicks and there was no one home. I bet there was no one home in the next two houses up the street and she knew it. Besides, if she just carried him out and dumped him over the edge, like I think she did, it would have taken no more than twenty or thirty seconds for her to do it, so I don't think there was much of a risk of her being seen. Anyway, she'd have to take the risk, she couldn't very well kill the kid and leave the body in the house. So far as I can see, this was killing the brother all over again, except instead of dumping him in the lake, she dumped him over the embankment."

Ben Harris spoke up. "Gus, I'd hate to have you on my case, that's for sure. When you sink your teeth in you just don't let go, do you?"

Gus nodded: "Well, Mr. Harris, I let go a few times before and it didn't work out too good. This is one time I ain't letting go, you can make book on it."

Chuck spoke next. "All right. I want Bert and Billy to go over that area tomorrow. Take your cameras and the laser gun. And measure out the exact distance from the top of the embankment to the tree. If Gus is right and she just dumped the kid over, we may get lucky and find some markings on the ground or twigs broken off or even some skin that might have gotten torn off as he rolled down."

"You got it, boss. When do you want us to start?"

"Well, the funeral is at eleven o'clock, so maybe that would be a good time. There won't be anybody home and the area should be clear for you then. And you'll have a good hour or more to get it done."

Hazel Stevens spoke next. "All right, I think that's about it for now. Why don't you all go home and see your families. The next few days are going to be long ones so you better relax while you can. Chuck, let's go into my office. I want to talk to you and Gus and Ben Harris. Thanks guys, we're going to wrap this one up and all of you have done a great job."

When they were all seated around Ms. Stevens's conference table she said: "I think we all believe Mrs. Hartwick murdered her own child. Our problem now is how do we prove it. All we've got is a circumstantial case and while it's pretty convincing, we have to get hard evidence. I doubt whether she's ever going to admit she killed anyone. She probably wouldn't even admit it to herself so we can't expect her to give us a confession. What I'm afraid of is she will get away with a plea of insanity and all we'll be able to do is to put her into a hospital and she'll get out and could kill again. It's happened before and I don't want to see it happen in this case. I believe Gus is right, that she killed all three of them and somewhere down the road we're going to have to convince a jury that she killed Bobby and put her away for life. That means no plea bargain, we're going to play this one out all the way, win or lose. Does everybody agree?"

Gus said: "I meant what I said in there, Ms. Stevens. This murder was premeditated. All three of them were. This woman deserves to die for what she did, killing helpless little kids."

"Gus, I don't disagree with you. But we have to be realistic. No jury is going to give the death penalty to a woman for killing her own child. It just doesn't happen no matter how much she may deserve it. What I'm after is to make sure we can convict her and put her away for good. And for that we need hard, physical evidence. I think our best shot right now is the medical evidence and I think we should get Sanchez in here, lay it out for him and see what help he can give us. That's what the county pays him for, so let's get him in tonight, is that all right with you?" They all nodded and Hazel said: "Chuck, why don't you call him and see if we can get him over here as soon as he is available?"

Chuck came back in a few minutes and said: "He's just finishing up over there and he can be over here in about a half an hour. He never had any lunch and he said to order him a sandwich or something unless we can find a Japanese restaurant around here who'll deliver some sushi. I never heard of a Japanese restaurant around Flemington, so he's going to settle for a sandwich."

Ben Harris said: "There's a place over in Somerville that serves some Japanese food. I ate there once when I had to see the prosecutor over there on a case. You think they might deliver over to Flemington?"

Ms. Stevens shook her head. "God, I hope not. I don't think I could look at raw fish right now. Chuck, just get him a ham and cheese and let him suffer."

Chuck looked around the table. "Anybody else want anything when I'm ordering?" They all shook their heads and Fahy went out and ordered for Sanchez.

Exactly thirty minutes later the medical examiner stuck his head in the door of Ms. Stevens's office. "This looks like an inquisition. Do I get something to eat, or do I get the rack before I eat?"

Hazel stood up and said: "Doctor Sanchez, I'm glad you could come. I'm sorry we couldn't get your first choice, but there's a sandwich on the way and we've got some coffee around here for you, if that's all right."

"My dear sweet lady, if you don't mind my calling you that, whatever you have is fine. Now, what can I do for you?"

"Doctor, this is Gus Bass. He's been working on the Hartwick case with us. As a matter of fact, he has found out a great deal about the mother, and we all agree that she murdered her child. We wanted to go over the material we have with you and see how it fits with your autopsy findings."

"Indeed, and I have some more results which may very well

help your case if it is the mother. We have identified the barbiturate the boy was given. It's secobarbital. It is the fastest acting of the barbiturate drugs and it's not available over the counter. It is classified as a narcotic and can't be sold without a prescription. It used to be prescribed quite frequently many years ago as a sleeping medication under the trade name 'seconal,' but it is very rarely prescribed today because it is highly addictive. However, it is available on the street. I think they call them 'reds,' but I may have my color wrong. Even more interesting than that, once we found a barbiturate in the blood samples, we analyzed the milk that he had for lunch and there were still traces of secobarbital in the milk. So whoever gave him the milk, in my opinion also gave him the barbiturate."

Fahy said: "Doctor Sanchez, is there any possibility this drug could have been given separately and was absorbed into the milk in his stomach?"

"Good question, Mr. Fahy. It is a remote possibility, but I don't think so. You see, once we found the drug present in his blood, we analyzed all of the milk we took from his stomach and the concentration of the drug was uniform throughout the sample. You wouldn't expect to find that if the drug was absorbed into the milk by contact in the stomach. I'm prepared to testify that the drug was administered in the milk he drank. Does that answer your question?"

Fahy smiled. "It sure does, Doctor. I'd say, Ms. Stevens, we've got our first piece of hard evidence."

Ms. Stevens nodded in agreement. "But remember, Chuck, we have to establish that she had access to the drug. If we can't prove that, it will present a problem. Doctor, if the drug is classified as a narcotic, I assume any pharmacy which filled the prescription for it would have to keep a record of it, wouldn't they?"

"Oh, most certainly. As a matter of fact, a special form has to be completed before any narcotic drug can be dispensed. If the drug was prescribed and you can find any pharmacy which filled the prescription, they will have the record of it all right."

Ms. Stevens turned to Fahy. "There's another assignment for tomorrow, Chief. Have two men check out all the pharmacies within a ten mile radius of Frenchtown. There can't be too many,

I'm sure. Is there one in Frenchtown, Gus?"

"Yes, Ms. Stevens, there is. It's called the Frenchtown Pharmacy and it's right on King Street just a short distance from where the Hartwicks live. Look, I know the guy who owns the store, and I'll check with him first thing tomorrow morning. Who knows, we may get a break for a change. But if that isn't the one, I'd suggest the guys try the drug stores across the river first. She's lived in Bucks all her life and might still use a drug store over there."

Chuck said: "You're right as usual, Gus. You take the Frenchtown drug store and I'll have the guys start with the ones over in Bucks."

Dr. Sanchez said: "Now, what else can I help you with?"

"Gus has a theory how she might have gotten rid of the body," Fahy said. "Why don't you tell the Doc, Gus? Maybe he can help us out there."

"It ain't any grand theory, Doctor Sanchez. Once we figured her as the killer, the next question is how did she get rid of the body, you know, how did the body end up in the woods in the park? She didn't have a car and she couldn't carry a body down the street. I climbed up that embankment near where we found the body. You must have seen it when you were over there that morning. Anyway, when I got to the top there I was right in the Hartwick back yard. So as I see it, there's two possibilities: she could just have dumped the kid over the embankment and he rolled down and ended up under that tree, or she could have climbed down with him and placed it there and then climbed back up. I guess if I could climb up it, she certainly could have climbed down and then back up."

Fahy interrupted Gus. "Doc, you remember the body had been moved before we got there, so we didn't have an exact crime scene. Maybe if those idiots had left the body alone, we might have a better idea. What do you think?"

"About moving the body before I got there? That's about as dumb as anything I've run into in a long time." Sanchez turned to Hazel Stevens: "My God, don't they teach these local cops anything about a crime scene?"

Ms. Stevens said: "They do now. Every cop who is hired is

required to attend a police training program. Unfortunately, some of the old timers who were appointed years ago never took the course because it wasn't required then and local politicians haven't forced them to go through the program. As a matter of fact, this case gives me an opportunity to write to every town which has a police department and tell them to have all of their police take the course, regardless of when they were appointed. How about that, Ben? Do you think I can do that?"

"Well, boss, you're the head of law enforcement in the county and if you tell them, they'll have to do it."

"Yes, and I can just hear what some of those characters will say about a woman ordering them back to school. It will go over big, I assure you. But we're digressing and we don't want to keep the doctor all night. How about it, Dr. Sanchez, can you give us any clue as to how the body got to where it was found?"

"Well, I'd have to agree with Gus. She could have carried the body out the backyard, and as to the two possibilities, I would think she probably dropped him over that embankment and he rolled down the hill and ended up against the trunk of that tree. Didn't you get a report from one of the men who moved the body that it was resting against the side of the tree?" Fahy nodded and Dr. Sanchez continued: "Certainly the wounds on the body are consistent with the body having rolled down a hill and through the underbrush. In my report I noted that there were numerous scratches and abrasions, all post-mortem, on the body. Those could have been inflicted either by the body rolling over that terrain, or being dragged through it. Either way would account for what I saw. Are there any more questions you have?"

Hazel Stevens answered: "Well, yes, there are, but it may not be in your field. It concerns the holes you found in the boy's stomach. Do they have any special significance?"

"I'm sure they do, but why do you ask?"

Fahy said: "You tell him, Gus. You found it."

Gus looked at Fahy skeptically. He had no choice but to tell the story about the death of Jimmy Hartwick and the bag with the three holes which certainly looked like the holes in Bobby Hartwick's belly. Gus ended up, saying: "We've got the autopsy pictures and pictures of the bag right here. Could you look at them and tell us what you think?"

Fahy opened the files and handed the doctor the photographs. He took them and studied them for a good five minutes before he spoke. "There's no question but that the holes in the bag and on the body are the same pattern. In each case they form an exact triangle and it certainly has a meaning, at least a symbolic meaning to the person who did it. What that meaning is, I couldn't tell you. I'm not a psychiatrist, just a humble pathologist. We had a course in psychiatry in medical school, but to tell the truth, and if you'll pardon me for saying so, I thought it was a lot of bullshit and I didn't pay that much attention. Looking at this, maybe I should have. I'll tell you what I can do, however. We've got a couple of good psychiatrists on staff over at the medical center and I'll arrange for a consultation with one of them. Have copies made of all your reports and the photographs and send them over to me first thing in the morning and I'll pass them on to one of the men on staff."

Hazel Stevens said: That will be fine, doctor. We're going to need a psychiatrist on this one soon. We'll be interviewing the mother Thursday, and if you could find someone to meet with us tomorrow afternoon or in the evening, maybe he could help us on how to proceed with her. That is going to be a very delicate confrontation, to say the least."

The prosecutor looked around the table: "Well, if we have no more questions, I think we should let Dr. Sanchez go home and get something to eat. Come to think of it, that sandwich never did get here. I'm sorry, Doctor, you must be hungry."

"Madam, if you must know the truth, I'm glad it didn't arrive. Now I have a good excuse to go over to Somerville and enjoy Japanese cuisine, starting with a large order of sushi. Would anyone care to join me? Well, if not I'll say good night, and I'll call you tomorrow about that psychiatrist."

After Sanchez left, Hazel Stevens stood up and looked at the faces around the table. Ben Harris was trying to stifle a yawn and Fahy's eyes were half-closed. "I think it's time to call it quits for tonight and go home. We've got tomorrow's assignments all set, so let's get out of here."

As they were filing out Gus said to Fahy: "Chuck, I'll call

178

you as soon as the pharmacy opens in the morning. Then I'll meet your guys and help them work Ridge Road, if that's okay with you, and I'll stop in and see that Aaron boy. He knows me by now anyway."

Chuck yawned and smiled. "Of course it's all right with me. You know, Gus, you're a glutton for punishment. I'll catch up with you sometime tomorrow."

THIRTY-ONE

Gus woke up the next morning at six and he felt lonely and he became depressed when he realized it was because Peg wasn't there. All his adult life he had lived alone and it had never bothered him. He had always wanted the independence and the freedom that came from living within himself and by himself. But now the loneliness was getting to him; he had never met any woman before Peg with whom he wanted to share his feelings. Peg seemed to be different from the others, she didn't make any demands, and she always seemed to want to help him and to share herself with him. As he lay in bed thinking about her, he decided he would be a fool not to ask her to marry him, or at least to start living together full time to see if things would work out. *What the hell, a lot of people lived together these days without getting married so why shouldn't they do it? The only real reason to get married was to have kids, and Peg doesn't want kids anyway.* He made up his mind to try the idea out on her today, if he got the chance.

By 7:30 he had showered, dressed, and had his coffee. When he looked in the garbage pail he was happy to see there wasn't enough there to bother taking it out and he wouldn't have to run into Mrs. Radcar. He called Peg, but there was no answer, she had left awfully early. He thought it was probably because of the funeral so he tried the school but there was no answer there either. He decided to go up to the Aarons' house to see if he could talk to their kid. He might as well get that out of the way and he was sure the Aarons would be up and dressed by the time he got there.

He pulled up in front of the Aarons' house at quarter to eight and he could see that Mr. Aaron's truck was gone. He went up and rang the doorbell and Becky came to the door.

"Oh, Mr. Bass, I am glad to see you. I'm having a terrible time with the boys. They don't want to go to the funeral, they think something may happen to them like it did to Bobby. They won't get dressed and say they're going to stay home from school, too. Maybe you could talk to them and explain it's something they really have to do. My husband tried, but they just won't listen to either of us."

"I'd be glad to, Becky, where are they?"

"In the kitchen, just follow me."

Before they reached the kitchen Gus could hear the boys yelling at each other. The older brother, Andy, was telling the younger boy, Jacky, that he had better not go to the funeral because Bobby might jump up and come after him and try to take him with him. Jacky was on the verge of tears. They both looked up at Gus when he walked into the kitchen.

Becky said: "See what I mean, Mr. Bass? You talk to them. You're a cop and you can tell them they're being silly."

Gus looked at each of the two boys in turn with a stern face. "What's all this nonsense I hear from your mother about you guys? Don't you know any better than this baloney about bogeymen? Look, your buddy Bobby died and when people die they don't jump up and grab anybody. They have to be buried and people go to a funeral just to say goodbye to the guy who died so he knows that you liked him and you're sorry he's dead. That's all a funeral is, just a way of saying goodbye to someone." Gus could see that he had their attention, and he continued: "What do you think Bobby would say if he thought you didn't care enough about him to say goodbye? I think he'd be pretty sore at you, that's what I think. I know I would if you didn't come to my funeral."

Jacky looked up at Gus: "Are you going to die, Mr. Bass?"

"Yeah, sometime, but not soon I hope. Look, guys, you do like your mother says and go up and get dressed. I'm going to the funeral myself and I want to see both of you there. And if I'm there, nothing's going to happen to you, I guar—an—f . . . I mean, that's a fact, okay?"

It was Andy who spoke: "Well, Mr. Bass, if you're going to be there I guess it will be all right. Will you have your gun with you?"

"You bet, Andy. Cops always have to have their guns with them at all times. That's the law. Now you get upstairs and get dressed while I talk to Jacky for a minute."

Andy ran out and Gus could hear him running up the steps.

He looked at Jacky and said: "Jacky, do you mind if I sit down? It's early but I'm tired already and I'd like to ask you a few questions, okay?"

Becky said: "So long as you're sitting down, how about a cup of coffee?"

"Gee, that would be great. Black, please. Hey, Jacky, do you drink coffee?"

"No, Mr. Bass, I'm too young to drink coffee. You have to be old to do that."

"Yeah, I forgot about that. How old are you, Jacky?"

"I'm six, but I'm going to be seven next month."

"You're not getting married or anything like that, are you?"

"Heck, no. You've got to be a lot older than that to be married. Don't you know that?"

"I guess you're right. You know you're a pretty smart guy. I bet you know a lot of stuff. You know, like all the stuff they teach you in school."

"Well, I really don't like school all that much. They've got too many girls there and they kind of louse things up for us guys."

"Well, Jacky, girls aren't so bad. You just have to get used to them, that's all. Jacky, speaking about school, you remember last Friday when you came home from school to have lunch? Did you walk home with anybody?"

"Sure, Mr. Bass, with Bobby. We always walk home together for lunch. We're in the same class so we get out together and we go home together. After school, too. Why do you want to know?"

"Oh, just thought I'd ask, that's all. Do you remember when you got to your house, did Bobby go into his house?"

"I guess so. He just kept walking on up to his house."

"This is important, Jacky. Did you see him walk into his house?"

"Nope, I don't think so. I just saw him walking up the street towards his house."

"Did you happen to notice if there was anybody else walking on the street or maybe any cars passing by?"

"I didn't see anybody else. Just Bobby."

"Well, I guess that's it. You'd better run along now and get dressed. And I'm going to look for you at the funeral, so you better be there. Is that a deal?"

"Do I really have to go, Mr. Bass?"

"I'm afraid so, Jacky. It's just one of those things we guys have to do. Don't worry about it, everything's going to be all right. I'll be there and your mom will be there and nothing's going to happen. Just remember to say goodbye to Bobby. Okay?"

Jacky ran out of the kitchen and Becky Aaron sat down at the table with Gus. Tears had formed at the corners of her eyes. "Do you have any children, Mr. Bass?"

"No, Becky, I've never been married."

"Well, I've got to tell you, if you don't already know, you've got a way with kids a lot of us don't have. It's too bad you don't have kids of your own. I think you'd make a great father."

"Becky, you're the second person who's trying to get me married off. Let's just say that I'm the bachelor type and the problem with having kids is you ought to get married first."

"Well, Gus—you don't mind if I call you Gus, do you—I've heard a lot of talk about you and Mrs. Shipley. She's a really fine woman."

"What is this, some kind of conspiracy you women have? The next thing you're going to tell me is if I get married, I won't have to take out the garbage."

Becky laughed. "I won't tell you any such thing. Stanley and I have been married for ten years and he always takes the garbage out. As a matter of fact, I think he likes to do it. But, would you mind telling me what getting married has to do with taking out the garbage?"

"It's a long story, Becky, and I'll tell you some other time. Listen, thanks for the coffee and for letting me talk to the boys. I really enjoyed that. I'll see you at the funeral."

"Gus, you're a strange man, but I'm glad you're around."

"I guess I am a little weird at that. Listen, Becky, while I'm here, did you see Bobby at any time last Friday? You know, like going back to school after lunch?"

"I did see him in the morning when he stopped by to go to school with the boys. Let's see, after lunch I think I was cleaning up in the kitchen and I'm sure I didn't see him then."

"How about Gladys? Did you see her at all on Friday?"

"No, I'm sure I didn't, except when you asked me to go over

183

and stay with her. What's this all about, Gus?"

"Nothing really, Becky. We're just trying to figure out when Bobby might have been taken. No one seems to have seen him on his way back to school and we need to know whether he got as far as the park and Creek Road. Listen, if some of the guys from the prosecutor's office stop in to see you this morning, just tell them I already spoke to you. Been good talking to you, Becky. Just one more question. Do you happen to know a Mrs. Radcar?"

"Gee, Gus, I don't think I ever heard the name. Should I know her?"

"I would think so. She's one of your co-conspirators."

"Well, then, I'd better look her up, hadn't I?"

Gus drove down to the pharmacy. He knew it wasn't likely to be open yet, but he figured he would stop next door and see Gene in the hardware store and find out if there was anything new in garbage pails. There wasn't, just the same old plastic barrels in assorted sizes. Gene suggested that if he was looking for something new in garbage, he should put in one of those compactors because it would save a lot of trips taking out the garbage.

"How do they work, Gene?"

"You put them in under a kitchen counter, just like a dishwasher, only a lot smaller. Then you put in a plastic bag and throw the garbage in. When the garbage gets to the top, you just press a button and the compactor comes down and squashes the garbage flat so you can throw more garbage in on top and keep squashing it down. They're not too expensive, would you be interested in getting one?"

"It sounds interesting, Gene, I'll think about it. Do you carry them?"

"Well I don't keep them in stock, but I can order one for you and you can have it in two or three days."

"Thanks, Gene, I'll let you know. Oh, I see Al's here. I've got to talk to him on something. I'll give you a call about that compactor."

Al Giaretta was just unlocking the front door of the Frenchtown Pharmacy when Gus walked up. "Hi, Al, can I talk to you for a minute? I need some information and maybe you can help out."

"Sure, Gus. Come on in and let me get the lights on and we can go in the back and talk."

Gus followed him intro the rear of the store behind the prescription counter. "What's on your mind, Gus?"

"Would you happen to have a customer by the name of Hartwick who gets prescriptions filled here?"

"You mean the mother of that boy who was killed last week? God, that was terrible. But to answer your question, yes, she does come in here from time to time. As a matter of fact, she was in just a few weeks ago and had a prescription filled. I remember because I had to order the drug from my distributor especially for her since I don't stock it."

"What was the drug?"

"It was a narcotic, seconal, and I've got the record right here on my computer." Al went over to his computer and typed some words in. He turned to Gus and said: "Here it is, you can see for yourself. May twentieth, I filled a prescription for her for seconal, one hundred milligrams, thirty ampules. That's the most you can dispense at one time. What's this all about, Gus, can you tell me?"

Gus was grinning. "Not now, Al. Maybe soon. Can you tell me what doctor prescribed it?"

Oh, yes, that's right here, too. Dr. Wilson from over in Riegelsville. I think he's their family doctor."

"Al, I've heard that drug isn't used much any more, is that right?"

"That's true. It used to be but not now. That's why I don't stock it."

"Well, thanks a lot, Al, you've been very helpful. I'll see you around."

"Sure, Gus, anytime."

Gus went out to his car and put a call into Fahy. This time he was in. "Chuck, you can save the guys a trip over to Bucks. I just left the pharmacy here in Frenchtown and she had a prescription filled on May twentieth for seconal. The druggist here has it all on computer."

"Good going, Gus. Maybe things are going our way for a change. They're already working on the search warrant. You'll have to come over here sometime this afternoon to sign your affidavit so we can get it to the judge today. What time do you think you'll be over?"

"Well, I promised some kids I was going to the funeral, so I can't get over until after that, say sometime around three, will that be okay?"

"No problem."

"Oh, and something else. I went up to speak to the Aaron boy this morning. He's really a bright kid. Anyway he says that he walked home from school last Friday with Bobby Hartwick and Bobby was headed for his house when he left him. And there were no cars or any people on the street."

"Did you get a written statement from him?"

"Hell, no. The kid's only six years old. There's no point in trying to get a written statement. Don't worry about that kid. He'll stand up and tell the same story he told me any time you want. Look, I'm going to head back up to Ridge Road now and see if I can help your guys out with the neighbors. Anything else you want me to do?"

"Gus, you put in a day's work already. You're on your own but just make sure you get over here to sign that affidavit. I'll see you then."

"One more thing, Chuck, before you hang up. The doctor who prescribed that seconal, his name is Wilson and he's from over in Riegelsville. That's the same guy who came to the house and said that Jimmy Hartwick's death was an accident. I think maybe it might be a good idea to have someone go over and talk to him. What do you think?"

"I agree we should try to do that. But I want to check that out with the boss-lady first and I'll let you know."

Gus drove over to Ridge Road for the second time that morning. He had no trouble spotting Amster and Walters' car and he waited for them to come out of the houses they were in. Cal came out first, from the house next to the Aarons'. "How's it going Cal, anybody see the kid?"

"No, Gus, I've been to three houses so far on this side of the block and only one person was home at all on Friday and she didn't see a thing. Says she was watching the soaps and didn't look outside at all. Christ, I think the Martians could have landed in her back yard and she'd never know it. You come up with any sightings?"

"Nope. I only been to the one house, the Aarons', so you can skip that one. I'll take the house next door to the Hartwicks and we'll keep alternating 'til we finish this side and then we can cross over and help Howie out. I've got to cut out by ten-thirty to go down to the funeral. So I'll catch up with you later over in Flemington."

Gus and Amster worked their way up the street and managed to find about a half-dozen people who were home, but no one had seen Bobby or Gladys on Friday. By 10:30, Amster and Gus had finished the west side of Ridge and Gus took off.

The funeral parlor was located on Bridge Street. It wasn't much of a place, but then they didn't get too many big funerals in Frenchtown. Gus spotted the chief's car parked across the street and he realized that he was sure to run into him sooner or later. The chief would probably insist upon leading the procession over to the cemetery. The thought crossed Gus' mind that maybe they could bury the chief there instead of Bobby, but he knew that was just wishful thinking.

Gus walked into the funeral parlor and signed the registry. The Hartwicks were already there sitting in a little alcove and receiving friends. He spotted Mrs. Degroat sitting across from them and her face was like an iron mask. He went over to the Hartwicks and expressed his condolences to them. Gladys looked up at him without any recognition. She looked exactly as he remembered her when he first saw her in her house last Friday— she just stared straight ahead looking right through him. He wished he could read her mind for just a minute and find out if she felt any guilt or even remorse for what she had done but her face and her eyes were a complete blank. He shook hands with her husband and leaned down and asked him if he could speak to him outside for just a minute. Bob Hartwick replied: "Can't it wait, Mr. Bass? I'd like to stay here with Gladys, she needs me."

"I really have to speak to you, Bob, and it'll just be a few seconds."

Bob Hartwick got up and went out the door with Gus. "Look, Bob, I hate to do this to you now, but we have to speak to you over in Flemington the first thing tomorrow morning. They'll send a car to pick you up at nine o'clock."

"I don't understand, Mr. Bass, why tomorrow and what do they want to speak to me about?"

"Bob, no one wants to do this to you, but it's necessary. We've developed some information and we have to talk to you about it."

"What kind of information? Does it have anything to do with Glad?"

Gus put his hand on Hartwick's shoulder. "I can't discuss anything with you right now. Look, just go back in and sit with your wife. I'll see you the first thing tomorrow morning."

Bob Hartwick bowed his head and shook it slowly as he walked back inside. Gus said to himself, you're a big shit, Gus, doing something like that to that poor bastard. But he knows or he suspects something about his wife, that's for sure. Just then he spotted Peg walking down Bridge Street toward him. "Peg, am I glad to see you. Can I give you a squeeze?"

"Mr. Bass, so nice to see you." Leaning toward him she whispered: "You'd better not, wait until later. There are too many people around. I've got a reputation to think about."

"For Christ's sake, Peg, half this town knows we sleep together. So what's a little squeeze?"

"Mr. Bass, I'll speak to you later. Is that all right with you?"

"It certainly is, Mrs. Shipley. As a matter of fact, I've reserved us a table at the Frenchtown Inn for lunch. I've got to talk to you about something, if that's all right with you."

"The Frenchtown Inn? My, Mr. Bass, you certainly are coming up in the world. Yes, I think I can join you there." Peg turned and walked inside and Gus followed her.

The ritual was over quickly. The Hartwicks' minister said the usual things about the slaughter of the innocents and accepting the will of "Gawd" and cherishing this little boy in our memories. And of course, he turned to the parents and told them they must bear their loss with faith in the Lord Jesus and the certainty that this boy's soul was now with the Lord in heaven. Gus wanted to stand up and yell at them about how this bitch had sent the boy's soul to heaven in a plastic bag with his penis cut off and holes in his belly. What a bunch of hypocrites.

As they started filing out, Gus went over to the Aaron boys.

"That wasn't so bad, was it guys? Did you say goodbye to Bobby?"

Jacky said: "Yeah, Mr. Bass, I did say goodbye. I miss him a lot. He was my buddy."

Gus looked away, he could feel tears starting. He choked back a sob and turned back to the boys. "Bobby would be happy, wherever he is, to hear you say that. Would you guys want me to come over and see you sometime? Maybe we could go to a ball game or something. You know they got a new team down in Trenton and I could try to get tickets for a game. Would you want to go?"

Andy looked up at Gus. "Gee, I heard about that team. Do you think you could get tickets, really?"

"Well, I'll try. You guys talk to your mother and make sure she says it's okay. Tell her I'll call her about it. She's waiting for you, you'd better be running along now. I'll see you around."

Gus turned to look for Peg, and there she was right behind him. "I heard all that, Mr. Bass, did you really mean that?"

"Of course, Mrs. Shipley." He leaned closer and said: "Come on, let's get out of here. I'm hungry and I've got to talk to you." He took her arm and they walked down Bridge Street to the Frenchtown Inn.

Gus had never been inside the Inn before and he was impressed by the long mahogany bar and the fancy bar stools. No one was behind the bar when they walked in and Gus smiled when he saw the sedate glass panel which said "Bass Ale." He said: "Look, Peg, they named a beer after me. I've got to try that."

A young woman came in, looked carefully at Gus, and said: "Do you have a reservation?"

"Yeah, miss, you named your beer after me. The name's Bass. Lunch for two."

She smiled very faintly. "Right this way, Mr. Bass. You're a little early, and I'll let you pick your own table."

They followed her into a handsome dining room, the tables all set with elegant glassware and tiny jars of flowers. Gus said: "How about that table over in the corner there? We'd like some privacy."

She led them to the table and pulled out the chair for Peg. "Would you like to look at a menu or would you like to order a drink first?"

189

"What will it be Peg?"

"You can bring me some Perrier, please."

"And you, Mr. Bass?"

"Just bring me a glass of my beer."

"Would you like it dark or light?"

"Any which way, so long as it's cold. And you can leave the menus here."

"Would you like me to tell you about our specials?"

"I don't think so. If they're so special they ought to be on the menu. We'll just order from here."

The young woman turned abruptly and stalked out. Peg looked at Gus and burst out laughing. "Gus, you were mean to her. She's only doing her job."

"Christ, I know that. I just wanted to be alone with you. I really missed you last night and when I woke up this morning I was thinking maybe it doesn't make any sense for us to be living so far apart. How about you moving in with me or I move in with you? What do you think?"

"Gus, you can't be serious. You've think I'd move out of my house and into that little apartment of yours?"

Gus's eyes blinked two or three times. "Yeah, I guess you're right. Sorry I mentioned it."

"You big idiot. You're going to move in with me, and that's the end of that. You go home right after lunch and pack up some things and come on over."

Gus grinned. "It's really all right with you? What about your reputation?"

"Gus, as you would put it, fuck my reputation. I'd rather have you with me without my reputation. That's settled."

"Honey, you've made my day. Tonight we celebrate. Oh, shit, I forgot. I've got to be over in Flemington tonight. We've got a meeting set up to go over everything. We're bringing the Hartwicks over tomorrow to question them."

"Go over what, Gus? What's going on with the case, have you picked someone up? You know I haven't spoken to you since Tuesday morning."

"I tried to reach you this morning but there was no answer at your house or the school. Listen, I probably shouldn't tell you

190

this, but we know who killed Bobby; it was Gladys Hartwick. But you can't tell a soul anything about this. After we finish questioning her tomorrow, she'll be charged with murder."

"Gus, I can't believe what you're telling me. His own mother killed him? That just can't be."

"Peg, believe me, it's true. Just this morning we nailed her for good. I don't think I told you this, but the medical examiner found that Bobby had been given a barbiturate called 'seconal' just before he was killed. Well, that's a prescription drug which is hardly ever used anymore. I checked with Al Giaretta just before I came over to the funeral and he filled a prescription for seconal for Gladys Hartwick just two weeks before Bobby was murdered. What got me onto her was that she had another child who died suddenly, did you know that? They were living over in Durham then and this kid, his name was Jimmy, was supposed to have stuck his head inside a plastic bag and suffocated himself. He was just a year and a half old at the time. Well, I went over to the state police up in Bucks yesterday and spoke to the guy who investigated Jimmy's death and he had the plastic bag. He showed it to me and it had the same three holes in the bag that were in Bobby's belly when we found him. We spent last night going over everything with the medical examiner and he agrees she did it. She killed two of her kids already. I tell you, over at the funeral parlor, when that minister was spreading all that bullshit, I wanted to stand up and tell them that this piece of shit killed her own son and pull her out of there."

Peg's eyes filled up with tears and she sobbed. "Oh, Gus, why did you have to tell me this? I don't know if I can handle it. Two minutes ago I was so happy, and now I feel all empty. Can we get out of here? I just want to go home and cry."

"I'm sorry, honey, I just thought you ought to know before it's public. I know what you're feeling, it hit me like that, too, when I heard the story from this guy and saw that fucking bag. I'm telling you when this is over, they can shove this job. I've had enough. Just sit there for a second, honey, and I'll tell the girl we've changed our minds and we'll get out of here."

Gus went into the bar and found the hostess. "Look, Miss, forget about those drinks. My friend isn't feeling too well and

I'm going to take her home. What do I owe you?"

"Well, Mr. Bass, you really didn't have anything, so there isn't any charge."

Gus pulled a five-dollar bill from his pocket and handed it to her. "Here, take this. I'm sorry we couldn't stay." He went back into the dining room and collected Peg and they left. He drove her home in his car and asked her where her car was and to give him the keys, he would have somebody pick up her car and drive it over to her house later. When they got to Peg's, he walked her in and said: "Look, Peg, do you still want me to move in with you? I know you're upset and maybe we should just wait a bit until you feel better."

"Gus, it doesn't have anything to do with you or with us. Of course I want you here. I just wish you didn't have to leave. Do you have to?"

"I'm sorry, Hon, I've got to get over to Flemington and get this thing wound up. It'll all be over in a few days, and then I start looking for a new job, I promise you." He put his arms around her and squeezed her tightly to him. "I'm coming back here tonight, no matter how late, okay? But don't you wait up. I can let myself in. I've got my own key now, remember?"

THIRTY-TWO

Gus pulled into the parking lot behind the prosecutor's office at two o'clock, and as soon as he was in the door the receptionist told him that Harris was waiting to see him and he should go right to his office. Gus went down the hall past Ms. Stevens' office and walked into Harris' room. Harris was sitting behind his desk with a stack of files and reports in front of him. He was just hanging up the phone as Gus sat down. "Gus, glad you're here. I was just speaking to Judge Benson and I made an appointment to present the search warrant application in about an hour. Here's your affidavit and I've put in the information you got from the druggist this morning. Better check the spelling of his name, I'm not sure I got it right, and if there are any changes you want made, let's do it quick so we don't keep the judge waiting."

"What's the big deal? Let him wait on us for a few minutes. It'll do him good."

"That's just the way judges are, Gus. They don't mind keeping you waiting, but they get very mad if they have to wait. It's part of wearing a black robe."

"Why, what the hell does he have to do that's so important? He's probably just sitting in his office snoozing anyway, unless he's got a golf date or something. Christ, Ben, all you lawyers ever do is play golf. It must be some kind of disease you get in law school."

Harris started laughing and then he said: "Gus, you're wrong on every count. I have never been on a golf course in my life. Second, Judge Benson is a she and not a he. And last, the judges don't play golf too much anymore. Tennis is their game now. They don't have enough time to get in a round of golf after court. It's not like the old days when they'd knock off at twelve-thirty or so. Do you play tennis, Gus?"

"Hell, no, they didn't have any tennis courts around where I grew up. We played baseball and football and the black guys played basketball. You know I batted over four hundred in my last year of high school? And after high school, I played semi-pro

193

ball for a year before I went into the army and I was hitting the ball pretty good there, too."

"So what happened after you got out of the army? Did you try playing ball again?"

"Yeah, I went back to the semi's, but somehow I kind of lost my eye and I couldn't hit a fast ball anymore. Still not bad on curve balls, but they found me out and all I saw was fast balls going by me, so I gave it up."

"Okay, Gus, get to work on that affidavit."

Gus read the document over carefully. When he finished he looked up at Harris and said: "You know, you write pretty good. You got it all down here and it tells the whole story just like it is. And you spelled Al's name right, too. Where do you want me to sign?"

"That's what I get paid for, Gus. Just sign there on the last page on that blank line."

Gus signed and handed the paper back to Harris. "Ben, did Fahy get a chance to talk to you or Ms. Stevens about this Dr. Wilson? He's the guy who gave Gladys the prescription for the seconal. I'd really like to talk to him and see if he knows something, and find out why he prescribed that drug for her. You heard what Sanchez said, no one uses that drug any more and the druggist over in Frenchtown told me the same thing."

"The only problem there is that he really can't tell you anything very much. There's a physician-patient privilege and he can't tell you what she told him or what he was treating her for, not even if he wanted to. It's the same as the lawyer-client privilege."

"I always figured you guys invented that privilege crap to cover your own asses. I don't know why you had to do the same thing for the doctors. Just the same, I would like to talk to him about their other son, Jimmy, and why he was so sure it was accidental, you know what I mean? That wouldn't be privileged, would it?"

"No, it wouldn't, that's true. He would have been treating the boy and not her, so he could tell you what he saw and what he did. As a matter of fact, he could tell you anything she said, too. That wouldn't be privileged."

"That's good. Christ, Ben, you really know the law, don't you?"

"Like I said, that's what I get paid for, Gus. Just like you get paid for doing your thing, and I've got to hand it to you, you're one of the best I've seen at your job. You just have a knack for getting people to open up and tell you things. I could never do that in a million years and most of the cops I've run into can't do it either. I guess you have to be born with it."

"Maybe, Ben. It's about the only thing I was born with besides being able to hit a curve ball. Look, can you clear it with Ms. Stevens for me to go over and speak to this Dr. Wilson?"

"She's not around right now. She had to go to a meeting down at the AG's office in Trenton. But you go right ahead and speak to Wilson. I'll tell her I gave you permission when she gets back. Just make sure you're back here for the meeting."

Gus shook hands with Harris and left. As soon as he reached his car he got Dr. Wilson's number from information and called his office. The receptionist said the doctor was in and asked if he wanted an appointment. "My name is Gus Bass, and tell the Doc I've got to see him right away. It's about Gladys Hartwick."

She came back on the line and said the doctor could see him at three o'clock. Gus looked at his watch, it was only 2:30, and he said he'd be there by three. The ride over to Riegelsville was uneventful and Gus had no problem finding his office, it was right on 611 just up aways from Sally's Place. When Gus walked into the office, the receptionist smiled and said that Dr. Wilson was finishing up with a patient and would be with him in a few minutes. Gus sat down and picked up a brochure about the danger of the silent killer, high blood pressure and he wondered what his blood pressure was. He didn't remember having his blood pressure checked since he had his physical when they pensioned him off down in Trenton. They hadn't said anything about it then, so it might have been all right. Maybe he should get it checked soon.

A door opened and an elderly woman limped through the waiting room and out the front door. Then a tall, gray-haired man with a substantial gut on him came towards Gus and introduced himself as Dr. Wilson. Gus followed the doctor into his office and was invited to sit, which he did.

. Wilson's hands were folded around his paunch. "Now, Mr. Bass, what did you want to see me about? Kate said it has to do with Gladys Hartwick."

"That's right, Doc. I'm with the Frenchtown Police Department and we're investigating the murder of Bobby Hartwick. You heard about that, didn't you?"

"Yes, I did. Bobby's father called me last Saturday morning and told me. If you want to know, I've been expecting someone from the police to come ever since, and now you're here."

"Geez, Doc, it must be something about Bucks County. Almost everybody I talk to over here on this case has been waiting for me to come see them. Why were you expecting me, if you don't mind telling me?"

"Because I was the one who signed the death certificate when Jimmy Hartwick died a long time ago. Did you know that?"

"Yeah, I found that out from Lieutenant Schoop yesterday. He showed me the file he had and that's one of the things I wanted to talk to you about. Did you know he kept the plastic bag you said the kid had suffocated himself in?"

"No, I wasn't aware of that. What difference does it make?"

"It makes a whole lot of difference, Doc, 'cause there's no way that kid could have killed himself with that bag and I think you knew it."

Wilson frowned. "To say I knew it is not correct, Mr. Bass. Let's say it puzzled me how it happened, but I'm not a policeman. I'm a doctor and the child was dead and nothing could be done to help him or the Hartwicks."

"That may be true, Doc, but if she killed Bobby, and we know she did, she never would have had a chance to kill him. And I think that's really why you were expecting somebody to come and see you, isn't it?"

Dr. Wilson's face sagged. "Mr. Bass, I know what you're saying and I won't argue with you. Even since I received that call last Saturday I've been telling myself the same thing and I am finding it awfully difficult to live with the idea. You've got to believe that."

"Oh, I do, Doc. That's one of the problems with playing God, isn't it? You've got a conscience to live with and He doesn't."

Dr. Wilson remained silent for some time. He looked away from Gus and finally he looked back at him. "Look, Mr. Bass, there's a lot more to this than you know about and I think it's about time I told the story of Gladys Wilkins Hartwick. It's not a pretty story but maybe it will help you understand why I did or didn't do what I did. The story goes back a long time ago, long before she was married. Do you have the time to listen?"

"I've got the time all right. But before you tell me anything, I've been warned about the doctor-patient privilege, and if it's anything Gladys told you as her doctor, then you can't tell me and I'd better not listen."

"I know all about the privilege that exists between doctor and patient. I can assure you that what I'm about to tell you is not privileged. It wasn't told to me by Gladys, but by her mother."

"Her mother? I was told she died a long time ago. How could she tell you this?"

"She told me shortly before she died. That was in 1984, almost ten years ago. Gladys and her mother—her name was Henrietta Wilkins—were living in Durham. Mrs. Wilkins was divorced from her husband by then, his name was Roger. After they moved to Durham I was treating the mother for a serious heart condition. She was an obese woman and her heart was extremely enlarged. She suffered from recurrent congestive heart failure and it was impossible to manage her care or to do anything for her because she refused to do anything to control her weight. You know, Mr. Bass, one of the hardest things we doctors have to deal with is a patient who is slowly killing herself and refuses to do anything about it. We do have patients, you know, who want to die and refuse to save themselves. That was Mrs. Wilkins."

"Did she have high blood pressure, too?"

"Yes, of course, her blood pressure was very elevated. Why do you ask, is that important?"

"Well, actually no, Doc, I was just wondering about blood pressure, that's all."

"Toward the end she was very ill and almost immobile. I saw her in the hospital shortly before she died and that was a day

197

I'll never forget. She knew she was dying and she said that she deserved to die and she wanted to tell me why. And then she told me the story. She hated her husband, Roger, and after her son, Roger Junior was born, she refused to have any marital relationship with her husband. Gladys was eleven years old at the time and she was a pretty girl. Within a few months after Roger Junior was born, he husband stopped making any sexual demands upon her, and she was relieved. Not long after that she became aware of the reason. Her husband was having a sexual relationship with Gladys. I told her that couldn't be true, but she said that she had actually seen them in bed together. She never confronted them and this relationship between her husband and Gladys continued until she separated from her husband and took Gladys to live with her in Durham. She did nothing to put a stop to it, because, as she said, it made her own life easier.

"After this had been going on for about three years, before the separation, Henrietta discovered that her husband's brother, Hiram, was also having sex with Gladys. The father used to take her to Hiram's house on Saturdays and Sundays and both of them would have sex with her. Mrs. Wilkins said she followed them there and actually saw what was going on, and still she did nothing to stop it.

"Not long after that, Roger Junior drowned and she had a confrontation of sorts with her husband. She told him she knew what was going on with him and Gladys and with Hiram. You see she suspected that maybe Gladys had something to do with her son's death, and that made her responsible because she had let the situation continue without doing anything about it and she thought they had probably driven Gladys insane.

"Those were her words, Mr. Bass, that Gladys was probably insane. She said she knew she was going to die and she had to tell somebody before she did so that whatever Gladys had done, someone would know it wasn't her fault, that it was her fault for not having stopped her husband when she should have. She said that she should have killed her husband and Hiram, but instead her son was dead and she was responsible for it, not Gladys. The last thing she said to me was that I should try to watch out for Gladys and help her if I could."

Dr. Wilson paused briefly and then continued: "By that time,

Gladys had married Bob Hartwick, and she was pregnant. Little Jimmy was born about six or seven months after Henrietta died, and for years I have kept a close watch over Gladys. She comes to see me once a month and we just talk. Jimmy died almost eight years ago and I really believed that if Gladys had caused his death, whatever illness she was suffering from which caused her to do it, she would never be capable of killing another human being. That's the story, Mr. Bass."

Gus sat with his eyes closed and there was complete silence in the room for a very long time. It was the doctor who spoke: "I know it's a horrible story, Mr. Bass, and you can condemn me all you want for what I didn't do eight years ago."

Gus' eyes snapped open. "Look, Doc, it's not my job to condemn anybody. My job is only to find out what the facts are and report them to the people who can do something about it. I don't give a rat's ass if she's sane or insane or something in between. I don't decide those things. But I got to tell you this woman killed three children already, and she's still got a three year old boy living in her house. And no matter what you may have thought, she ain't cured of anything and she could kill again. If she does, it's going to be Ricky. So Doc, you're going to have to tell the prosecutor across the river exactly what you told me so we make sure Ricky doesn't end up dead like the others. Are you willing to do that? If not, I'm sure those lawyers over there will figure out some way of making you, and it will be a whole lot easier for you and them if you just come over voluntarily."

"Mr. Bass, I'll do whatever you think best."

Gus stood up. "One more thing before I leave. You know the only thing we got is Mrs. Wilkins' statement to you. Maybe it's true and maybe it isn't. Maybe she was crazy herself and just told you a lot of crap. But there's one way we can check it out and that is to find her father. You have any idea where he or his brother might be?"

"Gladys has never mentioned her father to me and I'm sure she doesn't know where he is. Mrs. Wilkins once told me, after their divorce, that her husband was living somewhere out in western Pennsylvania with a woman young enough to be his daughter. As for Hiram, he's dead at least five years. He killed himself in an automobile crash. He was dead drunk at the time and drove into a tree on River Road down in Upper Black Eddy. The Wilkins were some family, weren't they?"

"Doc, do you think whatever is wrong with Gladys could be in her genes or something? I've read somewhere about there being criminal genes that get passed on from the parents to their children. Christ, that family had enough bad genes to fuck up a hundred kids."

"Mr. Bass, I really don't know anything about that. I'm just a family doctor and I'm not too good at that, as you can tell."

"I wouldn't say that, Doc, you can check my blood pressure anytime. Look, I'll get out of your hair now. I've got to get back for a meeting and you'll probably be getting a call in the next day or two from a guy by the name of Harris, he's the first assistant prosecutor over in Flemington and he's one hell of a lawyer. So long, Doc, and thanks for your time."

Gus walked out of the office, got into his car, and went back across the river.

THIRTY-THREE

Gus was at the prosecutor's office before six and went in to see if any of the guys wanted to grab a bite before the meeting. The front room was deserted and Gus walked down the hall and then he heard the sound of voices coming from Ms. Stevens' office. He stuck his head in the open doorway and Ms. Stevens, Harris, Fahy, Sloss, Carter, and a young, attractive blond woman were seated around Ms. Stevens' conference table on which there was a large platter of sandwiches, potato salad, cole slaw, and pickles. Ms. Stevens said: "I don't think you've met Susan Sturz, Gus. She our newest assistant prosecutor. Susan, this is Gus Bass who's been working on the case with us. Have you eaten, Gus? If not help yourself. It's not much but we'll do better when this is finally wrapped up."

"Thanks, Ms. Stevens, I am kind of hungry. I haven't had anything to eat since this morning and I forget what it was I had then." Gus sat down and loaded up a paper plate with a generous sampling of everything on the table and started eating.

Ms. Stevens said: "Gus, I heard that you have been busy. Ben told me you were going over to interview this Dr. Wilson. Did you get anything useful from him?"

"Yes, Ms. Stevens, he had quite a story to tell. Can I just eat a bit first, it's going to take a while to tell you."

"Sure, Gus, go ahead and eat. I was just about to describe my visit to the AG's office." She had received a call early in the afternoon from the AG's office to meet with the director of the criminal justice division, Matt Boylan. When she met with him, she had been told that Chief Winters had filed a complaint against Fahy and the office for interfering with his authority as the Chief of Police in Frenchtown, and Boylan wanted to know what it was all about. She told him the story of what had happened on Friday afternoon and Saturday morning with the chief and that she was trying to decide whether to press charges against him. He was simply incompetent to handle the job and should be replaced. Boylan agreed with her and said he would work on it. The chief had also asked for an investigation of Baumgart's death, and she told him he should send someone up to listen to the tapes of Gus' interrogation of Baumgart and the report on Baumgart's death. He said that it was really not necessary, but that for the record we should send him copies and the matter would be disposed of satisfactorily. "He asked how we were making out on the case, and I told him there would probably be an arrest tomorrow."

"That's my news, Gus, what do you have for us on Dr. Wilson?"

Gus put down the sandwich he was holding in his hand and proceeded to relate to them the story as he had gotten it from the doctor. By the time he finished, Ms. Stevens looked ill and the others were just sitting and slowly shaking their heads. Ben said: "It looks like it's going to be an insanity defense. I thought it would be, but if any of this is true, we're going to have a tough time getting a conviction. Is there any way we can check his story out, Gus?"

Gus shook his head. "It's going to be tough. The mother is dead, Hiram is dead, and no one knows where her father is or even if he's still alive. So how do we check it out?"

Fahy said: "Well, we can start with the Pennsylvania state criminal records and the FBI. If he's as much of a bastard as that, he's likely to have a record somewhere and we can trace him. If not, we can try to pick up his social security number and get a lead from them. We'll get started on that first thing tomorrow."

Hazel Stevens asked: "What plans do we have to bring the parents over tomorrow?"

Gus replied that he had told the father a car would pick him up at nine in the morning to bring him over to Flemington. "It's a funny thing. When I told him we had to talk to him, the first thing he asked was whether it had anything to do with his wife. Do you suppose he suspects something?"

Sloss said: "He damn well ought to suspect something. Two of his kids get suffocated in plastic bags. He'd have to be as crazy as she is if he didn't."

Ben said: "See what I mean, boss? Even Sloss thinks she's insane, and that's what a jury will think, too. And with this story

202

about her and her father, all the bleeding hearts will have a field day and say it's not her fault, she is the victim. There's going to be a hell of a sympathy factor here, you wait and see."

Gus put down what was left of his sandwich. "Ben, what the hell's the matter with you? This woman killed three little kids, and every one of those killings was planned and premeditated. Every time she made sure there were no witnesses around and she had a story all ready when the cops showed up. She knew what she was doing all right, and she made sure she wouldn't get caught, and she didn't until this time. Christ, you want to throw in the towel already."

The prosecutor looked at Gus. "Calm down. No one's throwing in any towel. We're going to prosecute her all the way. Ben's only saying that we have to be careful how we do it."

Fahy said: "I've got more news which should really tie up this case for good. Bert Williams and Amster went over that embankment behind the Hartwicks' house right down the slope to where the body was found. They found a kind of a trail from the top right on down to the bottom of the hill where the underbrush was still matted down and there were broken twigs and vines and pieces of torn flesh still on some of the thorns, which they took over to Sanchez and he is going to try to match them with samples of the boy's skin. There's no doubt she dragged or rolled the body down that slope and put him under that tree. You were right, Gus, how she got the body down there. I'm going to have a surveyor go over tomorrow and measure out the distance from the top of the embankment down to the tree and plot out that trail the guys found on a survey. They got a lot of photos and they're being printed up right now."

Stevens said: "Okay, let's be back at eight-thirty tomorrow morning. I think Chuck and Gus should start with the husband as soon as he gets here, and that will give you time to work out your approach. Let's assume we spend the morning with him and we bring her over around noon or early afternoon. I want Ben and Susan to sit in with you when you interrogate her and I want a court reporter taking it down. We'll have to mirandize her before any questioning begins and if she asks for a lawyer, we stop immediately. Ben I think you should alert the public defender's office that we may be calling them if she requests a lawyer. If she is willing to talk to us without a lawyer, I want Fahy and Gus to do the interrogation. If you get nowhere with her, then let's break for a while and speak to the husband and see if he can talk her into submitting to a polygraph examination. Remind him that he still has one son left and if she is left free, his son will be at risk. Find out if they have a minister or a priest and maybe we can get him in to help out. Anybody have any other thoughts about tomorrow?"

Fahy said: "I think maybe it's time we brought over that Miller girl, you know the one who found the body, and get a formal statement from her as to exactly what she saw so we can tie it in with what Williams and Amster found today. I'll send Howie over in the morning to pick her up when he picks up the husband."

The prosecutor stood up and said: "All right then, it's time to go home. We've got a long day coming up."

As soon as Gus was in his car he called Peg and told her he would be coming over after he picked up some clothes at his place. She asked if he had eaten and he said he had a quick bite, and maybe she could just heat up some of that pasta from the other night.

"There is some left, but are you sure that will be enough?"

"Absolutely, I'm cutting back on what I eat, remember?"

"I remember what you said, but I'm not sure you really meant it, Gus. If that's what you want, that's what you'll get."

"Okay, Honey, I'll see you in less than an hour."

Gus was at Peg's house by nine o'clock and as soon as he walked in he could smell the pasta. He was carrying a duffel bag with a couple of changes of clothes which he put down in the living room and he went into the kitchen. Peg was standing in front of the stove stirring the pasta and he went over to her and gave her a bear hug and kissed the back of her neck.

"Honey, that pasta smells better than the first time. I'm ready to *mangia*. Where's the Stoly?"

She turned to him with a frown on her face: "Is this what it's going to be like, you coming home at all hours and I've got to stay up all night and cook for you and get you a drink?"

Gus stopped short. "Honey, what do you mean? You know I had to go over to Flemington. The case is breaking wide open and we had to set everything up for tomorrow. I'm sorry. Look, you don't have to make me anything to eat. I told you I wasn't that hungry."

Peg's face broke into a smile. "Gus, don't you know when I'm teasing? Honey, I'll cook for you anytime you get home. Just make sure you get home. You know it's lonely around here without you."

Gus walked over to her and embraced her and they kissed passionately. "Time out, lover boy. You're going to eat this pasta first. The Stoly is in the cabinet next to the fridge so just pour yourself a drink and cool down for a bit."

Gus got his drink and sat down at the table in the kitchen. Peg brought over the pasta and set it down in front of Gus and she sat down opposite him. "So, what happened after you left me today?"

"That's a long story, Honey, and it ain't pretty." Gus proceeded to tell her of his interview with Dr. Wilson and the meeting at the prosecutor's office. When he finished there were tears in Peg's eyes just starting to roll down her cheeks.

"Gus, that's horrible. What a life that poor woman has had. To be raped by her own father and her uncle and then to end up killing her own kids. It's a nightmare, not a life. Do you think she knows she killed her boys?"

"Christ, Peg, she planned all three murders carefully so she wouldn't be caught. She had to know what she was doing, all right."

"I don't know, Gus. How could she live with herself, killing her own kids? If she wasn't crazy already, that would drive her crazy."

Gus shrugged. "Yeah, that's going to be the problem. The lawyers and the shrinks are going to have a field day with an insanity defense. Ben Harris sounds like he is all ready to cut a deal. I just don't buy it, that's all. When you are responsible for killing anyone, especially the way she did, you damn well know it and you don't forget it, believe me."

"Gus, you've got to get over what happened in Vietnam. This isn't the same thing. She actually killed these kids, you didn't kill anybody."

"Like hell I didn't. I killed my own brother and that's

something I will never forget."

Peg pushed herself back from the table. "Gus, what are you talking about, you never hurt a fly. You couldn't hurt anyone and you know it."

"I did, Peg, so help me I did. My brother was only three years old and I killed him." Gus put his head down on the table and started to sob convulsively. Peg got up and threw her arms around him, kissing the top of his head and started crying with him.

After a few minutes, Gus lifted his head up. "Peg, I've never told anyone this, but you have to know. It all happened when I was ten and my brother, Bobby, was just three. That kid idolized me. He would follow me everywhere he could and I really loved him. You know it really makes you feel good to have someone look up to you that way. I used to play baseball with him all the time, you know throw a ball to him and he would try to catch it. Well, one day we were playing in front of the house and I was throwing the ball to him and I guess I threw it too high for him. He missed it and the ball rolled into the driveway and down into the street. He ran after it and I yelled at him to stop, but he didn't, he just ran after that ball right into the street. A car was coming and the driver never had a chance. Bobby never knew what hit him. He was dead there in the street. And it was my fault. I killed him. We should never have been playing there. I shouldn't have thrown the ball so high he couldn't catch it. I should have been able to stop him. There it is and that's something I'll never forget. The sight of that kid running after the ball and the car and the sound of his little body being hit."

"Gus, you poor sweet Gus, you've been torturing yourself all these years for what? You didn't intend what happened. It was an accident, it was tragic, it was horrible, but it was an accident. These things happen, no one intends them. You didn't murder him. How can you compare what happened to your brother with what this woman did to her children?"

"Dead is dead. What difference does it make whether I wanted it to happen? It wouldn't have happened if I hadn't thrown him that ball."

"Gus, didn't you ever talk to your priest or anyone about this?"

"No, Peg. What was the use? When I saw that car hit Bobby, I knew there couldn't be a God or he wouldn't have let it happen. What could a priest do, tell me that God forgave me my sin when I knew there wasn't any God?"

"Gus, what am I going to do with you? You've condemned yourself because you wanted to be punished for something you didn't do. Haven't you punished yourself enough all these years? Forget about God or forgiveness. You're alive and you're just sacrificing your life, destroying it with all those ifs and shouldn'ts. Don't you see that? Do you think that little boy would have wanted you to die with him the way you have?"

"I don't know, Honey. It's been part of me for so long, it's hard to let go. God knows, I've tried to tell myself everything you've been saying, but it's just so deep inside me, maybe I don't want to let it go."

"Gus, we're going to work on it. You know, it's like a wound to your body. It can only heal if you treat it. And when it's your mind that's wounded, the only way to treat it is to talk about it. But right now, we're going to bed and we're just going to love each other. That can help, too."

THIRTY-FOUR

Peg woke up first and looked over at Gus. He was sleeping peacefully and snoring lightly. She made up her mind and nudged him until his eyes opened. "What time is it?"

Peg stroked his face gently: "Don't worry about the time, Honey, it's still early."

His eyes closed again. "Good, I can go back to sleep. Wake me up at seven, okay?"

"Gus, you're not going back to sleep. We've got to talk."

"I can't talk. It's too early to talk."

Peg sat straight up: "Gus, I want to get married, that's what we've got to talk about."

His eyes opened quickly, but his mouth remained closed. "Gus, I've decided I want to have a baby, and we have to get married."

Now Gus sat up: "Peg, you're not pregnant, are you?"

"Not yet, but I'm going to get pregnant and we have to get married first. Do you understand?"

Gus was wide awake now. "Christ, Honey, you're too old to have a kid." After a pause, he asked: "Aren't you?"

"What do you mean, I'm too old. There's a woman over in Italy who was in her sixties and she had a baby. I'm only thirty-eight and that's not too old. I've been thinking, Gus. I've always wanted a child. My whole career has been teaching children and trying to help them, and I've never had a child of my own. It doesn't make sense and I want my own child to love and to care for. And it's got to be your child, so we have to get married."

His brows knit and after a pause, Gus said: "I don't know, Peg. Getting married is one thing, but having a child is a whole something else. I don't know if I'm ready for that."

"Gus, for God's sake, you're forty-two years old. If you're not ready by now, when will you be ready, when you're seventy-five? Honey, we can have a good life together. We love each other or at least I love you, and we've got a lot to give a child. A lot of love, a good home, and caring for others and not just ourselves."

"Peg, Honey, you know I love you, but I'm not sure I like myself enough to be responsible for a child." Gus smiled for the first time since he was awake. "Besides, you know I swear a lot and that wouldn't be so good for a kid to grow up on."

Peg dove on top of him and pinned him down. She kissed him and her hand slid down his stomach. "Gus, we're going to start getting me pregnant right now, married or not, here I come. Start crowing."

It was after seven when Gus climbed out of bed. Peg was sleeping and he shook her gently. "Honey, I've got to get going. I love you. Let me know when we're getting married. I want to be there."

THIRTY-FIVE

By 8:15, Gus was walking into the prosecutor's office. As he walked down the hall he could smell the coffee and walked into the tiny kitchen. Fahy was there pouring himself a cup. "I figured it would be you, Gus. You're like me, I guess you couldn't sleep, either."

"Oh, I slept all right, Chuck. As a matter of fact, I slept so well I've decided to get married. You can't sleep any better than that. Pour me a cup, too."

Fahy stared at him. "Are you kidding me, Gus? You get married? I thought you had more sense than that at your age."

Gus grinned: "I thought so, too, but I kind of got talked into it. Someone made me an offer I couldn't refuse. You know how that is."

Shaking his head Fahy said: "Well, I'll be damned. Gus, what will happen next? You're certainly full of surprises. I guess I better say congratulations and who's the unlucky woman, that school teacher you've been hanging out with?"

"Christ, you heard about her? I thought they only knew over in Frenchtown. Anyway, she's the one and she ain't a teacher. She's the assistant principal over there."

Fahy grinned as he put his arm around Gus' shoulder: "Well, Gus, all I can say is you're marrying up in the world. Look, I think it's great and I'd like to meet her and tell her she's getting a real good guy. I mean that, Gus."

"Thanks, Chuck. I'd like you to meet her. Maybe we can all go out to have dinner when this mess is over with."

"Speaking of this mess, we've got some work to do. Let's go up to my office and start working. I'll be go to hell, Gus Bass, a married man. Next thing you know, you'll be having kids."

"We're working on that, too. Let's get this thing wrapped up and you'll be best man at the wedding, how's that?"

"As Sloss would say, you're on, pal."

By 9:15, Gus and Fahy were ready for Bob Hartwick and at 9:30 Fahy was buzzed by the receptionist that Mr. Hartwick was downstairs. He and Gus walked down to the interrogation room and Hartwick was brought in by Walters, who said that the Miller girl was down the hall with Carter giving a statement. Fahy asked Hartwick to sit down and when he had done so, Hartwick asked why he had been brought over.

Fahy's face had a blank expression as he said: "I think you know why you're here, Bob. You want to tell us about it?"

"I don't know what you're talking about. All I know is my son was murdered and now you want to talk to me. What about?"

"Bob, you know how your son was killed, don't you? He was suffocated with a plastic bag. You know that."

Hartwick stared down at the table and was silent. Gus said: "Look, Hartwick, you had a kid named Jimmy who was suffocated with a plastic bag almost eight years ago. You never said a word to us about Jimmy. How come? Why did you make us go all over Bucks County to find out you had another son who was killed?"

Hartwick looked up at Gus. "What do you mean, killed? It was an accident. The doctor said so."

Gus barked at him: "Why didn't you tell us about Jimmy?"

Hartwick looked away from Gus: "I just don't know why. It didn't seem to have anything to do with Bobby. Somebody took Bobby and killed him. When Jimmy died it was different, it was an accident."

"Nobody took Bobby. He was killed right in your own house and you know that. And you know who killed him."

Hartwick grabbed his head with both hands and was shaking from side to side. "No, no, it couldn't be. Somebody took him, she didn't kill him."

"Who's the she, Hartwick?"

Hartwick now looked up at Gus and Fahy: "I know what you're trying to do. You want me to say it was Gladys, but she had nothing to do with it. She couldn't have. You're all wrong. She didn't do it."

Fahy took over. "Bob, there's certain things we know that maybe you don't know. Like for instance, the medical examiner found that someone had given Bobby seconal in the milk he drank for lunch before he was killed. Did you have seconal in the house?"

211

Hartwick's brows knotted. "What the hell is that?"

"It's a drug that doctors prescribe sometimes for people who can't sleep. Did Gladys have trouble going to sleep?"

He nodded: "Yeah, sometimes she did."

"Why was that, Bob?"

Shaking his head Hartwick said: "I don't know, she just had trouble sleeping, that's all. It happens to a lot of people, doesn't it?"

Gus bore in. "You know a woman over in Springtown by the name of Jean Albertson?"

Hartwick's eyes almost popped out of his head. His voice was now excited as he said: "What does she have to do with this?"

"We don't know. Just answer the question. Do you know her or don't you?"

"I've seen her a few times."

"More than a few times, wasn't it? As a matter of fact, you and Gladys had a lot of fights about Jean, didn't you? And didn't Gladys make you move out of Durham to break it up between you and Jean?"

Hartwick seemed to be trying to withdraw himself from the scene by crunching his shoulders and casting his head down: "Who's been telling you all this?"

Gus said: "Never mind who's been telling us. Just answer the question. Did you and Gladys fight about this Albertson woman?"

Hartwick sat back in the chair and was silent. Finally he answered: "Yeah, I was seeing Jean and Gladys found out and we fought about it."

"And Gladys made you move out of Durham to break it up, didn't she?"

"Yeah."

"That was about a year ago, wasn't it?"

"I guess so."

"When did you start seeing Jean again?"

"Maybe two or three months ago."

"And Gladys found out about it, didn't she?"

"Yeah, she did. She raised all kinds of hell. She said she was going to leave me with the kids and take off."

"When was that, Bob?" Fahy asked.

"About two or three weeks ago. I was pretty pissed off. I told her if she wanted to go to get the hell out. I didn't need her and the kids didn't need her either. It was a dumb thing to say, but I was really pissed with her."

"So what happened then, Bob?"

"Nothing happened. She just stopped carrying on about Jean, and I figured I had called her bluff and she got off my back for awhile."

"Do you know Dr. Wilson?" Gus asked.

"Yeah, he's been Glad's doctor for a long time."

"Did you know Dr. Wilson had prescribed seconal for your wife to take if she couldn't sleep?"

"How the hell would I know that? I never saw Dr. Wilson and I don't know what he gave her. It could have been anything."

"Well, we happen to know that Dr. Wilson prescribed seconal for Gladys just a few weeks ago. For Christ's sake, don't you ever look in your medicine cabinet?"

"Yeah, there was something in there she got at the drug store, but I don't know what it was. I didn't look at the label."

"Is it still there?"

Now Hartwick was almost belligerent as he said: "How the hell would I know? You think I check to see what the hell is in the medicine cabinet every day?"

"If you want to know what I think, Hartwick, I don't think you think about anything but your friend Jean and fucking her up in that trailer."

Hartwick slumped down in his chair. "Christ, leave Jean out of this. She didn't have anything to do with what happened to Bobby."

"Then who did?"

Hartwick slumped over in his chair: "I don't know, I tell you. I don't know."

"We believe you, Bob. You probably don't know. But you sure as hell have an idea. Maybe you don't want to admit it, but don't tell us that you haven't thought to yourself she killed Bobby."

Hartwick shook his head violently: "She couldn't have. I'm telling you, she couldn't."

"And we're telling you she did. There's something else you don't know about. You know where Bobby was found? He was under a tree and that tree is right under the embankment from your backyard. Yesterday, two of my men went over there and they found a trail of broken vines and branches leading from your backyard right down to the tree. And they found pieces of Bobby's skin on thorns along that trail. So that's how she got rid of his body, she dragged him down that slope and left him there under the tree to rot."

Hartwick slumped forward throwing his chest and head onto the table with his arms stretched out in front of him. He began to sob and his voice was thick: "No, no, it can't be."

Fahy looked over at Gus: "I think it's time for a break. Why don't you get us some coffee, Gus?"

He looked down at Hartwick and said: "Just take it easy, Bob. Rest there for a few minutes." There was no response.

Gus was back in about ten minutes and handed Fahy a cup of coffee and placed another cup on the table alongside Hartwick, who hadn't moved since Gus had left. He had stopped sobbing and Gus said: "Hartwick, here's your coffee." Hartwick raised himself up from the table and slumped back in his chair. He still said nothing. It was Gus who spoke. "If you don't want the coffee, that's okay. But we got to talk now about your son Jimmy. I spoke to the cop who was on that case and he told me there was no way your son could have suffocated himself in that plastic bag. As a matter of fact, he still has the bag and we have pictures of it, if you want to see them. Now, what we want to know is whether you ever spoke to your wife about how Jimmy died."

The response was immediate. "She told me it was an accident, that she was in the kitchen cooking and Jimmy was in the living room playing with his toys. She didn't hear anything from him for awhile and when she went to check on him, he was dead on the floor with the bag over his head. That's what she said and so did the coroner."

"Hartwick, it was no accident. She killed him just as sure as you're sitting there. That bag was made of heavy plastic and there's no way your son could have killed himself by sticking the bag over his head. Besides, did you know there were three holes punched in that bag? The same three holes that she carved in Bobby's belly? Want to see the pictures?"

Hartwick lowered his head and the tears were streaming

down his face. "I don't want to see any pictures. I just want to get out of here."

"You know, Hartwick, I did some checking around over in Bucks, and I heard before Jimmy died, you were chasing broads. Is that true?"

"Who told you that? For God's sake, why do you keep harping on that stuff?"

"How about answering the question? Were you involved with any women around the time Jimmy was killed?"

"I don't know. That was a long time ago. Maybe I was staying out a few nights. What the hell, every guy does that."

"Did you and your wife ever fight about your staying out a few nights?"

"We may have. I can't remember exactly. That was a long time ago, you know."

"Cut the bullshit, Hartwick. You and Gladys were fighting about it and you know it."

"So what if we were, what's that got to do with it?"

"I'm not sure, but both times your sons were killed, you and Gladys were fighting about you chasing women. Did you ever think about that?"

Hartwick again slumped down in his chair and he didn't respond. They sat there for a good five minutes in complete silence. Finally, Fahy said: "Bob, drink some coffee. It'll help."

"I don't want any coffee. I just want out of here."

"Look, Bob, we need your help. Your wife is a killer and we're going to arrest her this afternoon for the murder of your son Bobby."

"Oh, no, you can't do that, it'll kill her."

Gus erupted. "Who gives a shit? She's killed three kids already, so what if it kills her?"

"What do you mean, three kids? You know you're crazy. Where the hell do you come off saying she killed anybody?"

"She had a brother who was four years old when she killed him, too. Want to hear about it? She drowned him in a lake."

"She never told me she had a brother."

"And I bet she never told you she was raped by her father and her uncle, did she?"

Hartwick stood up and turned to Fahy: "Mr. Fahy, what is

215

he talking about? This is all crazy. You've got to let me out of here."

Fahy grabbed him by the arm. "Bob, it's not crazy, it's a fact. She definitely killed both of your sons and we think she killed her brother a long time ago. But that's not why we're telling you all this. You've got a three-year-old in the house and he could be next. If we don't put her away now, she could very well kill him, too. We're only trying to protect him. That's why you've got to help us."

There was no response from Hartwick. He sat down in his chair and just stared at the table in front of him.

"All right, Hartwick, what's it going to be? Are you going to help or let your last son get killed, too?"

There was a prolonged silence in the room. Finally, Hartwick said: "All right, what do you want me to do?"

Fahy heaved a sigh of relief.

"We're sending someone over to pick your wife up and bring her over here. When she gets here, we're going to put her into a room with you and we want you to talk to her and tell her we know she killed Bobby and she has got to come clean and tell us what she did and how she did it. Then we're going to read her her rights and question her unless she wants a lawyer. That's what's going to happen and there's nothing you can do about it except to convince her she has to cooperate with us. Do you think you can do that?"

"I don't know. I still don't believe she did it, any of it you've been telling me. It just isn't Gladys. She couldn't hurt anyone."

Gus stood up.

"Okay, if that's what you think, let me bring you the pictures and you'll see what she did to your kids." Gus walked out of the room.

Hartwick started to sob and looked pleadingly at Fahy. He said: "Mr. Fahy, I don't want to look at any pictures. I'll do what you tell me, but please don't make me look at any pictures of Bobby."

Fahy reached over and put his hand on Hartwick's shoulder. "Okay, Bob, but we want you to be convinced that what we're telling you isn't bullshit. It's fact and you've got to face up to it."

Shaking his head, Hartwick said: "All right, I'll do what you

216

say, but I tell you it isn't going to do any good."

"All you can do is try, and that's all we're asking you to do. Just stay here and I'll let you know when Gladys gets here, is that okay with you?"

"Who's going to take care of Ricky while we're here?"

"That's all taken care of. Ricky will be at Mrs. Aaron's house and she'll look after him. Now stay here until I call for you."

Fahy got up and left the room and walked down the hall to his office. Gus was sitting there with Sloss. "He says he'll talk to her. Do you think it'll do any good?"

Gus: "I doubt it. I think she hates his guts anyway. I think we should go after her cold turkey and leave him out of it. All he's going to do is cry and tell her she didn't do it."

"I agree, Gus. I'm going to have one of the guys take him the hell out of here and waltz him around somewhere until we see what we can get out of her on our own."

Sam Carter walked in and told them the prosecutor wanted to see them in her office. They went down to the first floor and Ms. Stevens was sitting at her conference table with Ben Harris. She looked up when they walked in: "How did you make out with the husband?"

Fahy said: "He says she couldn't have done it. We told him what we have and he still says she didn't do it. He says she was having trouble sleeping lately and he recalls seeing a bottle in the medicine cabinet from the drug store, but he doesn't know what it was. Gus went after him about his girlfriends and he finally admitted he was having fights with her about the latest one and they were fighting around the time Jimmy was killed. He says he'll talk to her, but Gus and I have decided it may not be a good idea to have him talk to her first. We're going to take a shot at her and see what we get."

Ms. Stevens nodded. "I didn't expect you would get anything out of him. It's your call and do it whatever way you think best. But we've got press problems. The reporters are all over the place wanting a statement. They must have been tipped off that we had the husband over here and the word is out that there may be an arrest soon. If the leak came out of this office I'm going to have someone's ass."

Gus grinned. "Geez, Ms. Stevens, you sound like one of the

guys. But you know it didn't have to be from here. Everybody over in Frenchtown knows what everybody else is doing. It could be that Hartwick told someone he had to come over this morning or maybe some neighbor saw him being picked up by one of our guys. If that happened, you can bet half the town knew in five minutes what was going on and somebody would have called the *Del Val News* and told them."

"You may be right, Gus. In any event, I've got to get a statement ready but I'm not going to release it until you have had your go with Mrs. Hartwick."

It was shortly after noon when Sam Carter arrived with Gladys Hartwick. She was brought immediately to the interrogation room on the second floor. Ben Harris, Susan Sturz, Gus, and Fahy were already there waiting for her, and Noreen Walsh was sitting in the corner with her machine all set up. When Gladys entered the room, Fahy said: "It is now twelve-twenty-five P.M., June ninth, nineteen-ninety-four and Mrs. Gladys Hartwick has entered the interrogation room."

Gladys looked around the room and asked where her husband was. Fahy answered: "We're finished with him for now and he went out to get a bite to eat. He'll be back in an hour or so. In the meantime, I'd like you to please be seated and let me introduce you to the people here. You already know Gus Bass, and this is Ben Harris and Susan Sturz, they're both assistant prosecutors here in the office. The woman in the corner with the stenotype machine is Noreen Walsh. She's an official court stenographer and she's going to record everything we say in this room. In fact, she's already started. And we have a tape recorder going which will record everything. Do you understand and do you have any questions?"

Her eyes glared at Fahy as she said: "I'd like to see my husband."

"You'll see him shortly. Mrs. Hartwick, I have to inform you that you are a suspect in the murder of your son, Robert Hartwick, Junior, on June third, nineteen-ninety-four, in the Borough of Frenchtown. You do not need to answer any questions we would like to ask you, but if you do answer, anything you say may be used in evidence against you. You are entitled to have a lawyer present to advise you at any time. If you wish to

218

call a lawyer at this time, we will suspend this session and you will have the opportunity to call your attorney. If you cannot afford an attorney or if you do not have an attorney, the court will appoint an attorney to represent you. Do you understand what I have just told you or do you have any questions about it? If not, Mr. Harris will give you a written form which says in writing what I've just told you and we would ask you to read it and sign your name below to acknowledge that you have been advised of your right not to answer any questions and of your right to an attorney."

Gladys took the sheet of paper from Harris and sat back in her chair. Her face was expressionless, but her eyes were lit up as though she was staring at a fire.

"I don't know what you're talking about? How can you accuse me of killing Bobby? I didn't, I couldn't possibly have hurt him. Why, even you told me that someone had taken him, don't you remember?"

Ben Harris spoke: "Mrs. Harris, please don't say anything further. Read that paper and if you understand what's there, please sign it. If there's anything you don't understand, just tell me and I'll try to answer any questions you have."

Gladys looked down staring through at the paper she was holding in her hand. Finally, she said: "I understand, it's just like on those cop shows on television. I'll sign it and I don't want a lawyer. I haven't done anything and I'll answer your questions."

Harris said: "Fine, here's a pen. Just sign on the bottom line and put the date after your name."

Gladys signed the paper and handed it back to Harris who said: "Now, Mrs. Hartwick, if at any time you want to stop and speak to an attorney, just tell these men and either you can call your own attorney or we will have someone from the public defender's office over here immediately to speak to you. I have to leave now, but Ms. Sturz will stay here throughout the questioning." Harris stood up and left.

Fahy spoke first: "Mrs. Hartwick, is it all right if I call you Gladys?" She nodded. "Okay, Gladys, now your husband told us this morning that you were having trouble sleeping a few weeks ago and that Dr. Wilson may have prescribed a sleeping medication for you. Is that right?"

"Yes."

"Is Dr. Wilson your regular physician?"

"Yes."

"Did he give you a prescription for seconal to help you with your sleeping problem?"

"He gave me a prescription. I'm not sure what it was."

"Where did you have the prescription filled?"

"At the pharmacy over in Frenchtown. Why is that so important?"

"Gladys, we'll move along more quickly if you just answer our questions, all right? Now, did Dr. Wilson give you any other prescriptions when you saw him recently?"

"No, just the one." She raised her head and her eyes again had a burning intensity. "Look, aren't I allowed to ask you any questions? Why are you accusing me? I didn't touch Bobby, I swear it."

Gus said softly: "Look, Gladys, we don't like this any more than you do. But we've got to do it and all we want is answers. When did you find out about Jean Albertson and your husband?"

Gladys sat back in her chair and her eyes narrowed to tiny slits. She didn't answer.

Gus continued: "Gladys, we know your husband has been having an affair with Jean for a long time. He's admitted it and he says you two were fighting about it over the last two or three weeks and you threatened to walk out on him and the kids. Now is that true or not?"

Gladys started to rise up in her chair and then slumped back. There was still no response.

Gus now raised his voice: "Gladys, he had been seeing Jean for some time and you made him move over to Frenchtown to break it up. We know that, and your husband has admitted it, too. Then you found out not too long ago that he was still seeing her, isn't that right?" There was no answer.

Fahy asked: "Gladys, would you mind telling us where you were born and where you lived before you were married?"

Her eyes shifted from Gus to Fahy. "I was born over at Lake Nockamixon and we lived there until my mother and father separated. Then my mother and I moved over to Durham."

"What about your father, Gladys, have you seen him recently?"

Gladys lowered her head and responded almost in a whisper: "No, I haven't seen or spoken to my father since not long after we moved to Durham."

"Do you know where he is living now?"

Shaking her head violently she replied: "No, and I don't care."

Now Gus bore in: "Gladys, didn't your father have a brother Hiram who lived somewhere near you over in Nockamixon?"

Gladys started to stand up: "What the hell is going on here? What does Hiram or my father have to do with this? What are you after?"

"How about your mother, Gladys? Is she dead?"

"Yes, of course she is dead. She died right after Bob and I were married. You must know that. Why are you asking me these questions?"

"Well, Gladys, there's a lot we have to know and you're the only one who has the answers. Now would you mind telling us how long Dr. Wilson has been your doctor?"

"He was my mother's doctor and I've been seeing him since before I was in high school."

Gus continued in a softer voice: "Gladys, I want to ask you a few questions about your son, Jimmy. He died too, didn't he? How come you never told us about Jimmy dying?"

Gladys stared straight ahead as if she were in a trance. After a long silence, she finally said: "I guess I didn't think of it. Jimmy died almost eight years ago and it didn't have anything to do with what happened to Bobby. Jimmy died in an accident."

"What kind of accident, Gladys?" Gus asked.

Her voice was zombie-like. "He was playing in the living room and somehow he got a plastic bag from an album cover and stuck his head in it and he stopped breathing."

"Where were you when this happened, Gladys?"

Her face was now totally blank: "I was in the kitchen, cooking."

"Didn't you look in on him while he was playing?"

"I did and that's when I found him, with the bag over his

head. I tried to give him mouth-to-mouth and I called the ambulance and Dr. Wilson, but they couldn't do anything for him. He was dead."

"Yeah, I know. I checked into that and saw the whole file they have on it over in the State Police barracks. You know Lieutenant Schoop? I think he was a sergeant at the time Jimmy died."

"I don't remember. There was a state cop who came over to the house after they took Jimmy away, but I don't remember his name. It may have been that guy."

Gus: "Yeah, Gladys, it was. And you know, Schoop picked up the bag Jimmy stuck his head in and he kept it. I saw it just the other day. He says there was no way Jimmy could have killed himself with that bag and I'd have to agree with him. What do you think, Gladys? Is that how Jimmy was killed?"

For the first time since Gus had met Gladys she showed some emotion. She started to cry, not convulsively, just tears slowly forming and running down her cheeks. Susan Sturz spoke up: "I think Mrs. Hartwick can use a break now. Suppose we stop for five minutes."

"Just a minute, Susan. A few more questions and we can take a break. Gladys, I've been told your husband was running around with some woman not long before Jimmy died and you and he were fighting about that. As a matter of fact, your husband admitted that this morning. Is that true?" Gus asked.

There was no response. Gladys sat there, not sobbing or crying, just tears dripping down. "How about that, Gladys? Can you answer that question?"

"We're going to take a break now," Susan said.

Gus and Fahy stood up and Fahy said: "It is now one-o-five P.M. and this interview is being suspended. We will resume at one-fifteen. Is that all right with you, Mrs. Hartwick?" Gladys nodded, and Fahy continued: "The witness has nodded her head indicating it is all right with her." Gus and Fahy left the room.

They walked down the hall to Fahy's office. Carter and Sloss were sitting there. Sloss asked, "How did it go?"

"She's one tough nut. I don't know if we'll get anything out of her. What do you think, Gus?" Fahy asked.

Gus shook his head. "I can't get a read on her. Sometimes I

222

think she's playing us for suckers and then she seems like she's telling us the truth. But she's lying, that's for sure. You notice, Chuck, as soon as we get on to his chasing women, she starts to clam up. So, where do we go from here?"

Fahy said abruptly, "When we get back, I want to go after the day Bobby was killed and try to nail her down to her story. After that I was thinking we ask her whether she'll take a lie detector test."

Again Gus shook his head. "I don't know about the lie detector, I got a hunch she'll beat it."

"Gus, if she beats the polygraph, either we're crazy or she is."

"Who's going to run the polygraph?" Gus asked.

Fahy pointed at Sam Carter. "Sam will, he's the best around. I ought to know, I taught him."

Gus shrugged. "Okay by me, but I got to tell you I think she's going to beat it."

"I hear you. Let's go back and we'll play it by ear."

They got up and went down the hall to the interrogation room. Susan Sturz had moved her chair closer to Gladys, Noreen was still sitting in the corner and Gladys sat in her chair, looking as if nothing had happened. When they walked into the room Fahy nodded to Noreen and said: "It is now one-eighteen P.M. and we will resume the interview of Mrs. Hartwick."

Before Fahy could say another word, Gladys blurted out: "I'm telling you once and for all that I had nothing to do with Bobby getting killed. You can ask me any questions you like, but I had nothing to do with it."

"I hear you, Gladys," Fahy said, "but we'd just like to find out what you were doing last Friday. You know, take us through whatever you did that day."

Gladys looked up at the ceiling and then at Fahy. "There was nothing special. Bob got up and he went to work and I got Bobby off to school. Ricky had a cold and he stayed in his room most of the morning and then Bobby came home for lunch, and I fed him."

"What did you give him for lunch? Do you remember?"

"It was a peanut butter and jelly sandwich and a glass of milk."

223

"We know that, Gladys, the medical examiner found the remains in his stomach. Tell me, did you put anything in his milk?"

"What do you mean? It was just milk."

Gus said softly, "Look, Gladys, the medical examiner has positively determined that someone put seconal in the milk Bobby drank that day. And the pharmacist down in Frenchtown showed me the prescription he filled for you for seconal. How do you explain that?"

Gladys now screamed: "I don't know what you're saying. All I did was give Bobby his lunch."

"Gladys, you told me that Bobby left at about twelve-forty-five, remember? And you said you watched him walk down to the path and you waved to him. All right, what were you doing between then and when you called me around three-thirty?"

She cast down her head, staring at the floor as she said: "I was just doing work around the house and taking care of Ricky. That's all I was doing."

"Did you go outside anytime after Bobby left to go back to school?"

She continued staring at the floor: "No, I didn't. I stayed in the house until I went down to pick Bobby up. Why, did anybody say they saw me?"

"I didn't say that, did I? Did you see anyone, Gladys?"

"How could I? I was in the house the whole time."

Fahy broke in: "We're having a hard time believing you, Gladys. Maybe you could help us out here. Would you be willing to take a polygraph examination about what you were doing last Friday?"

She looked up at Fahy and asked: "What is that?"

"It's a test to see if you are telling the truth. You know, it's a lie detector test."

"What do I have to do?"

"Not very much at all, Gladys. We have a man right here in our office who is an expert at this. All you have to do is sit in a chair and he will attach small wires to you and he will ask you questions. All you have to do is answer his questions either yes or no. It doesn't hurt, you don't feel a thing. I've taken the test myself several times just to try it out."

Gladys cringed back into her chair: "Why do I have to take

this test? Don't you believe me?"

"Gladys, I know you are just as anxious as we are to catch the person who killed Bobby. Right now you are a suspect, and if the machine says you're telling us the truth, we can eliminate you and try to find the person who did kill Bobby. It's as simple as that."

"What kind of questions is he going to ask?"

"Oh, pretty much the same as we have been asking you, except he'll ask the questions so that all you have to do is answer yes or no."

Gladys was silent for a few minutes. Finally she said: "All right, if I take this test can I go home then and look after Ricky?"

"I can't promise you that, Gladys. First let's try the test and then we'll see. Okay?"

There was a long pause and finally Gladys said: "All right, I'll take your test. How long is it going to take?"

"I think we can set it up to start in less than an hour. You just sit there and rest and when we're ready we'll call you. Would you like something to drink while you're waiting?"

"Just some water please, and I'd like to use the ladies room."

"No problem, Gladys. Ms. Sturz will show you where it is. We'll come back as soon as we're ready for you. It is now one-thirty P.M. and we are terminating the interview of Mrs. Hartwick at this time."

Carter was still sitting in Fahy's office when they got there. "Okay, Sam, warm up the machine, she's consented to take the polygraph."

Carter's face lit up and he rubbed his hands in glee. "Good. Anything specific you want me to concentrate on?"

"I'd go after the time he got home for lunch, what she fed him and whether he left the house after he ate. Ask her if she had seconal or a sleeping medication that Dr. Wilson prescribed for her and whether she gave any to Bobby in his milk. Anything else you want in there, Gus?"

"Yeah, ask her if she stuck his head in a plastic bag. And cut off his penis."

"Leave it to you, Gus, to go for the jugular. I'm sure Sam will work that in, too. All right, Sam, Gus and I will grab a sandwich across the street and we'll be back in half an hour."

When they returned the receptionist told them that Ms. Stevens would like to see them and they went down to her office. Ben Harris was there and Ms. Stevens asked: "How did it go with her? I heard she is willing to take a polygraph."

Fahy said: "Well, we mirandized her immediately and she stuck to her story. She's got it down pat. He came come, she fed him and he left to go back to school. She never left the house that day. She admits having Wilson's prescription filled but she didn't put anything in his milk. And she won't give any answer if you ask her about her husband's chasing women. She started crying when Gus asked her about Jimmy's death, so we took a break. When we went back in, I asked her if she would take the polygraph and she consented."

Gus looked uneasy. "Ms. Stevens, what happens if she passes the test? Where do we go then and can we hold her?"

"What about that, Ben? Can we keep her here after the test?"

"Not unless you arrest her. You probably have enough to sign the complaint right now without the test. The physical evidence points to her as the killer, but since we asked her to take the test and if she passes, I'm just not sure. We may have backed ourselves into a corner."

Hazel Stevens frowned. "I see what you mean, Ben, but I think we've got to have a confession. As you said yesterday, there's going to be a major sympathy factor here with her background, and if there's the slightest element of doubt in a jury's mind, she could get acquitted. I've seen stranger things than that happen with a jury, even where the prosecution had compelling, conclusive physical evidence. I want to make sure this woman doesn't ever go free to kill again. That means no chances and no risks of an acquittal."

Gus looked upset. "Ms. Stevens, what do you mean about her not getting free again? Wouldn't you ask for the death penalty? For Christ's sake, she killed three kids, what does it take to get the death penalty?"

"I'm sorry, Gus, but you're all wrong there. In the first place we can only try her for killing Bobby. She killed the other two over in Pennsylvania and we couldn't prosecute her for those. Indeed, no judge would ever let us even suggest to a jury here anything about the other two. So, we're looking at one homicide, not three when it comes to what the penalty should be. And when did you ever hear of a mother getting the death penalty for killing her child? You know, over in England if a mother kills her child before he's a year old, they don't even call it murder. They just say she is *non compos mentis* and she just goes into an institution for treatment and not for very long at that. Besides, with our Supreme Court, even if we convinced a jury to recommend the death penalty, they would set it aside, and if they didn't, some federal judge would find a way to undo the whole conviction."

Gus looked perplexed. "What the hell is the death penalty for, then?"

It was Ben who said: "Gus, you should read some of the decisions our Supreme Court hands down in death cases. You know they set aside the death penalty in some twenty-nine cases in a row? They have only upheld it in three cases since the legislature reenacted the death penalty in nineteen seventy-one, and in one of them, a guy was convicted of hiring some people to kill his wife because he had another woman he wanted to marry and he wanted the insurance money on his wife's life. You can forget about the death penalty in this case. The important thing is to get her convicted and put her away for as long as possible. Another thing, we will probably be faced with a pre-trial hearing on whether she is sane enough to stand trial. You know the law is very tricky in this area. If she has no recollection of committing the crime and can't cooperate with her lawyers, we may not even be able to conduct a trial at all until she is restored to reason, as some of the judges like to say. If that's the case, all they can do is to put her into an institution for treatment and then maybe two or three years from now they'll say 'Okay, you can try her now.' No, the boss is right, we have to get a confession, get a plea, and put her away, hopefully, for thirty years."

Gus was shaking his head as he said: "For God's sake, don't those poor kids have any rights? Why should she be able to walk away and they're dead?"

Ms. Stevens reached out for Gus's hand: "Gus, she's not going to walk away. She is going to prison. But first we have to have a confession to make sure she doesn't walk."

Ms. Stevens turned to Ben Harris: "That brings me to the

statement I was going to give the press. I had intended to tell them that we had arrested her for Bobby's murder, but I'd better hold off on that until I see where we get with the polygraph. I've got to tell them something, so I'd just better give them yesterday's bullshit again and tell them we are still interviewing witnesses and following leads we have developed. Anything wrong with that?"

Gus said: "Ms. Stevens, when all this is over, Chuck should promote you to detective. You sure talk like us."

"Gus, I consider that to be a very high compliment and I may take Chuck up on that. In the meantime, I'm going to see if we can get Sanchez and his psychiatrist over here as soon as possible so we can fill him in on what's happened here today. So stick around and let me know as soon as Sam has anything."

They went back upstairs to Fahy's office to wait out Carter's exam results. Fahy said: "Gus, by the look on your face I can tell you don't like the way this is going. I kind of feel the same way, but all we can do is, like Sergeant Friday used to say, get the facts and then turn them over to the guys downstairs to prosecute."

"I hear you, Chuck, and I know what they say makes sense, I just can't help feeling for those kids. No one should have to die like that. Can you imagine what those kids must have felt having their own mother and sister kill them?"

"I don't think Bobby, at least, knew what happened to him. That's why she gave him the seconal to knock him out first."

"Oh, I don't think that's why, Chuck. I think she gave him the seconal so he wouldn't struggle and make any noise. Remember, there was another kid in the house and she had to keep it quiet. Even so, she was taking a risk little Ricky would walk in on her or hear something. You know, I've been thinking she probably gave Ricky some seconal, too, so he would be out of the way while she killed Bobby and disposed of the body. When I was there that afternoon, I never did see Ricky. She said he was playing upstairs and I never went up to take a look. Maybe I should have."

"Gus, there was no reason for you to check up on him. We all bought her story and the only thing that mattered then was to try and find Bobby. Look, I'm going to take a leak. Just relax for a while."

It was 3:30 when Sam returned to Fahy's office. As soon as he walked in the door, they could tell by the look on his face it wasn't good news. "Here are the readouts. She passed most everything, no indication she was not answering truthfully. The most I got was a few inconclusives on the seconal and whether she was fighting with her husband about his girl friends. When I went over that part again, she admitted they had been fighting and then she passed, but all of her readings on that were elevated. So now what?"

Fahy's face bore a look of dejection: "Well, we go downstairs and tell the boss lady and see what she wants to do. If I had my way, I'd arrest her anyway. Shit, I don't see how it's possible for her to pass like that. She killed Bobby and there's no doubt about that."

Sam accompanied Fahy and Gus down to Ms. Stevens' office and gave her the report. Ms. Stevens answered in one word: "Shit."

Chuck said: "Them's my sentiments, exactly. But what do we do now?"

"We hold them here. Put the husband and her in the same room and send out for dinner for them in about an hour or so. Sanchez and the psychiatrist are on their way over and let's see if they have any ideas."

Fahy and Carter started to leave to make the arrangements for the Hartwicks and Gus followed them out the door. As they walked out of the prosecutor's office, Dr. Sanchez was leading a short, well-groomed man with a tightly trimmed beard down the hall toward them. Dr. Sanchez introduced Dr. Weinstein to each in turn until he got to Gus. "I'm sorry, I remember your face from last night, but I forgot your name."

"That's all right, Doc. It's Gus Bass."

"Oh, yes, it rhymes with...." Dr. Sanchez paused and smiled at Gus. "I'm really sorry, Mr. Bass, it's just a mnemonic way of remembering people's names. Nothing personal."

They all laughed and Gus said: "Gee, I'm glad my name isn't Kitt, or something like that."

Dr. Sanchez put his arm around Gus's shoulder. "From now on, Gus, I'll just try to remember you by your first name—schuss, how's that?"

"Fine with me, Doc, but what the hell is a schuss?"

"That's a maneuver people use sometimes when they're skiing. You see, next time I see you, I'll think of skiing, then schuss, and then Gus. It's easy once you learn how."

"You know, Doc, I think it would be a whole lot easier to remember my name is Gus."

Ms. Stevens heard them talking and came to the doorway. Dr. Sanchez introduced Dr. Weinstein and when they were seated around her conference table she told them there had been some new developments. She nodded in Carter's direction and he related the results of the polygraph examination. When he had finished, Dr. Weinstein said: "I had been thinking when I read the material you sent over that a polygraph wouldn't work in this case."

Ms. Stevens said: "Why not, Dr. Weinstein?"

"I want to tell you first off, I'm not a forensic psychiatrist. By that I mean I don't testify in court, I treat people who are suffering from mental disease. I'm what they call a clinician, so please don't ask me whether this woman, Gladys Hartwick, is legally insane. That's something I frankly can't tell you. Based on what I saw I would have to agree with you that Mrs. Hartwick killed her son, Bobby, and her first child, Jimmy. I understand from what I have been told that there is a possibility that she also may have been responsible for the death of her younger brother as well."

Dr. Weinstein continued: "As you know, I've never interviewed the woman and I have never even seen her, so obviously I am in no position to give you a diagnosis of her condition. I can only tell you what the possibilities are and what you may be up against. I doubt whether anyone can give you a definitive diagnosis even if he spent months interviewing and treating her.

"We psychiatrists use a lot of jargon when we try to classify and explain mental disease, just like you lawyers do in a courtroom. One of the terms that was used early on to describe a person who to all outward appearances and who for prolonged periods of time acted rationally, but was prone to sudden outbursts of rage and violence, was 'psychopathic personality' or 'psychopath.' The term is still used among lay persons today. However, we have tried to refine the terminology we use and to be more precise in describing personality disorders, and today we usually refer to these people as suffering from a sociopathic or asocial personality disorder. You may also have heard the term 'sociopath' in describing such people. Just remember that whichever term is used we are referring to essentially the same type of condition. A sociopath is capable of manifesting his or her disease in an infinite number of ways, but the principal characteristic is that the person has no feelings or compassion for others and does not form loving relationships with others, including husbands, children, and parents. It is this lack of feeling toward others which enables her to engage in extreme acts of cruelty or violence and inflict physical harm upon her own children. Many studies have shown that the sociopaths make up a substantial part of the criminal population, particularly those who commit the most violent criminal acts. These are the people you, especially, have to deal with.

"Now under the heading of sociopaths, we find a special category of person who suffers from what we call the 'explosive personality disorder.' These people function normally and suddenly will explode in an act of violence, including the murder of a person close to them."

Gus's eyes brightened. "Doc, you mean like O.J.?"

Dr. Weinstein nodded. "If he's guilty of those murders, I'd have to say yes, like O.J. This is all speculation on my part, but I believe that this is the disorder which best describes Mrs. Hartwick's condition. From the evidence you have compiled so far, she is capable of leading a normal and uneventful existence and suddenly, and perhaps without any warning to those around her, she explodes with rage and kills. Some event occurs which, for other people might cause discomfort or unhappiness, acts as a trigger to an act of violence. What that trigger might have been for Mrs. Hartwick we obviously don't know, and possibly we will never know."

The doctor paused and looked around the table. "Now if you have any questions, I will answer them if I can."

Fahy was the first to speak: "Doctor Weinstein, how is it pos-

231

sible that she could fool the polygraph? I have heard of ways people can beat it by taking drugs, but I'm sure she hadn't anticipated being asked to take the test so she couldn't have prepared herself for it."

"If I'm right, she didn't have to prepare for it because she has no conscious recollection of having killed anyone and so she can truthfully deny it. I noted in the reports I read that in the case of both Jimmy and Bobby, following their deaths her emotional responses were practically nonexistent. She showed almost no overt reaction at all. I recall schuss—I mean Gus—saying in his report that she spoke like an automaton. That is typical of a person who suffers from an explosive personality disorder. Following the commission of the act of violence she is likely to be in a tranquil, almost catatonic state, barely able to function, like an athlete who has expended herself in extreme physical effort and then collapses when she crosses the finish line. Except that in this case, she has exhausted all of her emotional psychic energy. What you probably witnessed, Gus, was an act of self-preservation. In order to permit her to function as a person, she had to deny to herself what she had done. This is probably a long-winded way of saying, in answer to the question, that she most likely has repressed any memory or conscious recollection of killing her child and I doubt whether you will get her to confess to it because she has had to deny to herself that she ever did kill him. That's why a polygraph examination would probably be useless in her case."

Ms. Stevens said: "Isn't there any way we can get her to recall what she did?"

After a prolonged pause, Dr. Weinstein said: There's only one possibility that I know of, or perhaps two. If she were administered sodium amytal, it is possible that she might recall what she did and give you truthful responses. The other possibility is hypnosis. You've probably read in the press recently of cases where individuals under hypnosis have recalled memories of painful experiences they have repressed for many years. I don't know that I personally have much confidence in hypnotically induced recollection. The use of sodium amytal—which some of you may know as truth serum—has greater scientific acceptance but there is a lot of controversy about its use and effectiveness."

Fahy's face noticeably brightened: "If we could get her to consent to the use of this truth serum, can you do it for us?"

The doctor shook his head. "Oh, no. If this procedure were to be used, it would have to be done by an expert in the technique. And I have never done it. Are there any other questions?"

It was Fahy who now asked Ben: "If she were given truth serum, could we use a confession in court if we got one?"

Harris shook his head. "No way, Chief. There was a decision a few years back by the appellate court which said that sodium amytal test results are not admissible because they haven't been shown to be scientifically reliable, just like polygraph exams. But if she consented to the results being admitted into evidence, the court might allow it just like they have for lie detector results."

Fahy then asked Dr. Weinstein: "Doc, if we got her to consent, could you get someone for us to administer the test?"

"I believe so. But it couldn't be done locally. It is often used as a diagnostic tool in the case of people who are suffering from amnesia. The drug itself is a short acting barbiturate, somewhat similar to the seconal she used on the boy, but it has to be given in carefully monitored doses in order to sustain its effect without the patient completely losing consciousness. I observed a sodium amytal test once during my residency, and all it did was knock the patient out and we just sat around watching him sleep. But if you want to try sodium amytal and she consents, it could be done over in Philadelphia and I could probably arrange that for you."

"Do you think you could set it up for tomorrow?"

"I'll make a phone call as soon as we break up and see if it can be arranged."

Gus spoke next: "Doc, I don't understand. According to Dr. Sanchez, she killed Bobby by say one o'clock. I was up there talking to her by three-thirty and she gave me this cock and bull story about his not coming back after school. You mean to tell me that in two hours she could have forgotten what she had just done to her own son?"

"Gus—see, I remember your name now without thinking

about skiing—I'm sure that by the time you saw her she had no conscious memory of what she did that afternoon, and the polygraph results confirm that. Tell me, when you had your first interview with her, did you think she was lying about the boy being missing?"

"No, I just thought she was acting strange, that's all. I figured she was in shock. You know, she collapsed when I tried to give her the phone to speak to her husband."

"That's what I mean. The memory of killing her son no longer existed for her, and when she was asked to speak to her husband it may have started to trigger a memory of it and her mind wouldn't let it surface and that was accomplished by causing her to faint."

Gus leaned forward. "Speaking of triggers, Doc, do you think this explosion, or whatever you call it, could have been caused by her being jealous of her husband's having a girlfriend? You know, Jimmy was killed around the time he started chasing after girls, and a year ago she found out he was having an affair with one woman in particular and made him move over to Frenchtown. Then, within the past few months, she found out he was still seeing this same girl. When we questioned her, every time I asked about girlfriends she refused to answer. Then she finally admitted to Carter they had been fighting about it."

"That's a good point, Gus. It could well have been the trigger both times. But I doubt it if was jealousy on her part. More likely it was a feeling of being betrayed by a man who was the central figure in her life. That would be more consistent with the story you got from Dr. Wilson yesterday about her father. She might have accepted her sexual relationship with him on some level and felt betrayed when he forced her to have sex with her uncle. It was not long after that, as I understand it, that she may have killed her brother and that could have established the response pattern when she felt her husband had betrayed her."

Gus said: "All right, Doc, and now for my last question. What the hell do those three holes mean that we found in that plastic bag and carved into Bobby's belly?"

The doctor smiled. "Ah, Gus, that is one of the most intriguing facts of this case from a psychiatric standpoint. I'm not a Freudian analyst, but Freud did identify so called symbols that

234

the unconscious mind uses to express itself, particularly thoughts which have a prohibited sexual content, such as an incestuous relationship with a parent. The three holes, as you all know, are in the shape of a triangle with the apex at the top. Freud believed that such a triangle represented the male sexual organs, that is, the penis at the top of the triangle and the two bottom holes or points representing the testicles. If the triangle is inverted with the apex at the bottom, then it is supposed to represent the female organs, with the breasts or the ovaries at the top and the vagina at the bottom."

They all began to murmur and look at each other shaking their heads. Finally Gus said: "You got to be kidding, Doc. It's just a triangle, that's all. You shrinks can really dream them up."

Dr. Weinstein laughed. "You saw it, Gus, it was there on the bag and on the boy's abdomen. It clearly has to have a meaning for her. If I were a Freudian, I'd have to say that in her subconscious mind each killing represented the death of her father who was the first one to betray her and she used the triangle to express her hatred of him. And that may be why she cut off the boy's penis, because she was destroying the symbol of her betrayal.

"I started out by telling you that I was in no position to provide you with any diagnosis of this woman's condition, and that is still true. What I have told you is just speculation on my part, and while it may help to explain some of her actions and what happened here today, please bear in mind that what eventually emerges may be entirely different than the picture I have given you."

Hazel Stevens stood up and said: "Dr. Weinstein, I'd like to thank you for coming over. What you've told us should be very helpful. I'd appreciate your making that call to see if we can give her a sodium amytal test tomorrow. You can use the phone in Ben's office next door."

Dr. Weinstein stood up and extended his hand to the prosecutor. "Not at all, Ms. Stevens, glad to help out in any way that I can. And let me thank you for the opportunity of reviewing this most remarkable case." Ben led Dr. Weinstein to his office.

The prosecutor turned to Fahy and said: "Chief, I think you and Gus had better go to work on the Hartwicks, especially the husband, and see if you can talk her into the sodium amytal test. I'll try to keep Dr. Weinstein here so he can explain to them what's involved and answer any questions they have. If she is willing, I want you and Gus to take them both down to Philly so you will be available to answer any questions the doctors there might have. Is that okay? I must say, Dr. Weinstein is very persuasive, even if it turns out he is all wrong.

"In the meantime, we have to stop the leaks. If this story ever gets out, we'll have every TV network and every newspaper on our necks, and then we'll have no alternative but to file the complaint and arraign her. If that happens before we're ready and have a chance to obtain a statement from her, we'll be playing hardball all the way. Do I make myself clear? Pass the word around the office that this one stays in-house."

Ben and Dr. Weinstein were back and the doctor reported he had good news, the group down in Philly could administer the sodium amytal test tomorrow afternoon. "But you'll have to arrange to deliver to them the entire investigative file the first thing in the morning so they can review it and ask her the right questions."

Ms. Stevens said: "Doctor, would you mind waiting here for a short time? My men are going up to speak to the Hartwicks to see if they will consent to the exam and perhaps you could answer any questions they might have about how it is done and that kind of thing."

"I would be happy to do that." He looked at his watch and turned to Dr. Sanchez. "Yes, we have plenty of time, don't we, Michael? You see, Dr. Sanchez has arranged for a Japanese sushi feast for me tonight, but that's not until eight, isn't it, Michael?"

Dr. Sanchez smiled. "That's right, and if any of you would like to join us, you're more than welcome."

Gus groaned. "Gee, I would really like to try this sushi, Doc, but right now I'm on a diet."

"Oh, but Gus, that's the best thing for you if you're on a diet. Raw fish has very little calories and almost no cholesterol. You must try it."

"Some other time, Doc, but thanks for the invite anyway."

Fahy and Gus made their way upstairs to the room where the Hartwicks were sitting. Fahy led off, telling them they had consulted a psychiatrist who had explained a lot of things to them and had recommended that Gladys take a sodium amytal test and answer their questions.

Bob Hartwick spoke up: "What the hell is this sodium whatever you call it? Haven't you put her through enough already? What happened to the lie detector test?"

"Look, Bob, I've got to tell you that some of the results on the lie detector test were inconclusive. We asked the psychiatrist about it and he says that Gladys may have repressed any memories of what she may have done to Bobby. This sodium amytal is just truth serum. As I understand it, they just inject it and Gladys will relax and she may recall things that happened that she can't tell us about now. Look, we've got the doctor downstairs and he can explain the whole thing to you a lot better than I can. Let me call him up and he'll tell you."

Bob Hartwick looked at his wife: "How about it, Gladys? Is it okay with you? Maybe you can finally convince them you didn't do it and this whole nightmare will be over."

Gladys sat there staring at her husband. She said nothing. Gus said: "Look Gladys, for once your husband is telling you the right thing. We've got to get this cleared up once and for all and you're the only one who can do that for us. Besides, the Doc says that this drug they give you is just like the seconal you've been taking and all it does is relax you."

Gladys hesitated and then said: "I'd like to speak to the doctor."

Fahy: "Fine, Gladys, I'll have him right up here."

Fahy went out and returned in a few minutes with Dr. Weinstein. He introduced the doctor to the Hartwicks and the doctor said: "I understand you have some questions you want to ask me about the sodium amytal test you have been asked to take, Mrs. Hartwick. Let me explain that it is a drug, similar to the seconal I'm told you have been taking. The drug is administered intravenously, that is through a needle in your arm. The whole procedure is administered by doctors who monitor the dosage and your reaction to the drug very closely. There is absolutely no danger involved in the procedure. The worst thing that can happen to you is that you will fall asleep and not be able to answer any questions. I was telling these gentlemen that I saw that happen once when I was a resident, and there was a group of doctors standing around watching this person sleep. By the time he woke up, all of us were practically asleep. It is a procedure that is used frequently in treating patients who have amnesia and can't remember their identities or anything else about themselves. It is possible, I think, this may have happened to you and you may recall the events of last Friday under the influence of this drug. Oh, one more thing. There isn't anyone here at our hospital who is qualified to administer the test so it would be done down in Philadelphia, if that's all right with you. Is there anything you would like to ask me?"

Gladys and her husband looked at each other and it was her husband who spoke: "Doc, are you sure there is no danger to Glad if they give her this drug? Could it affect her mind in any way?"

"Positively not, Mr. Hartwick. The seconal she has been taking is much more powerful than the drug they administer during the test. And the dosage is a lot less. They don't want her to fall asleep, you know."

Hartwick turned to Gladys: "How about it, Gladys? What do you want to do?"

Gladys turned to her husband and said: "Well, if it's the only way they're going to be satisfied I didn't have anything to do with it, then I want to get it over with."

Dr. Weinstein said: "I'm sure you have made the right decision, Mrs. Hartwick. Whatever may have happened, it is better for you to know than to have this hanging over you for the rest of your life."

Gladys looked up at Doctor Weinstein. "Will you be there, doctor?"

"No, I'm afraid not. I have a full day scheduled for tomorrow but I'll be available by telephone if you want to speak to me. Will that be all right?" Gladys nodded. "If there's nothing further then, I'll say goodnight and I wish you well tomorrow."

After Dr. Weinstein left, Fahy turned to the Hartwicks. "We'll have forms for you to sign tomorrow before you take this test and we'll pick you up at your house around eleven o'clock, if that is all right with you? And I'll call Becky Aaron and ask her to take Ricky over to her house and take care of him while you're gone. If there's nothing else, you're free to go and I'll have

238

a car drive you back to Frenchtown."

The Hartwicks left and Gus and Fahy went down to see the prosecutor. As soon as they walked into her office, Fahy said: "She's going to do it. We'll pick her up tomorrow at her house and drive her down. Listen, I told her there was some form she would have to sign. I'm right, aren't I?"

Ben said: "Oh, I'm sure they'll have forms down there for her to sign. You know, those 'informed consent' forms they make you sign when you go into the hospital, that kind of thing."

"No, Ben, I was thinking about a form that would permit us to use her answers on the test in evidence if we have to go that far."

"Chuck, before we could do that we'd have to get her a lawyer and if we get her a lawyer, he sure as hell isn't going to let us give her the test in the first place. And if he ever did, not only wouldn't it be tomorrow, but any judge down the line would say he was so incompetent that she was denied the effective assistance of counsel and any conviction would be thrown out."

Gus shook his head and said: "Ms. Stevens, I hope you don't mind me saying this, but these goddamned lawyers can really screw up a good investigation."

Hazel Stevens' head went back and she started laughing. They all joined in. After she caught her breath, the prosecutor said: "Gus, I couldn't agree with you more. Now let's get out of here and go home. Oh, I almost forgot, Gus. There's a rumor going around you're getting married. Any truth to that?"

"You talk about leaks here, well, I got an idea who is doing the leaking, and his first name is Chuck."

Ms. Stevens smiled and said: "I'm taking the fifth on that, Gus, but I just wanted to say congratulations and best wishes. Now you better go back to this woman of yours before she changes her mind. Goodnight to all of you. I think we're almost there."

THIRTY-SIX

Gus had just turned on the ignition key when the car phone rang. It was Peg: "Where are you, I've been waiting for you to call me. I miss you like crazy."

"Honey, I just this minute got into the car and I was going to call you when the phone rang. You knew where I was. Why didn't you call me there?"

"Gus, I don't like to disturb you when you're working. Besides, I don't want any of your buddies over there to think I'm chasing you. I know how you guys talk about us."

"Well, Honey, you don't have to worry about that anymore. I told Fahy we're getting married and the word is all over the office. Even the prosecutor congratulated me. Everybody says you're a very lucky woman."

"Is that so? Get yourself home quick and I'll show you how lucky you are. I've got a real low-cal dinner all ready for you. A big salad, a can of tuna fish packed in water, and a low-fat yogurt. How's that?"

Gus groaned. "Gee, Peg, I turned down an offer to go and eat sushi with Dr. Sanchez, and now you want to give me tuna fish?"

"You'll love it and it's good for you. Just get yourself home."

When Gus walked in the table was all set and sure enough there was a big salad sitting in the middle of the table, but Peg wasn't in the kitchen. He called out for her and he heard her voice saying: "I'll be there in a minute."

Gus sat down and looked at the salad and thought about the sushi. The kitchen door opened and Peg walked in with a wooden platter in her arms on top of which was one of the largest steaks Gus had seen. "What happened to the tuna fish?"

"It got burned, so I decided you needed steak. Okay by you?"

"Come here, you. First you, and then the steak." He grabbed her as she set the platter down on the table. She sat in his lap and they hugged.

"Honey, eat the steak first before it gets cold. Don't worry about me, I'm not going to cool off." She got off Gus's lap and sat

240

down next to him and started to carve the steak. "So, Gus, how did you make out today? Get the confession?"

"Peg, you ain't going to believe this. We spent the morning with the husband and all he can say is his wife didn't do it. We hit him with what we have on her, and one minute he buys it and the next he's telling us she didn't do it. So we bring her in and she sticks to the same story she told me last Friday. We go round and round with her, but we get nothing. The only thing was when I hit her with his girlfriends and then she just clams up. So Fahy gets her to take a lie detector test, which I told him was a mistake, but they gave it to her anyway, and sure enough she passes. The shit really hit the fan then."

"Gus, she passed the lie detector? Does that mean she's innocent?"

"In a pig's ass it does. Those guys think they can hook up somebody to one of those machines and get a printout that says 'guilty' or 'innocent.' That ain't the way to conduct an investigation. You go out and dig and dig and you get the facts, and then you don't have to ask any machine for the answers. Christ, we got enough on her to charge her without any fucking machine."

"So now what do you do?"

"Well, right after that this shrink, Dr. Weinstein, comes in. He had checked all the reports and he gives us the lowdown on her. He says she's whacked out because her father and her uncle raped her and she has to get even with men. He says she exploded when she found out about her husband and his broads and she killed the kids to get even or something because of what her father did to her. That's why she cut off Bobby's penis, too, to send her husband a kind of message. I'm telling you, it's really weird. He says that she has repressed—I think that was his word—anyway she can't remember what she did to Bobby so that's why she could pass the lie detector. You know, Peg, I usually don't buy that shit, but listening to him I could kind of see maybe what he was saying made sense. Anyway, he says we should give her truth serum and she may get relaxed enough to remember what she did to Bobby and tell us the story. So tomorrow Fahy and I are going to take her down to Philly for this truth serum test. Christ, if that doesn't work, we may be up shit's creek. If I had my way, we'd just charge her with what we got, but the lawyers over there say we're going to need a confession to make it stick. You know, Peg, I sure as hell would hate to be a lawyer. All they know how to do is fuck up the works. As a matter of fact, I told that to Ms. Stevens."

"Gus, you didn't?"

"Almost, but I said 'screw up' instead of 'fuck up' and anyway, she got a big kick out of it and so did everyone else." Gus pushed his plate away and asked: "So where's the yogurt?"

"Well, Gus, it isn't yogurt. I happened to go up to Riegelsville today and I stopped in at a place called Sally's. The woman who owns the place and I started talking and she asked me where I was from and when I told her Frenchtown, she said that was funny, because there was a real nice guy, a detective, from Frenchtown who was in her place just this week and he was supposed to come back soon because he really loved her food. So I asked her if this nice guy was named Gus, and she said that's the guy. Then she told me what you ate for lunch and how much you loved banana cream pie. I told her you were coming over to my place for dinner tonight and she said I had to take home a banana cream pie to give you. And she refused to charge me for the pie. Gus, it's a good thing I love you. Maybe you don't lie, but you don't always tell the truth either."

Gus grinned: "Honey, you found me out. Where's that banana cream pie?"

THIRTY-SEVEN

They left Frenchtown at eleven o'clock. Fahy drove, with Gus beside him in the front, the Hartwicks in the back. There was little conversation except Gus talking about the new minor league team in Trenton and how he wanted to go down to see a game, and did they know who Daniel Bray was. Fahy said: "All right, I'll bite, who is Daniel Bray?"

"He isn't any more. He's been dead a long time. He was the guy who got all the boats together and took Washington across the Delaware to knock off those Hessians down in Trenton. They named this road after him, didn't you know that? As a matter of fact, we just went by the spot where they crossed the river. Didn't you see the park there?"

"That's very interesting, Gus. I didn't know you were a history nut."

"I'm not. It's just that I went to school in Trenton and that was something they kept telling us about and they always had it on the final exam so we all had to remember it and I never forgot it. It got me a 'C' in history and I needed that 'C' to graduate. It's funny how you remember little things like that."

By 12:30 they pulled into the parking lot across the street from the University of Pennsylvania Medical School, and fifteen minutes later they were in the office of Dr. James W. Thornton, III, Associate Professor of Psychiatry. The doctor came in a few minutes later with a kid and introduced himself and the kid as his assistant, a resident by the name of Philip Chadbourne. Both of them were wearing white frock coats with name tags, but neither one had a stethoscope in his pocket. The most distinguishing thing about Thornton, aside from the fact that he was about six foot six, was his completely bald head and his hawklike nose. The resident had a full head of blond curly hair and was about five-foot four. Gus thought to himself Chadbourne looked about fifteen years old.

After the introductions were made, Dr. Thornton said: "Mrs. Hartwick, I understand that Dr. Weinstein explained the procedure for this examination to you. Are there any questions you would like to ask me before we get started?" Gladys shook her head and the doctor said: "Fine, then if you just go along with Dr. Chadbourne he'll take you to the examination room and have you sign a form that you are consenting to the procedure we're about to perform." Dr. Chadbourne led the Hartwicks out of the office.

When they left, Dr. Thornton turned to Fahy and Gus. "Gentlemen, I have spent the better part of the morning going through the materials you sent down and I spoke to Dr. Weinstein shortly before you arrived. This is certainly an interesting case you've got on your hands. We may be able to help you with this procedure, but you have to be aware that it is not always successful. Sometimes it works and then sometimes it doesn't and we don't know why."

Fahy said: "How long does it take?"

"We'll have to proceed very slowly and keep adjusting the dosage she'll receive until we get the right level of sedation so she remains awake and can respond to questions."

"Can we ask the questions?" Gus asked.

"Oh, no. You will be in an adjoining room and you will be able to see her and hear everything that is said. We also have a television camera that will make a videotape of the entire session. I will be asking the questions and Dr. Chadbourne will be in the room with me. Do you want the husband to be in the room with you?"

"I think that would be best," Fahy said.

"All right, then, let's go down the hall and I'll show you where you will be."

They were shown into a small, dark room which had a half-dozen chairs facing a window which took up most of one wall. They could see into a much larger room which had a bed and an I-V stand next to it. Gladys was already lying on the bed and was talking to her husband and Dr. Chadbourne. They saw Dr. Thornton enter and he led Bob Hartwick into the room in which they were sitting.

Gus said: "How's Gladys? Is everything all right?"

"I guess so. They've got a needle in her arm connected to that tube. When are they going to start this?"

244

"Have a seat, Bob, it won't be long."

They saw Dr. Thornton re-enter the room and he started speaking by Gladys. "Are you comfortable, Mrs. Hartwick?" Gladys nodded. "Alright, then we'll get started. Just relax as much as you can." Dr. Thornton opened the petcock on the I-V and sat down on a chair alongside the bed. "Mrs. Hartwick, in a few seconds you'll start feeling drowsy and I'll ask you to start counting backwards from a hundred. Will you do that for me?" Gladys nodded again. "All right, you can start counting now."

"One hundred, ninety-nine, ninety-eight, ninety-seven, ninety-six, nine—"

"Mrs. Hartwick, can you hear me?" Gladys nodded her head very slowly, her eyes were closed. "Mrs. Hartwick, how old are you?"

"Thirty-one."

"When were you born?"

"April sixteenth, nineteen sixty-three."

"What was your mother's name?"

"Henrietta Wilkins."

"Where were you born?"

"At the hospital in Doylestown."

"And what was your father's name?"

A minute or two went by before Gladys responded: "Roger Wilkins."

"Where is your father now?"

Again a pause: "I don't know where he is."

"Is your mother alive?"

"No, she died."

"Where were you living when your mother died?"

"In Durham."

"Where did you go to high school?"

"Palisades High School."

"Did you have any brothers or sisters?"

A prolonged pause, then: "Yes, I had a brother."

"What was his name?"

"Roger Junior."

"Where is he now?"

"He's dead."

"When did he die?"

"A long time ago. He was only four."

"How did he die?"

"He drowned in the lake."

"Do you know how he drowned?"

Almost five minutes went by before there was any response, and then they heard her say: "I held his head under the water and then I let him go and he sank to the bottom."

Gus and Fahy looked at each other and then at Bob Hartwick. He was doubled over in his chair holding his head in his hands. Gus whispered to him: "Bob, maybe you had better go into another room. I don't think you should hear this." Hartwick shook his head almost violently. The questioning in the next room continued.

"Mrs. Hartwick, are you married?"

"Yes."

"What is your husband's name?"

Another pause, then: "Bob Hartwick."

"Are you living with your husband?"

"Yes."

"Where do you live?"

"Frenchtown."

"When did you move to Frenchtown?"

"Almost a year ago."

"Why did you move to Frenchtown?"

"We had to. My husband was running around with another woman and I told him we had to move so he couldn't see her anymore." Gladys started stirring and moving her head from side to side. Dr. Thornton gestured to the resident who turned the petcock slightly on the I-V.

"Did your husband see this woman after you moved to Frenchtown?"

"Yes."

"Did you fight about it?"

"Yes." Gladys started shaking and Thornton nodded to the resident who gave the petcock another slight turn. Dr. Thornton waited until Gladys was once again relaxed.

"Mrs. Hartwick, I want you to tell me what happened last Friday. Do you remember that day?"

"Yes, I remember. Bob went to work early and Bobby went to school."

"Were you in the house all morning?"

"Yes, I was cleaning and ironing clothes."

"Did Bobby come home for lunch?"

Gladys started writhing on the bed. Slowly her movements stopped but she didn't respond.

"Mrs. Hartwick, do you remember when Bobby came home for lunch?"

"Yes, he came for lunch."

"What did he have for lunch?"

"I made him a peanut butter and jelly sandwich and he had a glass of milk."

"Did you put anything into his milk?"

Again, a pause. "Yes, I opened up one of the sleeping pills and poured some of the powder in his milk."

"Did he drink the milk?"

"Yes."

"What did he do then?"

"He fell asleep at the table."

"You have another son, don't you?"

"Yes."

"What is his name?"

"Richard, but we call him Ricky."

"How old is Ricky?"

"He's three years old."

"Where was Ricky when Bobby fell asleep?"

"He was up in his room, sleeping."

"When did he go to sleep?"

"Before Bobby got home. I gave him some of the sleeping powder too and he went to sleep."

Chuck looked over at Gus and nodded. Bob Hartwick hadn't stirred, he was still bent over holding his head in his hands. Gus thought to himself, *Maybe he deserves to hear this.*

"After Bobby fell asleep, what did you do?"

"I carried him upstairs to the bathroom and put him in the bathtub."

"Then what did you do?"

"I put a freezer bag over his head and held it tight around his neck."

"What did you do then?"

"He stopped breathing, so I took the bag off."

"And then what did you do?"

"I saw his thing there and I went down to the kitchen and got a knife and cut his thing off."

"What did you do with his thing?"

"I flushed it down the toilet."

"Did you do anything else to Bobby?"

"I had the knife, so I punched some holes in his belly."

"Why did you punch the holes in his belly?"

"I don't know why. I had the knife and I did it."

"What did you do with Bobby then?"

"I carried him downstairs and put him in a garbage bag."

"What did you do with the garbage bag?"

"I took it outside to the edge of the hill behind our house and I emptied him out down the hill."

"Did he slide down the hill?"

"For part of the way, and then he got caught up on some branches and stuff."

"What did you do then?"

"I climbed down the hill and then I dragged him the rest of the way."

"Where did you leave him?"

"There was a big tree there and I put him under it."

"Then what did you do?"

"I climbed back up the hill and went into the house."

"What did you do with the clothes Bobby had been wearing to school that morning?"

"I hid them."

"Where did you hide them?"

"In a box of old clothes in the basement."

Dr. Thornton got up and gestured to the resident who now turned the petcock on the I-V back a little bit. "Mrs. Hartwick, just rest there a bit and I'll come back and we can talk some more."

Dr. Thornton came into the viewing room. "Well, it worked. Do you want anything more?"

Bob Hartwick looked up at the doctor, his face was almost unrecognizable. "I want to know whether she killed Jimmy, too. I got to know that."

"Mr. Hartwick, I don't know that it is advisable to continue this procedure any longer. She's been under a long time now and I'd suggest we stop now and continue the questioning at another time."

"I've got to know."

Thornton looked at Gus and Fahy and then back to Hartwick. "Mr. Hartwick, I'm sorry, but I won't take that risk. Perhaps we can schedule another session, but not now. Your wife will wake up soon, and she may have some recollection of what she has just told us. I don't want to risk her recalling what she did to Jimmy, too, when she awakens. Tell me, after what you just heard, is there really any doubt in your mind that she killed your son Jimmy, too?"

Hartwick lowered his head and began crying convulsively. Dr. Thornton said to Gus and Fahy: "This has been very traumatic for him and I will give him a sedative before you take him back. Did you all come in one car?"

Fahy said: "Yes, we did, but I don't think we should take them back together. I'll make a call and have another car come down and pick him up, but it'll be about an hour or so before they can get here. Will that be alright?"

"Oh, yes, that will be fine. What are you going to do with Mrs. Hartwick?"

"Gus and I will take her back and then we're going to charge her with the murder of Bobby. When will she be able to leave?"

"She should be fully conscious in about an hour, but I would like to keep her here under observation for a few hours after that to see what her reactions are. If she appears stable after that, then I think you can take her back. But I would suggest that you not subject her to any traumatic experience today, at least. I'm going to call Dr. Weinstein and he can examine her when you get back and see how she is tonight and again tomorrow morning. If she is still in a stable condition then, Dr. Weinstein will advise you if it is all right to have her formally charged tomorrow."

"But what do we do with her tonight? We can't let her go home."

"I suggest that you have her admitted to the hospital in Flemington. They have a good staff there and they can monitor her condition tonight."

"Fine, Doc, that's what we'll do. And thanks a lot. Between you and Dr. Weinstein, you've really delivered the goods to us. Is there a room where I can make some calls?"

"Just follow me, you can use the phone in my office."

It was just a little after five when the reception desk called up to Dr. Thornton's office that a Mr. Carter from the Hunterdon County prosecutor's office was downstairs. Gus and Chuck collected Bob Hartwick and went down with him to find Carter waiting for them in the reception area. Hartwick was half out of it and didn't utter a word.

Fahy said: "Bob, you know Sam Carter. He's going to take you home. Gus and I are going to bring Gladys back with us and Dr. Thornton wants her to stay in the hospital over in Flemington tonight. You'll be able to see her tomorrow morning and I'll have a car pick you up to bring you over. Bob, I'm sorry it all turned out like this, but this is the worst and from here on it'll get better. Just try and get some sleep tonight and we'll see you in the morning."

They walked out the door together and Sam led them to the car where Howland was waiting behind the wheel and Hartwick got into the back seat. Carter turned back to Gus and Fahy: "I heard from the boss lady it went pretty good, that you got the whole story out of her, chapter and verse."

Chuck's face was frozen into a mask. "Yeah, Sam, our end is over. Now it's up to the lawyers. We've got the whole thing on videotape. I tell you, Sam, I think I'd quit this job before I would go through again what we heard up there. Tell the boss we'll be over as soon as we check Gladys into the hospital and here's the videotape of the confession. They can play it before we get back. I don't want to see it." Carter got into the car and they drove off.

Fahy turned to Gus and said: "How about we get a bite to eat while we're waiting for the doc to check her out of here." They walked around the corner and found a deli less than a block away. There were a lot of people in there with white smocks and name tags on. Fahy looked at Gus: "I guess it must be all safe to eat here, a lot of doctors are here."

"Christ, Chuck, you should know better than that. These doctors don't know shit about food. They'll eat anything. Haven't you seen them in the hospitals eating hospital food? Who the hell could do that if he wasn't sick and had to eat that crap?"

Fahy laughed. "I won't argue with that, Gus. What are those guys over there eating? It looks pretty good."

"Geez, Chuck, haven't you ever been in Philly before? Those are cheese steaks. They're not bad if you got a strong stomach. Come to think of it, we ought to bring Sanchez down here. If he can eat raw fish, he ought to go for cheese steaks." They both ordered cheese steaks and beer.

When they got back to the hospital, Gus found a phone and called Peg and told her he would be late and not to wait up.

"But Gus, I want to see you. How did it go?"

"It worked like a charm. We got the whole thing on her brother and Bobby. It's all finished."

"Was her husband there? Did he hear it?"

"Yeah, he heard it all right. They had to sedate him, he was going crazy. We sent him home with Carter."

"How about Gladys? What happens to her now?"

"We're checking her into the hospital in Flemington tonight and then we play it by ear tomorrow. Let the fucking lawyers worry about it now."

"Honey, I'll try to wait up for you, but if I'm sleeping, what time do you want me to wake you up tomorrow?"

"Get me up by six-thirty, okay? Listen, Hon, when can we get married?"

"I'm ready when you are. Just say when."

"How about next week? I'm going to take some time off and what do you say we get married and go away for a few days."

"You're on and I mean you're on. How about Wednesday night? Then I'll take off Thursday and Friday and we can go away for four whole days together somewhere."

"Peg, I love you, and I may wake you up when I get home."

"That I look forward to. I love you too, Gus. Just don't eat too much down there."

*   *   *

251

It was after nine o'clock when they arrived at the Fleming-ton Medical Center with Gladys, who was still sedated and hadn't uttered a sound on the ride back. They led her in through the emergency room entrance and Dr. Weinstein was waiting for them. He walked up to Gladys and put an arm around her shoul-ders.

"I've got a private room for you, Mrs. Hartwick. This nurse will take you up there and I'll be up in a few minutes to see you. Are you feeling alright?"

"I'm very tired."

"I can see you are. I'm sure you will feel better in the morn-ing."

The nurse put Gladys in a wheel chair and went off down the corridor. Dr. Weinstein walked over to Gus and Fahy.

"I spoke to Dr. Thornton and he told me what happened. He said she did not show any signs of remembering what she told him during the procedure, but he thinks it can start to come back at any time. He suggested I put her under close observation tonight and I've made those arrangements. I'll examine her later, and if there's anything I should report to you, where can I reach you?"

Fahy said: "We'll be over at the prosecutor's office for at least the next hour. After that, just call the office number and there will be a message on the answering machine where to get in touch with me. Doc, I want you to know how grateful we are to you for your help. According to Dr. Thornton, you called it right on the nose."

Dr. Weinstein smiled. "Believe me, Mr. Fahy, it doesn't hap-pen too often in my line of work, just once every so often. I've got to tell you, if it weren't for the information you gave us, I wouldn't have had a clue to her problems."

Fahy said, "I've got to tell you, Doc, I didn't have anything to do with it. If it had been up to me, we'd still be chasing blue Ford pickups. It was Gus here who put it all together."

Dr. Weinstein nodded. "I gathered as much from reading the reports. Gus, you would make a good shrink, as I think you call us."

"Doc, I'm sorry about that. All I do is listen to people, that's all, and maybe ask a few questions."

"What do you think being a shrink is all about? That's what we do, too. Anyway, enough of this, I better get up to see her. If you don't hear from me tonight, you'll know everything's alright and I'll call you as soon as I see her in the morning. Good night."

Gus and Fahy drove over to the prosecutor's office and all of the lights were still on. The whole gang was in the grand jury room and they had seen the tape. As soon as they walked in, Ms. Stevens said: "I can understand why you didn't want to watch any replay. I almost threw up before it was finished. How is she?"

Fahy said: "When we left her she seemed to be alright. Dr. Weinstein is with her and he'll call us if anything is wrong. He's going to check her out in the morning and if she's alright then, he'll let us know and we can pick her up and bring her over to be arraigned. Has the complaint been drawn up yet?"

Ben Harris said: "It's all done. We've charged her with murder one. Who do you want to sign the complaint?"

Fahy replied: "I think Gus should. This has been his case all the way. Is that alright with you, Gus?"

"Absolutely, just show me where to sign. By the way, did the guys go back and find Bobby's clothes where she said they were?"

Bernie Williams said: "You bet, they were just where she said. A yellow polo shirt, a pair of jeans, and a pair of sneakers. We had Hartwick identify them as Bobby's when Sam brought him back to the house. I'm telling you, that guy isn't in good shape. I think he may be right on the edge."

Gus said: "Who wouldn't be after hearing what he heard today? Chuck tried to get him out of the viewing room as soon as she admitted killing her brother, but he wouldn't go. For my money he's a sleazebag anyway, so let him suffer."

Fahy looked at Ms. Stevens: "What about a lawyer for her for tomorrow?"

"We called the public defender's office and they'll be in court. The judge will ask her if she has an attorney when we arraign her and is she doesn't, he'll assign one then. I'm sure we'll end up with the public defender representing her. I'm going to re-lease a statement to the press early tomorrow morning announcing her arrest and the time of the arraignment, so you can expect it will be a zoo around the courthouse."

Fahy asked: "Who's the judge?"

"It'll be Abbott, he's assigned to criminal this month and we put him on notice so his calendar is all set. If Weinstein gives the okay, I think you should pick her up at ten o'clock and the arraignment will be at eleven. So that's it. I think we'd better go home and get what sleep we can. Gus, I think you did a great job on this, and Chuck and all of you, too. By the way, Gus, when are you getting married?"

Gus blinked. "Well, we were talking about maybe next Wednesday, and then we thought we'd take off for about four days and go somewhere, if that's alright with you."

"Gus, why don't you and your bride go down to my beach house? You'll be right on the ocean and this is the best time of the year there. I wasn't planning to go down next weekend anyway, and with all this going on around here, I certainly won't be able to get away. It'll be just sitting there empty, so you're welcome to use it. And there are some really good restaurants around there, and no sushi."

"Gee, thanks, Ms. Stevens. I'll speak to Peg about it and if it's okay with her, I'd sure like it. Speaking of Peg, I guess I'd better get out of here or she'll be calling the cops to find out what happened to me."

"Well, if she calls here, we'll tell her you left with a beautiful blonde two hours ago."

Gus laughed. "What was her name in case she asks me?"

"Get out of here, Gus, and go home."

Gus headed back to Frenchtown. As he drove into Peg's driveway, he could see the house was dark and he looked at his watch. It was after midnight. He sat in the car and started to think that if he went in, he would wake Peg up. He didn't feel like sleeping, he was still wound up. He started feeling uneasy about Hartwick and what Bernie Williams had said. He said to himself, *What the fuck, I'm not going to get any sleep anyway, so I might just as well do it.*

Gus backed out of the driveway and headed back to Flemington and made his way to the hospital. He went in through the emergency entrance and identified himself and asked what room Mrs. Hartwick was in. He went up to the third floor and walked down the corridor to the nurse's station. There was no one there, but he heard voices coming from a room just beyond and he opened the door. There were three nurses there and when he walked in they all looked up and were startled to see him. One of the nurses stood up and asked who he was and what he was doing there.

"It's all right, ma'am. I'm Gus Bass and I'm with the prosecutor's office. I just came over to check on Mrs. Hartwick to make sure she's okay. She is, isn't she?"

"Oh, you really gave us a scare. She's alright. Dr. Weinstein asked for a private nurse to stay with her and she's been resting quietly. She's in room three twelve. Mrs. Frostdyck is there with her if you want to speak to her."

"Thanks, I'll do that."

Gus walked down almost to the end of the corridor and found room 312. He pushed the door in slowly and saw Gladys asleep on her bed. A woman was sitting in the corner and she looked up when she saw Gus, who put his hand to his lips and gestured for her to come out into the hall. Mrs. Frostdyck did and they spoke in whispers outside the door.

"How is she doing?"

"Who are you?"

"My name is Bass, I'm from the prosecutor's office and I was just checking up on Mrs. Hartwick, that's all. We've got to take her to court in the morning."

"Why, what has she done?"

"She killed her kid, that's all."

Mrs. Frostdyck gasped and clasped her hand to her mouth. "Are you serious?"

"You bet I am. Look, I'm going to the sitting room over there and if anything happens, just let me know."

"They didn't tell me anything about that. I just got a call from Dr. Weinstein to come and sit with her for tonight and to call him if she woke up. Alright, I'll come and get you if anything happens."

Gus walked to the end of the corridor and into the sitting room. He found a lamp and switched it on. There were a lot of magazines on a table and he started looking for one to read. Then he saw something familiar, a brochure about high blood pressure, the silent killer. He said to himself, *Jesus Christ, maybe they're trying to tell me something.* Then he thought, *If I'm going to get married and have a kid, maybe I ought to get a physical first.*

He picked up a current copy of "Sports" and saw there was an article in it about new minor league teams. He sat down and started to read and sure enough, it mentioned the "Trenton Thunder" and their new ballpark. After about half an hour, he put his head back, closed his eyes, and drifted off. He dreamt he was playing for the "Trenton Thunder" and he was up at bat with a man on second. The guy stole the catcher's sign and signaled to Gus it was a curveball. Gus pulled his bat back and sure enough, as the ball left the pitcher's hand, he could see it was going to be a curve. He got ready and he swung. The contact felt good and he saw the ball headed out to deep left and the left field-er running with his back to him and he was stopping because the ball was headed high over that big wall in left field. Gus start-ed trotting down to first when the dream melted away and he became aware of someone shaking him. He looked up and saw it was Mrs. Frostdyck.

She whispered to him, "Mr. Bass, come quick. There's a man in Mrs. Hartwick's room. He's got a gun and he made me get out."

Gus was wide awake now and he ran to 312 and shoved the door open. Then he groaned. There was Bob Hartwick and he had a gun pointed at Gladys, who was sitting up in her bed and smiling at him.

Gus barked, "Hartwick, put down that gun and give it to me before you hurt somebody or yourself."

"Get out of here, Mr. Bass. I don't want to hurt you but I will if you don't get out."

Gus could see the wild look in his eyes and he knew he had to keep talking. "What good do you think you're going to do with that? What'll happen to you? It'll be murder and the least you'll get is life, for Christ's sake. Then what happens to Ricky? Did you ever think of that?"

"I don't care about that. I'm going to kill myself anyway. This lousy bitch killed my two kids and she's going to die."

Gus looked over at Gladys. She was still smiling. "Christ, Bob, can't you see she wants you to kill her. All you'll be doing is putting her out of her misery and destroying yourself. That's a hell of a way to get even. Did you ever think about that?"

Gus started slowly inching toward Hartwick. "Don't come any closer to me, Mr. Bass."

Gus stopped moving. "Look, Bob, you saw her today. Can't you tell she's crazy? You can speak to Dr. Weinstein and he'll explain the whole thing to you better than I can."

"What the hell can he explain? She killed my kids."

"But Bob, she didn't know she was doing it. Dr. Weinstein told us she is very sick. She was raped by her father and her uncle, did you know that?"

"I don't give a shit who raped her."

"That's why she killed her brother, to get even with her old man. And then when you started chasing all those broads, she had to get even with you by killing Jimmy. But she couldn't help herself, and the same thing with Bobby. You were shacking up with Jean and that drove her over the edge again. Look, just give me that gun and I'll call Dr. Weinstein and he'll tell you what I'm saying is all true."

Hartwick stared hard at Gus and the gun in his hand lowered slightly.

Gus thought he was wavering. "How about it, Bob, just back off until I can get Weinstein here." The gun was raised again and Hartwick turned toward Gladys. Gus saw his chance and leaped at Hartwick and grabbed his wrist. Hartwick was knocked backward into the chair the nurse had been sitting in and the gun went off. Gus started sinking to the floor still holding on to Hartwick's wrist and the gun went off again as Gus knocked the gun to the floor. Hartwick fell over the chair hitting his head against the wall and dropped to the floor right beside Gus.

All hell broke loose. The door was flung open and an orderly and three or four nurses charged into the room. Gladys was still sitting up in her bed but now she was laughing. Gus was lying face down on the floor and a pool of blood was spreading out from under his body. Someone yelled to get the doctor from the emergency room and they knelt down beside him. Gus was barely conscious and he kept muttering about a curveball and a home run. They turned him over and the whole of his shirt was soaked with blood. Within a minute a doctor was there and they lifted Gus onto a gurney and ran off with him to surgery.

THIRTY-EIGHT

Fahy got the call at 3:30 from Carter who was at the hospital.

"Chuck, Gus has been shot and it looks bad. I'm over at the medical center and he's in surgery. He got two right in his gut and it's touch and go."

"How the hell did that happen? Who shot him?"

"I'm trying to piece it together. There's nothing but confusion around here. For some reason Gus didn't go home, he came over to the hospital to check up on Mrs. Hartwick. There was a private nurse in her room and Gus checked in with her and then he went to this little sitting room next door. He must have fallen asleep. Bob Hartwick showed up with a gun and he was going to kill his wife. The nurse ran to get Gus, and Gus went into the room after Hartwick. The nurse was right outside the door and she says Gus was trying to talk Hartwick out of it. She didn't see what happened but Gus must have gone for the gun and the bastard shot him twice."

"Where is Hartwick now?"

"There's nothing wrong with him and I had the local cops take him over to the jail. I tell you, if Gus doesn't make it, I'm going to get a piece of that prick. Gus was right, he's nothing but a sleazebag."

"Just stay calm, Sam, and I'll get some of the guys over there to help you. We've got to get statements from everybody and run this one right. I'll call the boss lady and I'll try to get hold of Gus's girl and then I'll be right over."

Fahy made his call to the prosecutor. When he told her, he thought he could hear her starting to cry. She said she would be there in twenty minutes and to find Gus's girlfriend and bring her over. "That's my next call, Ms. Stevens."

When he hung up he realized he didn't know Peg's last name. It was almost four o'clock and he said what the hell and looked up Mary Trantino's number. He dialed and after a half-dozen rings he heard her voice.

258

"Mrs. Trantino, this is Chuck Fahy, remember me? I'm sorry to wake you up but this is an emergency and I need the number of Gus's girlfriend, Peg, but I don't know her last name. . . . Thanks. . . . Well, Gus has been shot, but I don't know how bad it is. Look, I want to call Mrs. Shipley so I've got to hang up now."

The phone had only rung twice when Peg picked it up.

"Hello? Who is this?"

"Mrs. Shipley, this is Chuck Fahy. I just got a call from the hospital. Gus has been hurt and I think you had better come over. I can send someone to pick you up if you want."

He heard her screaming, "No, no."

"Mrs. Shipley, they're doing everything they can. Let me send someone over to get you. I'll have a guy there in fifteen minutes. Listen, I've got to get over there myself. Will you be alright?"

After some silence, he heard her say she'd get there on her own. He hung up and headed for the hospital.

By 4:30, half of Fahy's staff was in the hospital and were taking statements. Ms. Stevens and Ben Harris were already there when Fahy arrived and minutes later Peg walked in. Sam Carter took them up to a family room down the hall from the surgical suites. When they were seated, he said: "I had a report from surgery just before you got here. He's lost a lot of blood and they're doing their best to sew things up. The bullets missed his heart and they told me he's got a good chance of making it if they can stop all the bleeding."

Ms. Stevens was sitting on a couch with Peg and had her arm around her. Peg was crying and her head was buried in Ms. Stevens' shoulder.

"Peg, he's tough and he's gong to make it. Did he tell you about going to my beach house for your honeymoon?"

After a few minutes, Peg lifted her head up. "No, I haven't seen him since this morning. He never came home last night."

Carter, who was standing next to them, said: "We don't know why he came back here. All we know is that he got here sometime after midnight and parked himself in the sitting room next to Mrs. Hartwick's room." Carter went on to tell them what had

259

happened. "You know when they got to him, he was still conscious and he kept saying something about it being a curveball and he hit a home run."

Ben Harris said: "I'll be damned, he was telling me just the other day about his playing baseball and how he could only hit a curveball. That is weird."

The hospital administrator walked in and introduced himself and asked if there was anything he could get for them. Fahy said they could use some coffee and maybe a doctor could take a look at Mrs. Shipley.

Peg lifted her head from Ms. Stevens' shoulder: "I don't need a doctor. I'll be alright."

Minutes later an orderly and a nurse came in with coffee, but no one drank any. They sat there in a numbed silence. Once every few minutes, Fahy would stand up and walk out of the door and come back again and sit down. An hour went by, and then another half hour. It was now full daylight outside and they could hear the sounds of cars pulling into the hospital parking lot.

Dr. Weinstein came in. He had been called by the head nurse on the third floor and had gone immediately to see Gladys. He told them Gladys was in bad shape. The nurses told him she had been laughing when they had gone to her room after they heard the shots. Now she was completely catatonic.

"It's my guess she became conscious of what she did to her sons and her brother and she has lapsed into a kind of psychic coma as a form of self-defense. God, what a tragic case this is. Have you had any word about Gus?"

Just then one of the surgeons walked in, clad in his green surgical costume. He pulled down his mask and said: "There's not much I can tell you. We've sewn up as much as we could, and we think we've stopped the bleeding. His vital signs are stabilizing and that's a good sign. There's a good chance now he'll make it, but to be perfectly honest, I don't know how he managed to last as long as he has."

Peg looked up at the surgeon: "Is he conscious?"

"No, but every so often he mutters something about curveballs and a home run. At least, that's what I think he's saying."

"Can I see him?"

260

"Not yet, not while he's still in surgery and we're going to keep him in there until we're sure we got all of the bleeding under control. We'll know better in another hour. If we move him into recovery, I'll arrange for you to see him there."

"Doctor, if you think he can hear you, just tell him Peg is here waiting for him."

"I'll do that. I'd better be getting back now."

As the doctor left, Sloss came charging into the room. "They called me at home and told me Gus has been shot. How is he?"

Fahy walked over to Sloss and whispered for him to go outside with him. When they were out of earshot, Fahy said: "It has been touch and go but one of the surgeons just left and things are better."

"Thank God for that. How the hell did it happen?"

"No one really knows very much except that Gus came over here last night after he left us, almost as if he had a hunch Hartwick might show up here. Well, he did and he had a gun and Gus tried to stop the bastard from killing his wife and he got shot twice before he could get the gun away from him."

"What about the wife, did she get hit?"

"No, but she's now flipped out completely. Dr. Weinstein came down and told us she's like a vegetable."

"Christ, why the hell didn't Gus just let him kill her? She deserved it. Gus said so himself."

"Who knows, Bob? I think maybe it's because he can't stand anyone being killed. You know, I'll never forget how he was when we saw the kid's body over there in the woods. And then when he found Baumgart that morning. I thought he might go over the edge then, too. He's hard to figure out. He can be tougher than any of us when he has to be, but I guess inside, he's different. God, I hope he makes it. I've really gotten to like the guy and he's one hell of a cop."

"How's his girl taking it?"

"She seems to be under control. You know, he told us last night they were going to get married next Wednesday. Christ, what a lousy break."

It was only fifteen minutes later when the surgeon came back with another doctor, their faces reflecting the good news they were bringing. The surgeon walked over to Peg and said he had told Gus she was waiting for him and he had seemed to smile.

"I have to tell you that's one tough guy you have there. They'll be moving him into the recovery room soon but he won't regain consciousness for a few hours. I have made arrangements for you to stay in the recovery room with him until we can move him down to intensive care."

Peg rose up from the couch and hugged him. "Doctor, thanks for giving him back to me."

"You don't have to thank me. It's Gus who deserves the credit—he has such a strong will to live, that's what pulled him through."

Hazel Stevens put her arms around Peg and held her. Fahy walked over to the doctors and together with Sloss walked them away, out of earshot. "Doctor, I'm Chief Fahy and this is Captain Sloss. We've been working with Gus on a really tough case and I just wanted you to know you saved a great guy and we're all grateful."

"It's like I told her, Chief, with the kind of wounds he had, I don't know how he made it. When you see something like this, you can't explain it medically except to say that the patient just didn't want to die and so he didn't."

"Is it too early for a prognosis, Doc?"

"Oh, much too soon for that. Let's see how he does over the next two days. If there are no complications and no infections, we should be able to get him on his feet shortly after that and maybe send him home in another week."

"That sounds just great. When will he be able to have visitors?"

"Let's not rush things, Chief. Give me a call on that tomorrow morning. Look, I'd better get back to him now."

Ben Harris walked out and was back five minutes later.

"I called Judge Abbott and told him what happened and that we wouldn't be arraigning Mrs. Hartwick this morning. I called the office and they are preparing a complaint against Hartwick, assault with intent to kill and unlawful possession of a firearm. Judge Abbott is ready to arraign him as soon as we're ready. Chuck, I told them to prepare the complaint for your signature. I figured you would want to."

"You bet, Ben. I'll meet you over at the office within the hour. What an irony this is. We're all set to arraign the wife for murder and now it's going to be the husband who's going to be charged. Christ, in this business you never know what's going to happen next."

Dr. Weinstein came back in and went over to Ms. Stevens. "I just heard and I'm so glad for him, he's such a fine man. I really felt I got to know him in the few times we met. Does he have a family?"

Ms. Stevens looked up and said: "Doctor, this is Mrs. Shipley. She and Gus were planning to be married next week."

"Mrs. Shipley, I'm very happy for you. He is really a very unusual man. You know, I read all of his reports and the interviews he did in this case, and he has a unique ability to deal with people and get them to open up. As a matter of fact, I told him just the other night I thought he would make a good shrink. Look, if there's anything I can do, or if you or Gus want to just talk, I'll be available for you anytime. All you have to do is give me a call."

Peg nodded her head and murmured thanks. As Dr. Weinstein left, a nurse came in to take Peg to the recovery room. Peg walked over to the chief and gave him a hug.

"Chief, do me a favor and call Mary Trantino for me. She'll want to know Gus is going to be okay. And I'll call you as soon as he wakes up and let you know how he is doing."

By seven o'clock they had all left except for Gus and Peg.

THIRTY-NINE

The arraignment of Robert Hartwick, Sr. on a complaint for assault with intent to kill and unlawful possession of a gun was held before Judge Abbott at eleven o'clock in the same courtroom of the Hunterdon Country Courthouse in which Bruno Richard Hauptmann had been tried for the kidnapping and murder of the Lindbergh baby. The courtroom was filled to overflowing with the press and the curious. One of the old-timers said there hadn't been this much excitement in the courthouse since the Hauptmann trial.

Hartwick was brought in through the rear door of the courtroom and Judge Abbott conducted the proceedings with dispatch. Hartwick acknowledged that he had been served with a copy of the complaint and that he understood the charges against him. Judge Abbott informed Hartwick that he had the right not to make any statement, but that if he did, anything he said could be used in evidence against him.

At that point, Hartwick blurted out: "But I didn't mean to hurt Mr. Bass. I only wanted to kill my wife."

Judge Abbott looked at Ben Harris who was appearing on behalf of the prosecutor, and then he looked back at Hartwick.

"Mr. Hartwick, I don't think it is advisable for you to say anything at this time. You have the right to be represented by an attorney, and you should confer with your attorney before you say anything else. Now, do you have an attorney?"

Hartwick shook his head.

"Can you afford to hire your own attorney or do you wish me to appoint someone for you?"

Hartwick looked up at the judge, who saw that he was confused.

"Alright, Mr. Hartwick, in view of the seriousness of the charge I shall appoint the public defender to represent you until it is determined whether you can afford your own attorney. In the meantime, you are remanded to the custody of the sheriff and you shall so remain until such time as an application can be made on your behalf for a bail hearing. Do you have any questions you wish to ask at this time?"

Hartwick didn't look up, just shook his head. "Alright, officers, you can take Mr. Hartwick away now." Two sheriff's officers took Hartwick by his arms and led him back through the door he had entered.

As soon as Hartwick had left, Ben Harris rose and addressed the judge.

"Your honor, the state filed with the court yesterday evening a complaint charging Gladys Hartwick with the murder of her son, Robert Hartwick, Junior, on June third, nineteen ninety-four, in the Borough of Frenchtown. We were prepared to arraign Mrs. Hartwick on that complaint this morning. However, we have been informed by Dr. Stanley Weinstein, who has examined Mrs. Hartwick on behalf of the prosecutor's office, that Mrs. Hartwick is unfit to proceed at this time. She is presently under guard at the Hunterdon County Medical Center and I would respectfully ask the court to appoint the public defender's office to act on behalf of Mrs. Hartwick and that an order be entered committing Mrs. Hartwick to a suitable facility for thirty days so that she may be examined and a report submitted to the court as to her ability to stand trial or participate in any further proceedings. If the court does appoint the public defender to represent Mrs. Hartwick, I shall confer with him and we shall submit an appropriate order and a list of qualified psychiatrists to conduct the examination of Mrs. Hartwick."

"Mr. Harris, I read the complaint and I will appoint the public defender to represent Mrs. Hartwick at this time. Please meet with the public defender as soon as we are finished here and make available to him whatever information you have received from Dr. Weinstein and submit an order to me for her commitment if the public defender agrees. If not, I shall conduct a hearing on your application this afternoon at three P.M. Is there anything further you have at this time, Mr. Harris?"

"No, your honor."

"Then we shall adjourn until I hear from you and the public defender's office. The court is adjourned."

Before the judge was able to leave the courtroom the press was storming around Ben Harris demanding a statement from him and barraging him with questions. Ben refused to answer and told them that the prosecutor would have a statement for them at noon. He ran out of the back door of the courtroom, down the stairs, and across the street to the prosecutor's office.

On June 16, 1994, the Hunterdon County Grand Jury handed up a bill of indictment charging Robert Hartwick, Sr. with assault with intent to kill and unlawful possession of a firearm. On July 15, 1994, Robert Hartwick, Sr. entered a plea of guilty to charges in the indictment under a plea bargain which required a sentence of fifteen years without parole eligibility for ten years. He also entered a plea of guilty to unlawful possession of a firearm for which he received a sentence of five years to be served concurrently with the sentence on the first count of the indictment.

On June 16, 1994, the Hunterdon County Grand Jury handed up an indictment charging Gladys Hartwick with murder in the first degree in the death of Robert Hartwick, Jr. On July 22, 1994, Judge Abbott conducted a hearing on the fitness of Gladys Hartwick to stand trial on the charges set forth in the indictment. At the hearing, the court received into evidence the report of the examining psychiatrist who stated, in substance, that Gladys Hartwick was in a catatonic state and was unable to communicate or to comprehend the nature of the charges against her. The report concluded that the prognosis for her restoration to reason was uncertain at this time and recommended that she be committed to the state prison for the criminally insane to receive such treatment as was appropriate to her condition. Neither the prosecutor nor the public defender contested the findings of the report, and Judge Abbott found that Gladys Hartwick lacked fitness to proceed and suspended all proceedings against her until the further order of the court.

Epilogue

Gus was discharged from the Hunterdon County Medical Center on June 19, 1994 and spent the next month recuperating at Peg's house. Among his first visitors were Becky Aaron and her sons, who wanted to know when Gus would be able to take them to see the "Trenton Thunder."

"I haven't forgotten, guys. As a matter of fact, Mrs. Shipley called and got tickets for us for a Friday night game the week after next. How's that?" The boy's faces lit up with broad grins.

Almost in unison they said: "See, mom, we told you he wouldn't forget."

"Mr. Bass, do you think you'll be well enough so soon?"

"You bet I will, Becky. I'm getting stronger every day and if I could just get Peg here to give me some real food instead of the pap I've been getting, I might even take batting practice with those guys down there and show them how to hit a curveball. God knows they could use some help."

Peg said: "You know, Mrs. Aaron, if there's one good thing that has come of all this, Gus has finally lost twenty pounds and I'm going to see that he keeps it off for good."

"Well, Mr. Bass, if you're feeling so good, when will the wedding be?"

Gus grinned. "We'll be getting the license next week and as soon as Ms. Stevens is sworn in as judge, she's going to marry us. She wants it to be the first official thing she does as a judge."

Becky beamed. "Well, I'm very happy for both of you. Now we'd better be going. Is it alright if I tell the folks down in Frenchtown about your wedding plans? Everyone has been asking about you, Gus. Even Sergeant Krantz asked me the other day if I had heard how you were doing."

Gus laughed and said: "Tell Krantz for me it's been a good way for me to lose weight and maybe he ought to try it himself. Sure, you can tell anyone you want. Right, Peg?"

"Absolutely. He's stuck with me whether he likes it or not, and he's not getting away."

The wedding was held at Peg's house a week later with Judge Stevens officiating and Fahy as the best man.